ANNE McALLISTER
KATE HARDY
FIONA HOOD-STEWART

Published in Great Britain 2014
by Mills & Boon, an imprint of Harlequin (UK) Limited,
Eton House, 18-24 Paradise Road, Richmond, Surrey, TW9 1SR

ISBN: 978-0-263-91203-6
eBook ISBN: 978-1-472-04498-3

05-1014

Harlequin (UK) Limited's policy is to use papers that are natural, renewable and recyclable products and made from wood grown in sustainable forests. The logging and manufacturing processes conform to the legal environmental regulations of the country of origin.

Printed and bound in Spain
by Blackprint CPI, Barcelona

THE NIGHT THAT CHANGED EVERYTHING

BY
ANNE McALLISTER

Award-winning author **Anne McAllister** was once given a blueprint for happiness that included a nice, literate husband, a ramshackle Victorian house, a horde of mischievous children, a bunch of big, friendly dogs, and a life spent writing stories about tall, dark and handsome heroes. 'Where do I sign up?' she asked, and promptly did. Lots of years later, she's happy to report the blueprint was a success. She's always happy to share the latest news with readers at her website, www.annemcallister.com, and welcomes their letters there, or at PO Box 3904, Bozeman, Montana 59772, USA.

For Peter, always.
And this time, especially, for Steve,
with thanks for the road trip and the memories.

CHAPTER ONE

He was Trouble. With a capital *T*.

From the look of him, Edie thought as she watched Mr. Tall, Dark and Drop-Dead Gorgeous flash his brilliant smile at her starlet sister, Rhiannon, the whole *word* should be capitalized.

TROUBLE.

The precise sort of trouble she knew it was her job to prevent.

So Edie hovered beside a pillar in the Mont Chamion state ballroom assessing the situation as the wedding reception of her royal highness Princess Adriana and her handsome groom, well-known actor-director Demetrios Savas went on around her.

The orchestra was playing and couples all around her were dancing. It would have been better—*safer*—if Rhiannon had been dancing, too. Instead she was standing still, her body nearly pressed into that of the man she was talking to.

Was it too much to hope that Mr. Trouble would simply smile at her simpering, eyelash batting sister, set her aside and move away into the throng? He was clearly out of Rhiannon's league. Her sister might be beautiful and flirtatious, but this man looked to be in his mid-thirties, worldly, sophisticated and clearly had far too much of the "male animal" for Rhiannon who was barely twenty.

And not a very mature twenty, at that.

Edie watched as her sister put her hand on his arm and stood staring up at him with rapt fascination. Edie recognized the look. It could mean she was actually interested in what he was saying to her. Or it could mean that Ree was doing what she did best—acting. In either case, unless Edie intervened it would cause no end of trouble.

Edie willed Mr. Trouble to turn away, to find another admirer. Dancing couples obscured her view for a moment. But when she caught sight of them again, she could see he hadn't moved an inch. His expression was bemused as he smiled down at her sister. It gave him an enticing groove in one cheek. Rhiannon reached up a finger and stroked it.

Edie stifled a groan.

An elbow suddenly collided with her back. She turned, expecting an apology. Instead she found her mother glaring at her.

"Do something!" Mona Tremayne hissed. She gave Edie a speaking look, then smoothly turned back to Danish producer, Rollo Mikkelsen, slid her arm through his and blinded him with one of her patent Mona Tremayne Sex Goddess For The Ages smiles.

All Edie could think was, "Thank God Rhiannon hadn't perfected that bit of their mother's repertoire yet." But she seemed to be doing well enough on her own. Behind her as the music ended Edie detected what she thought was her sister's lilting giggle. It was joined by a deep baritone laugh.

Mona obviously heard it, too. She turned back from Rollo Mikkelsen and glowered, first at Edie, then over Edie's shoulder to where Rhiannon was about to make a big mistake.

So there was no help for it. Edie set her teeth grimly and turned away from her mother, knowing her duty. "Right. On my way."

As her mother's and sister's business manager, Edie's job was to keep their careers on track. She dealt with the finances, the business appointments, the offers, the contracts and the myriad demands that the world made on one of America's leading screen actresses and her up-and-coming starlet daughter.

All that was a piece of cake.

It was the hands-on meddling that Edie hated. She didn't

have to do it for her mother. Over the years Mona had certainly learned to take care of herself. And if she made mistakes, she had the clout to make them go away.

Rhiannon was another story.

Rhiannon was young and vulnerable, emotional and flighty. She was also genuinely kind and loving. It was a scary combination. Making sure Rhiannon had lots of projects to keep her focused was the best way to be sure she didn't sabotage herself, her life or her career.

Ordinarily Edie could manage that by keeping her sister's calendar booked, and she never had to leave California to do it.

But Mona had rung two days ago from Mont Chamion and said, "Pack your bags."

When her mother spoke in that brisk no-nonsense tone, Edie knew not to argue. Where Rhiannon was concerned, Mona's instincts were almost always spot on. If she foresaw trouble, it was better to tackle it head-on than to hope it might not happen. So Edie had dutifully flown halfway around the world ready to put out whatever potential fire might erupt.

But she hadn't expected to attend the wedding.

"Why ever not?" Mona had demanded. "Of course you're coming to the wedding. And the reception," she'd added firmly. "God only knows what mischief Rhiannon can get up to there—especially now that Very Nice Andrew is gone."

Very Nice Andrew—*long-suffering* Andrew was how Edie thought of him—was Rhiannon's fiancé. Her first love, he was absolutely right for Rhiannon, and they both seemed to know it—most of the time. When he and Rhiannon were together and blissful, Edie's life was relatively blissful, too.

But a lovers' quarrel had sent Andrew stalking out yesterday. And Mona was right, disaster could easily ensue if Rhiannon was left feeling unappreciated and unloved.

But still Edie had protested that she wasn't attending the wedding.

"Of course you are," Mona had said firmly that afternoon as

she'd slipped into the gown she was wearing for the wedding and motioned for Edie to lace the back panel. It was a simple sheath, royal blue, setting off Mona's amazing eyes, with an open V at the back which, as Edie laced it, offered a glimpse of Mona's still-creamy flesh. It was quietly sexy and titillating, showing just enough to remind the world that, at fifty, Mona Tremayne was still a very appealing woman.

"I'm not invited." Edie pulled the laces together. "And I'm not crashing a royal wedding."

Mona's gaze met hers in the mirror. "Nonsense. You're not crashing. You're my guest."

"Oliver is your guest."

Sir Oliver Choate, English actor and Mona's most recent co-star, had flown in from Spain yesterday afternoon expressly to escort Mona to the wedding.

"Besides Oliver," Mona said impatiently. "You need to be there. And you might meet someone..." Her voice trailed off, but she looked at Edie hopefully.

Edie's teeth set. Exactly what she'd been afraid of. Mona—matchmaking. She gave a long-suffering sigh of her own. "I'm not interested in meeting anyone, Mother."

"Don't call me Mother in public," Mora admonished. "You're nearly thirty, for goodness' sake!"

Edie laughed and shook her head, then gave an extra tug to the laces, making her mother suck in a sharp breath. "We're not in public, and I don't think they have the bedrooms bugged. Besides, you don't get parts for ingenues anymore. People know how old you are."

Mona sighed, then stood up a bit straighter. "I try not to think about it. Anyway—" she shoved a hand into her artfully wind-blown auburn hair "—you must come—even if you don't meet a soul," she added piously. Then she spoiled it by saying, "But honestly, Edie, you need to get back on the horse."

Start dating again, she meant. Get a life again. Get over Ben.

But Edie didn't want to get over him. Why should she? Her

husband, Ben, had been the best thing that had ever happened to her. And yes, he had been dead two and half years. But so what?

"I did," Mona pointed out, not for the first time.

"And how did that work out for you?" Edie said dryly.

Edie's father, Joe, had been killed in a horse riding accident when Edie was five. He'd been the love of Mona's life, and she'd spent the next twenty years trying to replace him with a succession of men who'd become Edie's stepfathers.

"I have wonderful children," Mona said, defiantly meeting her daughter's eyes in the mirror.

That was certainly true. Edie couldn't complain about her younger brothers and sisters. In fact Rhiannon, Grace, Ruud and Dirk were the best part of her life, the family that had become for her the one she and Ben had never had.

"You do," Edie agreed solemnly. She might not have shared her mother's determination where men were concerned, but she loved her siblings dearly.

"And one of them needs you," Mona had said, playing the trump card. "Tonight. Lord knows what will happen if Very Nice Andrew breaks off the engagement."

"Do you think he might?" Edie thought Andrew was besotted with her sister, but she supposed even he could be pushed too far.

Andrew Chalmers was twenty-three, a three-event Olympic swimming medalist, cute as a button and an all-around nice guy, to boot. He had been head over heels in love with Rhiannon since they were in high school together, poor fool.

Though, to be fair, when she wasn't flirting outrageously with everything in trousers just because she could, Ree genuinely seemed to be in love with Andrew, too. He steadied her, brought out the caring, sweet side of her. And both Mona and Edie were delighted.

A month ago, Andrew had asked her to marry him. Instantly Rhiannon had said yes. They were getting married next summer.

Rhiannon was happily planning their wedding. Or had been—until yesterday's quarrel.

It hadn't been subtle. Right there in the middle of one of the Mont Chamion's most elegant royal reception rooms in front of the king and most of the royal family, Rhiannon had pitched a fit when Andrew had said he was leaving to go to a swimming competition in Vancouver.

"But what about me?" Rhiannon had wailed. "You're taking me to the wedding!"

"I'm not, actually," Andrew had said in calm, reasonable tones. "And you knew that, Ree. I said so last week when you wanted me to come over. I said I could come but I had to leave on Friday."

"But I want you to be with me!"

"You can come with me. I said so," he reminded her.

But Rhiannon hadn't wanted to miss the royal wedding. And she'd been sure she could twist Andrew around her finger once she got him here. But Andrew had more backbone than that. And no flood of tears or flurry of words had deterred him. He had stalwartly held his ground and soon thereafter caught a flight to Paris and then to Vancouver. Privately Edie had cheered him on, glad he wasn't knuckling under to every demand Rhiannon made.

But she had worried, too, because Rhiannon had been in High Drama Mode ever since.

"She'll 'do something,'" Mona predicted. "I know it. And so do you. She'll ruin it, shoot herself in the foot."

Shooting herself in the foot, literally, was not Rhiannon's problem. Doing something outrageous with an entirely inappropriate man just to spite Andrew was.

Rhiannon was one of the most beautiful young women Hollywood had ever seen. She was Marilyn Monroe at twenty. Betty Boop in the flesh. And she could flirt for England. Or Wales in this case as Rhiannon's father was the fiery Welsh poet,

Huw Evans. Rhiannon had dual-citizenship. And the ability to get into trouble no matter which continent she was on.

So here Edie was, lurking on the edges of the ballroom, clad in her sister's sparkly mauve dress that looked magnificent with Rhiannon's sun-kissed platinum-blonde tresses and deep golden tan, but made Edie's brown hair look dull and which washed out her fair skin, making her freckles stand out like spots. Even worse was the fact that Rhiannon's size seven matching heels were pinching Edie's size nine feet. It was like being stuck in a badly adapted version of Cinderella—and there wasn't a fairy godmother in sight. Of course there was no prince, either.

Only Mr. Trouble.

Even as Edie watched, Rhiannon cozied up to him, leaning closer, slipping her arm through his. Then she ran the fingers of her other hand down the front of his dinner jacket and giggled a breathless giggle at something he said. She tossed her head, making her hair dance in the light reflected from the crystal chandeliers. At the same time she tucked herself against him and reached up to playfully tousle his hair.

Edie swallowed a groan. Next thing you knew she'd start fiddling with his tie. *Undressing him!* Mona was right. Disaster was imminent.

Gritting her teeth against the blisters forming on her heels and toes, Edie pushed away from the pillar and made her way toward her sister.

"Ah, there you are!" she said cheerfully. She even managed to beam brightly though it felt more like a wince.

Rhiannon turned and tossed her hair again, obviously annoyed at having her flirtation interrupted. She was no fool. She had to know exactly why Edie was here. "What do you want?" Ree demanded.

Her tone had Mr. Trouble's dark eyebrows arching as he looked down his blade-straight nose at Edie, wordlessly asking the same question.

She flashed him a smile of polite acknowledgment, but focused on her sister. "I've had a text from Andrew." Which, fortunately, was absolutely true.

Rhiannon lit up, then remembered she was mad at Andrew and frowned. "Why's he texting you?" Her tone was accusatory.

"Can't imagine." Edie shrugged. "Maybe because you turned your phone off?"

Rhiannon's lower lip jutted out petulantly. "I didn't want to talk to him."

"Well, he wants to talk to you. Badly. He sounded desperate."

That might have been embroidering things a bit. The text had said, *Tell ur sister 2 turn her fone on. Need 2 talk.*

But he'd said "need." Didn't that mean "desperate"? Of course it did.

"Badly," Edie reiterated, to reinforce the point. Then she turned her gaze on the man still standing with his arm around Rhiannon. "Andrew is her fiancé," she said pointedly.

He let her go. Quite casually but deliberately, he eased his arm from beneath her hand and moved a step away. He looked at Rhiannon. "A fiancé?"

Ree lifted her shoulders in a sulky shrug. "He's not here," she said. But then she had the grace to appear a bit shamefaced. "We quarreled. He's not always right," she muttered.

Mr. Trouble didn't say anything, and Edie felt obliged to jump in and steer the situation. "Of course he's not," she said stoutly. "And now he's had plenty of time to think about things all the way to Vancouver. I'm sure he didn't mean to hurt you, Ree. He's probably missing you dreadfully."

"Do you think?" Suddenly Ree's tone was bright.

Edie nodded emphatically. "Call him."

But Rhiannon hesitated. She looked at the handsome man beside her, then her gaze measured the whole ballroom as if she were trying to decide what she'd be missing if she left: champagne, music, happy couples dancing past. Mr. Trouble who was, even in Edie's disapproving estimation, the handsomest man in the room.

Rhiannon looked disgruntled. "He should have stayed. *We* could have danced."

"Yes, but he wanted you to go with him, too," Edie reminded her. "It's a two-way street. He has a competition."

"But I'd have missed the wedding."

"And now you're missing Andrew."

Edie let that sink in for a few moments. Then she added almost offhandedly, "If you call him, you can tell him what Sir Oliver said about using his Scottish castle for your honeymoon."

It was the ultimate temptation. Ever since their engagement, Rhiannon's life had revolved around their wedding plans, and every detail had to be shared with Andrew. Sir Oliver's offer of his family's castle had been all Rhiannon could talk about last night—when she wasn't talking about how she was fed up with Andrew.

"Oh, all right." Rhiannon tumbled to the temptation exactly as Edie had dared hope. "I'll call him. I guess I should since he tried to call…and if he texted you…"

Ree sighed, then lifted her gaze to look at Mr. Trouble. "He loves me," she explained. "And I love him—even if he's maddening. So I probably should call him. But," she added a bit wistfully, "I really would have loved to see the architectural renovations in your bedroom."

"And I'd have been pleased to show them to you," he said gallantly.

Edie's jaw dropped. She slammed it shut at once. Rhiannon didn't notice. She gave them both a little wave and tripped gaily off toward the doors to the Great Hall where, please God, she would call Andrew and make up with him.

Edie watched her go, holding her breath until Rhiannon was out of sight. Then she turned to make her excuses and disappear, only to discover that the man Rhiannon had been pawing wasn't looking in the direction Rhiannon had gone.

His dark eyes were now on her. A slow smile touched his lips. And then he winked at her.

Winked!

Something kicked over in her chest. It was almost electric, as if she'd been dead and was suddenly jerked back to life.

Like Sleeping Beauty and the prince? she sneered at herself. But the sensation was so real and caught her so totally unaware that for a moment she couldn't speak. She hadn't felt this sort of awareness since Ben.

When she did finally find her voice, she said, "Architectural renovations in your bedroom?"

Next thing you knew he'd say he'd been going to show Rhiannon his etchings.

But Mr. Trouble just grinned at her and she felt another jolt. "Scout's honor," he said, eyes alight with amusement.

Edie refused to think it was funny. She glowered at him.

"You don't believe me? I'll show them to you." He offered her his arm.

Instantly Edie folded hers across her chest. "Don't be ridiculous! I'm not going to your room. And Rhiannon wouldn't have, either," she lied a second later, needing for some reason she didn't quite understand to deflect the focus back to her sister. "She does love Andrew. They just had a disagreement. And she…lost her head." Not to mention her sense of propriety. "She wasn't offering," she added firmly.

"No?" His brow lifted. "Apparently you didn't hear as much of the conversation as I did."

Edie's cheeks burned. "She wouldn't have—have…"

"Slept with me?" He was laughing at her now. "You don't think so?"

"No!" At least Edie hoped not.

"Well, don't worry, I wouldn't have slept with her."

Edie's eyes widened, and she was surprised again by another unexpected feeling, this time one of something akin to relief. "You…wouldn't?"

He shook his head, meeting her gaze. "Not on your life. She's a child."

"She's twenty."

He nodded. "Like I said, not my type."

"You have a type." It wasn't a question.

Of course he had a type. Men like him always did.

"Well, um, good," Edie said, because she felt obliged to say something in the face of the steady assessing look he was giving her. She started to back away.

He followed. "Who are you?" he demanded. His gaze was intent now, his eyes so dark they were almost black.

"Rhiannon's sister." No one ever believed it until Mona swore on a stack of Bibles that she'd given birth to them both. Her sister was blonde and busty, all curves and come-on. Edie was all angles, elbows and knees. Always had been. With nondescript brown hair and green eyes. Not the color of jade. Not the color of emeralds. Pretty much the color of grass. "Half sister," she corrected.

"Do you have a name, half sister?"

"Edie Daley."

Something else she and Rhiannon didn't have in common. Her sister was named after some ethereal mythological Welsh goddess. Edie was named after her father's mother.

"Ah. Edie." He grinned and reached out and tugged one of her nondescript locks of hair. "My grandmother's name."

Exactly.

"I'm Nick."

As in "up to the old nick," no doubt—as *her* grandmother used to say when describing the family's mischief makers.

"Nick Savas."

"Demetrios's brother?" Edie knew he had several, but she hadn't been introduced to any of them. She just knew that almost all of the tall dark-haired, sinfully gorgeous men at the wedding were related to the groom.

Nick shook his head. "Cousin."

Trust Rhiannon to flirt with a member of the groom's family. The most handsome member of the groom's family, come to that. All the Savas men were handsome as sin. But this one was definitely the most gorgeous of the lot.

That was doubtless why she'd felt the sudden jolt of awareness. She wasn't interested, but she wasn't dead! She was just able to appreciate a handsome man.

"I apologize if my sister's behavior was inappropriate, Mr. Savas—" she said politely, again beginning to edge away.

"Nick," he corrected.

She didn't repeat his name. She recognized it for what it was: an invitation to continue the conversation. And she didn't want to do that. Her awareness of him made her nervous, though she wasn't sure why.

"If you'll excuse me..." She turned abruptly to take the same route her sister had toward the doors. Her duty was done, she could go back to her room, shed the ugly dress, kick off the pinching shoes and spend the rest of the night with a good book.

But before Edie could take a step, strong fingers manacled her wrist, anchoring her right where she was. She looked back at him, eyes wide. "What?"

"You're not going to follow her and make sure she calls him, are you?"

"Of course not."

"So, why are you running off? Stay and talk to me." There was a smooth, persuasive note in his voice.

"I—" She stopped, wanting to say no, expecting herself to say no. She always said no. But now she couldn't seem to form the word. "About what?" she said finally, warily.

He raised a brow. "The architectural renovations in my bedroom?"

She couldn't help it. She laughed.

It was the sort of wry remark that Ben would have made. Her husband had never taken himself very seriously. And after years spent in her mother's world of overinflated egos, Ben's easy-going approach to life had been one of the things she'd loved the most about him.

She hadn't expected that same dry humor from Mr. Trouble, though. But Nick Savas laughed, too, then grinned at her. "There," he said. "See? I knew I could get you to smile."

Edie resisted the pull of attraction. "I've already smiled. I smile a lot," she contradicted him.

"But how often do you mean it?" he challenged softly.

"Often!"

"But not to me," he said. "Not until now."

She opened her mouth to protest, but he touched a finger to her lips to forestall her.

"Dance with me."

It was pure charm—the rough baritone voice, the slightly lopsided smile, the touch of that single finger against her lips. And its simplicity caught her off guard. So did the unexpected stab of desire she felt to do exactly that.

Disconcerted, Edie shook her head. "No," she said. "Thank you."

"Why not?" His fingers lightly pressed her wrist. His eyes wouldn't let hers go.

"You're not supposed to ask 'why not,'" she said irritably. "It's bad manners."

A corner of his mouth quirked. "I thought it was bad manners for you to say no."

She felt like a gauche teenager, her cheeks burning. But she managed a little shake of her head. "I'm sorry. I can't."

"Can't?" He cocked his head. "Or won't?"

Edie took refuge in the truth. She lifted her shoulders and said simply, "My feet hurt."

Nick did a double-take. Then he glanced down at the mauve leather pointy-toed high heels trapping her feet.

"Dear God." He scowled fiercely at them, then looked up to flash her a quick grin. "Come here." And he tugged her inexorably to one of the tables at the edge of the dance floor. "Sit."

It sounded more like a command than an invitation. But getting off her feet was a welcome prospect, so obediently Edie sat.

She expected he would sit down beside her or, even better and probably more likely, leave her there and go find some other woman to dance with. Instead he crouched down in front of her and, before she knew it, he'd taken both her shoes off and tossed them under the table.

She let out a little yelp. "What are you—?"

"I don't know why you women wear such terrible shoes." Nick shook his head, his dark eyes locking with hers accusingly, his fingers caressing her instep.

She started to say they were Rhiannon's, but his touch was robbing her of intelligible speech. And when he began to rub each of her pinched feet gently between his hands, she nearly moaned. It felt heavenly. And intimate. His touch sent bolts of awareness straight through her. She wanted him to stop—and at the same time nearly sobbed when he let go and pulled his hands away.

"There now." He stood up in one fluid movement. "Better?"

Edie looked up, dazed to see him looking down—imperious, in command, his gaze compelling.

All she could do was nod.

"Then dance with me." And he pulled her to her feet and straight into his arms.

It was magic.

He swirled her off her stocking-clad feet and led her into the waltz. She should have stumbled. She always stumbled when she danced.

Even when she'd danced with Ben at their wedding she'd felt self-conscious, always aware that Mrs. Achenbach, her cotillion instructor, had lamented that her clumsy pupil had two left feet. The words had taken up residence in her brain from the time Edie was ten years old. She absolutely believed them.

But tonight she had one of each—stocking-clad though they

were—and miraculously they did exactly what they were supposed to do: followed his.

Of course they did.

Because that was the sort of man he was. Nick Savas said, "Dance," and they didn't dare do anything else. Edie peeked down at her toes, amazed.

"Something wrong?"

Everything. Nothing. Edie shook her head, still dazed. It was like having an out-of-body experience. Or maybe like having an *"in-someone-else's-body"* experience. Like Cinderella's.

Certainly not her own.

She wasn't even supposed to be here. Didn't *want* to be here. Had no business being here—except for Rhiannon. And Rhiannon had already gone.

Instinctively Edie glanced around, looking for a clock. How close to midnight was it?

No way to tell. And Nick wasn't giving her a chance to look. They swirled and dipped and glided. Her liberated toes tingled and she would have wriggled them if she'd been able to do that and dance at the same time. It was the least likely thing she could imagine doing. She half expected someone to tap her on her shoulder and point out her lack of shoes, Or, worse, make a general public announcement.

But of course no one was looking at her. Especially not at her feet.

He had danced her all the way across the ballroom by this time. It was lovely, exhilarating. And yet she could only wonder how in heaven's name she was going to get Rhiannon's shoes back. She glanced around and couldn't even pick out where they'd left them.

"Now what?" Nick said gruffly.

"My shoes—"

"Not yours," Nick said with certainty.

"Well, no," Edie admitted. "Rhiannon's. But I can't just leave them there."

"We'll get them later." He dismissed the whole problem, but then he wasn't dancing at the royal wedding in his socks. "Smile," he commanded her. "I like it when you smile." And he smiled again, too, as if forming a smile of his own could prompt her.

It seemed that it could. Edie's lips curved. Apparently her mouth was as malleable as her feet.

Nick nodded. "Yes. Like that."

No wonder her sister had been pawing his dinner jacket.

Edie faltered at the thought. But the second her feet began to stumble, Nick caught her, drew her up again, pulled her close. Now her breasts pressed against his jacket. And as she was not overly well-endowed that meant all the rest of her was very close to him, too. Through the silk of her dress Edie could feel his legs brush against hers. If she turned her head, she could count individual whiskers on his jawline. And whenever she drew a breath, she smelled soap and a hint of woodsy aftershave.

Her knees wobbled. Nick held her closer still.

"I'm not a very good dancer," she apologized, trying to straighten and pull back.

But Nick didn't let go. "I'm enjoying it. Best part of the evening so far." His voice was a purr in her ear. The vibration sent a tingle all the way down her spine. And her brain leaped ahead, going exactly where she didn't want it to go.

So far?

How far was he expecting it to go?

"Now what?" he murmured as he must have felt her stiffen in his arms.

Edie gave a little shake of her head. "Nothing. I…I'm fine. I just thought of something."

"You need to stop thinking." She could hear the smile in his voice and as he turned his head, she thought she felt his lips against her hair. The shiver was back, sliding down her spine.

What on earth was wrong with her?

She hadn't felt like this in years. Hadn't felt the least flicker of interest in a man since Ben.

Her mother's insistence that she "get back on the horse" had fallen on deaf ears because she didn't feel any need to. And she refused to force things. But this wasn't forced. It was entirely involuntary—and very very compelling as Nick steered her closer to the orchestra. The music enveloped her, wrapping her in a ridiculous Cinderella fantasy.

Danger! her sensible self whispered.

But her dancing self, her wiggling-toes self, countered just as quickly: as long as she knew it was a fantasy, where was the harm?

It wasn't as if she believed in fairy-tale endings.

She'd learned at eighteen when heartthrob actor, Kyle Robbins, had broken her heart that fairy tales were fantasies, that real life romances didn't end in happily ever after. And if she'd dared to think that her marriage to Ben disproved that, well, she had only to remember the devastation of losing him.

So, she knew you couldn't count on happily ever after. She was immune.

So go ahead, she told herself. *Take it for what it is—a few minutes of enjoyment. It won't last, but who cares? It's one dance, one night. Nothing more.*

For the first time tonight her brain and her feet were in agreement. She smiled up at Nick Savas, wiggled her toes and gave herself over to the dance.

Nick Savas didn't do weddings.

Hadn't in years.

He hadn't wanted to come to this one, either. But when you were the cousin of the groom, on the one hand, and were currently restoring a wing of the bride's family's castle, on the other, you knew you didn't have a choice.

There was no way he could have continued working right through the royal wedding day—even though he would have preferred it. He didn't want to watch another happy couple make vows to each other for the rest of their lives. He didn't want to see the way they looked at each other with hope in their eyes and dreams in their hearts. Maybe it was selfish—all right, it damned well was selfish—but he didn't want to witness other people getting what he'd been denied.

Ever since his fiancée, Amy, had died two days before their own wedding, he'd turned his back on all that.

Savas weddings were particularly to be avoided not just because he would have to watch another of his cousins plight their troth, but because every single relative there seemed to consider it their responsibility to point out eligible women for him to meet. To marry.

Nick had no interest in marrying anyone.

No one seemed to get that. So ordinarily he took care to be on a different continent. But working on Mont Chamion's castle, meant he was here today. He'd had no choice.

"It will be lovely," his aunt Malena had assured him yesterday afternoon. "I think Gloria is bringing two of Philip's assistants. They're both young and unmarried," she added brightly, confirming his worst fears.

"Oh, yes," his aunt Ophelia gushed. "There will be lots of absolutely gorgeous women. You can take your pick."

But Nick didn't want his pick. So he'd arrived at the last minute, then sat in the back, avoiding the myriad Savas aunts, uncles and cousins, who, seeing him in attendance, would put one and one together. It was what they did. They couldn't help it. They had an ark mentality—the world was best arranged by twos.

Nick didn't dispute that. Hell, he absolutely believed it.

But there was no "best" for him anymore. Never would be.

When he heard the priest intone, "Do you take this woman…" his throat had tightened.

He shut his mind off, determinedly focusing instead on the various cherubim and seraphim floating above the congregation, studying them as if he were going to be tested on them which, once up on a time he had been, in a course on period architectural detail.

These were mid-seventeenth century from the look of them. Very baroque. Bernini would have been right at home.

"I now pronounce you man and wife."

Nick breathed a sigh of relief.

He would have escaped then, except his uncle Orestes had latched on to him before he could, determined to talk to him to see if he wouldn't like to come and restore the moldering gazebo on his Connecticut property.

At least it hadn't been an offer to introduce him to the new office girl. Silently Nick had counted his blessings as he went along the receiving line, congratulated his cousin, Demetrios, and kissed the glowing bride.

After the dinner, which he had contrived to eat in the company of his uncle Philip's triplet daughters because no one could expect him to be interested in them, he had propped himself against a wall near the dance floor where conversation would be difficult and no one would suggest that he dance.

He'd been counting the minutes until he could politely leave, when an eager young blonde had latched on to him.

"Rhiannon Evans," she'd announced breathlessly. And she'd looked at him as if expecting him to know who she was.

She was young, definitely stunning and determinedly sparkling. "I'm an actress," she'd explained, forgiving him because he admitted he didn't know the first thing about movies. Wasn't really interested. Didn't watch them.

He should, she'd told him. He could start with hers.

She was getting billing now—"though still below the title," she admitted—and bigger and better parts. She told him she was serious about her craft and that she didn't want to be known simply for being beautiful—she said this last with no self-consciousness whatsoever—but for being good at her work.

There was an edge to her bright girlish chatter. Nick was

well-versed in female body language and he could see she had An Agenda.

First there was the hand on his arm, then hers somehow linked around his. She leaned into him. She patted his lapel, then touched his cheek.

"I'm determined not to ride on my mother's coattails, either." And that was when he'd learned she was Mona Tremayne's daughter.

At least he knew who Mona was.

Nick doubted there was a male breathing who hadn't fantasized about Mona Tremayne at some point in his life—her early sex goddess movies had seen to that. Heaven knew as a young man he had, even if she was nearly old enough to be his mother.

He'd met her a few days ago at a dinner Demetrios had hosted. She'd been without her daughter then, thank God. Mona was still strikingly beautiful, still worthy of fantasies if he'd been so inclined. She was also warm and friendly, interested in what he was doing at the palace.

When she learned he was here not for the wedding, but to oversee the restoration of part of the palace, she'd said, "You don't do ranches, do you?"

"Never have."

"You should consider it." She'd smiled encouragingly. "I've got an old adobe on my property that needs to be restored before it crumbles back to primeval mud."

He'd laughed. But because old buildings of any sort interested him he'd asked her a few questions, then offered to send her the names of some colleagues.

Rhiannon hadn't been nearly as interesting. But as she kept on chattering. Nick contrived to look interested. At least she didn't have marriage on her mind. He was sure of that.

There had been an edge of fragile desperation to her frenzied chatter, and the way her gaze roamed the room, he thought she was desperate for someone to see her with him.

He didn't mind who saw them together. Nothing was happening. Nothing was going to happen. And her presence kept the Savas matchmakers at bay.

Finally she paused and focused on him. "What do you do?" she asked.

And so he told her—at length—about architectural renovation and restoration. Served her right, he thought, for pawing him. It was clear that she didn't care a whit. She had other things on her mind.

So he droned on about beams and joists, about weight-bearing walls, about matching the plaster using original techniques. He talked about dry rot and rising damp and wormy floorboards—which in the interest of her further education, he offered to show her as he was currently engaged in pulling up some in the palace's east tower. He'd even gone so far as to say he'd taken a bedroom there so he could continue to work on the wormy floorboards at all hours.

He'd figured he might bore her enough that she'd go find someone more inclined to take her up on what she seemed to have in mind. Or maybe the suggestion would scare her off.

In fact, that was when she'd run her hand down his lapel, looked dreamily up into his eyes and told him how much she'd "simply adore" coming to his bedroom to see the renovations.

Nick began to think it might be a better idea to dance with her—and step on her toes.

But it hadn't come to that.

He'd been saved. By Edie Daley.

A less likely savior would have been hard to imagine. A less likely sister to the ethereally beautiful Rhiannon was hard to imagine, too.

They looked nothing alike. Though Nick supposed he could detect the Mona Tremayne cheekbones in both her daughters' faces. But the similarity ended there. Where Rhiannon determinedly emphasized those bones with makeup, Edie did nothing to highlight them at all.

The little makeup she wore seemed more designed to cover

up than accentuate. Though he suspected that what she was covering up were freckles.

He thought he would prefer the freckles.

He certainly preferred her flashing gray-green eyes and tart tongue to her sister's blue eyes and breathless babbling. Edie didn't charm, she didn't flatter. She didn't paw, either. She kept her distance.

And she got right to the business at hand, which was clearly making sure that her sister had nothing to do with him. Used to having women thrown at his head, Nick found Edie's portrayal of a determined mother hen, intent on extracting her chick from danger, oddly appealing. Her words to her sister, though, revealed that she understood that Nick was not the entire source of the danger. Clearly she realized that her sister was capable of disaster with very little help at all.

Nick didn't envy whoever Rhiannon's fiancé was. The poor guy would have his hands full with her—which made Edie's ability to direct her back onto the straight and narrow all the more impressive. Obviously she was a woman to be reckoned with.

She had presence. And character.

While she may not have had the perfect ageless features of her mother or the ethereal beauty of her younger sister, Edie had the kind of bone structure a camera would love, as well as the liveliest eyes he'd ever seen.

Nick liked lively eyes. He liked her take-charge, no-nonsense personality. He liked the fact that she was intent on backing away from him.

It made him want to get closer.

And once her sister had disappeared, Nick stopped trying to think of ways to escape the reception and instead tried to find ways to keep Edie Daley talking.

For the first time he began to enjoy himself as he drew her out, got her talking, even teased her a bit. She responded, then backed off. He didn't want her backing off.

So he asked her to dance.

The request probably shocked him more than it had her. Nick didn't dance. Hadn't for years.

The last woman he'd danced with had been Amy, three nights before their wedding, the night before she'd died. He'd danced with Amy and it had been the last time he'd held her in his arms.

It wasn't the same, he assured himself. Nothing like the same.

This was a one-off, a turn around the dance floor with a pretty, vivacious woman. He was at a wedding, for God's sake. Dancing was expected! Just because he hadn't done it in eight years… It meant nothing.

Dancing was only moving your feet to music. Hardly something to hold sacred. He should have done it years ago, would have if it had ever occurred to him.

So he was shocked again when Edie said no.

In all his thirty-three years Nikolas Savas had never been turned down for a dance—which was undoubtedly why he'd demanded, "Why not?"

Her unexpected, yet honest answer had made him laugh. Her feet hurt.

No woman he'd ever met—not even Amy—had actually admitted that those stupid pointy-toed shoes women wore hurt their feet.

When he'd knelt to ease hers off, they were so tight he couldn't believe she'd even got them on. He wasn't surprised when she'd said they belonged to her sister. No wonder she didn't want to dance. It was astonishing she could even walk.

But once he'd freed her feet and tossed the offending footwear under the table—so she wouldn't dare crawl under and rescue them—she let him take her into his arms and swirl her onto the dance floor.

It was like riding a bike. Once you learned how to dance, you never forgot.

But it wasn't like dancing with Amy.

Amy had been tiny, the top of her head barely reaching his

shoulder. Edie's nose would have bumped his chin if she'd come that close. She didn't. She kept her distance and periodically glanced down at her stocking-clad toes.

So did he. They charmed him. She seemed shocked by them. Shocked to be dancing with him.

But she moved well, except for the fact that every once in a while she would stiffen and start to pull away.

When she did, he drew her closer, enjoying the feel of her soft breasts against his chest, of the silky dark hair that brushed his jaw when she turned her head. He brushed his lips against her hair.

She stiffened again. "Are you staring?"

No, that wasn't what he was doing. He grinned. "No."

"You are, too. You're ogling my feet."

He laughed and pulled her even closer. "There. Now I can't see them. Better?"

"Er, um," she muttered into the wool of his lapel. He felt her body stiffen again, but she didn't pull away. And seconds later, the tension seemed to ease, her body settled against his as they moved together.

Much better, he decided. Except that his body was becoming increasingly aware of how very appealing she was. Nick might have sworn off the idea of marrying after Amy's death, but he hadn't sworn off sex.

And thoughts of taking Edie Daley to bed were very appealing.

She seemed to fit in his arms, and as they moved together, he rested his cheek on her hair. She had amazing hair, not at all like the straight platinum curtain Rhiannon wore. Edie's was thick and dark and wavy. He suspected it had started out the evening tamed by a pair of gold hair clips just above her ears. But it was a long while since those clips had done their job. Even as she danced, her hair was escaping, curling wildly with a life of its own.

He wanted to thread his fingers through it, bury his face in it. He imagined what it would look like spread out against the sheets. He began to consider again how to get her there when the last strains of the waltz died away and the orchestra segued into something louder, faster and with a pounding of drums, which matched the thrum of his blood coursing through his veins.

"Well," Edie said, abruptly drawing back and pulling her hand out of his. "That was nice."

Nice? Nick stared at her, jolted.

She nodded, dimpling as she smiled. "Very nice. Thank you for the dance." There was something almost impishly polite in her tone, as if she knew the effect she was having on him—and wasn't going to even give him a chance to try his moves.

But Nick wasn't going to give up without an effort.

"I can do better than nice," he promised, holding out his hand, silently urging her to take it, to come with him.

Resolutely Edie shook her head. "Thank you, but no. And it isn't impolite to refuse a second dance," she informed him before he could claim otherwise.

"How about a glass of wine? We can sit this one out."

But again she shook her head. "It's been a pleasure, Mr. Savas. Thank you for being kind to my sister. And thank you for the dance. I…enjoyed it."

Had he heard an infinitesimal hesitation in her words? Before Nick could decide, Edie held out her hand and shook his politely. "Good night."

No!

He didn't say it. Blessedly his mouth stayed firmly shut. But a thousand things ran through his mind that he might say to stop her, to prolong the moment, to keep her there.

That he wanted to so badly surprised him. He wasn't used to feeling any such compulsion. Didn't *want* to feel it.

Bedding her, yes, he'd like to do that. But just keep her there to talk to him? There was no point.

So he tucked his hands into his trouser pockets and nodded.

"Good night, Ms. Daley," he said equally politely. "Thank you for the dance."

She turned away. But as she did so, he couldn't resist. "If you ever do want to see the architectural renovations in my bedroom, Ms. Daley…"

She spun back, her eyes flashing green fire.

Nick's heart kicked over. He turned on his best million-megawatt come-hither grin. Edie turned and, with a toss of her head, disappeared into the milling dancing crowd.

Only when the crowd had swallowed her up did he turn away. He felt oddly flat.

He should have gone back to his room then. It was nearly midnight. He'd done his duty. Showed up. Even danced. No one would remark on his vanishing now.

But he didn't go. He prowled the edges of the dance floor, restless and out of sorts. Edgy. Hungry. And not for food. His body was still aware of how neatly Edie Daley had fit into his arms.

"Damn it." Abruptly he turned and asked the nearest unattached female for a dance.

Why not? He'd danced once tonight already. It was just more of the same.

But it wasn't the same. This woman was nothing like Edie Daley.

She didn't settle into his arms with a reluctance that gave way to rightness. She plastered herself against him, locked her fingers together behind his neck and nibbled on his jaw. She didn't so much dance as slither and move against him until at last the music ended and Nick was finally able to peel her off again.

"Another?" she murmured.

"No." He'd had enough. More than. "I'm done dancing," he said firmly, though years of having good manners drilled into him made him try to look regretful as he stepped away. "I'm calling it a night."

Even as he did so, someone's hand touched his arm from behind. "I'm glad to hear it," an unexpected female voice said.

Nick spun around—and stared with shock into Edie Daley's gray-green eyes. She linked her arm firmly through his and gave him a blinding smile. "Because I've just decided that I'd love to see those architectural renovations."

CHAPTER TWO

NICK'S brows shot up. So did his heartbeat. And the spark of interest that had vanished when she had was back in spades.

But even as his libido was in favor of her suggestion, his brain was saying, *Hang on a minute.*

"Change your mind?" he asked her, careful not to sound too eager even though he damned well was.

Edie's smile, if possible, grew brighter. "Yes." Her voice was firm and clear. No hesitation at all. But he spotted a glitter in her eyes that he hadn't seen before. And was that a bit of her sister's desperation in her tone? He narrowed his gaze on her.

Her lashes flickered rapidly. Her smile amped up a bit more. Yes, this was desperation. And defiance, too. He could see that now. But exactly who or what had inspired it, he had no idea.

Carefully he let out a breath, drew another as he studied her from her flyaway hair to the tips of her stocking-clad toes. He wanted to take the stockings off those toes.

Would she let him?

Whatever was going on, taking her to his bedroom couldn't be a bad thing. Could it?

Nick guessed he'd find out.

Putting his hand over hers, he smiled down at her. "By all means." Then he turned to the blonde he'd danced with, the one who was still standing there and whom he'd completely forgotten about. "Thank you for the dance," he said to her politely. "Good night."

Then he laced Edie's fingers through his and started to lead her back to where they'd first met.

"The door is that way." Edie was practically dragging her feet.

"Shoes," he said and dived beneath the table. The miserable things were still there. He grabbed them and rose again, then slanted Edie a glance.

"You don't want to wear them, do you?"

She laughed, but it was a more brittle laugh than she'd shared with him before. Something had indeed happened. "I certainly don't," she said.

Nick tucked the shoes in his coat pockets so only the spiky mauve heels protruded. Then he offered her his arm. With no hesitation at all, Edie linked her arm through his and walked, head held high, along beside him, her bearing more regal than the queen of Mont Chamion.

Her posture was stiff and far more tense than when they'd danced, and she didn't speak again. But Nick knew better than to ask about it now. Edie kept her gaze straight ahead until they had nearly reached the door.

Then, near the door they came upon Mona and the small but inevitable knot of men clustered around her. Edie barely glanced their way, but she turned her gaze on him, focused a melting smile right at him and fluttered her lashes.

Nick almost laughed. He did smile at raised brows on Mona's face. There was a look of surprise and something else—consternation?—on Edie's mother's face. Whatever had sparked Edie's return, it had something to do with her mother.

Or, Nick realized as Mona said something to the man standing next to her who was staring at Edie and frowning, did it have something to do with him?

He was about Nick's age, fair-haired and handsome in a young Robert Redford sort of way. Familiar looking, but Nick couldn't put a name on him.

An actor, no doubt. Actor friends of Demetrios's were thick on the ground tonight.

This one transformed his frown into an engaging grin and stepped forward to intercept them as they approached. "Edie! Long time no see. I was so glad when Mona said you were here."

Edie's fingers tensed against his arm, but she smiled, too. "Not here for long," she said, still moving. "We're just leaving."

"But we haven't danced."

She kept smiling, but Nick could see it was tight. "Nice to see you again, Kyle. Good night."

"I'll see you in the morning, then," the man called Kyle said.

But they were already past him and headed toward the door when Edie said brightly to Nick in tones that were certainly loud enough to be overheard, "Which wing is your room in?"

Nick didn't think he imagined the sound of several people sucking air behind them. His own brows arched, but he said cheerfully, "I'll show you," gave her a melting smile for good measure and held the door so she could sail through it ahead of him.

Only when the door closed behind them did Edie seem to sag. But almost at once she pulled herself up straight and tall again, and kept right on walking until they'd left the reception area totally and were in one of the long walnut-paneled corridors. There at last she stopped and took a deep breath, then looked up at him.

"Thank you," she said, all her previous brightness gone. But the brittle tone had vanished, too.

Nick liked that. "My pleasure." She looked pale suddenly and he said, "Do you need to sit down?"

She gave him a wan smile, but shook her head. "I'm all right."

Still she looked rattled. Not at all like the Edie Daley who had come running to defend her baby sister. "What am I missing?" he asked her.

She looked down at her feet, then rubbed the bottom of one stocking-clad foot against the top of the other. They looked as vulnerable as she did. He wondered if she was going to deny that he was missing anything.

But at last she looked up at him and made a wry face. "My mother's heavy-handed attempt at matchmaking, I fear."

"The blond guy with the hundred-dollar haircut?"

Edie looked startled, then sighed and nodded. "Yes."

"You're not interested in him?" Nick was surprised how glad he was to hear it.

"No!" she said with a force that indicated more than indifference. She seemed to realize it because she muttered, "I'm not. I was just—I was afraid she'd try something like this."

"She being your mother?"

Edie nodded.

"She often sets you up?"

"She hints."

"And you don't like that?" He supposed she had a right to dislike matchmaking relatives as much as he did. But most women he knew welcomed the meddling. "Matchmaking is a bad thing?"

"Yes, it is," Edie said flatly. She didn't elaborate at first, and he thought she was going to change the subject. But then she sighed, "She thinks I need to start dating again."

"Again?" Nick prompted when she didn't explain.

There was another pause, as if she were deciding how much to say. Finally she looked around, then back at him and said impatiently, "Where are these architectural renovations?"

His brows lifted. "You really want to see them?"

"Do they really exist? Or were you flirting with my sister?"

"They really exist. And I wasn't flirting with your sister. Coming to see them was her idea."

"But you invited me—"

"I was flirting with *you*." And not giving her a chance to respond, not waiting to see what her reaction to that actually was, Nick grasped her hand in his and led her toward the tower.

She didn't speak as they walked, and Nick didn't say anything, either. He was too busy trying to assess the situation, trying to decide if she had been merely using him to avoid an unpleasant confrontation, no more no less? Or had she been angling for something else considerably more intimate.

He knew which he would prefer.

What she wanted he guessed he'd find out, he thought as he stopped and unlocked the east tower wing door. There was no one else staying in it but him so he'd only left a few lights burning, and the hall was cast in gloom when he pushed open the heavy door.

Edie paused at the entrance to peer into the shadows.

"Having second thoughts?" Nick asked. He wouldn't have blamed her.

But she took a quick breath. "No." There was a moment's pause and then she turned her head and met his gaze. "Are you?"

The question caught Nick off guard.

He'd slept with other women since Amy's death. It had been eight years, after all, and he had never claimed he would be a monk.

But it hadn't meant anything. Not the way it had with Amy. It was an itch he scratched. But only with women who considered it the same way he did.

He looked intently at the woman beside him now and wondered how Edie Daley considered it—she who wasn't even dating. That was when he realized that she was still looking at him, waiting for an answer.

Quickly Nick cleared his throat. "No," he said just as firmly as she had.

Edie smiled. It wasn't the smile she'd given her mother or the man named Kyle. It wasn't the brittle smile she'd given him when she'd reappeared and taken his arm. It was the smile he'd coaxed out of her before they'd danced—a genuine smile, he thought, and one that wasn't reluctant. It sent a shaft of desire right through him.

He wanted more of those smiles. More of her.

"Let me show you my renovations," he said, and he began to talk about the structure of the building. Several sentences later he realized that she was staring at him, wide-eyed, and he stopped. "What?"

"You really know all this stuff?" She sounded amazed.

Nick laughed. "It's what I do. My job. Why I'm here."

"I thought…the wedding…"

"I didn't come for the wedding. I came to restore the east tower."

And suddenly the smile he'd been hoping for lit her face. "How wonderful," she exclaimed. "Show me. Tell me everything."

He thought she might just be being polite, but as he turned on more lights and walked her through the main rooms, which were already finished, all the time telling her about the history of the place, explaining when it had originally been built and which parts were added on later, she asked eager, interested questions.

She didn't endure his lecture as her sister had done, but demanded to know more. Of course, to be fair, he'd deliberately droned on when he'd described his work to Rhiannon. He took pains to interest her sister.

But it wasn't long before he realized he needn't have bothered. Edie was clearly interested in the castle and in the work he'd done on it. She had studied history in college, she told him. She'd thought she might be a teacher.

"A teacher? Far cry from being your mother's business manager, isn't it?"

Her lips twisted. "One of those times when life happened while I was making other plans."

What plans? Nick wondered, but he didn't ask as there was something in the expression on her face that told him to leave it alone. So instead he asked, "Did you ever want to go into acting?"

She shook her head. "Never. That's not my world."

"But you work in it every day."

"In the business part of things. Not the glitz and glamour part. Not the movie star bit," she said adamantly.

"You don't like the 'movie star bit'?"

"It's not for me," she said simply, then added, "it's too difficult."

"Acting?"

"I suppose that's part of it. But I think really that it's harder being real. Being honest. If you act all the time, who are you? Really? Do you even know?"

Her voice rose when she asked the questions and they didn't sound rhetorical. Nick supposed, having a mother who was an icon of American film and screen, she'd probably given it considerable thought. Then, as if she decided she'd betrayed a bit too much emotion, Edie shrugged and said lightly, "I'm a behind the scenes person, that's all."

"Yeah. Me, too." When she blinked, clearly surprised, Nick explained. "When I'm working on a building, the building is what matters." He waved a hand to encompass the whole of the one he'd been working on. "Not who does the work."

Edie looked thoughtful, then she nodded. "Yes. I see what you mean." Then she ran an appreciative hand down one of the window casings. "You've done an amazing job. At least I guess you have. Honestly, it's hard to tell where the old stuff ends and the new begins."

"Exactly the way it's supposed to be."

"How do you start?"

"I case the joint," he told her with a grin. "I go over it all with a fine-tooth comb, so to speak. I learn who built it and when and why. Then I live in it."

"Hence the architectural renovations in your bedroom," she said with a grin. "Seriously?"

"Seriously." He pointed toward a door at the far end of the hall. "My digs."

Her gaze followed his gesture. Rhiannon would doubtless have rubbed up against him and suggested, "Show me."

Edie looked at the door, then turned back to him and asked, "When was the tower built?"

So Nick told her.

"It was a thirteenth century addition to the castle. It was designed to be a lookout and barracks for the soldiers who defended against the onrushing hordes."

"Hordes?" Her eyes got wide. "There were hordes? It's so small! Why would they bother?"

"The whole country was bigger back then. The royal family had more wealth and they had some good mountain valleys for cultivation. There are several natural springs as well as rivers. It would have made a nice prize for whoever could take it." He grinned and shrugged. "But no one could."

"I had no idea."

"The Chamion family are survivors. They knew how to pit one enemy against another. They also knew how to make alliances and how to make friends. There's lots of history here," he went on as he led her through the finished rooms to a heavy oak door at the far end. He pushed it open to reveal a hall where there was substantial scaffolding. "We're still working in here."

There were tarps and sawhorses—his concession to modern working conditions—all over, along with piles of lumber. But the tools were all primitive, ones that thirteenth century carpenters, joiners and masons would have used. Edie headed straight for them. She asked about every one, made him explain how he used them, where he'd found them. She looked at him with admiration when he said he often made his own.

"A matter of necessity," he said. "No old ones left."

"And you do it all yourself?"

Nick laid a proprietary hand on one of the scaffolds. "I started it. I did the first rooms on my own so I had a good feel for things. Recently I've been working up in the tower and there are a couple of local craftsmen doing this."

She walked around the room, noting where he'd replaced a joist. The new wood was evident. But she ran her finger over the chisel marks and shook her head. "It must take forever."

"Which is why it took generations to build places like this."

She smiled, then lifted her gaze from the wood to look at him again. He felt her gaze assessing him. "You look like such a 'modern' man," she said. "It's hard to imagine you spending your days doing this."

His mouth quirked. "Well, I don't usually wear a suit to work."

"How did you get into it? Kids usually say they want to be a fireman or a cowboy."

"I wanted to be an architect."

"Of old buildings?"

He shrugged. "I like them."

"Have you ever designed a new building?"

"Once," he said curtly, turning away.

There was a moment's silence. Then, "I'm sorry," Edie said.

Nick shot her a quick glance from beneath drawn down brows. She was leaning against one of the worktables, her gentle eyes on him, looking incongruous and desirable, both at the same time. "Sorry about what?" he said gruffly.

"Getting too close."

His frown deepened. "Close to what?"

"You." She smiled faintly. "Asking about how you came to do this. What you had designed," she added.

He felt an edginess between his shoulder blades. "It's not important." He picked up a chisel and balanced it on his palm, stared at it, then abruptly set it down again to look at her.

She looked back, her brows lifted a little. "I would have said it was very important," she countered quietly.

She would have been right.

Now Nick rubbed the back of his neck, kneaded the muscles, but they remained tense. "It was," he said tonelessly. It had changed his life.

This time she didn't ask. She didn't pry. She simply waited.

Nick shoved his hands into his trouser pockets, rocked back on his heels, stared into the middle distance, not at Edie.

"I designed a house," he said at last, unsure why the words were coming out of his mouth. He didn't talk about the house. Had never talked about it with anyone. But now he found himself saying, "I was getting married. I built it for my fiancée." He said the words almost defiantly.

Edie made a small sound. Otherwise she didn't move, didn't speak.

"It was supposed to be the perfect house," he went on, his tone as harsh as his feelings. He'd intended it to be his gift to her. He'd wanted it to be perfect. As perfect as she was.

Amy had laughed at that. "Don't be silly," she'd said. "I'm far from perfect."

But he'd thought she was. Absolutely perfect in every way. She was certainly perfect for him.

So he'd made her tell him everything she'd ever dreamed of having in a house—the expansive picture windows looking out across Long Island Sound, the winding staircase, the second-story balcony overlooking the naturally landscaped pool. The massive stone fireplace, the island-centered kitchen, the three upstairs bedrooms—a suite for them and one each for the children they would have—he was determined they would all be exactly as she wanted them.

"Her heart's desire," he said bitterly now.

"But it wasn't?" Edie ventured softly.

He shrugged. "She didn't care. Oh, she was delighted about the house, thought it was a great idea. But mostly she just wanted to get married. And I kept putting it off. I wanted the house finished. I wanted it all just right."

Not because he didn't want to marry her. He had. But he'd wanted to give her the very best he had to offer. He'd thought it was worth waiting for.

He'd been wrong.

The inadequacy of that house compared to the time he could

have had with her still gutted him. He ground his teeth, cracked his knuckles. Swallowed hard.

"What happened?" Edie asked quietly.

"She died."

He said the words baldly. Forced himself to confront the mistake he'd made. He didn't look at Edie. This wasn't about her. It was about him. And Amy.

For a long moment Edie didn't say anything, either. Nick wasn't surprised. What, after all, was there to say?

He should have kept his own mouth shut. He couldn't imagine what he'd been thinking, dragging out his private pain for a woman he'd known less than a couple of hours.

"Forget it," he muttered. "I shouldn't have said anything."

"I asked." She reached out, touched his arm. "I am so very sorry," she told him.

A lot of people had said they were sorry. But Edie's words didn't sound like a platitude. He could hear the earnestness in her voice, and there was something so close to pain in her tone that it surprised him. He turned to look at her.

"You lost her," Edie said, "and you lost your own future as well."

"Yes." It was something that no one else seemed to get. He wasn't the one who had died, after all. He should just get on with his life. If they didn't say it—and some did before many months had passed—he could see it in the way they looked at him, in the suggestions for dates, in the offers to set him up with eligible women.

"I understand," she said.

He doubted it. "Thank you," he said politely and looked away out the window.

"My husband died two years ago."

Nick's gaze snapped back, shocked, to meet hers. His "I'm sorry" felt as feeble and inadequate as a platitude now. "I didn't know."

"I don't generally announce it," Edie said lightly. Then she gave him a faint smile. "I don't suppose you do, either."

"No." It had been, literally, years since he'd talked about Amy to anyone. Now he paused, considering. "That was why you were upset about Mona's matchmaking?"

She thinks I need to start dating again. Nick remembered Edie's earlier words. Remembered wondering about the *again.* Now he knew.

She hesitated, then nodded. "Yes."

He understood. It made perfect sense. He didn't look at her. He didn't think she was looking at him. She was probably thinking about the husband she'd lost much more recently than he'd lost Amy.

And he was thinking about—her. About Edie.

He tried to think about her as someone's wife. He wondered what had happened, didn't feel as if he could ask.

She wasn't that close to him. Three feet, maybe even four. But even without looking he could feel her presence. There seemed to be a hum of awareness between them. Or maybe it only went one way. However it went, Nick felt a connection. He wanted to soothe away her pain, make her forget.

But he knew better than anyone that you didn't forget.

Now he heard her move, step away from the side of the table and he turned to face her again. She was smiling, but it was a faint smile. Sad, he thought. And why not? She had reason to be sad.

"I should go," she said now. "I've intruded on you enough."

But as she moved past him toward the door, he caught her arm. "Don't," he said. And when she looked up into his eyes, he said, "Stay."

Just one word. Low, rough, but laced with an urgency that surprised him. The very word surprised him. The request. The command.

He didn't know what to call it. Only knew he didn't want her to leave.

Edie looked surprised, too. Her lips parted, but for a moment no words passed through them. She seemed to be weighing her answer, deciding how to respond. Finally she said lightly, "You're not done with the tour yet?"

The question allowed them both to back off. Nick nodded. "You haven't seen the tower."

"The tower?" she echoed.

"I've been redoing the stairway up to the parapet, rebuilding the tower and the battlements. There's a fantastic view. You should see it." But he said wryly, "You're not exactly dressed for it." She was, of course, still in her stocking feet.

"I'll risk it," she said promptly.

"I'd carry you, but the passage is too narrow."

"It's all right. I can climb."

"The stones are too rough. Hang on. I'll get you something to wear on your feet."

He strode down to his own room and came back moments later with a pair of his flip-flops. He grimaced. "They're too big. But if you really want to do it, they're better than nothing."

"I really want to do it."

So did he. He crouched down to put the flip-flops on her, then realized at the same time she did that she would have to shed her stockings first.

There was a moment's pause. Edie's toes curled, then a second or two later slowly straightened again. Nick's mouth felt suddenly dry.

"Let me help you," he offered, lifting his gaze to her face.

It was shadowed. Her expression was hard to read, but he saw her touch her tongue to her lips. Then she bit down on the lower one and, looking down at him, held perfectly still.

He took that for agreement. "Hang on," he instructed her, and hoped to God he could do the same.

It was hardly the height of intimacy, sliding his fingers up beneath her dress to find the tops of her stockings or panty hose or whatever she was wearing.

On the other hand, it was pretty damned erotic. The stockings felt like real silk, smooth and warm against her legs, so fine that he was afraid his callused fingers would snag them.

So he proceeded slowly, trying to be careful, to move lightly. But the hint of firm flesh beneath that silken barrier was enticing. He loved to touch. He wanted to stroke as his hands snaked over her calves, past her knees, up her thighs. He could feel her legs tremble.

Fingers suddenly clutched his head, gripping his hair. He sucked in a breath. "S-sorry," she muttered. Her fingers loosened their grip, then as his continued their journey, hers tightened again. They sent a shiver down his spine.

But that sensation was nothing compared to the shaft of desire that shot straight to his groin as the silk beneath his fingers turned to lace and then, an inch later, to warm bare skin.

Nick sucked air, then tried to steady his breathing, to be matter-of-fact. This wasn't a seduction—unless he was the one being seduced.

Now he hooked his fingers inside the top of one stocking and drew it down, then slipped it off her foot. Then he skimmed his fingers back up the other leg. But knowing what he would encounter didn't make it any easier to feign indifference.

He *wasn't* indifferent. And when he stood up—provided he could manage to stand up—she would know it.

So he took his time, sliding her feet into the flip-flops, then picking up the stockings and folding them.

"I'll do that." Edie nearly snatched them out of his fumbling hands. Hers seemed to be full of thumbs as well. But at least her focus on them allowed Nick to wince his way to his feet and adjust his trousers so that his reaction was not immediately obvious.

He cleared his throat. "Right. We can go up this way." He picked up the flashlight on the worktable and headed toward a door at the far end of the room. "Be careful."

* * *

If she were being careful, Edie thought, she wouldn't be here now. She'd be back in her room listening to the faint sounds of the orchestra through the open window while she read a book.

But she wasn't. She was climbing a steep, winding, extremely narrow stone staircase behind a man who had just slid his hands up her legs. Her body was still tingling from the touch of his fingers. Her brain was still jangled from a hormone overload after over two years of complete disinterest. And her emotions were as unreliable as a teenager's. She *should* be in bed with a book—preferably one that would bore her to sleep!

Instead here she was trying to keep her eye on the beam of the flashlight that Nick was aiming at the steps as he climbed. He had angled it so that she could see it playing against the stairs and the wall without having to watch it through his legs.

But she preferred to study his legs.

She tried not to—and that was when she stumbled.

"Oh!" She gasped as her foot slipped. She reached out to grab at the side of the wall as she felt her footing fail. But before she could grab anything, Nick had spun around and grabbed her.

He hauled her up against him so that she was sure he could hear the pounding of her heart. She could certainly hear it. Or maybe that was his.

"Are you all right?" he demanded. Then, without waiting for an answer, because surely he could feel that she was fine—after all that was her body pressed against his—he said, "This is insane. I never should have brought you up here."

It might be insane, but climbing the stairs wasn't what made it so.

"I'm all right," Edie said. "Truly."

He made a sound that implied he wasn't convinced. If she lifted her face just a little, Edie thought her lips could probably brush his jawline. She couldn't see, of course. Other than the flashlight, which was now behind her in the arm he had wrapped around her, there was no light at all. And yes, his heart was hammering, too.

"You're sure?" He asked after a moment.

Edie nodded. She was right. The top of her head collided with his chin. "Sorry. Yes, I'm okay. I just slipped. Please, let's go on."

He didn't immediately agree, but finally he said, "Okay. But you're going ahead of me." And he eased her up the narrow stairway so that she was in front of him. Then, keeping one arm around her, playing the flashlight on the steps just ahead of her, he climbed the steps directly behind her.

He was so close his knees brushed her calves, so close she could feel the warmth of his breath against her back. And his other hand, big and warm and callus-roughened, wrapped her fingers. She'd wondered about the calluses when they were dancing. She understood how he got them now.

She remembered the feel of them sliding up her legs and touching the bare skin of her thighs. She wondered how those hands would feel against more sensitive skin on her body.

Once more she stumbled. Nick tightened his grip. "Careful."

"Yes," Edie said, breathless and mortified, taking another step and then another. "I'm trying to be."

Was she? Or was she actually being more reckless than she'd ever been in her life? She didn't know the answer to that yet.

"One step at a time," her grandma Tremayne always used to say. "You'll get there that way."

Edie supposed it was true. But it would have helped if she'd known where she was going.

"Here we are." They had reached a heavy wooden door. Nick reached around her and pushed open, then drew her up and out onto the narrow walkway.

"Oh!" Edie stopped stock-still and simply stared at the sparkling kingdom spread at her feet.

If the evening had felt like something out of a Cinderella fairy tale before, now, with the tiny lights of Mont Chamion's formal gardens spread out below her, Edie felt herself swept ever more fully into a sense of enchantment.

"Not exactly what it would have looked like in the thirteenth century," Nick said wryly.

"But beautiful," Edie murmured, putting her hands on the rough stone wall and leaning out to look down. "It's amazing. We have gardens back at home in Santa Barbara. But nothing like these."

"There aren't any like these. They're one of a kind." Nick's voice was quiet, almost reverent, as he came to stand beside her and together they stared out at the wonderland below. Neither of them spoke.

There were a few wedding guests outside in the gardens, and Edie could hear an occasional murmur of a voice or crack of laughter. From an open window came the lilting sounds of the orchestra playing a waltz. But as magical as it was, it was less enthralling than the man next to her.

He stood very close, but not touching her as he leaned forward, his elbows on the wall, the pristine white of his shirt cuffs peeking out from beneath his dark suit coat. His fingers were loosely knotted together. In the light of a three-quarter moon, she could, glancing sideways, see the light and shadow on the hard angles and planes of his face.

Her sister Rhiannon had casually and flirtatiously stroked his cheek. Edie's fingers curled into a fist so she wasn't tempted to do likewise. She turned her gaze away, too, tried to focus on the tableau below.

What Nick was actually thinking she didn't know. While moments ago in the stairwell she would have said he was as aware of her as she was of him, now he seemed so remote she doubted he was thinking about her at all. So she turned her head to risk another look.

He turned at the same time. Their gazes locked. The heat flared. And Edie's breath caught in her throat.

Nick cleared his. Then, deliberately he straightened. "It's getting cool up here. Shall we go down?" His voice was perfectly polite, but Edie thought she detected a hint of raggedness in his tone. The raggedness of desire?

Did she even know what that sounded like anymore?

"I'll go first on the way down," Nick decreed.

"So I can crash into you and knock us both all the way to the bottom?" Edie joked.

"Hang on to my shoulder if you want. I'll go slow."

He did go slow, but she didn't reach for him. She might have liked a hand, but clutching at him unnecessarily was something Rhiannon would have done, so Edie deliberately didn't do it. She just kept one hand on the wall as she made her way carefully down the steps behind him and tried not to stumble and crash into him. It was a relief to reach the hallway again and to have Nick turn and secure the door.

"That was lovely. Thank you," she said, slipping the flip-flops off and holding them out to him, smiling up at him at the same time.

Nick didn't smile back. His features were taut; there was almost a grim line to his mouth which, after a moment, he managed to curve into something resembling a smile. Then he stepped back and said briskly, "Well, there you have it. Nick Savas's two-bit architectural tour." He flashed her a quick glib sort of smile.

Edie's smile didn't flash. It remained firmly in place. But her heart was galloping and she had the sensation of walking on water. She dared not contemplate it too closely. She just needed to keep going. "It was wonderful."

Their gazes locked again. Nick's expression wasn't remote now. His eyes were intent. Focused on her. The silence went on. And on.

Until finally Nick said, "I want you."

His voice was rough. She heard an edge to it, a desperation almost. And something that sounded like annoyance. Edie wasn't annoyed. But she was shocked to hear him say the words so bluntly. At the same time, to her own astonishment, elated.

"Is that a problem?" she asked, keeping her tone light.

"Isn't it?" he challenged her, one brow lifting.

She blinked at the ferocity of his tone. "We're adults," she heard herself say mildly.

"There's more to it than that."

"Yes." She nodded, unsure where he was going with this.

"Usually," he amended.

Edie shook her head, not following. "I'm not sure what you mean."

"I mean," he said firmly, "that I don't want anything more than that."

"Than sex?" Edie said, wanting to be clear.

His jaw tightened and he looked faintly discomfitted by her plain-speaking, but nodded. "Exactly."

So much for fairy tales, Edie thought.

But really, she wasn't expecting a fairy tale, either. She knew better. So why not be frank? Why not set out parameters?

If Kyle Robbins had done so years ago, she wouldn't have been expecting a proposal of marriage when he'd simply wanted to go to bed with her. She wouldn't have had her hopes raised merely to see them dashed.

"I don't do relationships," Nick continued to spell it out. "One night. That's it."

"Those are the rules?" Edie said, smiling.

Nick nodded. "Those are the rules."

Their gazes met again, clear and unblinking. No starry-eyed foolishness here, Edie thought. No romance. No hearts and flowers. No expectations.

"Okay," she said at last, drawing the word out even as she came to terms with the implications.

Nick's brow rose a fraction higher. "You're all right with that?" He sounded as if he didn't believe her. "You're sure?"

"Well, I'm not expecting a proposal of marriage," Edie said sharply.

Nick raked a hand through his hair. "Good," he said with obvious relief. "Because I'm not making one." He shuddered and shook his head. "Never again."

"One day you might—" Edie began.

But he cut her off. "No," he said, absolutely adamant. "I won't."

Edie didn't think she ought to say she felt sorry for him, but the truth was, she did. She had loved Ben with all her heart and soul. But she would never say she wouldn't fall in love again, wouldn't marry again. She'd told Mona she wasn't interested because she hadn't been—then.

It didn't mean she wouldn't ever be.

Good grief, look how suddenly things could change. Two hours ago her hormones had been missing in action. She hadn't been remotely interested in a man. And now—now she was contemplating going to bed with a man she barely knew. Why? Because she was attracted to him, certainly. But mostly because she didn't trust herself not to do something even more foolish with a recently divorced, clearly interested Kyle Robbins. One night with Nick was far preferable.

"So if you're not interested, I'd completely understand," Nick was saying.

"I'm interested," Edie said. "One night. No relationship. Got it. That's what I want, too."

Nick stared at her long and hard.

Edie stared back, unblinking. *Don't look down. Don't look down.* The words echoed around her brain. Still he didn't move.

"I know what I'm doing," she assured him, with the slightest hint of irritation. "Do you?"

Apparently he did. Abruptly Nick closed the space between them and wrapped her in his arms.

Like when they'd danced, Edie thought for a split second.

But then as his hard, strong, warm body enveloped her in his embrace, she thought, *No, not like dancing at all.* A hundred, thousand, million times better.

Her whole body responded. Her knees wobbled. Her eyes

opened, then shut. Her lips parted and suddenly his mouth was on hers. Fierce, hungry, demanding.

I want you, Nick had said. His voice had been hungry, ragged.

But his subsequent words had seemed like some sort of impersonal negotiation of terms. There was nothing impersonal or negotiated about this. This was instinct, pure and simple. He was a man who wanted a woman—a man who wanted her.

And Edie wanted him, too. *Yes,* she thought, kissing him back. *Oh, yes!*

Yes, it was just one night. No, it wasn't going anywhere. She had no expectations. But where had expectations ever got her?

He wasn't Ben. But Ben was gone forever. He wasn't Kyle. And thank God for that.

He was Nick. And tonight—just tonight—he was hers. She was determined not to regret it.

CHAPTER THREE

SHE wasn't his usual sort of woman.

Nick didn't care.

He wanted her. And the desire that had been building all evening was the only thing that mattered to him now. She was tart and sweet, eager and tentative, cool and yet capable of burning him down to the ground.

She looked too closely, saw too much. And she wasn't afraid to talk about what she saw.

But they weren't talking now, were they?

No. They were kissing. God, yes, they were kissing! And her lips were as hungry as his. Her hands were as eager as his. They slid up his arms and around the back of his neck to hold his face to hers. He didn't complain. It was what he wanted, too.

Restless and eager, his hands roved over her back, tangled in her hair, loosening whatever pins she had anchored it with so that it fell in loose, heavy dark waves over her shoulders and down her back. He ran his fingers through it, buried his face in it, drew in the citrusy scent of shampoo and something exclusively Edie Daley.

It was heady, dizzying, and it didn't matter if she wasn't the sort of woman he ordinarily took to bed, a woman he could scratch a physical itch with and walk away from. He could do the same with her. He *would* do the same.

But first he would spend the night with her.

And yes, he knew exactly what he was doing.

"I missed a spot on the tour," he murmured against her lips.

Edie pulled back slightly, stared at him, disbelieving.

"My bedroom."

She smiled. Then she placed her hands on his arm and looked up into his eyes. "What a very good idea," she said. And there was a breathless quality in her voice that cranked his desire up another notch.

"Right this way." And he scooped her up into his arms and carried her down the hall to the room he'd been using as a bedroom, pausing only to kick the door open. Then he bumped it firmly shut again with one hip and then, in the darkness, lowered her onto his bed. He dropped down beside her, intending to pick up where they'd left off.

"Turn on the light," Edie said.

He pulled back and looked at her. "What?"

"If I'm getting a tour, I want to see everything."

Which wasn't a bad idea at all. He very much wanted to see her as he made love to her. He grinned.

"Or maybe there aren't lights," she reflected. "Do you use candles for an authentic ambiance?"

"It's possible to use candles," Nick said. But he reached over and flipped on a bedside lamp. "When they give tours at night, I imagine they do. But tonight I think a lamp will do."

It was a subdued light, but even so it threw the room with its utilitarian furnishings and spartan double bed into a pattern of light and shadow. Hardly the sight of a romantic seduction.

But Nick wasn't focusing on the room. He had eyes only for Edie Daley. He'd seduce her anywhere. She was half-reclining on his bed, the mauve dress dark against her creamy skin. The low light made Edie's peekaboo freckles entirely disappear and turned her skin to a soft gold while it made her dark hair look even thicker and more lustrous. Nick reached up a hand and ran his fingers through it again. It seemed to curl around his fingers with a life of its own. He rubbed a strand of it against his cheek, smoothed it over his lips, tasted it.

Then once more he buried his face into it, breathed deeply, knew the scent now—the hints of citrus and woods—and woman. This woman.

He wanted to give her a night to remember. He didn't want to erase her husband's memory. He knew she wouldn't forget just as he could never forget Amy. But equally, from here ever after, whenever Edie thought about making love, Nick wanted his face to come to mind.

He pulled back and undid his tie, then stripped off his coat and tossed it on the bureau. All the while he kept his gaze locked on hers. Smiling, Edie lay back against the pillow and watched him with a kind of hungry fascination that made his blood heat even more.

He reached for his shirt buttons, fingers trembling. As he did so, Edie raised a hand to touch his. "May I?"

Undress him? Nick wasn't used to giving up control. It seemed far too intimate. Risky. But Edie was smiling at him, looking hopeful, eager yet a little hesitant, too. And he knew he didn't want her hesitant. He wanted her to enjoy, to be involved, an active equal partner in their lovemaking.

So he gave a quick nod. "Be my guest."

Resolutely he dropped his hands to his sides and let her fingers do the work, certain his could have done in mere seconds. But the way they were trembling as she touched him, he wasn't sure that was true.

Edie sat up on the bed and leaned toward him, then began to studiously go to work on his shirt buttons. Her knuckles brushed lightly against the underside of his chin as she undid the top button. The soft brush of her skin against his made his chin tingle. As she moved lower, she caught her lower lip between her teeth as she concentrated on each one in turn.

His fingers clenched into fists to keep from pushing her hands away and doing it himself. It would be so much quicker and easier and he would get to feel her bare fingers on his skin that much sooner.

But having relinquished control he knew he couldn't wrest it from her now, knew she had to be the one to set the tempo.

So he let her—even as the tentative dance of her fingers damned near killed him.

Edie took her time.

She didn't know what was going to happen after tonight.

She didn't care. She didn't want to think about it. Since Ben had died, she'd spent too much of her life trying unsuccessfully to focus on the moment when she'd really never been able to do more than endure.

Not now.

Not tonight.

Not when this moment and those immediately following were going to be spent with Nick Savas—*making love* with Nick Savas.

She was going to savor it. Why not?

She'd missed the intimacy of the bedroom. Her first experience, with Kyle, had left her wondering what all the excitement was about. During the few weeks they'd been together, he had been fierce and hungry and demanding. He'd always directed things. Always taken charge. And with the eagerness of youth—he'd been twenty-three—Kyle had been more concerned with the end than the journey along the way. He'd never given her a chance to discover the subtleties of lovemaking.

With Ben it had been different. The two of them had learned together. They'd explored together. With Ben it had been about the journey, about pleasing, about loving, not simply about the orgasmic rush. It had been about knowing and being known.

She knew better than to expect that here. A single night meant nothing compared to the years she'd had with Ben. But until tonight she'd never even been tempted. She wasn't sure what that meant.

She wanted to find out.

Would she be in bed with him if Kyle hadn't turned up?

Probably not. Her well-developed common sense would likely have led her back to her room at a reasonable hour to her chaste single bed. And once there, then what? Would she have dreamed of Ben?

Lately she had not dreamed of him. For the past few months, she barely remembered dreaming at all. For all that she wanted to hang on to every memory, she knew he was slipping away from her. If she had gone to bed alone, would it have been memories of Ben that would have kept her awake? Or would she have tossed and turned all night thinking about this dark, handsome man who was holding so still now while she undid the buttons of his shirt.

The shirt was starched, the buttons stiff. It took a while. Edie enjoyed every moment.

It wasn't as if she was going to do it again, she told herself. Nick had been absolutely clear about that.

They were having a "one-night stand," she thought, and was appalled that those trite tawdry words could be used to describe what was happening at this very moment.

It didn't feel tawdry at all.

For all that it was unexpected, it felt—right.

So Edie shoved the words away, shoved all the rest of her life away, and focused on the man—and the moment.

She slid the last button loose, then eased the shirt off his shoulders and down his arms. Before she could decide where to go from there, Nick took it from her and tossed it aside. Then he yanked his undershirt out of his black trousers and started to pull it over his head.

Edie caught his hands. "Mine," she said, astonished at the word as it came out of her mouth.

Nick groaned, but he dropped his hands. "I get to undress you, then," he muttered, giving her a look that promised action.

"When it's your turn," she agreed, trying to sound as if it didn't make her shiver with anticipation. She was getting enough shivers just peeling his shirt over his head, then resting her hands for a moment on his shoulders before daring to rake her nails lightly down over his hair-roughened chest.

She could feel a tremor run through him as he remained still under her hands, his dark eyes hooded, watching her every move. She traced circles around his nipples, then arrowed her fingers down the center of his chest across his abdomen. They stilled when they came to rest at his belt.

"I suppose that's yours, too," Nick rasped, looking down.

Edie looked, too. "Sounds good to me," she said. "Do you want to stand up?"

He stood. She was just above eye level with the belt in question now. She brushed her fingers lightly over the front of his trousers as she began to undo the buckle. Nick drew a quick breath.

The buckle was easier than the buttons had been, and in bare seconds she had it undone. Without stopping to think about what she was doing, Edie skimmed down the zip of his trousers. Only when she did so, did she realize how close she was to the hot flesh that she wanted to touch, that she could tell, from its persistent press against the front of his shorts, wanted to touch her.

Belt undone, zip down, his trousers fell to the floor. Nick toed off his shoes and kicked them away, then stepped out of his pants and stood before her in only a pair of cotton boxers that did nothing to hide his arousal.

"Yours, too, obviously," he said gruffly, looking down. Then he lifted his gaze to meet hers. "Now it's my turn."

"I'm not done," Edie protested.

"Neither one of us is done," Nick said, grasping her hands in his, holding them loosely so she couldn't continue. "Let me catch up."

He bent his head and kissed his way down her bare shoulders, his hot mouth against her skin making her shiver as his fingers went to the back of her dress. Then he groaned and dropped his head against her shoulders.

"What?"

"There're five thousand buttons back here."

"Only forty, I think." But she remembered standing still for what seemed like forever as her mother had done up the dress. "Or maybe fifty."

"Fifty?" Another groan. But even as he did so, his nimble fingers set to work.

Nick Savas was a man of many talents, and he could multitask with the best of them, Edie thought, as his lips nibbled her jaw, her earlobes, her shoulders even as his fingers undid the buttons one at a time. Even his hair seemed to be actively seducing her as silky black strands brushed softly against her sensitized skin.

Then he sighed, pleased and lifted his head to smile at her. "Victory is mine," he murmured and hooked his fingers in the top of her dress and drew it slowly down.

The bra was part of the dress, and when he lowered the bodice, he bared her breasts. The cool air made her shiver. But so did the look on Nick Savas's face. Edie had never had the confidence in her bodily beauty that her mother and Rhiannon did. While she'd always known she had no major defects, she couldn't help feeling as if she suffered by comparison to her mother and sister.

But Nick seemed to be entranced by what he saw. His hands came up to cup her breasts, to weigh them gently in his hands. His thumbs rolled over her nipples heightening her awareness of her body's needs.

"Beautiful. You are so beautiful," he murmured and bent his head to lave first one breast and then the other. And Edie felt a shaft of desire clear to the center of her. She shivered.

"Are you cold?"

"N-no. I'm just—" But she couldn't seem to find words to express what she was feeling, so she just shook her head and savored the sensations.

Nick took his time as she had taken hers. He drew her off the bed, then as she stood before him, he pressed light kisses along her breastbone as he hooked his fingers inside the top of her dress, which was at her waist now. Kneeling, he continued to tug it down. The calluses on his fingers stroked her bare legs as he did so. She could still feel their imprint on her thighs from when he'd slid her stockings off. The dress pooled at her feet. He lifted first one and then the other, removing the dress completely. Then he skimmed the silk half-slip right down her legs, leaving her bare except for a pair of ecru lace bikini panties.

"Ah." He rested back on his heels and looked up at her. She could feel his gaze as it traveled slowly up her legs, past her belly, over her breasts to her face. He smiled at her.

He traced the lace at the top of her panties with a single tantalizing finger. Then he grasped them gently and pulled them slowly down.

Mindlessly Edie stepped out of them. Then, staring down at his head as he knelt before her, she felt his fingers begin at her ankles and stroke back up the length of her legs, teasing her smooth skin, making her tremble with need. Involuntarily she reached out and gripped his shoulders, hanging on for dear life.

His breath was warm on her belly. He kissed her there. Then his fingers slid slowly up the insides of her legs, reached the juncture of her thighs, brushed his fingers over the curls that covered her womanhood. Then he touched her there.

Edie swallowed a moan.

He didn't stop. On the contrary, he seemed to take it as invitation to go further, to part her legs and stroke between them. Her knees trembled. Her fingers tightened on his shoulders, dug into them.

"N-no f-fair."

He glanced up, smiling at her. "No?"

"You're not waiting for me."

He slanted her a glance. "Feel free to jump in anytime."

And so she did. Somehow he ended up on the bed beside her. Did she drag him there? Did he suddenly appear? She didn't know. She only knew that she couldn't get enough of him—even though, judging from the burgeoning of his shorts, there was a great deal of him. She hooked her fingers into the waistband of his boxers and dragged them down.

He shrugged them off, then settled beside her and began to explore her inch by inch. Edie was equally determined to take her time, to make this last, to wring every last moment of enjoyment out of the experience. But it wasn't easy because she was too eager, too hungry, too desperate.

Worse than Rhiannon, she thought.

But even thinking it didn't make her pull back. She wanted him. Her fingers dug into his hips as he settled between her knees. But still he took it slow, his fingers drawing light patterns of sensation as they moved up her thighs, brushed against her sex. His thumbs touched her, brushed her lightly, then slid back down her legs.

Edie swallowed a moan. She tried to lie still, not to squirm, not to lift her hips, not to seek his touch, not to betray how much she wanted him.

But he knew. He smiled, and his hands made the journey again. This time they traced small tantalizing circles on their way up, which he followed by pressing kisses first to the inside of one thigh and then the other. As he moved his head, his soft hair brushed against her sensitized skin. His lips were hot, but the moisture of his kiss was cool when he lifted his mouth and blew lightly where he'd just touched.

And every second he got closer. Closer.

Edie swallowed, tensed, waited, dug her heels into the mattress. Closer. Closer. Then his tongue touched her there—and she let out a little gasp.

"Nick!"

He lifted his head. "Yes?" Then he did it again. And again.

Edie's knees wobbled frantically, and her hands reached blindly to grab his hair. But she didn't pull away. She hung on. Desperate. Demented.

She twisted her head from side to side as he continued to stroke her, as his fingers followed his mouth, parting wet folds, sliding into her. His thumb found the most exquisitely sensitive spot and made slow firm circles as his fingers drove her mad with need. Her hips bucked.

"Oh!" She writhed on the bed. "Now! I—"

"Yes." The word hissed through his teeth. He kept one hand on her while he turned to the small cabinet by the bedside and took out a foil packet.

Protection. Edie understood. She was grateful he took the time and she helped him sheath himself, but she was almost equally grateful when, sheathed at last, he came to her, slid forward and slowly eased in, fitting exactly where he belonged, giving her exactly what she needed.

Instinctively Edie rocked up to meet him, dug her fingers fiercely into his buttocks and gave Nick what he needed, too.

She didn't know how she was so sure what he needed, but she was. Not just on a physical level—that wasn't hard to decipher at all. But on some other deeper instinctive level, she felt the connection between them.

She might have come to him for herself—to avoid the pull Kyle had always had on her emotions. But this had nothing to do with Kyle. This was only about the two of them—she and Nick as they moved together, slick and hard, eager and hungry, giving and taking in equal measure.

There was nothing tentative. No second thoughts. No thoughts at all. Just the sense of rightness—and completion.

They shattered together, breathless, weightless. Two made one.

And as he slid to the side and cradled her in his arms, Edie slept.

A few minutes. Half an hour, perhaps. But amazingly, she did sleep—deeply, dreamlessly—and when she awoke she felt remarkably refreshed as she snuggled in the smooth sheets and turned, coming up against a hard, warm body.

Nick Savas's body.

She felt a brief sense of shock. She waited for the feeling of impropriety. It wasn't there. Still she waited. It didn't come.

What came instead was a sense of satisfaction and an awareness of how good it felt to be with him. How right.

And how strange was that?

Edie didn't know. There seemed to be no limit to what she didn't know at the moment—like what she was supposed to do now.

Not get involved, she reminded herself.

Nick didn't want involvement. He didn't "do relationships." Well, yes. She'd gone into this with her eyes open. He hadn't led her on.

She wasn't changing the rules.

But somehow she wasn't prepared, either. The etiquette of the one-night stand was apparently beyond her. She'd never had one before.

She'd only slept with two men—Kyle and Ben. And with both she'd been in it for the long haul. Of course, Kyle hadn't been. But she hadn't known it at the time. And Ben had made her the happiest of women for their brief marriage. But he had wanted what she'd wanted: forever.

Whatever Nick Savas wanted, Edie was sure "forever" didn't come into it.

Probably he expected her to be sliding out of bed and out the door right now. But when she began to ease away, a strong arm curved around her and pulled her back into his arms.

"Where are you going?"

She turned her head to look at him. He was smiling at her, a lazy, satisfied smile. A smile she had put there, Edie reminded herself.

But even so, for the first time she felt a little awkward. "I should leave," she said tentatively.

"Why?"

"Because..." But the word trailed off and the reasons didn't come. There were undoubtedly plenty of them, but none of them seemed as important as staying right here.

"Not good enough." Nick's smile became a grin. "Do you want to leave?" he asked.

She considered it again, thoroughly, and came to the same conclusion: she didn't want to leave at all. She liked being in Nick Savas's bed, liked letting her eyes drift over his handsome face, memorizing his features, the feelings, this moment. She wanted to bottle it and keep it even as she knew that was impossible.

But staying a little longer, that was possible. Slowly she shook her head.

"Good. We took the edge off," he said. Then he smiled. "Now we can take our time."

Which was exactly what he proceeded to do. He settled beside her and moved over her languidly this time, pausing to taste, to tease, to touch wherever it pleased him.

It pleased Edie, too. Kyle had never been the lingering sort. He'd never explored, never particularly been interested in what she wanted. Ben had been. But Ben was little more experienced than she had been. And while they'd learned together, they'd still had much more learning to do when Ben had died.

Since Ben she'd had nothing—felt nothing.

Until tonight.

Tonight she had Nick—and Nick had her. He was experienced. No doubt about that. But he wasn't self-centered. He wasn't going through the motions in order to get what he wanted. He was focused. He was involved, as intent on learning her secrets as he was on learning the details of these buildings he took apart and put back together again.

She felt as if he was doing the same to her.

The featherlight touch of his fingers as he explored her made Edie aware of nerve endings she hadn't even known existed. The graze of his tongue on the inside of her elbow made her shiver. The soft stroke of his thumb swirling around first one nipple and then the other made her breasts peak. The dance of fingers down the middle of her abdomen, then brushing lightly through the curls that hid the place that longed for his touch roused her senses, made her quiver.

She wanted him to hurry, to touch her, to find her and shatter her and make her whole again. At the same time she wanted it to last forever.

What Nick apparently wanted was to drive her insane.

His fingers moved back up her body again. She swallowed her desperation. Then he traced her ribs, swirled circles round her navel, then with his thumbs he caressed the juncture of her thighs. Edie bit her lip as his hands slid around beneath her to cup her buttocks. He lifted her, spread her, stroked her.

Edie nearly whimpered. "Now," she urged him, reaching out to grasp his hips and draw him to her.

He came to her then, thrust into her with a desperation belied by his earlier slow, leisurely caresses. There was nothing casual or leisurely now. His need, like hers, was naked and urgent. His teeth clenched. The skin drew taut across his cheekbones. His breathing grew quick and hard as did his movement. And Edie moved to meet him, to join him. She dug her nails into his back just as he gave a hoarse cry, and they shattered together again.

This time there was no edge taken off. There were no edges at all—just bone-deep contentment, relaxation, a sense of serenity and well-being as Nick's weight settled against her. He would have moved off. She held him where he was—wasn't ready to let go. Not now. Not yet.

Their hearts were still hammering in unison. His sweat-dampened cheek rested against hers. Midnight shadow whiskers abraded her sensitive skin. Instinctively Edie turned her head toward them, pressed her lips to his cheek, breathed in the scent of him.

Slowly he turned his head, too, so that they lay facing each other, sharing the pillow, their noses nearly touching, their eyes open, watching each other silently.

There were no words. At least Edie couldn't think of any. So she smiled. It said everything she couldn't find words for.

Nick didn't smile. He looked like a man who didn't know what had hit him. That made Edie's smile widen.

His eyelids flickered shut. He opened them again, seemed to focus on her once more. But within moments his eyes shut again, and this time they stayed shut. His breathing slowed and deepened.

He was asleep.

This time Edie didn't sleep at all. Her breathing, like Nick's, slowed and settled into a regular peaceful rhythm once more. But she felt no exhaustion now, no lassitude. She felt centered. Settled. Physically a little sore because she hadn't done this sort of thing in a while. But on the whole she felt astonishingly good.

Great sex will do that for you, she thought, remembering similar feelings after she'd made love with Ben. But with Ben it hadn't only been great sex. There had always been something more.

There had been a connection between them, the sense that together they made beautiful music, that together they created something greater than the two of them could on their own.

Could that happen with Nick, too?

The thought came from out of nowhere—or from some well-spring deep within. Edie didn't know where. She knew only that even thinking such a thing was a mistake.

Nick didn't want that. He'd made it absolutely, perfectly clear that he wasn't interested. And she had agreed to that. She'd assured him—and herself—that she wasn't interested in anything else, either.

She wasn't. She hoped.

And if she was?

Well, Edie acknowledged, that was her problem.

Now she lay quietly and allowed her gaze to trace Nick's sleeping features. He looked younger asleep, his hard features gentled. Was it the "great sex" that had softened them? Edie wondered. Or was it the great sex *with her?*

Had he felt the sense of connection, too?

Or—Edie forced herself to confront the possibility—was she just a lonely widow trying to rationalize a night of very uncharacteristic behavior?

She didn't have the answer to those questions. All she knew is that she wouldn't get those answers tonight. Maybe she never would.

But lying here was not helping. It was only making her want things she had no right to, with a man she didn't really know.

Except a part of her thought she knew Nick Savas very well indeed.

He had showed her tonight that it was possible to find life after Ben. And she certainly knew she would be thinking about him—and not about Kyle Robbins—for some time to come.

But now she needed to get up and get dressed and go back to her own room—to her own life.

There, over the next days or weeks or months, she might discover the answer to what she'd been doing tonight.

Carefully Edie eased herself from beneath his arm, then slipped out of the bed, wincing as she began to move about and gather up her clothing. Muscles she never knew she had were reminding her of their existence now.

In the bathroom—thank heavens for some modern conveniences!—she put on a small light and dressed as quickly as she could, which wasn't very as she had to slither into the dress since no one was available to button it up the back for her, and she could hardly saunter down the corridors of Mont Chamion castle with her dress hanging half open.

Fortunately it was still the middle of the night. Even the earliest risers would not be in the hallways just yet. But she had a plane to catch in a scant six hours.

So she slipped back out of the bathroom and started toward

the door, then stopped. She couldn't just leave—not without looking back. Not without one last memory.

So she crept back to the bed and stood over Nick's sleeping form, drinking in the sight of him. He'd rolled onto his back now. The sheet barely covered the essentials, but she had indelible muscle memory of them—and the soreness to remind her for a while at least.

Now she memorized the rest of him—the broad, hair-roughened chest, the strong shoulders, the blade-sharp nose, the sensuous lips, the hard planes of his cheeks, the delicate black half-moon lashes and the tousled dark hair. She wished she could see his eyes—sometimes laughing, sometimes haunted—again. The mirror of his soul.

Tonight he had touched her soul as well as her body. He had given her back a part of herself that had died with Ben. She hoped she had given him something, too. She took her time, imprinting him in her mind's eye now the way he had imprinted himself on her body during the night.

She looked. And looked. And then, because she couldn't help herself, she bent and brushed a kiss over his mouth. His lips moved, sought hers. But when she pulled away, when he didn't find her, his lips parted. He sighed.

Edie did, too. "Good night, Nick," she whispered. "Thank you." She allowed herself one last light touch on his bare shoulder. "I think."

And then she turned and slipped silently out into the night.

CHAPTER FOUR

THE unexpected sound of the front doorbell of her mother's Santa Barbara mansion startled her.

"Blast!" Edie shot a helpless glance in the direction of the living room, then turned a malevolent one on the computer screen she'd been staring at forever.

She was in the middle of making the latest of Rhiannon's many plane reservations. She was almost to the last screen. If she stopped now, it would "time-out" and she would have to start over.

God knew, she probably would anyway. Rhiannon had been changing things almost daily for the past two months. Ever since she and Andrew had had their meltdown in Mont Chamion, even though they'd made up, Rhiannon had been edgy and wired, worried about whether Andrew would dump her one minute, and whether her career was over the next. She was constantly changing her priorities and her mind, and today's rearranged schedule was just the latest indication of her turmoil.

It did not give Edie restful days, either. Fortunately Rhiannon was in the Bahamas shooting a music video today. If she hadn't been, chances were good she'd have been perching on the edge of Edie's desk talking a mile a minute, fretting about Andrew, and changing her mind even as Edie was rebooking her reservations. Now Edie glared at the hourglass, which still hung on the screen.

The doorbell rang again.

At its insistence, the dog, Roy, a gigantic Newfoundland—all black glossy fur and lolling red tongue—looked up with vague interest. As a pup he'd have been at the door already, barking like mad. Now at nine, he had a more casual approach to visitors. They had to be persistent or he wasn't interested. He lay his head between his paws and closed his eyes again.

The doorbell chimed again. Emphatically. Twice.

Well, whoever they were, Roy would give them points for persistence. Ah, at last. The new screen finally appeared asking her to confirm the ticket purchase. Edie clicked. The hourglass reappeared. She waited.

And the doorbell rang. Once, twice. Three times now.

Not many people got as far as Mona Tremayne's front door. Tucked away high in the mountains behind Santa Barbara, the acreage Mona had bought with Edie's father, Joe, was far off the beaten path.

Everyone else had urged Mona to move after Joe died. The acreage was too big, they said. It had been Joe's dream to have the cutting horse operation on rural Santa Barbara ranch land. But Mona had stayed true to that dream.

She and Joe had bought it not just for the horses, but because they'd wanted a place to get away to, a place where they could be themselves without coming face-to-face with the fanfare of Mona's growing celebrity on an hourly basis. Of course it hadn't had the present house on it then, only the now sadly decaying old adobe ranch house even farther from the road.

This house had come later, after Joe's death. In her grief Mona wouldn't leave the place they'd had together. But the crumbling old adobe was no place to be with two small children. Without Joe to keep things together, the roof would have fallen in on them at the very least. So Mona had had a new house built and a year later she and five-year-old Edie and nine-year-old Ronan had moved down the hill several hundred yards to what Ronan still called "Ma's movie star house."

It was big and lavishly decorated, parts of it definitely elegant enough for spur-of-the-moment entertaining of Hollywood moguls and the world's rich and famous. At the same time it had eleven bedrooms, even more bathrooms, a butler's pantry big enough for Edie's twelve-year-old twin half brothers Dirk and Ruud to roller skate in, a swimming pool, tennis court and, oh yes, a doorbell.

This time whoever it was didn't just ring it, they leaned on it. Long and hard and far too shrilly.

Annoyed, Edie was tempted not to answer it at all. But Mona's "open house" policy extended to whomever among her hundreds of "close" friends turned up in the vicinity. Even when Mona was on the other side of the world, she—or, basically, Edie—welcomed all and sundry. The Tremayne hospitality was legendary, and Edie was quite happy to do it, though usually her mother warned her before guests were expected.

Now the hourglass gave way to a "confirmed" screen. Gratefully Edie punched a button to print Rhiannon's itinerary, then, with Roy at her heels, she went to answer the bell—which was still ringing

"All right! I hear you!" she shouted as she hurried down the hallway from her office at the back of the house, across the living room and grabbed the handle of the oversize dark oak door. "You can stop now!"

It stopped.

She jerked open the door. Her jaw dropped. Her fingers clenched on the door handle. She stared in disbelief. *"Nick?"*

Because it was—Nick Savas in the flesh. As tall and gorgeous as she remembered. And as unexpected as—well, Edie couldn't think of anything she had been anticipating less.

She clutched the door handle with one hand and Roy's collar with the other, as if they would anchor her in a storm. And there was a storm—of emotions, of memories, of questions and answers that she'd put behind her because she'd never managed to sort them out.

Not that she hadn't tried. For weeks after she'd got back home after the wedding in Mont Chamion she'd thought about that night—about the man she'd spent it with. She thought about what she'd done and tried to understand why.

As near as she could come to an explanation was that somehow that night he had awakened her.

After two and a half years of going through the motions of getting on with her life—and yet never really finding the spark that would make her recognize that she was alive and fully functional again on all levels—that night she had.

Something—and she never did put her finger on what—about Nick Savas had touched something elemental in her. In her most fanciful moments she thought it was what the prince's kiss on Sleeping Beauty's lips had done—brought her back to life.

It wasn't Nick's kiss that had done it for Edie. It wasn't his lovemaking, either. It was simply him—his energy, his charm, his wit, his dazzling smile. And his eyes. His eyes were eloquent. They spoke to her without words. They laughed with her, they teased her. They bore witness to his suffering. They anguished with her about her own. They drew her in.

They woke her up.

The kisses, the lovemaking grew out of that. She thought maybe she'd gone to bed with him out of gratitude for her awakening. She was grateful. But it was more than that.

She'd felt a connection she couldn't explain—as if he'd given her something that night and, in their lovemaking, she had given him something in return.

She'd tried over the past couple of months to articulate what. She hadn't been able to. Not really. If he'd come after her, she might have been able to. But of course he hadn't.

It had been a one-off, just as he'd said it would be.

So what was he doing here now?

His mobile mouth tilted into a conspiratorial smile and his eyes—those dark, sometimes laughing, sometimes brooding eyes—were just as intent as ever as they focused on her.

Once more Edie felt the connection she'd felt that night in Mont Chamion.

So whatever it was, it had lasted—for her at least—longer than one night. Edie felt her breath catch.

"What— What are you doing here?"

The Cinderella inside her wanted him to say he was here for her. The other sane sensible 99.9 percent of her brain told herself to get a grip. Things like that didn't happen in real life. She wouldn't want them to happen!

"Nice to see you, too," Nick said amiably. Then he cocked his head and looked quizzically at her. "I don't remember us parting on bad terms. Actually I don't remember us parting at all. I woke up and you were gone." Now his eyes accused her.

Edie felt her face warm, her fingers tightened on Roy's collar. "You were asleep. I had a plane to catch." She tried to sound matter-of-fact. In fact she knew she just sounded defensive. "Sorry," she said after a moment. "It was…" She hesitated, trying to find the right word. "It was a lovely night."

That was inadequate. But what else could she say? And the situation wasn't one she'd ever been in before—or since.

He was still smiling at her, every bit as gorgeous as he had been that night, only this time in an easy California casual way. This Nick wore a pair of jeans, faded nearly white at the knees and thighs, a long sleeve sage-green oxford cloth shirt with the cuffs rolled half up his forearms and a pair of aviator sunglasses parked atop his midnight-black, wind-ruffled hair.

"It was," Nick agreed. His gaze moved over her slowly, as if he were undressing her again now. Edie felt her whole body warm.

And then he said, "I've been talking with your mother."

"My mother?" He was undressing her with his eyes and he'd been talking to her mother? Dear God, what had Mona done now?

"We were talking about an old adobe ranch house she's got."

Edie stared at him, feeling a total disconnect. "What?"

"She mentioned it when I met her in Mont Chamion," Nick went on. "She said it was in need of work. So I told her I'd give her an evaluation." He gave Edie an encouraging smile.

"Evaluation?" Edie echoed. He was here because he'd talked to her mother? It was business. It had nothing to do with her. She felt oddly deflated and off-kilter. She didn't know quite what to say, but Nick was watching her, clearly waiting for her to say something.

Finally she said the only thing she could think of. "Mona's not here. She's in Thailand."

"I know. I talked to her yesterday."

"Really?" Edie had talked to her mother yesterday as well, and Mona hadn't said a single word! The name *Nick Savas* hadn't crossed her lips. Nor had any mention of the adobe.

"We discussed renovations a couple of weeks ago," Nick said. "But I didn't know when I was going to be finished then. She said it didn't matter, just to come on ahead whenever I got my last job done." Nick spread his hands.

Pennies were slowly beginning to drop.

"Come ahead?" Edie echoed again, wondering if he thought it was strange that she couldn't seem to form a thought he hadn't already said. "For what?"

"The evaluation. Working on the house, if it warrants it." He reached out a hand to the dog, letting Roy sniff to make sure he was a friend.

Edie wished that was all the assurance it took. She felt pole-axed. And betrayed. Obviously when dangling Kyle in front of her didn't tempt Edie, she'd moved on to the man Edie had gone off with the night of the wedding.

Had she tracked Nick down and called him? Twisted his arm? Edie was mortified beyond belief.

"You won't want to bother with the adobe," she said shortly now. "It's not worth saving."

That wasn't true, of course. Or at least she hoped it wasn't. She loved the old house where she'd lived as a small child. But that didn't mean she wanted her mother to hire Nick Savas to restore it!

Unfortunately Roy seemed to have accepted him as a friend. He began to slowly wag his tail. Edie anchored him firmly with a hand on his collar. She ground her teeth, trying to keep a polite smile in place.

"She made it sound as if it had possibilities," Nick said. "We won't know until I look at it, though," he added, as if to mollify her. "When I have, I told her I'd have a look and give her a call and talk to her about it. If it looks like a go, I'll do up a plan and explanations, then submit it for approval. There may be historical commissions to talk to, people to get on board. We'll cross those bridges as we come to them." This was Nick the professional talking, detailing all the steps with easy confidence.

Edie barely heard them beyond registering that all these bridges he was going to have to cross would take time. And time meant—

"Where are you staying?" she asked abruptly.

Nick blinked, then the lopsided smile reappeared. "Well, Mona invited me to stay here."

Edie felt as if she'd been punched in the gut.

"Is that a problem?" Nick asked. He was looking at her speculatively.

"I—" Edie managed one word, then her speech dried up.

Problem wasn't precisely the word. Try *awkward,* she thought. Try *disconcerting.* Or *mortifying.* But how could she explain? She'd told him that Mona was matchmaking back in Mont Chamion. She didn't want to have to admit it again. She didn't want him to think her mother was trying to serve him up on a plate!

Deliberately she pasted on her best *mi casa es su casa* smile. "Of course not," Edie lied and stepped back to open the door wider. "Not a problem. I was just surprised. Come in. This is Roy, by the way."

Nick hunkered down and ruffled Roy's ears. The dog, a

sucker for ear rubs, moaned his pleasure. The sound made Edie remember all too well how Nick's hands had made her moan, too.

She was sure her cheeks were flaming when he gave Roy's ears one last rub, then stood up. "I'll just get my bag from the car."

Edie waited by the door and tried to gather her wits, to find a proper emotional leg to stand on from which to handle the sudden appearance of Nick Savas into her life.

He wasn't here for her, she reminded herself. At least not in his estimation. He'd come because her mother had given him some song-and-dance about renovating the adobe. And he didn't care enough about her one way or the other to let it sway him.

"It's business," she told herself firmly. "Remember that," she muttered under her breath as he strode back up the driveway with a leather and canvas duffel in one hand and a battered laptop case in the other.

"What's that?" he asked, obviously having heard her saying something.

Edie shook her head. "Just talking to myself. I need to remember something."

"You should write it down."

Yes, Edie thought. *I should. I should emblazon it on the insides of my eyelids.*

"I'll do that," she told him briskly, then took a deep breath and turned to lead him back into the house. "Right this way."

"Amazing place," Nick said appreciatively as he followed her.

The living room, with its high ceilings, thick cream colored rough plastered walls and terrazzo floors, opened through a series of French doors onto a broad patio with a trellised canopy sheltering it from the sun. The doors at this time of year were open, and the light afternoon breeze drifted in, stirring a set of shell wind chimes as they passed.

"It's hardly authentic," Edie said over her shoulder, glad that he was looking around rather than at her. "It's what my brother calls 'Movie star Spanish.'"

Nick laughed. "I recognize it." Then he shrugged. "But it pays homage to the real thing in an impressive way. The purists hate it, but it celebrated the heritage and the history in its own way. It's made it popular and accessible."

"You're more forgiving than my brother." Edie was surprised at his attitude. She would have thought an architect, especially one who dealt with authentic historic preservation and restoration, would be more judgmental, not less.

"It is what it is," Nick said, running his hand up the smooth dark bannister as she led him up the broad staircase, then looked back at the room below them. "A romantic idealization. It's not pretending to be authentic. Maybe your brother is responding not to the house but to what it means to him."

Which was probably truer than he could know, Edie thought. And Ronan wouldn't like being called on it, either.

"You could be right," she said as they reached the open hallway on the upper floor.

"You can pretty much have any of these that you want." She gestured at the several open doors. She showed him all the ones that were available, at the same time pointing out her mother's suite at the far end of the hall, then her youngest sister, Grace's, room and the twins' room overlooking the pool. "They're in Thailand with Mona right now," she said. "For the summer holidays."

She used to do that herself when she was young, trail after her mother and watch the filming from the sidelines. Those experiences had made her certain she never wanted to do what her mother did, at the same time it had made Rhiannon long to get in front of the cameras.

"How about this one?" Nick said, looking into a spare masculine looking room. It was almost Spartan in its lack of decor.

"Ronan, my older brother, uses this one when he's here. But

he won't be here for months, so you're welcome to it. Or," she added with a grin, "you can have the tower room."

"Tower?"

"Surely you noticed our pseudo-Moorish tower when you drove up." It was the most romantic of all the romantic elements in the house.

He grinned. "I'd forgotten that. There's a bedroom up there?"

"A small suite. Rhiannon loves it." She pointed at the narrow staircase that curved upward.

"Why am I not surprised? Does she use it when she's here?"

"Yes. But she's gone right now. You're welcome to it."

"I'd have thought you'd have first dibs on it."

"Never wanted it."

He raised a brow. "Not a romantic?"

"No." Not about rooms, anyway. And she tried to be realistic. At least most of the time. "That was my room." She tilted her head toward one that looked up toward the woods.

"Was? Which one is yours now?"

"I have an apartment over the carriage house."

It was a small, cozy one-bedroom flat that had been the caretaker's place when Edie was growing up. But then the caretaker left, and Ronan had taken over the carriage house during college. He'd kept it even after he got his first job as a journalist. But eventually he was out of the country so much he decided he didn't need it.

Edie had moved in there when she came back after Ben had died. She would work for her mother willingly, but she wasn't going to live with her, too. She'd been a married woman, Now she was a widow. She wanted her independence.

For all the good it was obviously doing her!

"So who's sleeping in your bed?" Nick asked.

Edie opened her mouth and promptly shut it again, face burning. Then she realized he meant the bed in the room that had been hers. "No one," she said hastily, which was in fact the answer to who was sleeping with her in the carriage house, too. Not that he would care.

"Then I will," he said and walked in and dumped his duffel bag and laptop on the bed.

She wouldn't let herself read anything into his choice. It was a fine room, and there was nothing of hers left in it. At least she hoped there wasn't. Not that Nick Savas would care if there was. To him it was a place to sleep.

"Great," she said with all the brisk indifference she could muster. "Well, I'll just leave you to get settled in."

"Who else is here?" he asked.

"Just you. But don't worry. Clara—she works for Mona, cleaning and sometimes cooking—will come in and cook for you. She lives in Santa Barbara, but she comes up every day and cooks for the family when Mona and the kids are home. She regularly does it for guests, too."

Nick shook his head. "Not necessary. I can cook for myself. Besides," he reminded her, "I might not be staying. Gotta see if it's worth it."

"Of course."

He might be gone before nightfall. Life would go back to normal. Edie crossed her fingers.

"Do you want to take a look at the old house today, then? Or are you tired from traveling?"

"I'm fine. Just flew up from L.A. I was visiting my cousin."

"Demetrios?" She knew he and Anny kept a place there for when his work took him to Hollywood.

But Nick shook his head. "Yiannis."

If Edie remembered right from the wedding, he was Demetrios's youngest brother. Another lean, dark, handsome Savas male. "Is he an actor, too?"

Nick laughed. "You wouldn't catch him dead acting. He works with wood. Makes furniture. Imports and exports everything from raw lumber to finished pieces. He's done some pieces for restorations I've worked on. Talented guy."

"Apparently." Edie smiled and began to back toward the door. "Come down when you're ready and I'll take you to see the adobe. I'll be in my office. It's in the back of the house, beyond the kitchen. If you get lost, follow the sound of the phone."

It was ringing now. And so she had the excuse to dart off to answer it. She gave him a quick smile and a little waggle of her fingers, then hurried back down the stairs.

It was the first time in weeks she was glad to hear Rhiannon's voice when she picked up the phone. Even when her sister said, "I've changed my mind," Edie didn't snap.

She just grabbed a pencil and said, "Okay. Tell me what the new plan is."

If Rhiannon noticed that Edie wasn't peevish, she didn't remark on it. But then she rarely seemed to pick up on other peoples' reactions. Now she just began explaining her most recently changed decision, which was to go meet Andrew in Miami next weekend instead of following up on meeting with a director about a film set in Turkey.

"So you can change it, right?" Ree demanded.

"I can change it," Edie assured her. It just meant starting over from scratch, canceling the reservation she'd made an hour ago. But at least she'd have something to occupy her mind that she could handle—unlike the man upstairs.

No, she told herself firmly. She could handle him, too. She just needed a little space and a little time to regroup.

She was just surprised, that's all. She hadn't expected to see him again. She might have hoped, yes—just a little—but she hadn't really considered it. And then when he did turn up, she'd dared to believe he had come to find her, to explore the connection she had sensed between them.

And then she'd discovered he'd come because her mother had asked him to—on the flimsiest of pretexts!

"Edie! Are you there?" Rhiannon's voice broke into her mental conundrum.

"Of course I'm here. Did you think I'd hung up on you?"

"You're not talking." It sounded like an accusation.

"I'm writing down the information you just gave me," Edie said. It wasn't totally a lie. She'd made a couple of notes. "I'll make the reservations now. I'll send you an email and forward them."

"Great. Thanks. You're the best. Don't tell Andrew," Rhiannon added quickly. "I want to surprise him."

"Are you sure?" Surprises were sometimes not the best idea.

"I need to make a gesture. To show up when he's not expecting me, when he's given up all hope!"

Ah, the drama of it.

"Whatever," Edie said vaguely.

"Thanks, Ede. Love you!" Rhiannon trilled and rang off, leaving Edie to muster her wits and check her watch. It was the middle of the night in Thailand or Mona would be getting an earful.

The phone rang again, distracting her. And two more calls after that forced her mind back to her work so that she actually jumped when a voice behind her said, "So this is where you work."

She spun around to see Nick standing in the doorway, hands braced on the uprights as he looked around and then let his gaze come to rest on her. There was a smile on his face.

Business, Edie reminded herself sharply. *Just business.*

"This is my office," she agreed with a sweep of her hand taking in the room. Mona called it "command central" but it really looked more like a comfortable den than anything else. There was a wall of bookshelves on either side of the fireplace, wide planked floors with a deep burgundy and navy blue Turkish rug, a pair of upholstered armchairs, a comfortably saggy sofa, a double-length heavy Spanish style oak desk with Edie's computer, printer, scanner and a stack of in-and-out boxes without which she would not be able to survive.

But most impressive of all was the view.

One wall was mostly glass, comprised of floor-to-ceiling

windows around the Spanish-style equivalent of French doors, which opened onto a terrazzo-tiled ramada overhung with bougainvillea. It looked out onto a broad rolling expanse of lawn with an inset naturally landscaped nearly Olympic-size swimming pool. Below the sweep of lawn and the pool, the land fell away steeply so that a grove of eucalyptus treetops were at eye level. Beyond them you could see the rooftops of Santa Barbara and, in the distance, the bulky shape of the Channel Islands in the sea.

"Not bad," Nick murmured, taking it all in. He slanted her an amused glance. "I'm surprised you get any work done."

"You get used to it," Edie confessed as she stood up. "It seems a sacrilege to say so, but unless I consciously stop and look—and sometimes I do—most days I don't see it. I see work."

Nick nodded. "Understandable. It's the same when I'm working on a building. It's usually some massively impressive place in all the guide books, and all I see is rising damp and rotting timbers."

"Were there rotting timbers in the stave church?" she asked him. When he'd given her his "tour" in Mont Chamion he had mentioned that his next project was to be a Norwegian stave church restoration. Edie hadn't been familiar with stave churches then, but as soon as she got home, she'd looked them up online. Now she knew they were medieval wooden churches, and she could well imagine they'd have a few rotten timbers after all these years.

"There were." Nick nodded. And then he did what she hoped he would do—he began talking about the project.

As long as he kept talking about the church, she could focus on that. She could remind herself that he was here on business, and that it had nothing to do with her.

But then, on the way out of the house, she grabbed a baseball cap and yanked it on. In the summer Santa Barbara, particularly away from the ocean's edge, could be hot in midafternoon. Once the sun broke through the fog that usually blanketed the coastline until late morning, it beat down relentlessly. And while inside fans were enough to keep things cool, outside Edie regularly wore dark glasses and an old baseball cap of Ronan's to shade her eyes.

"Very fetching," Nick drawled, a corner of his mouth tipping in a grin as he studied her. Then he reached out and tugged the bill of the cap.

And suddenly remembering this was just business wasn't so easy.

"I sunburn," she said, trying to sound matter-of-fact. Then she headed out the door. "This way."

She headed across the driveway and up the path past the carriage house. The groomed lawns didn't extend to this side of the property. It was brush and chaparral and eucalyptus, with a sort of vague path through it that led up the hill. Roy ambled on ahead, nosing in the under brush.

"No road?" Nick said, striding alongside her, easily keeping pace.

"There's a rough one," Edie told him. "But it doesn't come past the house. It goes around the side of the hill and winds a bit. So it's generally faster to walk—unless you'd rather not."

His hair was ruffled and damp on his tanned forehead and she thought he did look a bit tired. But he just laughed. "Is that a challenge, Miz Daley?"

Something in his drawl made Edie's skin prickle with awareness. It was perverse, really. For two and a half years after Ben died, she felt no interest, no awareness of the opposite sex at all. Then, that night in Mont Chamion, the very sight of Nick Savas across the ballroom with her sister, had jolted her awake. His appeal as the night went on hadn't lessened, and it had certainly taken her mind off thoughts of Kyle Robbins. Still, she'd expected that, not seeing him again, her reawakened hormones would have noticed another man in the meantime.

But they'd gone right back to sleep—until now.

Now she tried to ignore them as best she could. "Just asking. We can drive if you want."

He shook his head. "I'm good," he told her and started walking again. "I was just wondering how I'd get materials to the house."

Right. Business.

So Edie pointed out where the road went as they climbed the hill. Once there had been a path through the woods that led from the new big house back to the old adobe. But in the past fifteen years or so, it had overgrown as the family had gone back there less and less.

It meant something to Ronan and Edie. But the rest of Mona's children had been raised in the new one, so they had no memories and little interest in a derelict run-down ranch. Even the twins, who thrived on the prospect of adventure, especially where mud and dirt were involved, had really never shown much interest in it. It wasn't exactly exciting, though Edie loved it.

Occasionally she had thought she would love to restore it and make it into the family house it had once been for them when she was a child. She hadn't said anything to Ben about it, though. There had been no point when they were in Fiji. And she'd always thought there would be time.

Now she was glad she hadn't. She had only come back a few times since his death—mostly to bring the twins and Grace to the house, to try to interest them in it, to tell them stories there and give them a sense of connection to a past they were only peripherally part of.

"I thought you didn't do houses," she said now as she and Nick made their way up the path.

"Maybe I won't," he said. "I have to see it first."

"Of course. It was nice of you to come all this way to look at it and give Mona an opinion," Edie said, striving to sound properly businesslike. "I don't know why she is so keen on doing it now."

Well, she did, actually. And it had nothing to do with the

house itself. But just how blatant had Mona been in her attempt at matchmaking? Edie slanted a glance at Nick as they walked, but he didn't reply, and the look on his face didn't give anything away.

"When did you finish at Mont Chamion?" she asked.

"I left a week or so after the wedding. There were some talented local craftsmen who continued the work while I was in Norway. I went back a couple of times to make sure everything was going well, but I've been in Norway and Scotland most of the past two months."

"Scotland?"

"Mmm. Tell me about the ranch house."

So much for getting him talking. But the ranch house was business, too, so Edie did as he asked.

"I think it's from the mid-nineteenth century. Pretty primitive to begin with, I think. My dad used to tell us stories about the ranchers who lived here. I don't know how true it was. Dad liked to tell stories." She smiled now as she remembered the delight Joe Tremayne had taken in gathering her and Ronan onto his lap and regaling them with tales of early California.

"Was it in his family?" Nick asked.

"No. My mom and dad bought it right after they married. It was pretty run-down already by then, but the land was what my dad wanted. He was raised on a ranch north of San Luis Obispo. His dad was a foreman there. Dad wanted to raise cutting horses. That was his dream. He dabbled in winemaking, too. He wasn't a Hollywood sort of guy." In her mind's eye she could still see her tall, handsome father with his shock of dark hair and wide mischievous grin. "He was a good balance to my mother. Solid. Dependable. Steady." She caught herself before she went any further. "But you don't care about that. You want to know about the house."

"I want to know it all," Nick said, his eyes on hers. "About the house, of course. But it's important to understand the people who live—or lived—in it. What mattered to them. What they valued."

Edie thought about that. She remembered him telling her about the history of the castle at Mont Chamion and about the royal family there. She guessed it was the same here.

"Family," she said firmly. "That's what they both wanted. Even Mona," she said before he could raise his brows in doubt "My dad's death changed her. He was her anchor. When he died, it was like she'd been cut adrift. She was lost. She wanted what they'd had—what we'd all had—and she kept trying to get it back."

Telling him about it now, she could see it all again—the happy days they'd spend as a family in the old adobe followed by the painful dark days after the car accident that had taken her father's life. Her voice trailed off as they crested the hill and headed down the other side. The old house came into sight beyond a stand of eucalyptus.

"Hence the marriages?" Nick ventured.

"Pretty much," Edie agreed. "She wanted to be married. She wanted a man. And men want Mona. They always have. So they kept proposing, and she kept saying yes. And she kept having babies," she added a little wryly.

"That must have been difficult for you."

"No. It was great, especially after she got to be so famous. It was easier that there were six of us. It diluted the paparazzi's attention."

They were approaching the house now, and Edie was appalled at how run-down it looked. Tried to see it from Nick's perspective. She imagined he was mentally packing his bags, ready to declare it worthless. It certainly didn't look salvageable to her. And it had an empty forlorn air very much at odds with how she remembered it.

"It's a lot worse than I remembered," she said. "It wasn't like this when I was growing up here."

Nick didn't say anything. He just stopped on the slope and

studied the sprawling one-story adobe structure with its broad front porch and deep-set windows.

"It wasn't in the best shape when they bought it," Edie said quickly. "I remember Mona saying they got it cheap as a 'fixer-upper.' But my dad did a lot of work on it," she added defensively. "But he was busy making a go of the ranch and the horses. He didn't have a lot of time."

"Understood." Nick made his way down the rest of the dusty slope and began a closer inspection.

Edie, following him, recognized how very neglected the house had become. The broad front porch covering sagged. Pieces of the *zaguán* were broken or altogether missing. Places that her father had tried to patch with stucco had crumbled away and the adobe beneath them was crumbling as well.

Nick took his time, walking around the building slowly, looking at it from all angles while Edie followed, looking at the house, but also at him. He moved with the easy grace of some sort of jungle cat. Last year when she'd taken Ruud and Dirk to the San Diego Zoo, she'd been fascinated with the grace of a tiger moving through the brush. She thought of that tiger now as she watched Nick prowl around the house. He took hold of one of the timbers that poked out from the roof and jerked it. The crack of the wood made Edie wince.

"Probably not worth restoring," she ventured.

He didn't reply, just kept moving. He paused to pick at some of the stucco her father had used to repair part of the crumbling back wall, then watched it flake and fall to the ground. Another reason to wince.

It was good, she tried to tell herself. With all these things wrong with the house, the less likely he was to stay and Mona's heavy-handed efforts at matchmaking would come to naught. But at the same time she didn't want the house to fall down. And the Cinderella gene she was trying to ignore still wanted Nick Savas to stay.

"Is it unlocked?"

So the outside hadn't totally discouraged him?

"I have a key." She dug into her pocket and pulled out a set of keys, then chose the one to open the front door. Nick took it wordlessly from her. Their fingers brushed. Yes, heaven help her, even with a simple touch the awareness was still there.

In one long leap Nick vaulted onto the porch and opened the door.

Edie followed him more carefully, picking her way past the broken wooden steps up to the porch. "The electricity's off," she said. "I'm afraid you can't see much."

With a forest of towering eucalyptus all around, the house never received the brunt of the direct sun. It was far cooler that way, but the interior, shrouded in shadow and with only very deep-set windows, was barely visible when Edie followed him in the front door.

Apparently Nick was used to doing things by feel. As she watched, he moved around the room, running his hands over the walls, peering up at the ceiling, crouching down and studying the floor.

Edie didn't know what he was seeing, but the longer she stood there, the more she saw memories of the house she'd been happy in as a child. This living room was the place where her dad had crawled around on the floor giving her horsey rides. Over by the window was where they'd put up the Christmas tree. In the big kitchen they had eaten meals her mother had actually cooked instead of those a cook made for them.

The memories made her throat ache as she looked around.

She walked around, touching things, recalling things. She ran her hand over the kitchen countertop and remembered standing on a chair helping her mother cut out cookies there. By the back door there were still the marks on the wall where her dad had marked her height and Ronan's every few months. How small she'd been.

She rubbed her thumb over the last, highest pencil mark and remembered how she used to stretch as tall as she could, and her dad would press his hand on the top of her head, laughing. "Stop that! You're growing too fast already!"

"You okay?" Nick appeared in the doorway, looking concerned.

Edie mustered a smile. "Just remembering." She gave the wall a little pat. "It's been a long time. This was a good place. I was just remembering how good it was."

Nick nodded as if he understood.

Maybe he did. She didn't know that much about him. The trouble was, what she knew she liked. And seeing him here made things somehow even more difficult.

When she'd had one night with him in a completely foreign setting, it was easier to tell herself she wasn't really interested, that her awareness of him was a momentary aberration, that back in her own life, she wouldn't really notice.

But she did.

He was opening the cupboards now, peering inside. And she allowed herself to study him because he wasn't paying attention to her. She had run her fingers through that tousled hair. She'd nibbled her way along his stubbled jaw, then pulled off his tie and unbuttoned his shirt. Now, as he shut the cupboards and crouched down to look at the floor, she watched the muscles in his thighs bunch and flex beneath the worn denim covering his thighs and remembered that she had touched him there. And he had touched her, too.

Not just her body—but something fundamental deep inside her. Something that she hadn't managed to forget.

"I have to go," she said abruptly, her announcement rather louder than she intended. "I have work to do."

From where he was crouched on the floor studying the boards, Nick glanced up at her and nodded. "Yeah. Sure. Fine. Go ahead." He sounded as if he'd already dismissed her from his mind.

No doubt he had, Edie thought. She turned and hurried out

of the house. "Come on, Roy," she called to the dog who was nosing curiously around the edge of the porch.

Roy looked at her, then back at the house, as if he expected Nick to join them.

"He's not coming," Edie said, more for her own good than for the dog's. "He's here on business. And then he's leaving."

She hoped.

At least she thought that was what she hoped. He wasn't here for her. He had awakened her, but he didn't want her. He thought he was here for work, but it was really because Mona had been playing matchmaker again.

Edie glanced at her watch. It was early yet in Thailand, but so what?

If Mona thought she was going to get away with meddling in Edie's life, she deserved an early wake-up call!

He'd hadn't made any promises.

"I'll take a look at the adobe," Nick had told Mona on the phone last week. "You don't want to throw money down the drain. If it isn't a good candidate for restoration, I'll tell you."

"Fine. Good. Whatever you think," Mona had said. "You can stay at my place. There's plenty of room."

"I'll do that," he'd said. "But it might not be worth it."

"Understood." Mona had sounded impatient. "Got to go. We're shooting now. Discuss it with Edie. She can show you around. You remember Edie."

He remembered Edie.

She hadn't changed a bit.

Her utilitarian ponytail hardly recalled the sophisticated upswept hairstyle she'd worn to the wedding. And her casual canvas pants and open-neck pink shirt might mask the curves the purple dress had highlighted.

But Nick was willing to bet that, unloosed, her hair would cascade down her back in those wondrously silken waves. Just as he knew damned well that underneath whatever Edie Daley wore, he would still find her petal-soft skin and the womanly secrets he'd only once had a chance to explore.

"Hell," he muttered, scowling toward the door she'd walked out of moments before.

Hell—because she was just as appealing as she had been back in Mont Chamion. He'd hoped she wouldn't be. That was why he'd been at pains to make sure Mona understood he might not stick around.

Maybe the house wouldn't be worth working on—or maybe he'd take one look at Edie Daley and decide that their one night in Mont Chamion was the extent of her appeal.

No such luck.

Now he stood in the shadows of the window and watched her until she was out of sight.

She was still wearing the baseball cap, with her hair pulled back into a ponytail and poking out through the space above the adjustable strap at the back of the hat. And she really didn't have any noticeable curves. In fact, from the back he was disconcerted to discover that she could probably pass for a tall, slender twelve-year-old girl.

So why, for two and a half months, had he not been able to get her out of his mind?

Nick had never dwelt on the women he bedded. Had no interest in them beyond the night they spent together. They were fun and attractive and he had a good time with them. But as soon as they were gone, he moved on and never looked back.

End of story.

He couldn't even have told you half their names. But he couldn't forget hers: Edie Daley.

Edie of the long dark curls and flashing green eyes, of the wide mobile mouth and the very kissable lips. Lithe and limber Edie. Eager and passionate Edie. Her spark, her charm, her curiosity, her vulnerability, all had haunted him every night, and plenty of days. Since he'd shared his bed with her.

Two and a half months and he hadn't been able to forget her. It was absurd.

At first Nick thought the memories kept coming back because they'd spent the night in *his* bed. He had always made a point of never sharing his own bed with a woman.

He didn't bring them onto his turf.

Hell, he didn't even have turf. He didn't own a house, didn't rent a flat. He had no place to call his own. He'd sold the house he'd built for Amy as soon as he could after her death. He wanted nothing more to do with it.

He left what little personal gear he didn't carry with him at his uncle Socrates's house on Long Island. And he stayed on the move, living in someone else's house while he renovated it. It suited him perfectly. He had no reason to have a house.

He had no wife. No kids. No dog nor cat. No encumbrances at all.

He didn't need them. Didn't want them.

And he didn't want Edie Daley, either!

Well, he did. Carnally, at least, Nick admitted, he wanted her a hell of a lot. But that was all.

The desire was an itch he needed to scratch. So, he'd scratch it and it would be gone, and that would be that.

CHAPTER FIVE

"WHAT do you mean she's gone?" Edie demanded.

The Thai woman on the other end of the phone connection didn't speak particularly good English, which gave Edie hope that she might have heard wrong. But when the woman repeated her words, the meaning was the same the second time around.

"Miz Tremayne go away for work. Not here."

"But it's barely light," Edie protested. "What on earth time did she go?"

"She go last night."

"Last night? But she didn't mention anything yesterday."

"Change of plan," the woman said. She didn't sound as if it was any big deal. Probably for her it wasn't.

"When's she coming back?"

"Don't know. Three, four, five days maybe. They go to mountains."

"Mountains?" That didn't sound good. And they were going to be gone days? "But I need to talk to her."

She was only calling the phone at the house Mona had rented because she had already tried Mona's mobile phone half a dozen times. Each time it had gone directly to voice mail.

At first she'd thought her mother was simply avoiding her. But after two hours with no reply, she knew something else was going on. Mona was a stickler for returning messages. The only time she didn't call back was when she was in the middle of a scene or completely out of range.

Obviously now she was out of range. But for *days?*

"Where are the kids?" Edie asked. Ordinarily her mother would have sent for her to take care of them while she was gone. Surely she hadn't just left them with the woman who cared for the house.

"They go, too."

"Ah. Well, um, good." At least Edie hoped that was good. There was no doubt that Mona loved her children. But she also had a career that demanded she put it first most of the time. Taking the twins and Grace with her this summer—without having Edie along to keep an eye on things—was something of a first.

"Did she even take her phone?"

"She take it," the woman said. "But hard to get calls. You try," she suggested cheerfully. "Maybe you be lucky."

Luck, Edie could have told her mother's housekeeper, was not on her side at the moment.

She thanked the woman, tried Mona's number twice more, then gave up. There was no point in filling her mother's in-box with messages she wouldn't see until she got back to civilization. Besides, when she confronted Mona about her matchmaking, she intended to do it live and, if not face-to-face, then at least ear to ear.

She'd given Mona a piece of her mind after the Kyle Robbins incident at the wedding. She thought Mona had learned her lesson. Apparently not.

Still grumbling, Edie stared at the computer screen and tried to focus on the rest of the afternoon's work. She had phone calls to return, some correspondence from Mona's contracts lawyer to deal with and Rhiannon's plane reservations to cancel and rebook. Surely she had plenty to keep her busy—enough so that she wouldn't spend the rest of the afternoon thinking about Nick Savas.

Easier said than done. She got the reservations rebooked. She looked up the answers to the questions Mona's contracts lawyer wanted. She returned that call and several others. But all the while she did so, she had one ear cocked toward the door, expecting to hear it open, expecting the sound of footfalls heading toward the office.

Time passed. An hour. Two. By five-thirty he still hadn't come. Perhaps he'd taken a look around, then simply left. When she closed up the office she actually walked out to the front room to look out the window to see if his car was still there.

Of course it was. He couldn't have left without her knowing because he'd have had to come back for his bag. He'd already taken his duffel upstairs.

So did he expect her to simply sit in her office and wait for him?

Probably not, Edie admitted to herself. Probably he hadn't given her a thought at all.

"And you should stop thinking about him," she counseled herself.

So she did what she always did after work. She changed into her bathing suit, went out to the pool and dived in.

It was just past six when Nick got back to Mona's house.

He had gone over every inch of the adobe, had walked around kicking the foundation, prying up floorboards, clambering onto the roof. He was grimy, filthy, sweaty and hot and he needed a shower. Bad.

Now he went around the house to go through the doors closest to the stairs so he wouldn't track in dirt and dust. And so he could stop by Edie's office. But before he got there, out of the corner of his eye he saw movement that caught his attention.

Beyond the bank of oleanders growing partway down the lawn, someone was in the pool.

Before his brain made a conscious decision, his feet were already heading across the lawn toward where Edie's lithe form cut through the water as she did laps. Her stroke was smooth and even, but it wasn't her stroke Nick was focused on. It was her body, her mile-long legs, her tanned back—all that lovely golden skin he remembered so well.

If he'd needed a shower before, he needed one worse now. A long icy cold one.

Or, he thought, he could dive into the pool, take Edie into his arms and solve all his problems at once.

Not a difficult choice.

He had unbuttoned his shirt by the time he reached the terrazzo-tiled patio where the pool was. He opened the gate, tossed the shirt onto a chaise longue and was toeing off his shoes and tugging his undershirt over his head at the same time.

"You're back." Edie's voice startled him.

Nick jerked the T-shirt the rest of the way off to see her, out of the pool now, coming toward him. She had a towel wrapped around her waist and she was rubbing her hair dry with another. He couldn't see her legs anymore, but her bare midriff was enticement enough. As Nick watched, half a dozen droplets of water slid down her abdomen from beneath the top of her bathing suit.

He swallowed, staring as the drops disappeared into the towel knotted at her waist.

"So what do you think?"

"Think?" He wasn't thinking. Not with his brain anyway.

"About what?" he asked dazedly. She had to have seen him coming. Why the hell hadn't she stayed in the pool? Was she trying to avoid him? he wondered, nettled.

"About the house." She lowered the towel from her hair and peered at him over the top of it "Time to raze it? Cut our losses?" She sounded almost hopeful.

Was she hoping? Surely not. He'd seen the wistful look on her face this afternoon. He'd watched her move from room to room, running her hands over the woodwork and the cabinets, touching those little pencil marks by the back door.

"No," he said sharply, with more force than he intended. He moderated his tone. "No. It's quite salvageable."

"Really? And it should be?" Now she sounded surprised.

"It's an interesting piece of vernacular architecture," he said firmly. "Not all of a piece, of course. And not of huge historical significance," he added honestly. "But the fact that it's not a mansion, but a surviving example of small ranch architecture makes it worth restoring."

Also true. To a point. From a purely historical significance standpoint, the old adobe ranch house was such a pastiche of different styles, periods, restorations, disastrous additions and bad workmanship that, as a bonafide professional historical restoration expert called on to choose which buildings were worth preserving and restoring, he ought to have been running in the other direction.

But he wasn't.

He was standing here saying, "It can be salvaged," with an absolutely straight face.

And he was rewarded by seeing her face light up. "I thought you'd say it wasn't worth the trouble."

It wasn't. At least not solely on an architectural basis. But there were other reasons to restore things.

"It's worth it," he said.

She gave him an instant brilliant smile. But it faded quickly. "So what does that mean?" she asked, sounding almost wary now.

We make love right here on the chaise. Of course he didn't say that. He cleared his throat. "I put together a plan, talk it over with Mona, then get to work."

"So, you're…going to be staying a while?" She didn't sound thrilled.

"Yes," he said firmly.

Now she smiled again, but it still didn't seem to reach her eyes. "Well, um, great. That's just great."

"You don't want the house salvaged?"

Something flickered in her eyes. "No, I do. It's—" she hesitated, then the smile appeared again "—it's lovely."

"Then why don't I take you to dinner and we can celebrate?"

Edie blinked. She opened her mouth. But then she just stood there looking at him. No sound came out.

"Edie?" he prompted when seconds went by and she didn't speak.

"Celebrate?" she echoed at last.

"Sure. We have a lot to celebrate. That the house is worth fixing. That I'm going to be here a while. That we're both here," he added pointedly and turned the full heat of his gaze on her. "I think that's worth celebrating, don't you?"

He saw her swallow. Then she bobbed her head a little jerkily and took a breath. "Yes. Of course." Another breath, a brittle smile. "That would be nice."

"Nice?" He cocked his head, regarding her from beneath hooded lids. "Nice?" he repeated, teasingly.

Edie shrugged awkwardly. Her smile stayed in place but it looked even more superficial. Nick was reminded of the smile she'd worn when she'd reappeared at his side at the reception, when she had taken him up on his offer of a tour of his renovations. There had been a tense edginess about her then, too.

Then she'd been avoiding the hundred-dollar-haircut man and her mother's expectations. Was she nervous now? Uncertain? Wishing she could avoid him?

Nick scowled. Why would she feel that way? Didn't she remember how good it had been between them? If she didn't, he'd be happy to remind her.

"I need to get dressed," she said now, and she began edging toward the gate.

"Not on my account." He grinned.

A blush suffused every bit of Edie's visible skin, telling him that she certainly hadn't forgotten.

Even so, the look she gave him was pained. "If we're going out to dinner, I need to shower and wash my hair."

"We could get take-out, stay in, celebrate here." He could

think of excellent ways to celebrate that wouldn't require her dressing at all.

Edie shook her head. "No. If we're going to stay here," she said, "I have work to do."

"Then we're going out."

"But—"

"Go take your shower and wash your hair, Edie Daley. Get dressed if you must," he said. "I'll swim and change and be at your place in an hour."

All evening long it felt like a date.

Edie knew better, of course. Her mother had engineered the whole thing. But, knowing it didn't entirely save her. The minute she had opened the door to Nick standing on her small front porch, it felt as if he were courting her.

Wishful thinking, she'd chastised herself even as she let him open the door of his car for her and, for a moment, brush his fingers over hers as she got in.

Though her fingers tingled with awareness, Edie tried to keep things pleasant and businesslike. That's what it was, after all.

Business. It was like a mantra. She needed to keep the word going over and over in her head all the time—because the way he smiled at her, the way his eyes seemed to heat when his gaze met hers, the way, every time he refilled her glass of wine and handed it back to her, their fingers touched—all of it made her want more than she knew was really there.

It was a beautiful, cloudless California evening with the lightest of breezes, perfect for sitting at a table outside. The ambiance was casual, the food was fantastic and Nick was charming and flirtatious. She was sure he was like that with every woman he ever met, but telling herself that didn't make her any less susceptible to him.

He was too easy to talk to, too gorgeous to look at. He answered her questions about the stave church in Norway and another project he was working on at a Scottish castle.

"And yet you came here?" she said. Mona's powers of persuasion were legendary, but Edie was still surprised Nick had agreed, especially since he had to know she'd be here—and he didn't "do" relationships.

Or did he? The thought was tantalizing.

He had awakened her, after all. Perhaps she had done the same for him.

Edie leaned in to study him more closely, as if an intent examination of his features would give her the answer to the question.

"I came here," Nick agreed. He lounged back in his chair and regarded her from beneath hooded lids.

"Why?"

He blinked, as if her blunt question surprised him. But then he shrugged easily. "It's what I do. And," he added, one corner of his mouth quirking, "I like a challenge."

And there it was again—the hum of awareness that seemed to arc between them.

Physical attraction? Oh, yes. Anything more? Edie couldn't tell.

The noise of the dinner hour had abated and, as other diners left, their table, which was at the far end of the patio of the downtown Santa Barbara restaurant, became more isolated and intimate.

"Cup of coffee?" Nick murmured. He was watching her from beneath slightly lowered lids. A smile played at the corners of his mouth. Edie had no trouble remembering the taste of that mouth and the way his lips had felt pressed against hers.

It was time to go. Edie knew it. But going meant confronting the awareness sooner rather than later. And she wasn't ready yet. She needed fortification. So she said yes to the cup of coffee. It was strong, black, a full-bodied Colombian roast. Meant to be savored. Meant, she suspected, to give her the stamina—and the caffeine—to stay up all night making love with him.

Which she would dearly love to do. Except…

She clutched the cup like a lifeline, stared into it, trying to find the words to say what she needed to say. Finally she lifted her gaze and met his. "We need to get something straight."

At her tone one of Nick's brows lifted. "Oh?"

She gave a jerky little dip of her head. Her fingers strangled the coffee mug as she plunged straight to the heart of the matter. "I'm not sleeping with you."

Now both of Nick's brows shot up. He sat up straighter, looking first surprised, then almost bemused. After a moment, he settled back in his chair and picked up his own cup, holding it easily. "Aren't you?" His tone betrayed only mild interest, making Edie feel like an idiot. But she'd already begun, so she forged ahead.

"No. And yes, I know, you haven't asked." There, she'd pointed out the obvious, too. "But since we did once—" she took a quick breath "—I thought the issue could come up again."

"It could," Nick agreed. His tone was still mild, but there was a hint of something else, something deeper, yet definitely suggestive that told her she hadn't entirely misread the situation.

She met his gaze head-on. "So I thought I should make it clear up-front that it's not going to happen."

For a long moment Nick didn't say anything, but his gaze never wavered. Then finally, after what seemed like an eon, but was probably less than half a minute, he asked, "Why not?"

Edie swallowed. Her mouth was dry and her palms were damp, and she was already regretting having opened her mouth. She didn't do confrontation. Ever. She was a negotiator, not a battler.

Now she said, "It isn't that I didn't enjoy it." Her gaze dropped. She couldn't look at him squarely now. "I did," she admitted. Her cheeks were on fire.

"I'm glad." Nick's tone was grave, but when she dared look up, Edie thought she saw his lips twitch.

"You're laughing at me."

He shook his head. "I'm not. I'm...baffled." He set down his cup and seemed to draw himself together. "I was under the impression that we had both enjoyed it."

"Yes, well, um," Edie said. "I'm glad you did, too. But that was it."

"It?"

"A one-off. You said so yourself."

She thought his jaw tightened fractionally, but in the shadows she couldn't be sure.

"It wasn't a hard and fast rule." His tone was gruff. "I don't turn into a pumpkin if I make love to a woman two times."

Edie's mouth curved into a reluctant smile. "I'm glad."

"Do you?" he challenged her.

Slowly she shook her head. "Not a pumpkin, no."

"Well, then?" he demanded. Their eyes met again. She didn't see anger in his, thank heavens. It was more curiosity.

"I could fall in love with you."

"What?" His cup hit the table with a decided *thump.* Then he went absolutely still. "In love with me?" He sounded at worst appalled, at best disbelieving.

Edie shrugged. Too late to turn back now. "After…after Ben died," she explained, "I felt like I'd died, too."

Nick nodded almost impatiently. "Yeah."

"Months passed. I wasn't interested in going out. I didn't care about dating again. I…wasn't interested in any man." She hesitated, then spelled it out. "Until you."

"You don't love me," he protested.

"I know that!" Edie said fiercely. "But I like you."

"Yeah, well, I like you, too," he said, frowning. "But I'm not falling in love with you!"

"Exactly," Edie said. "And if I am starting to feel things again, I don't want to fall for someone who isn't interested. I've already done that," she told him.

He scowled. "When?"

"I was eighteen. Young, foolish. I should have known better. You remember the actor with my mother at Mont Chamion?"

"Him?" Nick looked appalled.

"He was charming. We dated. It meant more to me than it did to him." She refused to go into all the bloody details. "It wasn't like that with Ben," she said. "So I know how it's supposed to be."

"You do, do you?" His dark eyes glittered with challenge.

But Edie had no doubts about that. She wrapped her fingers around the coffee mug and met his gaze squarely. "Yes."

Nick's mouth twisted. His fingers drummed lightly on the tabletop. With his other hand he carried his coffee cup to his lips, his eyes never leaving hers. He still didn't speak.

Neither did she. Just as well. She'd probably already said far too much.

The waiter came and refilled Nick's cup, but Edie put a hand over hers and shook her head with a smile. "I've had enough," she said. "I won't sleep if I drink anymore."

The waiter shot a conspiratorial male look in Nick's direction. "Sleep is overrated."

Nick made an inarticulate sound, then said harshly, "Could you bring the check, please."

Edie reached for her purse. "I'll get it."

Dark eyes flashed. "The hell you will."

"It's business," Edie protested. "My mother—"

"Your mother has nothing to do with this!" Nick pulled out his credit card and thrust it at the returning waiter before he could even reach the table.

"Really, Nick—"

"Stop arguing, Edie." His tone was flat and uncompromising. "And put your wallet away."

Reluctantly Edie put it away. "I don't expect—"

"You've already made what you expect and don't expect quite clear. Let me make something clear, too—when I invite a woman out to dinner, I expect to pay. Got it?"

"Got it," Edie muttered.

The waiter came back with the tab, which Nick scanned

quickly, nodded and signed, then tucked his card and the receipt back in his wallet.

"You can tax deduct it," Edie suggested.

Nick glared at her. Then he stood and came around the table to pull out her chair for her before she could push the chair back and get up herself. All very gentlemanly and polite. Just as if she couldn't hear him grinding his teeth.

"Thank you," she mumbled as she stood. "And thank you for dinner."

"My pleasure," he lied. It had to be a lie. The hum of awareness was still there, but so was a sizzle of annoyance.

Edie quickened her steps as they headed for the exit. But the toe of her sandal caught on a protruding chair leg. She stumbled. Nick's hand shot out to catch her arm and keep her from falling.

"Thank you," she said, breathless.

"No problem," he said, tersely.

The problem was that he didn't let go. He walked beside her as they headed toward the lot where he'd parked the car, his fingers stayed on her arm. Through the thin cotton of her dress, she could feel them as if there was no barrier at all between them.

Once in the car, she gave him directions on how to get out of Santa Barbara and back up into the hills to Mona's house. He'd found it himself during the day. She knew it wasn't as easy at night. He didn't argue. He didn't discuss. He didn't talk at all. He followed her instructions without comment.

He didn't speak again until he'd parked the car and they were climbing the steps to her apartment.

She would have protested that she didn't need to be escorted to the door, but there was an implacability about him now that made her hold her tongue. If he wanted to walk all the way up, so be it. He wasn't coming in.

The porch wasn't big. As she got out her key, he was close enough that she could smell the woodsy scent of his aftershave. He was close enough that if she turned, she could go up on her tiptoes and kiss his lips.

She didn't turn. In fact she was glad she managed to stick the key in the lock without fumbling as her hands were trembling slightly. Only when she had the key in the lock, did she look around. "Thank you for dinner," she said politely.

Nick grunted, his lips pressed in a thin line. So much for all that Savas charm.

She gave him a quick smile, pushed open the door and went in. Roy came bounding to meet her.

"Edie."

She caught Roy by the collar and looked back at Nick. "Yes?"

His dark eyes bored into hers. "It's not a given, you know."

It? "What's not?"

"That you'll fall in love. People *choose* whether or not to fall in love. It's always a choice."

"It's—"

"Always a choice," he repeated firmly, cutting her off. "You just need to choose not to."

Edie opened her mouth to protest, but even as she did so, she knew there was no point. If Nick believed that, they would have to agree to disagree. "Good night, Nick."

"Good night, Edie." His tone was ever so slightly mocking. A corner of his mouth lifted slightly. "Let me know when you change your mind."

In the morning, he was gone.

She wasn't surprised to look out the window and see that his car wasn't there. He'd obviously decided that if bedding her wasn't going to be a perk of Mona's renovation job, he didn't want to be bothered.

In some perverse way, Edie thought perhaps she should be flattered.

At least it meant he had enjoyed their night together in Mont Chamion. But of course it also meant that he saw her presence as nothing more than an opportunity for physical release.

Maybe not so flattering after all.

"So I'm glad I said what I did," she told Roy over her morning oatmeal.

The dog cocked his head and grinned at her, then looked hopefully at the toast she was buttering.

"You've had enough," she told him. "And I don't feed you from the table."

But try convincing Roy of that. He made a low whining sound and didn't budge or blink an eye as long as the oatmeal and toast lasted. Edie rolled her eyes at him.

He grinned happily, then ambled over to Mona's house with her when she went over at nine to start work. She knew what he was thinking: it was always possible she would stop for a snack midmorning. He wouldn't want to miss that.

There was no sign in the kitchen that Nick had eaten before he'd left. It was just the way she'd left it yesterday—as if he'd never been here, as if it had all been a dream.

It hadn't been a dream. Perhaps, though, Edie thought, it was a wake-up call.

Maybe Mona was right. Now that her hormones had been reawakened, maybe it was time for her to stop sitting at home and waiting for the right man to appear in her life. After the disastrous end to her relationship with Kyle, she hadn't sat home and moped. She'd gone back to the university where, a few months later, she'd met Ben.

He'd been the right man, just as clearly as Kyle had been the wrong one.

Maybe, now it was time to do that again. She had loved Ben, but she didn't want to spend the rest of her life alone. Ben wouldn't have wanted her to. So if Nick Savas was the wrong man, it was up to her to find the right one.

He'd done her a favor.

She kept telling herself that.

She even acted on it. When Derek Saito, a local English teacher, called that morning to ask if Mona would come and talk to the drama class when school started, she didn't just take down the information and promise to check with Mona and call him back. She actually chatted with him.

Derek was Ronan's age. They'd been in the same class in school. They'd been surfing buddies and had played tennis together. He'd been Ben's friend, too. And she remembered well how kind he'd been to her after Ben's death. Now, after she caught him up on what Ronan was up to, he asked about her.

"I'm all right," she said. "Working hard."

"Too hard, I'd guess." Derek knew her well. "As usual."

Every other time Edie had disagreed. But today she said, "You could be right. I need to get out more."

There was a pause, as if Derek hadn't been expecting that. But then he said, "So, want to go out with me?" There was a quick pause, then he said, "I'm not hitting on you, Edie. Not yet," he qualified. "Ben was too good a friend. But there's a concert on campus Friday night. Old-timers. Couple of eighties rock groups. Pure nostalgia…if you're interested?"

It sounded like fun. And Derek was a friend. She doubted he'd ever be more than that, but why not go? What was there to stay home for?

"I'm interested," she said. "Yes."

"Great!" There was a sudden spike of enthusiasm in his voice. "Dinner first?"

"I could cook," Edie offered.

"No. We'll grab a burger or something. I'll pick you up at six."

"Shall I meet you at the restaurant? You wouldn't have to come all the way out here." Derek lived in town. The university was several miles on the other side.

"I'll pick you up. My pleasure," he said. "See you then."

But the moment Edie hung up, she sat there a moment thinking, *What have I done?*

"Nothing," she said out loud with all the firmness she could muster. "You're going out with a friend. You're getting a life. Mona will be proud," she added wryly.

Speaking of whom, she had a few words to say to her mother. So she picked up the phone again and tried to ring Mona. Again she got no answer.

She'd already tried twice this morning, right after she'd come into the office. There had been no answer then, either, so apparently Mona was still out of range.

She supposed Nick had sent her an email to say he had decided not to do the renovations. Serve her right, Edie thought, for all her meddling.

But a part of her felt a little bereft because the adobe wouldn't be salvaged. Going back over there with Nick had reminded her that once upon a time it had been a nice house, that she had made lots of good memories there. She had hoped to make more with Ben, though, to be honest she wasn't sure that ever would have happened. She'd thought that maybe when they'd come back from Fiji they could have fixed it up as a vacation house, even though they'd probably live elsewhere close to wherever Ben worked—somewhere right on the water.

Now none of it would happen.

Life was what happened when you were making other plans. She thought it was John Lennon who had said that. But Mona said it, too. Her mother was just a fount of wisdom these days, Edie thought grimly.

At least she had made a plan. She was going to a concert with Derek on Friday. And this afternoon she was going to finish doing the filing she'd intended to do yesterday when Nick Savas had been the "life" that had interrupted her plans.

The phone rang. Edie picked it up. "Edie Daley."

"Hey," a gruff masculine voice she hadn't expect to hear ever again said into her ear, "can you meet me at the adobe with your key? I've got tools and a truckload of roofing tiles to unload."

CHAPTER SIX

SHE was still an annoyingly attractive woman, even when she stood there, hands on her hips, watching him back a truck down to the adobe, with her mouth opening and closing like a fish.

Nick gave her a wave and a cheerful grin through the open window as he passed. "Thanks."

If she replied, he didn't hear her. He didn't see her mouth move, either, but he was focused on getting the truck as close to the house as he could. When he had, he flicked off the engine and hopped out.

Edie was still standing in the yard. "What are you doing?" she demanded as he walked toward her.

"Going to start with the roof. Figured while I was in town, I'd see if I could get what I needed." He shrugged and spread his hands. "I did."

He couldn't get all of the tiles he would need. But he got all they had at the moment with more on order. By the time they arrived he would be ready for them. In the meantime he had to finish pulling the rest of the old roof off.

"You left," Edie said.

"No. I went into town. Had to file permits, pick up materials." He gave her his best sunny smile.

She still had her hands on her hips. "I thought you'd changed your mind and gone."

He'd considered it. Half the night, which he'd spent either restlessly prowling the house or swimming laps in the damn pool to take the edge off his frustration, he'd thought about cutting his losses, packing his bags and hitting the road.

God knew he had plenty of other jobs he could be working on. He had commitments lined up for the next two years. He'd had to do some serious shuffling to fit Mona's little ranch house in.

Which was why he was staying, he told himself. He'd said he would. But in fact he hadn't told Mona yet. She was unreachable—off somewhere at the ends of the earth in Southeast Asia shooting a film. She wouldn't even know he'd changed his mind until he was gone.

But he didn't go—wasn't going—because of the expressions on Edie's face when she'd walked around the old adobe yesterday afternoon. He'd been examining the walls, the roof, the foundation. But even more, he'd been studying Edie.

Her face was such a mixture of wistfulness, yearning, happiness and sadness as she'd drifted through the rooms, run her fingers over the woodwork, stood staring out the windows, that he'd spent far less time going over the bones of the house and far more time watching her.

And last night after her "I'm not sleeping with you" announcement, after which he'd been ready to leave, he remembered the way she looked, and he couldn't go.

Instead he'd gone downstairs and wandered around Mona's house looking at all the photos on the piano, on the bookshelves, on the walls.

Mona had her share of fine paintings and prints by well-known and not-so-well-known artists. But by far the most numerous framed pieces were family photos. Not one of them was of Mona alone—they were all of her children, her spouses (Edie's dad and the exes, he gathered) or family group shots.

There were a lot of Edie.

In the kitchen there were magnetic snapshots on the refrigerator—of all the kids, but he only noticed Edie. In one she was playing in the pool, her head thrown back as she laughed. In another she had her arms looped over the shoulders of a pair of identical redheaded young boys. They were freckled and gangly, but they had Edie's eyes. In a third she was sitting on the patio with her arms around Roy. She was smiling, but the wistfulness was there in this one.

He found others as well. He looked at them all—Edie as a girl on a pony with a boy who had to be her older brother, Edie suited up to play volleyball at some high school, Edie and Rhiannon, Edie and another girl who was also probably a sister, more of Edie and the twins. Edie and a handsome young man with their arms around each other and expressions of pure delight on their faces. It had to be Edie and her husband.

He almost couldn't look at that one, knowing what he knew. He wondered that she could. But there were several, including a larger more formal portrait that must have been taken on their wedding day. It was in pride of place on the piano. She must see it every single day.

He hadn't looked at a photo of Amy in years.

The photos—and the memory of Edie's face that afternoon—made him stay. She wanted the house salvaged. He could give her that.

Besides, he wasn't a quitter.

If she thought she could just say no and make them both miserable—well, she was wrong. He'd leave when he was good and ready to leave, when he could turn his back and walk away, which he would.

Because, as he'd told her, love was a choice. And he'd done it once. He wasn't doing it again. Ever. But that didn't mean they couldn't enjoy their time together.

He started off-loading the tiles. "You could help," he suggested, slanting her a glance. "Or not."

Edie didn't move for a long moment, but then he heard her footsteps coming toward the truck. "Ten minutes," she said. "Then I have to get back to work."

* * *

He was *staying?*

Still poleaxed from his phone call, Edie stared after Nick as he carried an armful of tiles to a spot near the side of the house. She still felt as if the breath had been knocked right out of her. She was giddy and panicky and perversely elated. At the same time she was trying not to feel anything at all.

She knew what he was doing.

He was calling her bluff. He was going to make her prove she could resist him. She ground her teeth, glaring at his back. But then, having put down the tiles, he straightened and turned and looked right at her, and she felt the giddiness again, and hoped to goodness she could do what she'd told herself—and him—was necessary.

It *was* necessary!

She knew herself. She knew how invested she became in relationships. She knew the pain that her unrequited love for Kyle had caused her. Even having gone to bed with Nick once had undermined her ability to remain uninvolved. She had told herself she could—but in the end, she'd cared.

She hadn't fallen in love. But she hadn't been able to forget him, either.

Now once more she tried to imagine taking Nick to her bed for as long as he was here, then smiling and saying goodbye whenever the house was finished.

Or sooner.

There was no guarantee he wouldn't get bored with her much sooner than it took him to finish the house!

He could share a bed with her once more or five times more and then decide it was time to move on, find another woman. He wouldn't even have to flaunt her in front of Edie. He could simply find a new bedmate.

And she'd be left, gutted, heartbroken.

In the end Nick was right—it *was* simple.

But he was wrong, too. He might find it easy to choose where he loved. But could she?

Again the answer was simple: no.

So she turned her head, refused to let her gaze linger on his easy walk, his lean muscular body, his smile, the gleam in his eyes. She helped him move the tiles, and tried to think about something else.

And when they had the truck unloaded, she said, "Goodbye."

"Au revoir," Nick said cheerfully. "That means I'll see you again."

"I know what it means," Edie said shortly. She felt like saying, *Not if I see you first.* "Come, Roy."

But Roy, perversely, was too busy following Nick around, watching what he was doing, deftly catching the occasional treat Nick tossed his way.

"I saw that," Edie accused him. "Roy, come on!"

But Roy only had eyes for Nick.

"He's my friend," Nick told her, grinning.

"Because you're bribing him," Edie said indignantly.

"You haven't ever heard the old saying, 'The way to a dog's heart is through his stomach'?"

Edie shot him a glare to keep from laughing. "Fine. Keep him with you. Just don't overdo it," she said irritably. "And don't lose him."

"No fear. We'll both be back for dinner," Nick promised.

Edie grunted her lack of enthusiasm about that and started up the hill.

"I'll pick up a pizza," Nick called after her. "What kind do you like?"

She didn't answer that. "I'm going to be busy." Busy avoiding him.

But if Nick got the message, he ignored it. "See you later."

She tried to make sure that wouldn't happen. She finished up at work early. She swam her laps early, so she would be done before he got back. And she was in her apartment making a salad for dinner when she heard his car.

The only reason she looked out the window was to see that

Roy was with him. Once she saw the big black dog, she turned away. So she wasn't prepared for the knock on her door.

"We're back," Nick announced unnecessarily. He had a pizza box in one hand.

She didn't invite him in. Apparently she didn't need to. He came in just the way Roy did, without an invitation. Only while Roy went straight to the food dish, Nick paused to look around at the overstuffed sofa and chair, the craftsman style bookcases and the library table that doubled as her dining room table. He nodded his approval. "Nice place. Suits you." He spotted the cat on the windowsill. "Who's this?"

"Gerald," Edie told him. "What are you doing here? I didn't invite you," she said pointedly.

"No, I invited you," Nick agreed. "For pizza," he reminded her when she looked blank.

"I said I was busy."

He looked around at the evidence of her doing absolutely nothing other than tearing up some salad greens. "Yeah, I can tell."

Breath hissed through Edie's teeth. "I don't want to have dinner with you."

"Because you'll fall in love with me." He paused, then the grin flashed again. "Or am I making myself so obnoxious that you can't stand me?"

"Getting close," Edie said, determined not to smile.

Nick shrugged equably. "Well, if you don't want to share the pizza with me…" He waved the box close enough that she could smell sausage and other mouth-watering pizza sorts of smells as he moved toward the door. Edie's stomach growled.

"Oh, fine. Sit down," she snapped.

He beamed. "Will do. Gotta clean up a bit first. You take care of this while I grab a quick shower." He thrust the pizza box into her hands. "Don't eat it all before I get back." And he ran lightly back down her stairs and headed for Mona's house.

She put the pizza in the oven and turned the heat on low

to keep it warm. Then she finished making the salad, adding enough for him now, and set the table for two. Roy looked hopeful. Gerald came over to see if there was something for him. Edie fed them both.

Then she told them sternly, "That's all you get. No sitting around watching us, looking hopeful."

"No, that would be me."

She whipped around to see Nick standing in the doorway. He gave her what was undeniably a hopeful look, tempered with a grin, as his gaze slid over her, making her all too aware of what he was hoping for. Edie steeled her heart—and her hormones.

"Don't," she said firmly.

He shrugged. "Okay," he said easily, dropping the hopeful look and heading straight for the table with the same single-mindedness Roy and Gerald had shown. "Starving," he said as he put a piece of pizza on her plate and one on his. Then he dished her up some salad and took some for himself. "This looks great."

It did. And she was hungry. So she ate.

For the first few minutes there was silence as they were both focused on the meal. But eventually Edie had had enough to be far more aware of the man than of the meal he'd brought.

When he finished his fourth piece of pizza, he leaned back in his chair and sighed. "Ripping off a roof gives a guy an appetite."

She'd noticed that he'd already begun when he'd called her to bring the key. Now she reached over to the counter and plucked it up and held it out to him. "You'd better have this. Then you won't have to keep calling me."

His lips twisted, but he took the key and stuffed it into the pocket of the canvas shorts he was wearing. "Thanks."

Their gazes met again. His dark eyes regarded her warmly. A slight smile played across his lips. She abruptly got up and carried her plate to the sink. "Thank you for the pizza," she said, running water to wash the dishes.

"Thank you for the salad," he said equally politely. He came up behind her, set his plate on the counter. He was so near she could feel the heat of his body. She added dish soap to the water, then began putting the dishes in, all the while aware of him right behind her. And equally aware when he moved away.

She breathed again.

"I've got some planning to do," he said. "So I'll say good night."

She looked over her shoulder, surprised.

Nick shrugged. "Unless you have a better idea?" There was that hint of hope again.

Edie shook her head. "No. No. I—good night."

It was the right thing to do, she assured herself when the door closed behind him and she heard his feet going down the steps. It was safer—far far safer—this way.

Nick finished ripping the roof off the next morning. The following day he cleaned and sorted tiles. It had been a while since he'd worked on a roof like this one. Putting new and old tiles together was a tricky business. He wanted to take his time.

And he wanted Edie to come back.

She hadn't been here since the first day. He barely saw her except at dinner. Somehow they managed to eat that together every night. Either she cooked and apparently felt obligated to feed him—"Mona's hospitality is legendary," she said, making it clear the meals were an extension of it—or he went into town and picked up take-away.

But other than at dinner, he didn't see her. She didn't come around the adobe at all. Well, no, that wasn't true. She was certainly there in spirit—in his head—even if she didn't set foot in the place.

On Friday as he removed the last of the rotten front porch beams before he put the new one up this afternoon, he could look across the roof line and see the rusty swing set near the trees.

Edie hadn't gone near it when she'd shown him the house, but he knew she must have played there as a child.

It took no imagination to envision her swinging high, short legs pumping furiously, long dark hair streaming out behind. He smiled as he saw it in his mind's eye because he knew exactly what she'd looked like. The dark-haired little girl who had been Edie graced half a dozen pictures in the upstairs hall at Mona's place.

Later when he ate his lunch in the kitchen at the rickety table, he thought about her eating meals here with her family. It was intriguing to think of Mona Tremayne cooking in this kitchen, of her not as a megastar but as a young wife and mother.

But it was more intriguing to think about Edie as a child.

As the sun spilled through the dirty windows, making patterns on the dusty floor, Nick tried to imagine her playing there with her brother. He was sure she had. He'd seen the flickering expressions on her face when she'd brought him here. He wondered about those memories.

Ordinarily when he thought about the earlier occupants of a building he was restoring, they were distant historical figures. They weren't the woman he'd had pizza with on Tuesday and meat loaf with last night, the woman he'd made love with in Mont Chamion, the proper, tart-tongued woman who had melted in his arms, the woman he couldn't stop wanting to take back to his bed.

But when he studied the vertical row of little ink marks climbing the wall by the back door—dark blue Rs for her brother Ronan, and bright red Es for Edie—once again she became the little dark-haired girl she had been when she'd lived here. He bet she had stood tall while her father measured her.

If he shut his eyes he could see them now in his mind. There was a photo in the hall of Edie and her dad. She had been sitting on the adobe's front porch steps, snuggled close under her father's arm. She'd had her head turned so that, instead of staring into the camera, she was looking up at her father as if he regularly hung the moon just for her.

The memory made Nick smile until he realized that within a year of that photo, Joe Tremayne had been killed in an accident and Edie's life had irrevocably changed.

It was a wonder she wanted to come back here at all.

The noise of clicking on floorboards jolted him back to the present, and he turned to see Roy pattering in from the living room across the dusty floor. His mood lightened and he looked up, expecting—hoping—to see Edie at last.

But no one was there.

"Where is she?" Nick asked the dog.

Not surprisingly, Roy didn't answer. He was more interested in what remained of Nick's sandwich, and he whined hopefully. Nick gave the crusts to the dog, stood up and went outside to look for her. "Edie?"

But no one answered. He called her name again. Nothing. Except that Roy, having swallowed the crusts in one gulp, had come outside, too, and stood on the porch, wagging his tail.

"You didn't come without her, did you?"

But apparently he had. Hope faded. Nick sighed and rubbed the back of his neck, kneading taut cords of muscle. "Well," he said to the dog, "make yourself at home. I've got work to do."

If Mona ever got back to civilization, Edie thought irritably, she'd be amazed at all the work her business manager had accomplished while she had been out of touch.

Edie always worked hard. But working all day and a good part of the night, determinedly refusing to let herself think about Nick Savas, was having an extraordinary effect on her work output.

Even in the instances where, previously, there would be half a dozen phone calls waiting to be returned when she got to work in the morning because people all over the world were involved with Mona, now Edie almost always picked up the phone regardless of the time of night.

Why not?

She wasn't sleeping.

And talking about whatever they wanted to talk about was safer by far than lying in bed, tossing and turning and thinking about the man asleep in Mona's house—the man who could be in her bed if only she'd let him.

But she wouldn't let him. Couldn't.

But she thought about him. Couldn't help herself.

She looked forward to their dinners every evening. Couldn't seem to help that, either. She was eager to learn what he'd done on the house every day.

"You should come and see," he said each evening.

But she always declined. "I've got too much to do," she said. But she was curious.

So was he. While she asked about his work, every evening he asked questions about the years she'd lived there.

Which had been her bedroom? When had the swing set been set up? Whose birthday present had it been? How had they celebrated Christmas when they'd lived there?

At first Edie was reluctant to answer. For years she had bottled up the memories because it had seemed safer that way. But under Nick's gentle questioning, she found herself talking more, remembering more—and finding joy in the flood of memories she'd kept close to her heart.

Why hadn't she done it sooner?

Because talking about her father had always caused her mother pain. Ronan, too, shied away from discussing their father. But then Ronan shied away from talking about everything. And no one else shared those memories. No one ever asked about them. Not even Ben, she realized. He hadn't probed, didn't want to make her sad. And Ben had always been busy looking forward.

But Nick asked.

And Edie talked. When she protested that she was talking too much about herself, that it was his turn, he obliged with stories about his own childhood—about summers on Long Island—he and his brother Ari with their Savas cousins, especially Demetrios who was his age and George who was the same age as his brother Ari.

"We were wild and crazy kids," he told her. "If there was trouble to get into, we found it."

He told her stories that made her laugh and he showed her scars that made her wince. And she realized that not going to bed with Nick wasn't stopping her falling in love a little bit more every night they shared a meal.

Each evening the dinners lasted longer, and it was harder to pull herself away and say she needed to get back to work.

But she did. She had to. It was all she could do for self-preservation.

But by Friday she knew it was a very good thing she had agreed to go out with Derek that evening.

Midafternoon, after she'd taken four high-pressure phone calls in a row and spent another hour fruitlessly trying to contact Mona about a script, she decided to take a break, go back to her apartment and figure out what she was going to wear.

"Come on," she said, turning to look for the dog as she hung up the phone, frustrated at still not reaching Mona. "Let's get out of here."

And that was when she realized Roy wasn't there.

"Roy?"

She got up from her desk and went out to the kitchen. Sometimes on hot days he would go lie on the cool tiles there. But not today.

"Roy?"

She went back to the office, and pushed open the door to the patio and called his name again. Since she'd adopted him from a rescue organization shortly after she'd come back to the States following Ben's death, Roy had been her shadow.

If she was in the office, he was by her chair. If she was stretched out on a chaise beneath the *ramada* making notes on scripts, he was always there. If she was swimming laps, Roy was lying on the tiles, one eye open, watching her. If she was eating a salad for lunch, he was sprawled on the kitchen floor looking hopeful—though admittedly salads weren't his favorite meal.

She tried to remember the last time she'd seen him. It had been at lunch, she thought.

He hadn't been enthralled when she'd begun to tear up salad greens. Had he wandered back toward her office? He could push the door open to go outside, but he rarely did—only if Clara was there cleaning or if her grandkids had come and were swimming in the pool would he leave Edie's side.

Roy was a social animal. He liked to be with people, and Edie was the only one around.

Except…

"No," she said aloud. "Roy, you didn't."

And, truthfully, she didn't believe he had gone all the way to the adobe to see Nick. Why would he?

But if he wasn't there, where was he?

Had something happened to him?

Please God, no.

But even as she thought it, the words formed a knot in her gut, bringing back the memory of Ben's disappearance all over again.

Rationally she knew it wasn't the same, Roy was a dog in his own territory. Not a man in a small boat on a stormy sea. Roy was capable and competent. But bad things happened even to the capable and competent.

Ben had been both. And he'd been a skilled sailor besides. He'd simply been in the wrong place at the wrong time. In high school, Edie's friend, Kelly, had lost a dog to rattlesnake bites. It wasn't common, but it certainly happened. And without warning.

Edie knew there was nothing she could have done to save Ben. But if something had happened to Roy…

He wasn't by the pool. He hadn't gone to the cutting horse arena. He was nowhere in the house or the carriage house. There was no place else to go but the adobe. It was close to half a mile away. She couldn't believe he'd gone that far.

But she had to check. Maybe at least Nick had seen him.

"Roy!" she called his name over and over as she went.

The first response came when she was not quite at the top of the hill. She couldn't see the adobe yet. The voice that responded was loud enough for her to hear, but strained.

Just two words. "He's here."

"Oh, thank God," she said aloud as she hurried over the rise.

She was elated to see Roy standing in the yard in front of the house, tail wagging happily, and horrified to see Nick, shirtless, halfway up a ladder, a huge heavy beam on one shoulder as he tried to climb.

One end was already in place, which must have been a chore in itself. But the other needed to be lifted up and slotted into the opposite end of the porch.

Even as she watched, the ladder seemed to teeter.

"Wait!"

The second she shouted she thought she'd made a mistake, that she could startle him and he could drop it, could fall and have it come down on top of him.

Fortunately he didn't. He stopped, then turned his head to look up the hill toward her.

Edie was already scrambling and skidding down. Roy, enthused at the sight of her, began barking and frolicking in joy.

"No! Roy, stop!" She could just imagine him hurtling against the ladder and sending Nick flying.

For once in his life, Roy listened. He stopped at the bottom of the broken steps and squirmed, wagging his tail furiously as she reached the yard and glared up at the man on the ladder.

"What on earth are you doing? You could kill yourself!"

"I've done it before." His voice was still strained, undoubtedly from the load he was bearing.

Edie could see the sweat trickling down the side of his face and making paths through the dust on his shirtless back. "And lived to tell about it, apparently. But that doesn't make it sensible. You need help."

"You volunteering?"

"Yes, I am." And she brushed past Roy and took hold of the ladder, standing behind Nick, bracing her hands on the sides to keep it steady as he climbed.

Startled, Nick looked down at her. "Get out of there. You're right in the line of fire if I drop this thing."

"Then you'd better not drop it." She stayed right where she was, nose to the back of his denim-clad knees.

"Edie!"

"Nick!" she countered, still not moving.

"Damn it," he muttered under his breath. But when she still didn't move or relinquish her hold, she saw the legs of his jeans shift as he tensed his muscles and climbed another step. The ladder trembled. She gripped it for all she was worth. Now she could study the smears and scuff marks on his steel-toed work boots. Above her Nick breathed raggedly.

"You're an idiot," she told him conversationally, more to keep her brain engaged, thinking about the bigger picture than about what could happen if the beam slipped or he did.

"So—" he went up another step "—are you."

The boots went out of her line of sight. She had to look up if she wanted to see him at all. She did. The view was pretty spectacular—apart from the beam, which was downright scary.

She wanted to look away and was mesmerized at the same time. Nick was beginning to shift his weight, easing the beam forward off his shoulder and into place. As he did so, the ladder tilted. Edie clutched it with white-knuckled fingers, her breath caught in her throat.

And then he said, "Got it," and in the time-honored behavior of proficient ladder climbers everywhere, he skimmed back down before she could unlock her fingers from the uprights.

And there she stood, her hands locked to the ladder, her knees weak with relief, her nose pressed to the back of his neck, her arms bracketing him.

Exactly where she wanted to be.

She was so stunned she didn't move away. Just hung on. Clutched the ladder for dear life and breathed in the scent of sweat and dirt and something so elementally Nick.

For a moment Nick didn't move, either. He stayed absolutely motionless within her arms, as tense as she was boneless. She could see the tension in the quiver of the muscles of his back. Then his head dipped as he rested his forehead on one of the rungs and took a deep shuddering breath. The movement closed the millimeters of distance between her lips and the hard damp skin of his back.

She kissed it.

Tasted salt. Tasted Nick. Couldn't help herself.

It was a split second. That was all.

Yet at her touch he spun around. "God, Edie!"

Then he was kissing her back. Not a taste. He was determined to devour her. He wrapped her hard in his embrace and his mouth met hers with a fierce hunger. "Yes," he said, exultant. "Yes! I knew it. I told you." He pulled back to look at her, eyes glittering, triumphant.

And Edie grabbed for the shards of her sanity and shook her head. "No."

Hard fingers gripped her upper arms. "What do you mean, no? You kissed me!"

She wouldn't deny it. "Your neck," she said. "That's all."

"It's enough," he said. Then, "No, it's not. Not nearly. But you can't claim you don't want me."

"I never said that," Edie told him. "I did…want you," she admitted. She owed him that.

"Do," Nick corrected firmly, as if daring her to dispute it. "You do want me."

Edie pressed her lips together. "Yes," Edie admitted. "I do. But I told you—I want more than that." Her voice quieted. "And you don't." Their eyes met again and now she gave him a look that dared him to argue with her.

His teeth came together. A muscle in his jaw ticked. She dropped her gaze to watch the steady rise and fall of his hard, tanned chest. Then slowly she lifted her eyes once more. He met them squarely. He didn't say a word.

His silence said it all.

Somewhere in the treetops Edie could hear birds calling. A long way off the faint sound of a motorcycle broke the silence. By her knees Roy was panting.

She stepped back, drew in a breath and let it out slowly. "I have to go."

Nick's shoulders settled slightly. His fingers, which had been curled into fists, eased open and hung loosely at his sides. His dark eyes accused her.

She'd made the move. She'd changed her mind, they seemed to say.

She hadn't. She only wished she could.

CHAPTER SEVEN

THERE was gone—and then there was *gone*.

When Edie had said, "I have to go," Nick assumed she meant back to the house, back to the safety of her work schedule where she could pretend that the desire that had just flared up between them could be dialed back to a simmer she felt comfortable ignoring.

He didn't realize it meant she'd *left!*

But when he got back to the house that afternoon, still fuming, still horny, definitely determined to confront her, to tell her she could damned well stop saying one thing while her body wanted something else, she wasn't there.

Roy was there—in the house, waiting.

So was a note on the kitchen counter: *Out this evening. Lasagna in the refrigerator. I fed Roy.*

She hadn't even bothered to sign it.

An irritated breath hissed through Nick's teeth. He didn't eat the damned lasagna. It was Friday night. He wasn't going to spend it with a dog for company. He took a shower, then went into town in search of a good meal—and a little companionship. A woman. Someone to take his mind off Edie Daley.

If she wasn't going to share his bed, he was willing to bet he could find a woman who would.

He found a very good meal with no trouble at all. Santa Barbara had its share of fine dining. And afterward he met several young women at a sports bar just off State Street.

They were all too chattery and giggly or too blowsy and flirty. Their hair was too short or too blonde. They were too tall unless they were too short. Not one stirred his hormones in the slightest.

He drank a beer, talked a bit to the bartender and watched some baseball. Then, feeling more out of sorts than ever, he drove back to Mona's. Alone.

Roy was delighted. The dog wagged his tail madly, bumping his head against the back of Nick's thighs as he followed him into the sitting room. What it told Nick was that she hadn't come back yet. If she had, she would have reclaimed him.

It was past eleven. Hardly the witching hour, but where the hell was she?

He prowled the downstairs of the house, the dog at his heels. All evening he hadn't let himself wonder where she'd gone. It was her business. Not his. He didn't care.

Every time his thoughts had veered in her direction, he'd turned them away again or skipped right over them. Easy enough while he was watching the ball game. Not quite so simple when he was struck by the endless shortcomings of women who were not her. Even less so now that it was going on eleven-thirty and she wasn't here.

Did she expect him to babysit her dog all evening?

Nick jammed his hands into the pockets of his jeans and glowered out through the French doors at the sparkling turquoise of the pool set in the darkness of the garden. Then he jerked as his phone vibrated against his hand.

Surprised, he pulled it out of his pocket to stare at the number calling. It wasn't one he recognized.

He felt a quick skip beat of his heart as he flipped the phone open. "Savas. Where the hell are you?"

"Thailand. Where the hell are you?"

"Mona?"

It was, of course. No one else, not even Edie, had that sultry, sexy, immediately recognizable voice.

"Where are you?" she demanded again. "Are you in Santa Barbara? Working on the house? Where's Edie?" The questions came fast and furious.

Nick rubbed a hand against the back of his neck. "Yes, I'm in Santa Barbara," he said impatiently. "Yes, working on the house. And I don't know where Edie is."

"Why not?"

"I'm not her keeper," he snapped.

"No?" Mona said with just enough inflection in her voice to raise the hairs on the back of his neck.

"No," Nick said shortly.

"Whatever you say, dear." Mona brushed him off. "But you have seen her? She is there?"

"She was this afternoon," he said gruffly.

"Ah." One syllable. It was no wonder she was an actress. She could put layers of meaning into two letters.

Nick didn't reply. Wherever she was taking this conversation, he wasn't going willingly.

"Has something happened?" From her first fast and furious questions, Mona now sounded concerned.

Nick flexed his shoulders, kneaded the back of his neck, remembered that Edie's lips had touched him there and abruptly dropped his hand. "Happened? No, of course not."

Whatever happened—or hadn't—it was none of Mona's business.

"Well, she's not answering her phone," Mona said, clearly put out. "Edie *always* answers."

"That's ridiculous. It's almost midnight here," Nick reminded her. "She should have some time off. Maybe she's asleep."

"She'd hear her phone."

Or has a life, Nick wanted to press the issue, but didn't. Instead he said, "Maybe she didn't want to answer it."

Mona dismissed that idea with a mere *pffft* sound. "I need to talk to her. Tell her I need to talk to her."

"I'll tell her."

"Tell her to call me." And Mona rang off.

In the silence afterward, Nick stood glaring at the phone, not sure who he was most annoyed at—Edie or her mother.

Or himself—for not having taken up an invitation from one of the too giggly, too flirty, too blonde, too short or too tall women he'd met this evening.

Derek Saito was a nice guy. He was funny and charming and better looking than Edie remembered. He'd grown up, filled out and developed an easy, wry sense of humor since she and Ben had spent time with him back in their college days. He taught high school English, was unattached—"Heart whole"—he assured her, and he was obviously interested in her.

Equally obviously Derek was the steady nonmercurial sort of guy she should be interested in if she was seriously considering a relationship.

But she wasn't—interested, that is. Not in Derek.

It was as if the hormones that had been all wide-awake and raring to go when she'd been in Nick's arms this afternoon, had taken a sleeping potion as soon as Derek picked her up at her apartment.

Not just her hormones, either. Her brain.

They went out to dinner before the concert, and try as she might to follow Derek's conversational leads, her mind kept clicking back to that other man, the one who was going to walk out of her life sooner rather than later, the man who made it clear he wanted to bed her—but wanted nothing else.

She tried to keep focused, be alert, ask appropriate questions. But she knew she'd blown it when Derek, telling her about a summer high school theater production, asked if she'd read it.

She said, "Who wrote it?"

"Romeo and Juliet?" The pained smile on his face would stick in her mind forever. Or if it didn't, it should.

Her cheeks burned. "I'm sorry. I'm sorry. I don't know where my brain is. I—" she shook her head "—I haven't been sleeping well."

No lie there.

Derek's expression softened and he nodded understandingly. "I'm sure it's still difficult," he said, reaching across the table to give her hand a light pat. "I'm just glad you came out with me tonight."

"I am, too," Edie said fervently, though certainly not for the same reasons. "Which scenes are they doing?" she asked, and managed not to make any more grievous gaffes for the rest of the evening.

The concert was loud and raucous, but with enough beach and surf music as well as later rowdier stuff that meant pretty much everyone there had a good time.

Edie did, too. But she couldn't help wondering what sort of music Nick liked. They had never discussed music. And never would—because after today she was going to have to stay completely away from him until he finished the house.

Or maybe this time, she thought as Derek turned off the winding road and into the estate grounds, when she got home, he really would be gone.

The night was dark with a bit less than half a moon casting silver light amid deep shadows as they drove up the curving lane through the eucalyptus. Ahead, through the tree trunks, as they climbed the hill, Edie could see lights on in Mona's house. She reached for her purse on the floor of the car, and rehearsed her best, well-brought-up thank-you for the lovely evening speech as Derek took the last turn.

Nick's car was parked in front of the garage. The sight made her heart do a wholly undesirable cartwheel.

Deliberately she turned her attention on Derek. "It's been great."

He cut the engine and turned her way, smiling, too. "It has. I'm glad we did it."

She couldn't see his eyes, but she heard genuine friendliness in his voice, and perhaps a hint of regret. "So good to see you again. And the food was terrific."

Derek nodded. "Best place in town for fish tacos." His grin flashed in the moonlight. "Don't let anyone tell you I don't know how to give a girl a good time."

"It *was* a good time, Derek." She put her hand on the door handle. "Thank you."

He got out, too. She knew he would. Didn't know how to prevent it. Hoped he wouldn't be offended by the faintest of kisses good-night. Keeping a smile on her face, Edie headed toward the carriage house and stopping at the bottom of the steps, she turned. "Thank you again, Derek."

He smiled, a sort of wry, understanding smile. "It was my pleasure."

There was a moment when she thought she might not have to kiss him. But when he leaned in, she knew she couldn't turn her head away. It was the faintest brush. Nothing more. Her hormones didn't even notice.

"I'll ask my mother about talking to the class in the fall," she said. "But I don't know when I'll talk to her again. She doesn't seem to be answering her phone."

"Oh, she is now," a gruff, wholly unexpected voice said.

Edie jumped and spun around to see Nick come striding toward them out of the darkness. "She wants you to call her. Tonight."

She didn't know how he did it, but somehow he was standing between her and Derek, looming like some interfering father whose daughter had missed curfew.

"This is Nick Savas," she said to Derek. "He's working on restoring the old adobe ranch house. For my mother," she added pointedly, though she wasn't sure who she wanted to get the point—Derek or Nick.

"She wanted to know where you were," Nick went on as if she hadn't said a word. "Who you were out with." His tone made it clear he wasn't impressed with Derek.

"Thank you," Edie bit out. She didn't bother to introduce Derek. Nick was obviously in no mood to listen. "It was kind of you to stay up and relay the message—"

"Oh, I wasn't sleeping," Nick drawled. "I've been out. On the town. Just got home myself." He gave her a hard smile.

Edie felt the dart. He certainly hadn't wasted his time.

Derek, who had been watching their exchange as if they were on center court at Wimbledon, spoke up. "Well, don't let us keep you up," he said easily to Nick.

Edie looked at him in surprise and not a little admiration for his willingness to go nose to nose with Nick's impersonation of a pit bull guarding his bone.

Now Nick's teeth came together with a snap. His whole body seemed to almost vibrate with tension. And Edie thought that, interesting as it was, watching men trying to mark their territory, she really didn't much like being the "territory" in question.

And she didn't want Derek getting his butt kicked.

So she said to him, "I think I will just go call her now. How about if I call you in the morning and give you her answer?"

Derek seemed to hesitate a moment, but then nodded. "Appreciate it." His dark eyes held hers and he gave her a long, assessing look, as if he were reevaluating everything he'd thought earlier this evening.

As well he might.

Then he looked at Nick. "I'm a friend of Edie's—and her husband's," he added, establishing his right to be protective. The air seemed to hum between them. Then apparently Derek felt he'd made his point. He turned and walked back to his car.

Edie stood right where she was until Derek had got into his car, turned it round and driven off. Beside her, Nick stood like a sentry. She felt a serious urge to kick him.

"You could have waited," she said through her teeth.

Nick shrugged. "You could have said where you were going."

They didn't look at each other, both stood on the gravel in

the darkness watching Derek's car move down the hill around the bend until the taillights were out of sight.

Only then did Edie move away briskly toward Mona's house to get Roy. "I didn't imagine you'd care," she tossed over her shoulder.

"Your mother cared."

Her mother cared. He didn't. And that was the long and short of it, right there.

"I'll call her," Edie said, opening the door to Roy who shot out eagerly and danced around her. She ruffled his fur. "Come on then," she said.

With the dog by her side, she walked past Nick toward her apartment. All the way there, up the stairs, until the door shut behind her, she felt his eyes on her back.

"You rang," Edie said when her mother finally answered her phone. She said the words with considerably more acid than she usually used when talking to her mother. Ordinarily she simply smiled and let Mona's behavior, Mona's theories, Mona's view of the world sluice over her like water over a duck's back.

She'd learned long ago that she was her own person.

She just wished Mona would learn it, too.

"Are you all right?" her mother demanded now, surprising her.

There had been eleven messages from her mother when she'd got back to her apartment and turned on her phone. The first few had been long-winded directions of things Edie needed to do and who she needed to call if she hadn't done so already (which she had).

After the fifth the messages began to get shorter and edgier, until the last one said, "My God, Edie! Answer your phone or I'll think you're dead!"

"I'm fine," Edie said. "I had a date."

"Nick said he didn't know where you were." Mona's annoyance came through loud and clear.

"I wasn't out with Nick," Edie said through her teeth. "And I don't need you throwing men at me!"

There was a moment's silence and then Mona said, "What?"

"You heard me," Edie said, fed up with guilelessness that was anything but. Her mother might be an award winning actress, but she couldn't fool Edie. "I said I don't need you throwing men at me! I know you think I should date again. I know you think I need to get on with my life. But understand one thing, it's my life! I'll find my own man when I want one!"

This time the silence lasted longer. Then Mona said almost meekly, "I'm sure you will."

Edie ground her teeth. "I mean it. I thought I'd made it clear after the night of the wedding in Mont Chamion. Didn't you hear anything I said?"

"You said," Mona parroted carefully, "I don't want you finding men for me. I especially don't want you setting me up with Kyle Robbins. Do not ever do that again."

It was a scarily accurate impersonation of the short version of what Edie had said to her mother that night.

"And?" Edie pressed when Mona didn't say anything else.

"Don't tell me you went out with Kyle Robbins?"

"No, damn it! I didn't go out with Kyle. Did you send him, too?"

"Too?"

"Besides Nick," Edie spat, furious that Mona wouldn't just admit to setting her up. Again.

"Say what?"

"Why else would he be here?" Edie demanded.

"Well, when he called, he said he was interested in looking at the house I'd told him about," Mona replied.

Edie opened her mouth. No sound came out. *He'd* called Mona? He'd said...*what?*

"*Nick* called? You?"

"Nick called me," Mona affirmed.

"You...didn't call him?"

"Edie."

"I'm just…trying to understand." Edie thought she must have been standing too long. Her knees felt wobbly. She sat down and tried to think.

"I should think it would be obvious," Mona said dryly.

Was it?

Edie shook her head. "No," she said, the single word soft and uncertain.

"Oh, for goodness' sake," Mona said, exasperated. "Why do you think he wanted to renovate my tumbling down adobe ranch house? To pad his résumé? To impress another king? I suppose you imagine an inconsequential ranch is going to do that? I don't think so!"

"But then—"

"He came for you." Mona put it in words of one syllable.

"But—" Once more Edie stopped, dazed, shaking her head. She'd jumped to that conclusion herself when he'd appeared on the doorstep. Her heart had leaped. Her hopes had danced. And then she'd asked, "What are you doing here?"

And Nick had replied…?

What *had* Nick replied?

She racked her brain. He'd said nothing direct at all. No straight out statement that he'd come for her. But no denial, either. He'd said, *I've been talking to your mother.*

Edie went perfectly still, tried to think it through. Didn't breathe. Didn't dare hope.

And yet…

"Edie?"

She was still thinking. Her mind whirled. It didn't make sense. Why would he have suggested he renovate the adobe unless…?

"Are you sure he called you?" she asked her mother.

"What is going on there?" Mona demanded. "Should I have said no? You went off with him the night I 'threw' Kyle at you," she reminded Edie forcefully. "I thought you liked him."

"I barely knew him," Edie said. "Then," she added hastily, lest her mother get even worse ideas than she was already apparently entertaining. "And yes, I—I like him."

"So," Mona said archly, "I'm forgiven?"

Edie supposed she was lucky her mother wasn't asking for an apology from her! "Yes," she said. "As long as you don't do it again."

"I'm hoping I won't have to." Mona's meaning was crystal clear.

"It's...not as simple as you might think," Edie said.

"I know you loved Ben—"

"This isn't about Ben," Edie said.

"Because loving Ben is no excuse to turn your back on life," Mona went on as if Edie hadn't spoken. "I loved your father with all my heart." She stopped abruptly, and Edie was surprised to hear a break in her mother's voice that had nothing to do with Mona's legendary acting ability. "I loved him," she said again, more quietly, but no less fervently.

"I know that, Mom," Edie said. "I've always known it."

But she was grateful for the words all the same. Mona so rarely stopped to look back that it was good to hear that reaffirmation. "But," she said again, "this isn't about Ben. Or Dad."

"Then what's it about?" Except in her layered acting performances, Mona wasn't one for subtlety.

"It's about Nick."

"What about Nick?"

Indeed, what about Nick? "That's what I'm trying to figure out. I'll call you back in the morning. My morning or your morning or something," Edie qualified. "I'm tired now. I've got to sleep. And I've got to think."

"Try not to do both at the same time," Mona said dryly.

But she didn't make any more comments—and she let the myriad work questions slide. All she said was, "If you need to talk, Edie..."

"Thanks," Edie said absently, already thinking. It wasn't

Mona she needed to talk to. Still. "Thanks, Mom," she said now because for once the term seemed right.

They called it a paradigm shift.

When phenomena could not be explained by the laws of the world as one knew it, one had to rethink.

That night Edie rethought.

She lay in bed and stared at the ceiling and looked at the events of the past week through a lens created by a new piece of information: Nick was the one who had called her mother, not the other way around.

Nick was the one who had proposed coming to see the house, to evaluate it, to see if it was worth renovating it.

Why?

Mona admitted having told him it existed. Edie knew that already. When they came back, she had handed Edie a piece of paper Nick had given here with the names of a couple of possible architects she might want to call to see if they'd be interested in the project.

But instead he came himself.

Why?

Because he desperately wanted to renovate an old adobe ranch house?

Hardly. Mona was right in scorning that notion. Owners of significant old buildings worldwide regularly attempted to hire Nick Savas. When she'd come home from Mont Chamion, despite her better judgment, which told her to forget him, Edie had looked him up on the internet instead. Nick Savas was a recognized, sought-after authority in architectural reconstruction and renovation. He could—and did—have his pick of projects.

So why had he picked this one?

If Mona had asked him, he might have considered it. There was, Edie knew, no discounting the pull of her mother's star power. But since Mona hadn't asked—and Edie trusted that she hadn't—it made no sense.

Unless Nick had another reason for coming.

Her.

The thought felt odd—daring—and came with the expectation of being slapped down for even venturing to voice it. After all, that was the unspoken hope she'd felt when he showed up at the door.

And he'd shot it down with very nearly his first words.

Why?

Because she'd shown that hope. She'd indicated that she cared and could care even more, and Nick hadn't wanted that. He wanted a physical relationship, and nothing else.

But when she said no to that, he could have left. He could have said the adobe wasn't worth saving. He could have said he didn't have time. But he didn't say that.

He stayed. Which meant…

Edie felt a renewed shiver of hope as she pushed that idea to its conclusion: whether he wanted to or not, Nick Savas cared—about her.

He hadn't stayed for the joy of working on a project he could easily have passed over. He hadn't stayed for the red-hot sex they were having—because they weren't having any.

He'd stayed for her.

It was about that point—at 3:12 in the morning, according to the bedside clock—that Edie realized she was grinning madly at the ceiling. She stopped grinning. Now was not the time to grin.

Now was the time to think some more, to figure out what to do next—because if Nick really cared, it changed everything.

Nick's stomach was not happy.

Neither was Nick, but that was beside the point.

What *was* the point was that he was starving. He'd grabbed a bagel and some coffee at seven after a not particularly restful night spent wondering what the hell was going on between Edie and the man who'd brought her home, and it was now going on two in the afternoon, and he'd left his lunch at Mona's.

He wasn't going back after it, either. If he did, Edie would doubtless think he'd done it on purpose so he could come back to check up on her. Or maybe she wasn't even there. It was Saturday, after all. She probably took weekends off.

She'd certainly taken Friday night off!

Then he reminded himself for the hundredth time that what she did was her own business, damn it. Just like he'd told her mother. But he didn't like Mr. Proprietary's "I'm a friend of hers—and her husband's." As if that meant he had rights Nick didn't have.

Nick wished he were doing something more physical and demanding than setting tiles on the roof. Tearing out a wall sounded like a far more satisfying occupation.

He pulled a bandanna from his pocket and wiped the sweat off his face, and was just putting another tile in place when a voice called out, "Hungry?"

His head whipped around. For a moment he thought he was hearing things. His stomach growled as if in reply. And then he heard footsteps as well and looking around, he saw Edie and Roy coming down the hill through the eucalyptus.

She was wearing canvas knee-length shorts and a bright green T-shirt, not the sort of casual, but professional, attire she wore during the workweek, so she must in fact have the day off. Her hair was pulled back and banded at the nape of her neck. She wore a floppy red straw sunhat on her head, and she was carrying a basket over her arm. When she reached the front yard she squinted up at him on the roof. "You forgot your lunch."

"Yeah."

"So I brought it." She shrugged, smiling. "And mine, too."

Hers? Nick's brows lifted, then his eyes narrowed.

Edie didn't move, just kept smiling, kept looking up at him. He didn't move, either. There was something wrong with the picture. His brain was scrambling to figure out what it was. Last night she'd been spitting nails at him. And today she was…

"Or maybe you're not hungry," she said when he stayed where he was. "Oh, well. You don't mind if I eat here, do you?"

And with that, she carried the basket up the plank he'd laid over the broken steps and disappeared into the house.

If he'd been a weather vane on this roof, Nick figured he'd have been blown around about 180 degrees. He rubbed his head. It was hot and the sun was beating down. Maybe he had sunstroke. He gave his head a little shake, then picked up a tile again.

His stomach growled.

"Oh, hell," he muttered. "All right."

It was all right, too. He expected either an apology for snarling and spitting at him last night or more snarling and spitting today. But he didn't get either. He got little Miss Mary Sunshine.

Cheerful, bright, tart, funny—not to mention as appealing as ever, Edie was once again the woman he'd spent that unforgettable night with in Mont Chamion.

She'd brought his sandwiches and his apple. But she'd added a thermos of iced tea, a couple of bottles of cold beer and some potato salad. "I wasn't sure what you brought to drink at lunch," she said. "So I brought both. And I was feeling domestic this morning, so I made some salad."

She'd cleared off the kitchen table, where he'd laid hammers and rasps and a crowbar, and had wiped it down with a damp cloth. She set it with paper plates and forks for the salad, and sat down as he came in, then gestured at the place opposite for him to take a seat.

Somewhere amid wary, perplexed, bemused and intrigued, Nick sat.

She told him she had talked to her mother. That was as close as she came to acknowledging their encounter last night.

"She's very enthusiastic about the renovation," she told him brightly, and her own eyes were shining. "But since you talked to her, you obviously know that."

He and Mona hadn't talked about the adobe at all, in fact. The only reason Mona had called had been to demand to know where Edie was. But that would have meant talking about how he'd come to be here in the first place, and Nick didn't want to get into that again. So he simply nodded and washed a bite of his sandwich down with a long swallow of beer. He didn't bring beer to work, but it was Saturday—and if Edie was going to bring it, well, he wouldn't say no.

"Are you working all day?" she asked.

"You got a better idea?" He grinned, expecting her to get flustered.

But she said, "I was thinking of going to the beach."

"With lover boy?" Nick bit out before he could stop himself.

Edie blinked, looking momentarily confused, then said, "You mean Derek?" She shook her head. "No. I was going by myself. Unless you want to come." She made the invitation offhandedly, then got up and fetched herself a glass of water from the sink.

Nick hesitated. Then he nodded. "I wouldn't mind. Got a bit to finish up here first. An hour?"

"Perfect." Edie's smile flashed again as she got up and started gathering up the paper plates and silverware to carry out in the basket.

Nick finished his apple, drained his bottle of beer, then headed outside to go up the ladder again. But before he got to the door, he turned back. "Thanks for lunch." He paused, then had to ask, "What's changed?"

Edie finished putting the bowl of salad and the other things back into the basket before she looked up. "Changed?" Her tone was just a little too casual.

So he pressed. "You were avoiding me. Now you're not."

She smiled faintly. Her gaze warmed and under the heat of it, so did he. "No," she allowed slowly, "I'm not."

"Because," he prompted when she didn't elaborate.

Edie ran her tongue over her lips, then shrugged and met his gaze head-on. "Because I only have one life," she said quietly.

CHAPTER EIGHT

THEY went to Leadbetter's Beach where Edie used to go to when she was in high school.

It was a city beach not far from the marina, a picture postcard sort of place with light surf, white sand and blue skies in one direction, and the Spanish architecture and red tile roofs of the city and hills of Santa Barbara in the other. She chose it because it was a place where she had good memories, but wasn't where she habitually went with Ben.

Nick enjoyed it, as she'd hoped he would. They swam, they bodysurfed, they walked on the beach. Edie hadn't known if he was a "beach person" or not. There was so much she still had to learn about him. She was eager to know more.

And she was glad that she had found the courage to do it. Glad that what Mona told her gave her a promise to build on. She could work with that.

Thanks to Ben she knew how. He had done the same for her.

After her painful unrequited love affair with Kyle, Edie had shied away from men, afraid to trust, scared of putting her heart on the line.

She'd resisted Ben. "I don't want to go out," she told him more than once. "I don't want to get involved."

Ben had just looked at her and smiled. Then he'd said, "Let's go ride some waves," or "Let's go fly a kite."

Ben had been full of suggestions. But he only suggested. He

never demanded. And in the face of such good-natured perseverance, Edie hadn't been able to resist.

They had done simple things together. They'd gone to the beach, went for bike rides, raked leaves, cooked meals.

They were friends first.

Perhaps that was why it had worked—*because* they had been friends since grade school. They'd been friends long before they were anything else. And that easy friendship had given Edie a chance to be with Ben in circumstances that, at first, didn't feel like dates.

"No expectations," he had promised her solemnly. But then he'd grinned. "Which doesn't mean I'm not hoping."

Edie understood. And the truth was, she felt something, too, something initially less heated and consuming than the sizzle she'd felt with Kyle, but still real. More real, if possible, because what she and Ben nourished together didn't flare brightly, then scorch and die.

The more time they were together, the stronger it grew.

It was different with Nick, of course. He wasn't Ben. They hadn't known each other forever. They hadn't been friends.

Before everything else, they had been lovers.

And from that very moment there had been something between them—a spark, a hum, a hint, a promise.

She'd tried to ignore that promise, but it hadn't gone away. And now she was no longer determined to resist it. On the contrary, she was making the choice Nick had told her was hers to make.

Not whether or not to fall in love with him—that had already happened. But whether to run from it or to try to create a relationship from it—that was her choice. And she chose to stop running, to turn and hold out her arms.

And Nick?

Nick was where she'd been before Ben had brought her back to life. He was locked in the past with the pain of his fiancée's death. He had turned his back on hope, on dreams, on possibilities.

And yet, he felt something for her. She was sure of it. If he didn't, he wouldn't have come.

It was a very slim hope on which to begin to build a future.

She should be afraid, Edie told herself. Risking your heart wasn't for sissies. But she knew from loving Ben it was worth the cost.

And if Nick didn't know that, well, she'd just have to teach him.

Nick didn't know why Edie had changed her mind.

But he was damned glad she had. Since she'd stopped going out of doors when he came in them, stopped being distantly polite when they talked and started coming around to see how things were going on the adobe restoration and actually stayed to talk about what she remembered about growing up there, the days got a whole lot brighter.

And the nights? Well, the nights were everything he'd imagined.

Nick hadn't known what to expect about the nights—or rather what Edie intended to do about them. It didn't take him long to find out.

That very evening after dinner she put the last of the dishes in the dishwasher, then said, "I was thinking I might take a swim."

"Swim?" He'd been thinking about how to convince her to stay around, talk a bit longer, hoping her change of heart wouldn't have her heading off right after dinner. And now she was suggesting a swim?

She nodded and smiled an even more dazzling smile than the one she'd given him when she'd hooked her arm through his that night in Mont Chamion. "Join me?"

She didn't have to ask him twice.

The night was clear and still warm though the sun still hung like a great orange ball above the city's rooftops and the sea.

Edie had gone back to her place to change, but as Nick headed toward the pool, she ran past him down the sloping lawn. "Can't catch me," she sang.

Grinning, Nick watched her run. He had seen the look on her face well enough to recognize the promise. He didn't hurry. There would be time.

When he got there she was already churning through the water, doing laps. He settled himself on the side of the pool and dangled his feet over the edge as he watched her lithe form cutting through the cool turquoise water.

Several laps done, she veered off course and swam over to look up at him. "That's not swimming," she said.

"I'm watching." He smiled. "And conserving my energy."

She tossed her hair back out of her face, a smile touching her lips. "Think you're going to need it?"

"Hoping."

Their eyes met. Gazes locked for a brief moment.

"Me, too," Edie said quietly, and Nick felt his body go hard in an instant. Then quick as a flash Edie's body bent. She ducked her head and dived beneath the water. A hand caught his ankle, gave a hard tug and pulled him in!

By the time he sputtered to the surface, she was half a width of the pool away.

Grinning, Nick swam after her. Again he didn't hurry. The anticipation was part of the game.

It was a game—and more than that, too. She was grinning as he caught her, laughing as he pulled her back against him, then turned her in his arms and set his mouth on hers. He meant to tease, to taste, to tempt. To play her game and raise the stakes a bit.

But it had been so long since he had held her—really held her. His hands moved up her back, sliding over the wet silk of her skin to press her close. His tongue traced her lips, opened them, delved in. One kiss wasn't enough. Nor two, nor three. Kisses would never be enough. He groaned.

"You're supposed to swim," she said against his lips.

He shook his head. "Can't. I'm drowning." In desire. In sensation. In need. In *her*. "Edie." His hands moved down now to splay across her bottom and press her closer, let her feel how urgently he wanted her.

Her legs twined around his, bringing him still closer, pressing them together. Her hands clutched his shoulders as her heels bumped the backs of his knees. His thumbs hooked the back of her bikini and began to draw it down, his fingers smoothing over the curve of her buttocks as he did so. Edie pulled back, shifted a little, letting go of him with first one leg and then the other, so he could slide the garment down until she could kick it away.

Then his hands moved back up her legs, teased her inner thighs, brushed the soft folds at their apex, then stroked her there.

It was Edie's turn to groan, to wrap her legs around him and press her mouth to his, to devour him as hungrily as he was kissing her. But still it wasn't enough. She squirmed against his touch. She pressed harder. His fingers slipped inside her and he felt her clench around them.

"Nick!"

"Mmm." He wanted her badly. But to take her now would be a matter of moments. He had waited too long, knew that he would shatter at the merest touch. Now…now he wanted to give to her, to prove to her that she had made the right choice.

So when her hands had slid down his arms to reach his waist, intent on slipping beneath his trunks to free him, he stopped her.

"But—" Edie protested.

"There will be time. This is for you." Then the only things that moved were his fingers, giving her pleasure, making her dig her heels into the backs of his thighs, making her arch her back and let her head fall back. He felt her body tense, clench and shudder against him. Then her head came forward, her forehead dropping on his shoulder as she collapsed against him. Then the only thing moving was the lap of cool water against fevered bodies—and the pounding of their hearts.

Edie moved first, shifted slowly in his arms, would have pulled away, but he was loathe to let her go. He liked the warmth of her, the weight of her in his embrace. So he held on, but lightly, giving her space. She didn't take much, just enough to stroke a hand down his chest. "That was—" she shook her head "—amazing."

"Better than swimming?"

She smiled, kissed his jaw. "Oh, yes." Her hand stole lower, brushed across the front of his swim trunks. "And now?"

"Not here," Nick said, lifting her and settling her on the side of the pool, then hauling himself out as well. "I think we could use a bed for the second round."

Edie's eyes widened, her mouth laughed. "We're having rounds? How many?"

He kissed her. "As many as we can get."

Edie didn't regret changing her mind. If she regretted anything, it was that she hadn't changed it sooner. If she'd been braver, they could have had spent more days together at the adobe, more nights sharing a bed.

But they were together now. They spent a lot of every day together. The beauty of her job was that she could do it from almost anywhere. So while Nick worked on the adobe, most afternoons now Edie took her cell phone and her laptop, and she and Roy went over the hill to bring Nick lunch and spend the afternoon with him.

They ate together, sitting on the front porch if it was cool, or inside with fans on if it was a bit too warm. And she asked questions about what he was doing and he asked questions about what she remembered.

The more they talked, the more she was able to explain the hold the house had on her. It was, as she told him, "where it all began." It was a reminder of the core values of love and commitment and allegiance to family that her parents had given her. They were values she wanted to share with her own children, values she wanted to share with Nick.

She didn't say so outright. She simply explained the best she could.

"It's a touchstone," Nick said.

She nodded. "Exactly. The best of times," she reflected, but then remembered the day the sheriff's car had driven up and the man had got out to talk to her mother. Her smile faded. "And the worst of times," she whispered.

But then Nick took her hands in his and leaned over to kiss her. "We'll make it right," he vowed against her lips.

He made her happy. Whatever else he did, Nick Savas did that.

He seemed to delight in making her smile. He even went so far as to figure out what mattered to her without her even telling him. She mentioned once how she'd love to play on the high, wide back porch under the kitchen windows.

"It was my place," she told him. "Ronan preferred trees. But I loved it there. I played house there and school there, with my friend Katie. It was special because I could be on my own. My mom only had to look out the window."

Thinking about it now, it seemed strange that international movie star Mona Tremayne had once been just like all the other moms who kept an eye on her children. But she had—at the same time she'd known to give her daughter space.

"I'd like to do that for my children," she'd reflected.

The next day when she came back with lunch, he said, "Why don't we eat out on the back porch?"

"It's filthy," she protested, because it certainly had been the day before.

But when she came through the house into the kitchen, the back door stood open onto a porch of brand-new wood. Edie let out a little scream. She dumped the basket on the table and hurried outside, looking all around.

"Oh! Oh, yes!" Her eyes were shining as she spun around. "Yes, exactly! And the stairs—" She crossed the porch and peered down the back steps. There had been six of them, she'd told Nick yesterday. They'd played school on them—each stair being assigned a different grade. Now she counted them, then turned back to him, beaming. "Six! It's perfect!" She knelt down and ran her hands over the sanded wood. "Better than," she told him, "because the old wood was rough and we were always getting splinters."

"No splinters in this," Nick assured her.

"Thank you." She flung her arms around him and kissed him hard. He returned the kiss with equal fervency—and she suspected that things would have got scandalous then and there, but he pulled back, grimacing and said, "I've got a couple of plasterers coming after lunch."

"Bad planning," Edie told him, laughing.

"I'll make it up to you tonight."

"Is that a threat or a promise?"

"What do you think?"

Edie thought life was wonderful—and getting better by the minute. "I'll be looking forward to it," she told him, getting out a cloth to spread on the new wood so they could picnic there. Afterward she left him to his plasterers and took Roy back home for the afternoon. But before she left she turned to him and took his hands in hers, then looked up into his eyes.

"Thank you for the porch, Nick. I love it."

He nodded. "I'm glad."

"My children thank you, too."

He blinked. But he didn't say anything else because she went up on her toes and kissed him.

Her children?

He'd done it for her—for the memories she had told him

about—and now all he could envision were her children. Little dark-haired girls and grinning boys with freckled noses.

It made him hot—and cold—at the very same time. He'd never thought about Edie in the future before. It had always been now—and the two of them—together.

But suddenly he could see her surrounded by children.

Whose?

He shook the question off as soon as it occurred to him. It didn't matter, he told himself. It wasn't his problem. They weren't his children.

But the notion stuck with him all afternoon. The plasterers showed up and they discussed how to best deal with the interior walls. He'd intended to have them working in the bedrooms. Now, walking into Edie's old room, he imagined it not as hers but as the room her daughters might use. And Ronan's bedroom somehow seemed to be populated by little boys who would be Edie's sons.

He didn't hear everything the plasterers said. He wasn't sure he communicated at all what he wanted them to do. They said, "Sure. Fine," and they could start on Monday. He said uh-huh or something like that.

He was glad when they left. He left right after they did, heading back to Mona's earlier than usual.

Edie was on the phone. She looked up surprised when he came in. She waggled her fingers at him and smiled, then kept listening, occasionally murmuring something that sounded comforting.

He was grimy and sweaty, and on the way back to the house he'd been planning for Edie to take a shower with him and wash his back. But now she was obviously deep in a conversation, so he went up the stairs by himself, took a quick shower, put on clean clothes and went back down.

She was still listening. And listening. She was moving around the kitchen as she did so, putting together something for dinner. But her attention was obviously on the person she was talking to.

"I know," she was saying. "Yes, I remember."

Nick ambled out to the den to turn on the television and catch up on the baseball scores. It was another half an hour before Edie joined him.

"Grace," she said by way of explanation.

"From Thailand?"

She nodded. "Her boyfriend dumped her."

"She had a boyfriend in Thailand."

"No. Here. He read something in some gossip blog online about her and Matt Holden. He's an actor," she explained, in case he didn't know. He'd heard the name, but that was about it. "About twenty. A heartthrob-to-be. David took exception."

Why this was Edie's problem, Nick had no idea. But obviously she'd spent a long time talking to and listening to her sister. And he could tell from her expression and the few remarks she made that it was important, that Grace mattered. All her siblings mattered.

Edie wasn't just her mother's and Rhiannon's business manager. She was the glue that held the family together, the one that everyone turned to when things went awry.

Rhiannon, he realized, had things go awry on a regular basis. A day rarely went by that he didn't overhear Edie soothing and settling her sister, making arrangements and then rearranging them with what seemed like endless patience and good cheer when Rhiannon couldn't manage to make things work.

Mona made fewer demands. Her requests were generally in line with the work Edie was hired for. But the younger children—Grace and the twins, Ruud and Dirk—all turned to Edie, not their mother, for support. They might have been half a world away in Thailand, but they called Edie almost every day. She might as well have been their mother. She would make a wonderful mother.

And there he was, facing the Edie of the future again.

"Do you expect to live in the adobe?" he demanded.

She was going back into the kitchen to put the pan of lasagna she'd been making into the oven. But now she stopped and looked at him surprised. But then she tilted her head and seemed to give it serious thought.

"I hadn't thought about it recently," she said. "Until today. But since there's such a nice new back porch..." She nodded. "Yes, I think so. Not all the time, of course. I would hope to have a place *not* at my mother's. But it would be a good place to bring the family, don't you think?"

Fortunately she didn't wait for a reply, which was just as well, as he didn't have an answer.

"That way the kids could be near Mona and not be underfoot. Good for everyone concerned," she added with a smile. "Mona loves kids, but the day to day isn't really her style."

But it was Edie's style. And now that Nick could see it, he couldn't seem to forget it, especially because, besides Grace's ongoing soap opera, later in the week Edie spent an evening talking to Dirk who was trying to set up a connection so he could listen to baseball games from Bangkok. Between the two of them, they accomplished the task—fortunately right before Nick carried her off to bed.

"You're very eager," she commented as he drew her with him up the stairs.

"I am." He was kissing her as they went, then tugging her scoop-necked T-shirt over her head.

"Why is that?" she asked, though she seemed to be equally eager, fumbling to undo the button at the waistband of his shorts.

"Can't get enough of you," he murmured, bearing her back onto the bed.

He didn't know why it was true. He only knew it was. The more time he spent with Edie—in bed and out—the more he wanted to be with her. He certainly hadn't tired of her. If he was going to get his fill of Edie Daley, he was going to need every available minute between now and when the restoration was done.

Getting his fill wasn't easy to imagine. He kept devising

more and more ways to spend time in her company. They spent lunches together, afternoons at the adobe, dinners every evening and nights in her bed or his. Far more time than he had ever spent with anyone.

But far from sating his desire to be with her, he was annoyed one afternoon at the end of the third week they'd shared, when she packed up the lunch basket and said she'd see him at dinner.

"Dinner?" he frowned. "Where are you going?"

He was surprised how much it mattered. But he'd grown used to having her there. Until Edie he'd never invited anyone to be there while he was working. Not even Amy when he'd been building the house he'd designed for her.

Nick willingly listened to other peoples' input. He valued their ideas, but he didn't like interference, and he'd always worked alone. So he was probably more surprised than Edie the first afternoon he'd suggested she stay. And he was equally surprised now to discover that he cared when she wasn't going to be here today.

"I promised Ruud that I'd get the skateboard wheels he wants and put them in the mail this afternoon."

Of course it would be on account of one of her siblings. He should have known. Still he raised his brows. "You know skateboards?" He understood now that there was quite a bit more to Edie Daley than he'd first imagined, but—skateboards?

She smiled. "I have explicit instructions." And she pulled a paper out of the pocket of her shorts and waved it at him.

Nick took the paper and scanned it over. "How will you choose? He's got four different options."

"I'm supposed to pick the best." She sighed. "He's got them ranked. Or, he said I could ask someone who knew something." She looked at him hopefully. "What do you know about skateboards?"

Nick grinned. "I rode my share in olden times."

"Really?" She was delighted. "Come with me, then. I could use an expert."

He hadn't ridden a skateboard since he was in his teens. He was a Neanderthal in the skateboard world.

But if it meant spending the day with Edie…

"All right." Something else he rarely did, take time off during the workweek. When a man worked for himself, he had to be a tough taskmaster.

So he made it a work trip, stopping at the building supply place and picking up some materials as well. But after they'd checked several skate shops and picked his choice of the perfect wheels, then mailed them, Edie suggested they go for a walk along the beach before going back to the house.

"It's beautiful down here. And it's too late to go back to the adobe and work. It's nearly five. We can take a walk, then stop somewhere for an early supper." She turned to him, eyes shining, and said, "We could go to the Biltmore."

The Biltmore was an old Santa Barbara landmark right on the beach just a ways down the coast from downtown. Built in the 1920s at the height of Santa Barbara's determined celebration of its Spanish colonial heritage, the Biltmore embodied what idealists believed neo-Colonial buildings should look like. With its thick adobe style walls, red-tile roof, wrought-iron gates and Moorish archways, the place looked more like a romantic movie set than a hotel.

"Think of it as inspiration," Edie said, grinning.

For once Nick couldn't think of a reason to argue. He shrugged and laced his fingers through hers. "Why not?"

Tempting fate—that's what it was—asking Nick to go to the Biltmore.

But the words were out of her mouth before Edie could stop them. Truth was, she didn't want to stop them. She wanted to go to the Biltmore with him, have a meal there with him, wanted to share the romantic ambiance, the special setting and—this was the part that tempted fate—add to the family history in the process.

The Biltmore was where she had come with Ben to celebrate their engagement. It was, thirty odd years ago, where her parents had had dinner the night that Joe had asked Mona to marry him. It was where, thirty years before that, Joe's own mother and father had met when she was working in the kitchen and he was the chauffeur of a wealthy Bostonian who had come west to spend the winter in milder climes.

Memorable days at the Biltmore were something of a family tradition.

Not that Edie told Nick that.

She certainly didn't intend to ask him to marry her there—and she would be shocked if he asked her. Not tonight. Not yet. But soon.

Yes, she dared to hope it would be soon.

What they'd shared these past weeks had not weakened, had not diminished. It had only grown. The time they spent together, the tales she told him of her childhood and the stories of his youth that Nick shared, showed her how much common ground they had. They had as well a love of history, an appreciation of family, friends and big black dogs, of restoring houses and swimming races, of walks on the beach and picnics between mornings and afternoons working, and nights in each other's arms.

They'd both loved—and they'd both lost. She didn't expect to replace Amy in his heart any more than she knew he could ever replace Ben. There was room for both. In her perhaps foolish, but still admirable willingness to risk again and again, Mona had shown her that. Ben had taught her to trust, to dare to love.

She *loved* Nick.

Back in Mont Chamion, she'd told herself she wouldn't. When he'd first come to Santa Barbara and had promised nothing but the moment, she'd resisted. Or tried to.

But she couldn't resist forever. Didn't want to.

She loved him.

And, yes, perhaps it was tempting fate to suggest the Biltmore, to know in her heart what that meant, but she couldn't help it.

Edie believed. Edie hoped.

They parked the car across the street from the hotel, next to the sidewalk that ran along the beach. Because it was still too early for dinner, they took off their shoes and climbed over the low wall to walk on the beach. It was when she was jumping off the wall that he caught her and, afterward, hung on, that kept her hand in his.

Edie smiled and rubbed her thumb along the side of his hand and tipped her face to let the afternoon sun warm her even as Nick warmed her heart. They walked all the way to the marina and back, holding hands, hips brushing. They talked as they walked, shared stories, laughter. And then there were times they walked in silence. Both were comfortable, both felt right.

And when they got back to the Biltmore, they wiped their feet and put their shoes back on, and Edie combed her hair. She had no doubt that her grandparents would have been scandalized at the lack of dress code at the Biltmore these days. Some things had indeed changed.

But others—like two people staring into each other's eyes over a candlelight dinner—had not.

The meal was lovely—fresh caught seafood, pasta cooked to order, fresh salad greens. The wine was superb. Nick chose it, raised his glass and clinked it against hers, his gaze smoldering as he said, "To you, Ms. Daley." His voice was ragged.

Edie raised her own glass, looking deep into his eyes. "To you, Mr. Savas." In her heart she said, *To us.*

They skipped dessert. All the tortes and flans and tarts and cheesecakes looked delicious. The zabaglione, Edie knew from experience, was to die for. But she didn't even hesitate tonight.

Something better waited for them at home.

They barely spoke as Nick drove them back. He held her hand even as he drove. The only time he let go was when they reached the house and they got out of opposite sides of the car. But Nick caught her hand in his before they climbed the stairs.

They had made love in his bed in her old room in Mona's

house. They had made love by the pool. Once they had even made love at the adobe on the old madras cotton bedspread Edie had brought to lay out their picnics on.

But mostly they came here—to her bed. And while Edie would have loved Nick anywhere, she liked making love with him here best.

Her carriage house flat was small and not at all lavish. But it was her home and, as much as anywhere on earth, it held pieces of her heart. Here was the photo of her dad with his arms around her and Ronan, taken on Christmas morning, just a month before he died. Here was the photo of Mona with all her children around her—a motley crew, but deeply beloved. Here were the memories she had of Ben—a carving he'd done for her when they'd lived in Fiji, a tiny outrigger he'd made when he'd been researching on one of the small islands and she'd spent three whole weeks without him, a box containing all the postcards she'd sent her mother while she and Ben were abroad. Mona had given them to her just last year.

"Because you can handle remembering now," her mother had said. "You can look back with love. And you can move on."

At the time Edie hadn't been sure. But though Mona's gift might have been a bit premature, she was right. Edie was ready now. And she was glad Nick was willing to make love to her here.

Roy went shooting out the door the minute they came in. But in a few minutes, he was back looking for dinner. Gerald, the cat, meowed plaintively and wove his way between their feet, indignant that he hadn't had his evening meal.

"I know you're hungry," Edie said to him. She reached for his bowl and a can of cat food.

Nick stood behind her, kissing her neck, making her shiver with longing. His hands played lightly over her breasts. "In case you haven't noticed," he murmured, "I'm hungry, too."

"Gerald would say you had a wonderful meal," Edie told him,

opening the can and scooping food into the dish. "Fresh swordfish. Yum."

"To a neutered feline, the food of gods, no doubt." Nick nibbled along the her partially exposed shoulder. "I've got better things to feast on."

She put the dish of food down for the cat, and felt herself scooped into Nick's arms and carried through to the bedroom.

Nick dropped her lightly onto the bed, then fell down beside her, stroked her clothes off and in a matter of moments shed his own. Then, at her urging, he settled his hard muscled body over hers. And Edie opened to him, wrapped her arms around his neck and let him feast his fill.

They loved with fierce intensity, their bodies hot and slick with sweat as they drove each other to frenzied completion. But after their coupling, neither of them slept. They held each other close. They slept and woke and loved again, then slept some more.

It was close to dawn when she stroked his whisker roughened jaw. He threaded his fingers through her hair. She kissed her way along his collarbone, then down the center of his chest, to nuzzle his navel, then moved lower.

Nick sucked in a sharp breath. "You're going to kill me," he said raggedly.

"I'm hungry, too." Edie lifted her head to look at him through the curtain of her hair. Then she went back to kissing and nibbling, touching him with her tongue, making him groan, wringing him out, until he pulled her up and settled her over him and drew her down to take him in.

His breath hissed between his teeth as she rode him.

They shattered together, and Edie collapsed against him, heard his heart thundering against her ear. His arms held her close, circled her back, his lips pressed against her hair.

"Dear God, what have you done to me?" he whispered.

And Edie lifted her head and looked up at him, then reached up to brush a lock of hair off his forehead as she smiled and, trusting her instincts, gave him her heart as she had just given him her body.

"I love you, Nick," she told him. Then she eased away and drew herself across his chest to touch her lips to his. "I love you," she told him. "I love you."

He went still. Rigid. His gaze, which moments ago had been fierce with passion, was blank now. Dark and unreadable. Remote. His fingers, which had tangled in her hair and played along her spine, moved away, pulled back.

All that was left was a strained, haunted look in his eyes as he rasped out a single harsh word. "Don't."

CHAPTER NINE

"Don't what?"

Something was different. Wrong.

She could feel it. Could see it in Nick's face. A muscle in his jaw twitched. His teeth seemed clenched, and when he opened his mouth he drew a slow breath before he said evenly, "Don't fall in love with me."

Edie swallowed. Then she smiled and tried desperately to recapture the intimacy of their lovemaking, saying gamely, "Too late. I already have."

She would have rested her head against his chest once more, but he reached out and caught her arms, lifting her away from him, settling her on the bed while he shoved away.

"Nick?" She reached out a hand to him.

But he didn't see it. He was already off the bed with his back turned, reaching for his clothes, his voice still harsh as he muttered, "Damn it."

Damn it? Damn what?

Edie sat up, drawing the sheet around her naked body, suddenly cold as she stared at Nick's back. It was the same back, broad and strong and smooth, that she'd run her fingers over only minutes ago, the same whose spine those fingers had tripped lightly down.

Now it was a wall, keeping her out, his hard, tense muscles almost quivering with emotion. "Nick."

He spun around to face her. "You knew better," he said harshly.

Knew better than to fall in love with him, he meant. She understood what he was accusing her of. But she knew something else with even more certainty.

"I know you," she said with quiet conviction. "You love me, too."

He gave his head a quick, sharp shake. "No."

The flat denial was like a blow. Emotionally it rocked her, but outwardly she refused to flinch. "No? Then what are we doing here?" She waved her hand to encompass not just the room, not just the bed where they had just spent the night in each other's arms, but everything that had happened between them since he'd come to Santa Barbara. "What have we been doing this past month?"

He met her gaze. "Enjoying each other."

Now it was Edie's turn to shake her head. "No. It's more than that."

But Nick folded his arms across his chest. "You're dreaming," he told her. "You're seeing what you want to see."

What she wanted to see—love, commitment, honesty, a future, the two of them together for the rest of their lives—yes, indeed, that's exactly what she was seeing.

"What's wrong with that?" she asked him. When she had given him those words a few minutes ago, warm and languid from their lovemaking, the world had seemed golden, full of promise. Now, in the face of his implacability she felt as if a cloud had crossed the sun.

"It's not going to happen."

"You're saying you don't care?" she said slowly.

"I care." At least he would admit that. "You're a friend. You're a wonderful woman." His words were awkward, but the sentiment was worse. It came out stilted and insincere, stabbing her like a knife.

But she managed a brittle smile. "A good lover?" she suggested with saccharine sweetness. All her earlier euphoria was evaporating now. She felt cold and hurt and scared. Worse, almost, than when she'd learned that Ben had died. Ben couldn't help what had happened.

But Nick—Nick was choosing to reject her love, to deny her and himself.

"A good lover. A great lover," he corrected, not hearing or admitting to hearing her bitterness. He had stepped into his shorts, but he paused and smiled at her now before pulling on his trousers, as if she might forget this nonsense, invite him back to bed and give him an encore.

Not a chance.

Edie got out of bed, too. She felt sick. Her whole body was trembling. She didn't believe what he was saying, but she knew that didn't matter.

What mattered was that *Nick* believed it.

She began dressing quickly, as if putting on clothes would somehow warm her. But of course it wasn't the day that was cold, it was the feeling growing inside her. "I'll be sure to put that on my résumé." She could barely get the words out past the lump in her throat. She struggled into her shirt and began to fumble with the buttons. Damn her fingers, anyway.

Nick's gaze narrowed. "What's that supposed to mean?"

She turned her back to him and stepped into her canvas pants. "Just saying." She tried to toe her sandals out from under the bed. Somehow getting dressed fully was important. It was like putting on armor. Too late, perhaps, but she did what she had to do.

She had her pants zipped up when Nick reached out and caught her by the arm. "Edie."

She tried to pull away, but he held her fast, drew her around so that he looked down into her face. His dear face. His beloved face. His resolutely, implacably closed face.

"You're making too much out of this."

"No."

"Yes," he insisted. "We have a good thing."

"I thought we did," she agreed, her throat aching. "I hoped." Her voice broke.

Damn it! She didn't want to betray how badly this was hurting her. But then, why not? She'd already admitted to loving him.

"You knew that wasn't on. It wasn't what I wanted. Ever," he insisted. "We discussed it."

"What about what I wanted?" she demanded.

He just looked at her. "You're changing the rules."

"Me? You changed them when you came after me!"

He opened his mouth, and for a moment she thought he might deny it. But then he just pressed his lips together in a grim line and shrugged. "It was a good night."

As if he'd done it all because of that. "You came halfway around the world! You took on the restoration of a third-class adobe ranch house when you could have been doing an historically significant Scottish castle."

"I'm going to do the castle. It's where I'm going next."

"When you finish here?"

"Yes."

"When you finish with me!"

Her words made a muscle in his jaw jump. His eyes flashed at the deliberate provocation. Deny it, she begged him silently.

But he didn't. "Yes." The word hissed furiously between his teeth.

She wrenched out of his grasp. "Fine. I'll save you the trouble." She jammed her feet into her sandals, grabbed her phone off the bedside table and clattered down the stairs.

Nick hurtled after her and caught her at the door. "What are you doing?"

"Leaving."

"What? Where are you going? You live here!"

"Yes, well, I don't want to be here right now." And she

grabbed a sweater off the back of a chair and her purse and car keys off the kitchen table.

"Come on," she said to Roy.

"Edie! Stop it. Don't be ridiculous. If someone needs to go, I'll leave."

"Fine. Leave. Go to hell. I don't care." Which was a lie, of course. She wouldn't be close to tears if she didn't care, if she didn't love him with all her heart. She wrenched open the door and clattered down the stairs, Roy following.

Nick came after her in hot pursuit. "Edie! Damn it!"

But she didn't stop. She didn't listen. And she had no intention of standing there listening to Nick tell her that she was being unreasonable. Reason had nothing whatever to do with this. Her response to him had been gut-level since the moment she'd seen him across the dance floor talking to her sister. It had been gut-level when he'd come back, though she'd tried her best to avoid allowing her emotions to control things. For the past month, after learning it had been his idea to come here, not her mother's to bring him, she had dared to believe that he had trusted his emotions as well.

Apparently not. Apparently he was as determined not to care as he'd ever been. So she wasn't staying here. Couldn't. Not now. Not when there was no future for them.

"Edie! For heaven's sake!"

But Edie wasn't listening. She opened the door of her car, let Roy jump in, then climbed in beside him, stuck the key in the ignition and started the engine.

"Don't be an idiot!" He grabbed the door, but not soon enough. She'd hit the power locks an instant before. "Edie!"

But she put the car in gear and took off, refusing to look back, blinking away tears as she went. So much for trusting her instincts.

He let her go.

There was no point in jumping in his car and going after her.

He didn't want her doing something reckless, something foolish. Though it seemed, despite his warning, she already had: she'd fallen in love with him.

There was no point in trying to talk to her, to make her see that wanting too much was asking for trouble, tempting fate. Though God knew, she of all people, having lost a husband, ought to understand about tempting fate.

So be it, he thought as he stood there, staring as the taillights of her car disappeared around the curve in the driveway. But even as he did so, he willed her to slow down, to turn the car around, to come back and wrap her arms around him, to let him wrap his around her, to be grateful for what they had.

It was enough, damn it! She ought to be satisfied with that. He was, he told himself as he punched his fist into the garage retaining wall.

She drove to the beach out by the university, parked her car and began to walk. And walk. It would clear her head, she told herself. It would give her some perspective. It was where she had gone after the debacle with Kyle.

She'd been standing there, staring out at the water, wallowing in mortification, when Ben had jogged by her, stopped and grinned and said, "I know you."

What followed, of course, had changed her life completely.

She wasn't the same person she'd been in those days. At eighteen she had been innocent and idealistic. Kyle's perfidy had wounded her pride and made her feel foolish for having believed they had something when they hadn't.

But at twenty-five she had a great deal more life experience. She knew what was real and what was a pipe dream. She was sure she wasn't wrong believing that she and Nick could have something special. She was sure he loved her just as she loved him.

Nick was the one who was wrong. He didn't believe. He didn't trust.

And she couldn't make him.

Neither could she take back the words she'd spoken. There was no going back, no way of pretending.

She wasn't sorry. She couldn't have lived that lie. She wouldn't live it.

But she couldn't stay here, either. Not if he was going to stay.

She sighed and stared out toward the islands, tried to think what to do, where to go, how to handle the disaster her life was becoming.

Down the beach toward her, a man came jogging. He had dark shaggy hair like Ben. He was lean and slightly knock-kneed like Ben. He came closer. And closer—and ran straight past her without even glancing her way.

Edie smiled a wry self-deprecating smile. There was no Ben to rescue her this time. No Ben could. Not this time. Because this time her love was real, and no amount of serendipity would allow her to deny it.

But that was the thing about serendipity. You couldn't predict it. Never in a million years would she had guessed her mobile phone would ring that moment and Mona would say, "Ruud's broken his leg."

Bangkok was hot and steamy and crowded. Edie was crumpled, exhausted and hollow-eyed, wishing she was numb twenty-four hours later when Mona fell on her neck in gratitude.

"Oh, thank God, you're here!"

Edie stood in the middle of the main room of Mona's beautiful old teak house and let herself be swept into her mother's embrace. She tottered a little under the impact of Mona's enthusiasm, then got her balance as Mona gave her one more squeeze and stepped back to assess her from head to toe.

"Good heavens, you look terrible."

Thank you very much, Edie thought. *Terrible* was actually an improvement on how she felt. She was exhausted physically, shattered emotionally and still unable to get Nick out of her head.

"Surely the flights weren't that bad." Mona was towing her toward one of the rattan sofas and pushing her down.

"No," Edie said. The flights had nothing to do with it.

"Rhiannon?" Mona guessed. "I know she and Andrew have been having a set-to again."

"Have they?" Edie didn't know that. She supposed Rhiannon might have said, but she'd been too busy with Nick to pay much attention.

"Don't cover for them," Mona said firmly. "And I know I have wanted you to make things right in the past, but honestly, Edie, don't worry about them. If they can't solve their own love life problems, it's not your job to do it for them."

Right. Especially since she couldn't even deal with her own.

"And I didn't expect you to drop everything and fly halfway across the world just for Ruud and his leg," Mona added. "Not that I'm sorry you did," she added cheerfully, "because we both know Ruud behaves better for you than for me. And he and Dirk and Grace have missed you terribly. But," Mona added, "I did think you had more pressing things in your own life…" And her perfectly plucked brows lifted in silent query.

Edie knew exactly what they were asking. And she had no intention of answering.

"I was glad to come," she said firmly. "I've missed you—all of you. Where's Ruud? I'm so eager to see them."

And even more eager not to be subjected to more questions. She must have convinced Mona that she really was thrilled to be here because after directing the houseboy to put suitcases in her room, she beckoned to her daughter to follow.

"I didn't tell any of them you were coming," she said. "I wanted them to be surprised."

They were surprised, and as thrilled as Mona had promised they would be. Ruud's face lit up. Dirk flung himself at her. And Grace gave her a hug and said, "I'm sooo glad you're here."

Edie assured them she was glad, too. And, of course, they believed her. Why shouldn't they? They had been the focus of her life since she'd come home after Ben's death. They had no reason to think anything was different now.

And, really, it wasn't different, was it?

Certainly when she'd announced she was leaving, Nick had done nothing to stop her. True, he'd raised his eyebrows. But ultimately he'd just shrugged.

"You do what you have to do," he'd told her.

Short of killing him, which was seriously tempting, she did what she had to do: she left. She moved on.

She knew that if she stayed, she wouldn't be able to do that. She'd be stuck wanting what she couldn't have. And she wasn't going to settle for the affair he was willing to allow her.

No, damn it. It wouldn't be easy, but she was going to forget him.

Forget her!

It should have been a mantra, Nick's mind repeated it so often. He felt sometimes as if the words were emblazoned on the insides of his eyelids. They weren't, of course.

There wasn't room. That was where all the images of Edie resided—the ones that plagued him every time he closed his eyes.

There was Edie in the swimming pool, her dark hair streaming, her eyes alight with mischief. There was Edie in the adobe, prowling, poking, looking wistful, reminiscing. There was Edie tossing a salad, Edie across the dinner table, Edie at the Biltmore, smiling at him over her wineglass, offering him a bite of her pasta. There were visions of Edie romping with Roy, Edie feeding Gerald, Edie standing on the parapet at Mont Chamion, looking out over the fairy lights. There was Edie dancing barefoot. Edie in his arms.

Edie in bed.

So many, many memories of Edie in his bed. In *her* bed. Dear God, he couldn't get them out of his mind.

The memories should have been enough. More than enough. He should have had his fill of her by now, be ready to move on.

But he hadn't. He wasn't.

And though he'd gone to the adobe to work the afternoon she'd left the house, he felt as if she were with him, humming in the other room, just out of sight. He couldn't believe she was getting on an airplane, going to Thailand, for heaven's sake!

It was stupid! Insane!

What they'd had together was amazing, marvelous. Unlike anything he'd ever had before with any woman—except for Amy.

No…not even Amy had been like Edie. *No one* was like Edie. No one made him laugh the way she did. No one was quite as enchanting. No one teased and tempted and at the same time gave so unstintingly of herself.

She had made him happy. And he obviously had made her happy because she claimed to have fallen in love with him.

And yet the stubborn woman threw it all away.

Fine, he told himself angrily. *So be it.*

If he'd got over Amy's death, he could certainly get over Edie walking out. He didn't need her. He didn't want her. Permanence, commitment—*love!*—was the last thing he wanted!

So he'd forget her. He'd finish up the adobe because it was his job—and he'd never mix business and pleasure again.

Never.

"Miss? There is a gentleman…" Malee, the housekeeper, opened the door a crack to the room Edie was using for an office. She smiled apologetically when Edie looked up, startled.

"A gentleman?" Edie felt the bottom drop out of her stomach at the same time hope went winging heavenward. She shut her eyes. Thank God. "Show him in," she said, wiping damp palms on the sides of her linen trousers as she stood up and tried to compose herself.

It had been a week. She'd almost given up hope. She took a deep breath as Malee pushed the door open wider and stepped back.

Kyle Robbins walked into the room. "Edie!" The trademark gorgeous Robbins grin lit his face.

Edie felt the light go out of hers. "Kyle," she said dully. Her stomach felt like lead.

He raised his brows as he read her body language. "Good to see you, too," he said with obvious irony.

"I—wasn't expecting you." Edie hoped she didn't come down too hard on the "you" part of that sentence. "What are you doing here?" she demanded. "If Mona put you up to this—"

"Mona invited me," he said, "to go over a script with her. We're doing a film together next month. You know that," he reminded her. "You set up this meeting." Which, now that Edie thought about it, was the absolute truth.

Mona habitually asked to spend a week or so going over a script with the other actors she'd be working with. Kyle was one of those actors. And now that he mentioned it, Edie did vaguely remember setting up this meeting.

But she'd done it when her every thought had been revolving around Nick. And it was testimony to how little Kyle mattered anymore that the emails she'd exchanged with him had barely even registered on her radar.

"I forgot," she said, shrugging lamely.

Kyle grimaced wryly. "Which pretty much shows me where I stand."

"Yes," Edie said frankly.

He nodded. "I'm sorry. Many years too late. I was an idiot. I handled things badly."

"You were unfaithful," Edie corrected.

He winced, but then he nodded. "Like I said, I was a fool. But—" he sighed "—Jake is the one thing about my marriage I don't regret."

And he turned and through the doorway, Edie could see that Kyle hadn't come alone. Out in the other room a young boy sat on the sofa. The baby Serena had been expecting, the reason Kyle had broken off his relationship with Edie.

"If I'd known you were here, I would never have—"

But Edie shook her head. "I'd like to meet him," she said quite honestly.

Kyle's eyes lit up. "He's a great kid. You'll love him. Maybe you and I—"

"No," Edie said.

But she would like to meet Jake. And she imagined Jake would like to meet the twins. If he was going to be around for a week or so, they could have a good time—and she could keep even busier.

She needed to stay busy—because Nick wasn't coming after her. She'd hoped. But he'd had a week. If it were going to happen, it would have happened by now.

She needed to face facts, needed to face the truth.

She might love Nick Savas fervently and foolishly, but however much she might wish it was otherwise, Nick wasn't willing—or wasn't able—to return her love.

She wasn't coming back.

He'd thought she would. Even though he'd told himself to forget her, that she didn't matter, that he was better off without her, deep down somewhere inside him, Nick couldn't quite manage to convince himself.

So he did the next best thing. He told himself she'd realize she was wrong, that she was throwing away something good—and she'd come back.

He would be gracious about it. He wouldn't say, "I told you so," even if he had. He wouldn't point out how foolish she'd been to run or how much time she'd wasted that they could have been spending together.

He'd just smile and hold out his arms to her. He'd catch her up in an embrace and carry her off to bed and show her what she'd been missing.

Every time he thought about doing that, he smiled.

It was pretty much the only time he smiled all day. He spent almost every waking hour at the adobe working his tail off. He might as well. He had nothing else to do with his waking hours. And the hours he was supposed to be sleeping—well, he wasn't doing much of that. He might as well have been working then, too.

When she came back, he'd show her how much he'd accomplished. She'd love it. She'd smile and tell him about growing up there. She'd make him see it in his mind's eye. But then every day that she didn't come back, his hopes faded a little bit more.

And then a week after she left, he was dragging himself back, grim and exhausted, to Mona's house one evening, when Roy ran ahead, barking.

Nick came around the corner of the garage and saw a strange car in the driveway. The trunk lid was up. The front door was open.

He stopped and stared. Hope soared.

Then he started to grin, and scrubbed eagerly at his filthy face with the T-shirt slung round his neck. He began to sprint toward the door—and skidded to a halt as a woman came out of it.

"Rhiannon?"

It was, with Roy bouncing eagerly around her. Edie's sister paid Roy no attention at all. She was staring at Nick, equally stunned.

"Where's Edie?" she demanded.

"In Thailand."

Rhiannon frowned. "In Thailand? Why? Who are you?"

She didn't *know?* He guessed he shouldn't be surprised. "Nick Savas. We met at my cousin's wedding. What are you doing here?"

Whatever answer he might have thought he was expecting, he wasn't expecting the one he got. She burst into tears.

"I need Edie!" Great noisy sobs erupted and her face grew blotchy and red. It seemed far too theatrical to be real, but a moment's reflection told him that she couldn't possibly be doing this on purpose. These sorts of sobs made her far too ugly.

"For God's sake, Rhiannon," he said, caught halfway between wanting to pat her on the back and wanting to run in the other direction. "Stop that! What's wrong?"

She gulped, started to speak. Then started crying again and he had to wait for her to stop to get an answer at last. "Andrew's b-broken our en-g-gagement!" And, of course, the tears started up again.

Nick shifted from one foot to the other. He debated offering her his filthy T-shirt to mop up her face, then decided against it. "I'm sure he didn't mean it," he said awkwardly, not sure at all.

"H-he did!" Rhiannon dug in the pockets of her jeans and came up with a handkerchief that looked as if it had seen her through earlier bouts of tears. "And—and I deserve it. It's all… all my f-fault!"

Now that Nick could believe.

"I was trying to make him jealous. He spends so much time swimming! Matt doesn't mean anything!"

Uh-oh.

"He's just a f-friend. But Andrew got the wrong idea. Edie s-says I don't think Andrew has feelings."

He could believe that, too. "Go inside," he ordered her. "I'll bring in your cases, then make you a cup of tea."

Rhiannon managed a watery smile. "A cup of tea?"

He shrugged, feeling stupid and awkward.

But she nodded and sniffed. "Tea would b-be good. Edie makes me tea. You're like Edie."

He wasn't, God knew. On the other hand, it might be the biggest compliment he'd ever received.

He brought in her cases, put on the kettle, then went upstairs, scrubbed his face and pulled a clean shirt over his head. He wished she'd go away, and yet at the same time, he was glad she was here. She was a link to her sister, even if she obviously hadn't spoken to Edie in days.

When he came back downstairs, Rhiannon was coming out of the powder room. She'd washed her face, too, but it was still blotchy and her eyes were bloodshot.

"I don't know what to do." She trailed after him into the kitchen, like a lost soul. "What should I do?"

Nick made tea and thrust the mug into her hand. "Drink this."

She took a sip. Then, clutching the mug as if it were a life preserver, Rhiannon carried it to the sofa and curled up in one corner. "Edie would know what to do." She sobbed into her tea mug, then lifted her gaze and fixed it on Nick. "What should I do?"

As if he were some love-and-marriage guru. As if he were Edie. What would Edie do?

He asked, "Where is Andrew?"

"Here."

Nick looked around, wondering if somehow he hadn't noticed Andrew in the room. "Where's here?"

"At home. His parents live about a mile from here. He's with th-them." She was sobbing again. "He won't talk to me."

"Have you tried?"

"N-no."

"Well, then—"

"He says h-he's done. That he's getting a new girlfriend! He says he hates me."

That was the first thing that sounded promising. "He doesn't," Nick said firmly. "Go talk to him."

"But—"

"Listen." Nick sat down beside her on the couch and leaned toward her, absolutely earnest. "If Andrew says he hates you, he's trying not to love you. He's not there yet."

Rhiannon looked at him, eyes wide. She sniffed. Twice. "Are you s-sure?"

Was he? What the hell did he know about love?

A lot, came the wholly unexpected answer. He'd been in love once. He was in love now—with Edie.

The recognition hit him like a fist in the gut.

"But what if he has a new girlfriend?" Rhiannon was demanding.

It didn't matter. Just like it hadn't mattered that Derek WhatsHisName had tried to muscle into Edie's life. "What if he does?" Nick challenged her. "Are you just going to sit back and let her have him?"

"I—" She stopped and looked at him helplessly.

"You can," Nick said, "if he doesn't matter to you. Or if you can pretend he doesn't matter." He let the words sink in. "Or—" his eyes bored into hers "—you can take a risk."

Take a risk. Take a risk. Take a risk. The words pounded inside his head.

Rhiannon didn't answer. She stared at him. Then she stared into the mug of tea. Nick didn't care what she did. The words were beating a tattoo in his brain.

Then Rhiannon lifted her gaze and met his. "I'm going to take the risk."

Her words dropped like stones in a quiet pool. Nick could almost see the ripples. Certainly he could feel them.

She didn't finish her tea. She put the mug on the counter, ran a brush through her hair, dabbed her cheeks dry again, but at the last minute grabbed a tissue box to take with her.

"Just in case" she told Nick who was still sitting on the couch, her words—a reply to his own challenge—still echoing in his head.

She paused beside him, then bent to kiss his cheek. "Thank you," she said. "I hope you're right."

Nick watched her go. As soon as she was out the door, he picked up his phone and called the airline, hoping to God that he was right, too.

CHAPTER TEN

THE problem with running away when you were an adult was that, eventually, you had to go home.

Edie knew that. She accepted it. She'd just hoped she would have done a better job of putting Nick behind her before she did so.

God knew she'd tried. She'd thrown herself with a vengeance into life in Thailand. Besides doing her regular work for Mona, she'd spent vast amounts of time with the twins and Grace. And because he was there, and he really didn't matter to her now, she even found herself going out with Kyle and his son, Jake.

But however much time she spent with them all, it wasn't enough.

No matter where she was, no matter what she was doing, Nick was always with her.

She wouldn't be able to move on until she'd gone home and faced him—or at least faced the renovation of the adobe he'd left behind. That might not work, either. But since Mona's film was finished and they were all leaving the country, it was the only hope she had.

"You don't have to go home," Kyle told her when she brought him his boarding passes that afternoon. He and Jake were going to the Caribbean for a couple of weeks before Kyle started work with Mona on the new film. Now he was sitting in Mona's garden watching Jake roughhouse with Dirk. But after tucking the boarding passes into his pocket, he turned to her with a brilliant smile and said, "Tear yours up. Come with us."

Edie shook her head. "Thanks, but I can't."

"You're not happy," Kyle pointed out. That had been obvious to everyone, though Edie had done her best to pretend.

Now she shrugged. "So I should bring my unhappiness to you?" She laughed a little ruefully. "Thanks, but I don't think so."

"I could make you happy," Kyle said with his customary confidence. But then his grin faded a little and he said, "I could try, Edie."

"Kyle—"

"I know you said forget it. But we were good together once—until I screwed it up. I was a fool." He shook his head. "I'll always regret that."

"But you don't regret Jake."

And he turned his gaze to watch his son playing with the twins. For a long moment he watched, and then he turned back to her. "No," he said quietly. "I don't regret that."

They both stood silently then, and Edie wondered if she was being a fool, too, throwing away a chance at some sort of happiness just because it wasn't with the man she really wanted?

But there was only one answer to that.

"Thank you," she said, looking up into his eyes, smiling and shaking her head. "But I can't. I will always be your friend, but I don't love you."

Kyle's expression was rueful. "Nothing more than I deserve," he allowed. "Still, if you change your mind, you'll know where to find me." Then he dipped his head and kissed her on the lips.

"What in the hell are you kissing him for?"

Edie spun around. *Nick?*

Yes, Nick! Stone-faced and furious, Nick was standing in the living room glaring at her. Behind him by the open front door, a nervous Malee was wringing her hands.

Edie stared, stunned, her mind reeling. What was he doing

here? Her pulses started to pound. More to the point, why did he care who she kissed? He didn't want her—except in his bed.

Now she bristled. "I'll kiss whoever I want!" She drew herself up and glared right back at him. "And for that matter, what the hell are you doing here?"

His jaw worked. He was still holding a duffel bag, which he dumped on the floor. "I need to talk to you." His gaze was glittering, his chest heaving.

"About what?" Edie asked, afraid to hope. She'd already done that. Couldn't do it again.

"You don't have to talk to him," Kyle said quietly.

"She damned well does," Nick bit out.

"You don't," Kyle insisted, stepping between her and Nick. She thought Nick might pick him up and throw him into the pond.

"Do you want to talk to him?" Kyle asked her. "Or should I beat him to a pulp?"

"Like to see you try," Nick ground out.

Kyle didn't back down. Nick took a step forward. Malee, the twins and Jake all sucked in a collective breath.

"Let him talk," Edie said unsteadily. "What's so important that you came halfway around the world?"

His eyes were fixed on her, still glittering. "Rhiannon needed you," he told her. "You weren't there."

His words crushed any hope she had left. She felt numb. "And you came all the way to Thailand to tell me that?" It didn't make any sense.

Nick shook his head. "No, but it got me here."

"I don't understand." Had something happened to her sister? There had been messages from Rhiannon. Lots of them. But Edie had taken a page out of Mona's book. She'd made up her mind to stop trying to fix Rhiannon's love life. Now, all of a sudden Edie felt dread.

"What happened to Rhiannon?" she demanded.

"I'll tell you," Nick answered evenly, "but I'd prefer it without an audience."

"You don't have to listen to him, Edie," Kyle reminded her.

Nick opened his mouth, but Edie cut him off. "It's all right. Come on," she said to Nick. "We'll go in the office."

She led the way, aware of him right behind her. But she didn't look back until he'd shut the door behind them.

Then she turned and demanded, "Tell me! What about Rhiannon? What's happened?"

Nick grinned faintly. "She's fine. All patched up with Andrew. Married to him, as a matter of fact."

Edie's legs felt suddenly like jelly. "*What?!*"

Nick shrugged. "I wasn't quite expecting that, either. But she came home three days ago. No, maybe four—what day is it?"

"Friday," Edie said absently. "Tell me." She had to be hearing things.

"Right." He dragged a hand through his hair. He looked terrible. Sleepless, pale, with dark circles under his eyes, hair rumpled and at least a couple of days stubble on his jaw. And beautiful, too. She wanted to reach out to him, to touch him. She didn't dare. So she balled her fingers into fists.

"She came looking for you," Nick said. "Crying. The world had ended. Andrew was finished with her. It was all her fault. She loved him so." Nick looked harassed at the memory.

Edie nodded. Yes, that sounded pretty much like Rhiannon.

"Wanted to know what she should do," Nick went on. "I mean, how the hell should I know?" Now he looked beyond harassed. He began pacing around the small office, rubbing his hand through his hair, kneading the muscles at the back of his neck.

"You who don't do relationships, you mean?"

He shot her a glance and then hunched his shoulders. "Pretty much. So I thought, what would you do?"

"And what would I do?" Edie asked curiously.

He shrugged. "I made her a cup of tea."

Edie swallowed a smile. She didn't feel like smiling. She felt like crying. "I'm sure that helped," she said gravely, past the lump in her throat.

"It did," Nick said shortly. "And then I told her to go talk to him. Told her he still loved her."

"How would you know a thing like that?"

"Because, damn it, she said he'd told her he wasn't going to. Like it was a choice!"

"I thought it was a choice," Edie reminded him quietly.

"That's rubbish," Nick said flatly. "You can't stop it. It's destiny." He was looking square at her. "Like I love you."

The world stopped. Sound stopped. Well, maybe not sound. Edie could hear the twins and Jake yelling in the garden. But all the rest of the sounds in the world.

And her heart. Her heart stopped, too.

She stared at him. Mute. Disbelieving.

"I love you," Nick repeated, his voice ragged. He looked miserable.

"And that's what you came to tell me?" Edie ventured, unsure, though her heart was singing, whether this was a good thing or not. Nick certainly didn't look as if he were thrilled by the discovery.

He looked as uncertain as she felt. And then he demanded, voice cracking, "Whatever happened to 'I love you, too'?"

And then Edie understood. She saw his pain for what it was—fear. But he had vanquished it. He had said the words. He'd believed them!

And that was what mattered. She flew to him then, and threw her arms around him. "I love you, too!" And she kissed his rough chin, his stubbled jaw, his warm, hungry mouth.

Nick caught her to him, kissing her, wrapping her in an embrace so tight she could barely breathe. It didn't matter. What breath she had was for him. She kissed him back, hungry for him, desperate for him. She wanted him here and now, but there was one office chair in this room—and one small desk.

He looked around at the same time she did, saw what she saw and came to the same conclusion, saying ruefully, "Bad planning."

She laughed unsteadily. "Later," she promised. Then, "There will be later, won't there?"

"Please, God," Nick said fervently.

"There will," Edie vowed. "There will," she said again, knowing he needed to hear it. "It won't be like Amy."

"You don't know that," Nick said roughly.

"You're right, of course. I don't. I don't know what happened."

"She had an aneurysm," Nick said. "No one knew she had anything wrong. Then, two days before the wedding, she just—" He stopped, couldn't go on.

Edie kissed him again, then rested her cheek against his. "I'm sorry. So very sorry."

"So am I. It was my fault."

"Aneurysms aren't anyone's fault," Edie protested.

"Not that. Putting off the wedding. She didn't care about the house being done. I shouldn't have made her wait."

"You can't second guess that," Edie told him.

"I know. And yet—" he shook his head wearily "—I couldn't help it. I wanted to die, too. I never wanted to go through it again. I chose not to." He raised his head and met her gaze now. "At least I tried to."

"I'm glad it doesn't work like that," Edie said softly. She still had his fingers wrapped in hers. They lay against his chest, and beneath them she could feel the steady solid beat of his heart.

"I am, too." Nick turned his head and his lips touched her forehead. He kissed her. He kissed her hair. "Will you marry me?"

As much as she wanted to hear the words, when she did, they were unexpected. "Is that what you want?" she asked, needing to be sure.

Nick nodded. "It is." A corner of his mouth quirked. "I asked Rhiannon if she was going to fight for Andrew, if she dared to take the risk. She did. And I knew that if she had enough guts to go after what she wanted, I should damned well take the risk for you." He bent his head and touched his lips to hers. "I love you, Edie."

And Edie believed then. Trusted. And put her heart in his keeping. "I love you, too. And yes, please, I'll marry you."

His wedding day scared the hell out of him.

Not that Nick let on.

He figured Edie knew. She seemed to know what he was thinking even before he thought it. But everyone else was focusing on the bride. So was he. He wasn't superstitious. He didn't think lightning struck in the same place twice. But he couldn't stop worrying. He didn't want to lose her.

If Amy had been his first love, Edie was his forever love. She was his heart and his soul. She gave the meaning to every breath he took.

And as he waited for her to come down the stairs of her mother's house and walk out onto the *ramada* in her bridal gown to marry him, he knew that his heart was hammering, his collar was strangling him, his fingers shook.

Next to him, his cousin Yiannis, the best man, murmured, "You're not going to faint, are you?"

And the terrible thing was, Nick couldn't promise that he wouldn't. He couldn't say anything at all. He could only wait.

And then, there she was—his beautiful dark-haired bride, his Edie—coming to meet him, her eyes alight with joy, her smile just for him.

He breathed again.

"Thank God," Yiannis murmured.

"Have you got the ring?" Nick asked under his breath.

"Ring?" Yiannis looked blank. Then at Nick's look of pure terror, he grinned. "I've got it right here." He patted his pocket. "No getting out of it now."

"I don't want to," Nick said as Edie reached him and he took her hand in his. "Let's do this."

They did it.

Short, sweet. An absolutely perfect wedding with only family and close friends around, followed by a reception for Rhiannon and Andrew as well as for them. It had been going on for hours.

But Nick and Edie weren't there.

They were going on their honeymoon.

"Where are we going for our honeymoon?" she asked. "Why won't you tell me?"

"You'll see soon enough," he said.

"Will I like it?"

"I hope so."

They were in her apartment getting ready to leave. They could hear the music and the dancing and the celebration across the driveway in the house. Rhiannon and Andrew were enjoying it immensely. Nick was glad they had been there. He was ready to move on.

"I don't even know what to bring," she said plaintively. "I don't know what to wear."

"I've packed for you. And what you've got on is fine for now," he told her. She'd changed out of her wedding dress into a pair of shorts and a T-shirt just to relax.

"This?" She looked askance.

"Perfect," he told her. He grabbed the bag he'd packed in one hand and took hers in the other. "Come on."

He took her down the stairs, but when she would have gone toward the car in the garage, he turned the other way, toward the trees.

Suddenly Edie stopped, and Nick knew she understood. "Nick?" She had a stranglehold on his hand and was looking at him, her eyes wide, wondering.

He gave her a gentle tug. "Come on."

She hadn't been to the adobe since they'd come back from

Thailand. She hadn't had much time. They'd arranged the wedding in less than a week. And the few times she had suggested going to check out his progress, he'd found reasons to put it off.

Now he felt a flicker of the old familiar fear as he took her hand and led her up the hill and down the other side to where the old adobe waited.

A softly glowing porch light welcomed them in the waning twilight. It looked good. The front steps were solid, the porch wide, with low-slung wood and leather Spanish style chairs for sitting outside on a warm afternoon.

Edie looked at it, her lips parted in amazement. The outside walls had all been finished with lime plaster. All the *vigas* and corbels had been repaired or replaced and the roof was whole again. Lights shone from within through the deep-set windows.

"It's beautiful," she murmured. "It's far more beautiful than I remembered." Now she grabbed his hand and, instead of going up the steps to the porch, she dragged him around the back to beam at the porch now painted and finished. She hugged him hard, her eyes shining. "It's perfect." Then she went up on the porch and peered through the windows.

"Furniture?" She turned back to look at him.

"Some. You didn't think we were going to sleep on the floor, did you?"

"I didn't think we were going to spend our honeymoon here!"

"Are you sorry?" He'd thought it would be perfect, but now he wondered if perhaps he'd been mistaken.

But Edie was smiling. "Not at all. It's the best place." She ran her hand down one of the support beams. "It's how I knew you loved me."

He stared at her. "What?"

"You would never have suggested renovating a third-rate run-down old building if you didn't," she told him cheerfully. "Would you?"

He thought about it, logically, analytically, sensibly—and knew that she was right. "I guess I wouldn't."

Now it was his turn to take her by the hand and lead her around to the front of the house, to take her up the steps onto the wide front porch. There he stopped and took down the envelope that had been tacked to the door. He handed it to Edie. "It's for you."

Edie's fingers trembled as she took it. Slowly she fumbled it open. Then she bent her head and read it—at first silently, then aloud.

"My darling daughter," she began, her voice wavering. "There was always love in this house when your dad and I lived here. I wish you and Nick a lifetime of the same sort of love. The house is yours. I know you and Nick will make it a wonderful home. I hope the memories you already have and the memories you make are as wonderful as you are. I love you, Mom."

Tears slid down her cheeks. Sniffling, Edie tried to wipe them away.

"Here," Nick said gently, and he bent his head and kissed them away one by one.

"Mom," Edie said, with a quiet laugh. "Mom." She hadn't called her mother that in years. But it was right. Everything was right.

"Not Mona," Nick agreed.

"Just wait until there's someone to call her Grandma," Edie said with sudden glee.

Nick laughed, too. "I can't wait. I love you." And he swept her up into his arms, kicked open the door and carried her over the threshold into the home of her past and of their future. "In fact, Mrs. Savas, I think we should get started on that someone right now."

* * * * *

[illegible] was just [illegible] to take [illegible] the [illegible] and [illegible] around to the front of the house [illegible] the wide front porch. [illegible] and [illegible] that had been [illegible] to the door [illegible]. "It's for you."

Pete's [illegible] again [illegible]. [illegible] opened it. Then she bent her head and read [illegible] aloud.

"My darling daughter, [illegible] to give [illegible]. There [illegible] always [illegible] in this house [illegible] and [illegible] you and Nick [illegible] the same [illegible]. The house is yours. I know you and Nick will make [illegible] wonderful home. I hope the memories you already have [illegible] the memories you make are as wonderful as you are. I love you, Mom."

[illegible] down [illegible] sniffling. Pete [illegible] away.

[illegible]," Nick said gently, and he bent his head and kissed them away [illegible].

"Mom," Pete said with a quiet laugh. "Mom." She hadn't called her mother that in [illegible] Everything [illegible].

"Not Mom," Nick corrected.

[illegible] someone to call her [illegible]," Pete said with a [illegible].

Nick laughed [illegible]. "I can't [illegible]. I love you." And he swept her up in his arms, [illegible] the door and carried her over the threshold into the house of her [illegible] and of their future. [illegible] [illegible], I think we should get married in the [illegible] [illegible]."

CHAMPAGNE WITH A CELEBRITY

BY
KATE HARDY

Kate Hardy lives in Norwich, in the east of England, with her husband, two children, one bouncy spaniel, and too many books to count! When she's not busy writing romance or researching local history, she also loves cooking—see if you can spot the recipes sneaked into her books. (They're also on her website, along with excerpts and the stories behind the books.)

Writing for Mills & Boon has been a dream come true for Kate—something she's wanted to do ever since she was twelve. She's been writing Medical Romance™ since 2001, and also writes for Modern™; her novel *Breakfast at Giovanni's* won the Romantic Novelists' Association's Romance Prize in 2008. She says she loves what she does because she gets to learn lots of new things when she's researching the background to a book: add warmth, heart and passion, plus a new gorgeous hero every time, and it's the perfect job!

Kate's always delighted to hear from readers, so do drop in to her website at www.katehardy.com.

CHAPTER ONE

WE'LL have to wait and see. The phrase that Guy had come to hate most in the entire world. How the hell could he be patient about this, when it could turn his entire world upside down?

But this was the second specialist to say it. His third medical opinion in as many months. And while 'we'll have to wait and see if your sense of smell returns' might be perfectly acceptable advice for most people, it absolutely wasn't fine for a parfumier. Guy couldn't do his job properly without his sense of smell.

He'd been covering it up for three months now. It was only a matter of time before someone found out. And then things would get seriously difficult; as it was, his business partner wanted to accept a huge conglomerate's offer to buy out the perfume house. Guy had resisted, so far—he wanted to keep them focused on what their customers wanted, and continue to support local suppliers—but this would give Philippe the ammunition he needed to force the sale. How could GL Parfums possibly continue as it was, when its head of research and development had lost his 'nose'?

Hell, hell, hell.

He'd been banking on this last specialist being able to help him. On being able to offer him something more than just waiting to see if it cleared up by itself, because the only possible reason for it was damage caused by the virus. He'd sat perfectly still and gone through the truly nasty procedure of having a camera on a tube fed up his nose and into his sinuses. He'd taken vitamin supplements. He'd spent hours online, scouring every possibility, reading the forums of every support group. And still he was being told, 'We'll have to wait and see.'

Worse, the specialist had added that it could take up to three years for his sense of smell to come back, and even then it might not come back fully.

Three *years*?

The last three months had been bad enough.

The prospect of spending three years like this was torture.

Besides, he couldn't wait for three years. The perfume house couldn't afford to stand still—if they didn't develop new fragrances or extend their current lines, they'd have no chance of competing in the market. And then it would go under and everyone would lose their jobs. His staff had supported him and believed in his dreams so much that they'd even taken a pay cut, in the early days, to keep the perfume house going. How could he let them down?

Unless he hired someone to be his 'nose' at the perfume house in his stead…and then his own role would have to change. He'd have to shoulder a lot more of the admin and the marketing—the things he'd always been relaxed about delegating, because he'd been happiest in his lab developing new fragrances. Hiring another parfumier would mean that he could keep the perfume house going; but it also meant that the perfume house would stop being his dream. It'd just be a job. He'd be living half a life, unable to do what he loved most: the thing that got him up in the mornings and made him glad to be alive.

He knew it was selfish of him—and unfair—but he really didn't think he could bear that.

Thank God he'd finalised the formula for the new perfume before his sense of smell had gone. That would buy him a few more months. And then he'd just have to hope to hell that whatever the problem was with his nose could be fixed. That he could find a specialist who could help him.

And somehow he had to drag himself back from the brink so he could be smiling, urbane, sweet-natured Guy Lefèvre, best man at his brother's wedding. He wasn't going to drop the vaguest hint that his life was turning into a nightmare: no way was he going to ruin Xav and Allie's happiness with his own misery.

'Smile,' he told himself harshly, 'and look as if you mean it.' And he was supposed to be out here cutting roses for the table arrangements, not making clandestine calls on his mobile phone to an ENT specialist and brooding in his garden. Better get on with it, before someone came to find out what was taking him so long.

'Sheryl, it's gorgeous. It's just like what I expected a French château to be like. Did you get the photo I sent you?' Amber asked.

'Yes. All tall windows and old stone. Very glam.'

'It's a bit shabby inside,' Amber admitted, 'but a little bit of work could fix that. Change the faded drapes for voile and light damask, paint the walls white with just a hint of rose, and get someone to polish the parquet and the panelling. And there's this amazing chandelier in the hallway. Needs cleaning, mind, but it's a stunner.'

Sheryl laughed. 'Don't tell me you're going to persuade Allie to lend you the place for a party?'

'I'm tempted,' Amber admitted. 'How much would

people pay for a weekend house party in France, do you think? Or maybe a Marie Antoinette–themed dinner?'

'I don't believe you. You're meant to be having fun at a wedding, and you're spotting locations for a possible charity ball.'

'Well, yeah. It's gorgeous, Sher. The kitchen's to die for. It's enormous. There's this old terracotta floor, cream-painted cabinets—and they're obviously handmade—gleaming copper pans and a scrubbed wooden table.' The kind of kitchen she would love to have, herself.

'Just as well the paps can't hear you,' Sheryl teased. 'If only they knew that Bambi Wynne the party girl likes being all domesticated.'

'Just as well you won't tell them, then,' Amber retorted, knowing that her best friend was completely trustworthy and would never betray her to the media. She pushed away the thought that she'd actually quite like to be domesticated, pottering round at home with a family to settle down with. Being the centre of someone's world.

How ridiculous.

She had a fabulous life—one that most people would envy. A nice flat in a fashionable part of London; good friends to meet for lunch and go shopping with; invitations to celebrity parties and cinema premières. Her time was her own, and if she fancied shopping in Milan, Paris or New York she could just hop on a plane without having to worry. She was on decent terms with all her family, so why on earth would she have this hankering to be tied down?

She shook herself. 'And the rose garden here. I've never seen so many in one place before. You know that corner of the handmade soap shop we like in Covent Garden? Walking through here's even better than that. Like drinking roses every time you breathe in.' On impulse, she wandered over to one choice bloom and picked it. She sniffed deeply and sighed. 'This has to be the most beautiful scent in the world.'

Guy rounded the corner and stared in disbelief.

Véra?

Common sense kicked in. No, of course Xav wouldn't have invited his ex to the wedding. Even if Allie knew her through work, he very much doubted that she and Véra would be friends. Allie wasn't in the least bit princessy, whereas his ex-wife had turned out to be a demanding, selfish diva. More fool him for letting his heart rule his head and not letting himself see what she was really like before he'd married her.

Then the woman turned, and Guy realised that he'd actually been holding his breath.

It wasn't Véra.

Though this woman was physically very like his ex: tall and slender, with legs that went on for ever. She wore her hair the same way, in long, dark spiral curls; even though Guy knew better than to act on the impulse, his fingers tingled with the urge to find out if they felt as silky as they looked. And he'd just bet that under those dark glasses she'd have huge blue eyes, enhanced by coloured contact lenses and super-volumising mascara to make them even more striking.

She was obviously one of the wedding guests. One of Allie's friends, he guessed, because she looked the media type—she was beautifully groomed, even in jeans and a T-shirt. And she was chatting happily on her mobile phone as she strolled through the roses, gesturing with her free hand. She looked absolutely carefree.

And then, to his shock, she stooped and snapped off one of the roses.

Oh, now this really *wasn't* on. He didn't mind people wandering in his garden, but he *did* mind them interfering with his roses. What would she do next—toss it to the ground and tread on it, now it had served her whim?

He strode over to her. 'Excuse me.'

She looked up. 'Oh. Got to go, call you later,' she said swiftly into her phone, and ended the call before giving him the most dazzling smile. 'Sorry about that. Was there something you wanted?'

He gestured to the rose in her hand. 'Don't you think you should ask first?'

She frowned. 'It's beautiful, and flowers are for sharing. I didn't think Allie and Xav would mind if I picked a single rose for my room.'

'It's not their garden,' he pointed out. 'It's mine.'

'Oh.' Colour bloomed in her cheeks, making her skin look as pink and as soft as the rose in her hand. 'Well, in that case, I apologise.' She gave a disarming shrug and another of those sweet, sweet smiles. 'I guess it's a tad late to ask permission now.'

She pushed her sunglasses up over her forehead to the crown of her head, and Guy felt his body tighten. She didn't have blue eyes. They were a deep, deep brown, and absolutely enormous. And, from his time with Véra, he could tell that she wasn't wearing much make-up at all: not even mascara to define those amazing eyes. Just the barest sheen of lipstick. Then again, she didn't actually need make-up. She had to be the most beautiful woman he'd ever met, including the days when Guy had been married to a supermodel and had mixed with some of the most gorgeous women in the world.

And no doubt she knew just how stunning she was, because she bent her head slightly to sniff the rose, looking up at him. The perfect coquettish pose—one that was very close to his ex's trademark.

'This really is the most amazing scent,' she said.

He knew that. Except he couldn't smell it any more. Only something like the ghost of a scent—so it was more likely that he was simply remembering what they smelled like instead of actually smelling them. And memory wasn't enough. 'Yes,' he said, through gritted teeth.

'I didn't think roses would still be blooming at the end of September.' She shrugged and smiled. 'Still, I guess this is the Med. Or near enough.'

He knew he ought to be polite. She was a guest in his home. It wasn't her fault that he couldn't smell, and it certainly wasn't her fault that she reminded him of Véra. But she'd pressed all his buttons; he was nearly crazy with the frustration of not being able to fix the two biggest problems in his life; and the strain of keeping it from those he loved most—because he knew they already had enough on their plate and didn't need the extra worry about him—wasn't doing a lot for his temper.

'If you don't know where we are, try looking at a map,' he suggested. 'And kindly don't damage any more of my roses.' He turned on his heel and walked off, without a backward glance. He needed to get out of here. Now. Allie's roses would just have to wait.

Amber stared at the man's retreating back.

Wow.

What had she done? Were these prize-winning roses and he was the gardener, or something? It would certainly explain why there were so many roses around here. Didn't posh gardeners have lots of different varieties though, and pride themselves on breeding different ones? Most of these roses seemed to be the same colour, cream at the centre shading to a deep blush-pink at the edges.

And what did he mean, it was his garden? Surely it belonged to the château and the vineyard? Or maybe he'd been the gardener here for years and felt that it was 'his' spiritually.

All that suppressed anger, over one little rose.

Crazy.

Though she felt a tiny bit guilty. He was right about one thing: she was a guest, and she should've resisted the impulse to pick a rose for her room. Or at least asked first.

Never mind. She'd ask Allie about her gorgeous sexy gardener—and if he ever smiled. Because, even though he'd been all brooding and simmering, she'd noticed how gorgeous he was. Sun-bleached fair hair, eyes the colour of a summer evening sky and a mouth that promised passion, all wrapped up with a seriously hot body.

She rolled her eyes. Picking a rose, without asking, was enough of a gaffe. Seducing her friend's gardener would definitely be off limits. Besides, after that embarrassing feature in *Celebrity Life* a month ago—detailing every single one of her boyfriends over the past year, how long they'd lasted and how they'd dumped her—she'd decided to steer clear of men for a while.

She headed back to her room, filled the glass in her bathroom with water and put the rose in it, then placed it on the table next to her bed.

This place was so gorgeous. OK, so the walls needed a lick of paint and the heavy gold damask curtains were faded and the rug was a bit threadbare, but the half-tester bed was like a fairy princess's. The whole place screamed 'shabby chic' and history. And her room had the most amazing view over the rose garden. It was the kind of room where you'd be quite happy to get up early in the morning, because you'd get to see the sun rising over the garden.

Lucky Allie, having all this at her disposal.

And definitely lucky her, having a friend who could invite her to stay somewhere so fabulous.

She wandered down to the kitchen; Allie was sitting at the kitchen table with someone else she recognised and hadn't seen for ages. 'Gina!' She gave the designer a huge hug, kissing both cheeks. 'When did you get here?'

'The taxi dropped me off ten minutes ago.'

She rolled her eyes. 'You should've texted me. I could've waited at the airport for you and given you a lift. Never mind.' She hugged her again. 'It's so lovely to see you.'

'The coffee's hot, if you want some,' Allie said with a smile.

'Yes, please.' She poured herself a mug from the cafetière and added a splash of milk. 'By the way, Allie, I'm sorry. I'm afraid I've just upset your gardener.'

'My gardener?' Allie looked surprised.

'He caught me picking one of the roses. He was a bit cross with me.'

Allie frowned. 'I don't have a gard—oh, wait. Was he tall, blond and gorgeous?'

'Tall and blond, yes.' Amber shrugged. 'Gorgeous…' Definitely. 'He might be, if he wasn't scowling.'

Allie blinked. 'Guy never scowls.'

'Who's Guy?' Amber asked.

'Xav's brother. It's his château.'

Oh. So it really *was* his garden. Amber bit her lip. 'In that case, I owe him an apology.'

'Sorry, it's my fault. I should've warned you that he's precious about his roses, so don't touch them.'

'He's a garden expert?'

'Parfumier,' Allie corrected. 'You've heard of GL

Parfums?' At Amber's nod, she said, 'That's him. Guy Lefèvre.'

'GL Parfums? They do that fantastic shower gel. The citrussy one,' Gina said. 'They were going on about it in *Celebrity Life*, the other week, about how it was the best pick-me-up ever.'

Amber groaned. 'Don't mention *them*.'

Gina hugged her. 'They gave you quite a mauling last month, didn't they?'

'Mmm, and how the hell did they find out that Raoul the Rat dumped me by text? I swear they must be tapping my mobile.' She deliberately kept her voice light, but that feature had hurt. And Raoul had hurt her badly. She'd thought he was different, that he might be The One—but he'd turned out to be yet another of the liars and losers she always seemed to date. Sometimes she thought it was as if she had a tattoo on her forehead that was invisible when she looked in the mirror, but was written in neon colours for everyone else. *Shallow and heartless? Take me, I'm yours!*

She shook herself. 'Let's talk about something nicer. So that's his fragrance, is it?'

Allie nodded. 'That was the first scent Guy made for the perfume house. Originally it was an aftershave, but then he extended the line. Actually, Gina, I know he wants to talk to you because he likes what you did for our labels. He said something about a new project.'

'Really? Oh, I'd love the chance to work with him,' Gina said, looking enthusiastic. 'His perfumes are brilliant and it'd be a fantastic opportunity for me to be involved in designing packaging or what have you for a new perfume.'

Xav strolled into the kitchen, wrapped his arms round his wife-to-be and kissed her. 'Have you seen Guy anywhere, *ma belle*?'

'No, though we were just talking about him being a genius with scent,' Allie said.

'Then he's probably sneaked off to his lab,' Xav said, and kissed her again. 'I'd better go and fish him out, because we have a hot date with a barbecue lined up.'

'That's a terrible pun,' Allie said, laughing. 'Hot date with a barbecue, indeed.' She glanced at her watch. 'We'd better get started on the salads, I guess.'

'Count me in for kitchen duties,' Amber said as Xav left the kitchen. 'Important things first: what are you doing for pudding?'

'Pudding?' Allie's eyes went wide. 'Oh, no. I forgot pudding. How could I do that?'

'Because you're getting married tomorrow and have a dozen more pressing things to think about?' Amber suggested.

Allie sighed. 'I'd better run down to the village and get something from Nicole's. She makes the best *tarte tatin* in the world.'

Amber couldn't resist the opportunity of getting her hands properly on this kitchen. 'I could make pudding,' she said. 'We had this amazing one at the ball last month.' She pulled up some of the photographs on her phone to show them.

'Oh, wow, that looks fantastic,' Gina said.

'And it tastes even better. Is there somewhere in the village that'd sell raspberries and passion fruit?'

'Nicole's farm shop,' Allie said.

'Righty—I'll go shopping. Allie, if you could chat up your scary brother-in-law and wheedle three roses out of him, I'll be right back.'

'Are you sure you don't mind?'

'Course not. Is there anything else you need?'

'No.'

But Amber could see in her face that Allie was having an attack of butterflies. If this Nicole made great pastries, hopefully she'd sell chocolate as well. Cake would do, at a pinch.

It didn't take long to buy the ingredients she needed. She drove back to the château, then put her hair into a ponytail, ready to start cooking. 'Oh—before I forget. Butterfly-taming material,' she said with a smile, handing over the chocolates.

'You're wonderful. And I got what you asked for.' Allie produced three roses.

'Fantastic. I'm going to play.' Amber carefully painted the petals with egg-white, dipped them in icing sugar and set them to dry while Gina and Allie were in charge of the salads. She cooked the meringue and prepared as much of the filling as she could. 'I need to assemble this at the very last minute, or it'll be soggy and disgusting,' she said, 'so I'll do it when people have nearly finished eating, OK?'

'More than OK,' Allie said, giving her a hug. 'I don't know why *Celebrity Life* keeps making you out to be an airhead. They really have no idea about who you really are.'

Amber knew exactly why they did it. She'd turned down a date with one of the journos and, even though she thought she'd been tactful in her refusal, he'd really taken a huff. As a result, the magazine's favourite sport seemed to be Amber-baiting. She tried her best to ignore the snide headlines—When will Bambi be a Wynne-r in love?—but it was starting to rankle. After that last nasty feature, she'd had to stop herself going to the office and punching him on the nose. Ignoring him was the best policy. She'd just have to grit her teeth; someone else would do something indiscreet, soon enough, to take the spotlight off her.

'Who cares about *Celebrity Life*?' she said lightly, and picked up a platter of bread to take out to the terrace.

Xav was already cooking things on the grill, and Guy was pouring wine for all the wedding guests who were staying overnight at the château.

He handed her a glass in silence.

Time to fix things, she thought. She was definitely in the wrong about the rose, and it wouldn't be fair for Allie and Xav to have needless tension at their wedding. 'Guy, may I have a word, please?' she asked.

He looked wary. 'Why?'

'I owe you an apology,' she said, 'for picking your flowers without asking. Especially as I didn't have the manners to introduce myself when we met. I know your name and that you're Xav's brother. I'm Amber Wynne. Nice to meet you.' She held out her hand to shake his.

For a moment, she thought he was going to refuse, but then he took her hand and shook it. The second his skin touched hers, desire jolted through her, shocking her with its intensity; judging by the surprise in his eyes, quickly masked, it was the same for him.

Interesting.

Except, she reminded herself, she was off men. Her love life was a disaster area, and she'd promised herself a break for the next six months.

'I owe you an apology, too, Amber,' he said, surprising her. 'You're a guest and I shouldn't have snapped at you. My only excuse is that you caught me at a bad time.'

'And your roses are important to you. I thought you were maybe the gardener,' Amber said, 'but I take it that you grow them for your perfume?'

Guy looked slightly taken aback, clearly realising that she'd talked to Allie about him. 'Well, yes.'

'May I?' She gestured to the chair next to him. At his

brief nod, she sat down. 'You have a beautiful garden,' she said, 'and a beautiful home.' And she really hoped he hadn't overheard her telling Sheryl that it needed a bit of work. 'Thank you so much for letting me stay here.'

He shrugged. 'You're a wedding guest—any friend of my sister-in-law-to-be is a friend of my family.'

Guy had been prepared to dislike Amber, because she reminded him so much of Véra, but there was an easy warmth about her; to his surprise, he found himself relaxing and chatting to her. And when she encouraged him to talk more about his roses, for one crazy moment he thought he could smell them. On her skin.

No. Of course not. The virus he'd caught three months ago had put paid to that. But, all the same, she intrigued him.

And attracted him. An attraction he wouldn't let himself act on—not while his life was in chaos and all his energy seemed to be used up in fighting the fear that the career he loved was over. Besides, she was only here for the wedding. It wasn't as if their paths were likely to cross again in the near future. There was no point in starting something he had no intention of continuing.

When Allie and Gina started to clear away, Amber stood up and started helping—something else Guy hadn't expected. Véra would have considered herself a guest and therefore someone to be waited on, not someone to help with the waiting.

As if she read the expression on his face, she said, 'I'm in charge of pudding. Back in a minute.' She smiled, and was gone.

And what a pudding. She came back holding a platter containing two soft meringue roulades, filled with what looked like some kind of cream-and-fruit mixture; the top was decorated with candied rose-petals and a drizzle of passion-fruit seeds, and she'd found some indoor sparklers somewhere and stuck those in, too, so her pudding could make a real entrance.

'So that's why Allie wanted three more roses,' he said when she brought him a slice neatly plated.

She looked awkward. 'Sorry, but they were so perfect for this—cream in the centre shading out to deep pink at the edges.'

'And candying them must've taken you a while.'

'It's the little details that make the difference,' she said simply.

'And you pay attention to them.' Again, he hadn't expected that. He'd pigeonholed her as a careless, thoughtless diva. How had she managed to wrong foot him so completely? He gestured to the pudding to cover his awkwardness. 'This looks good. Are you a chef?'

She shook her head. 'I like messing about in the kitchen. But being a chef would mean working crazy hours. Not my thing.'

'So what is your thing?' he asked, suddenly curious.

'I organise parties.'

He blinked. 'You organise parties?'

'It's how I met Allie. She came to one of my parties, a couple of years back, and we hit it off. We've become friends.'

'You're a party girl.' So he'd been right, at heart. She *was* a media darling—just like his ex-wife.

'Uh-huh.' She sighed. 'But don't believe everything you see in the press about me.'

'You're in the press a lot?' Although her face seemed familiar, he couldn't quite place her. He skimmed the business news, most of the time online because it was quicker; he certainly didn't read the gossip and celeb pages in the newspapers, and the only time he saw one of the celeb magazines was if the cuttings agency sent it over because it contained a piece about GL Parfums. One of the things that drove his business partner, Phillipe, crazy was Guy's insistence on low-key product launches—but Guy had already been burned by the media. Badly. And he wasn't giving them a chance to dig around in his life again.

'She's the darling of the celeb mags, our Bambi,' Gina said, coming over and draping her arms round Amber's neck.

'Bambi?' The question was out before he could stop it.

'Because of those big brown eyes and the legs up to her armpits. If she wasn't so nice,' Gina said cheerfully, 'we'd all hate her for looking this good. Everyone else has to work at it. Not her. She could be wearing a sack after having no sleep for a week, and she'd still manage to look glamorous and start setting a trend! Life just isn't fair.'

Amber laughed. 'Thank you for the compliment, Gina, but you have to credit my mother for giving me her genes. And if you'd let me get you out of your "I'm an artist so I must wear black" uniform and put you in some colour to show off that porcelain skin, beautiful auburn hair and those gorgeous eyes, there'd be a queue of men from here to Paris.'

'No chance. I'm an *artist*,' Gina retorted, returning the grin.

'Hopeless,' Amber said, rolling her eyes. 'Tell her, Guy. She's gorgeous.'

'She's gorgeous,' Guy said dutifully. Gina was pretty enough. But Amber was stunning: next to her, all the other women seemed plain.

And that unsettled him. He'd been here before. Lost his

heart and his head to a gorgeous media darling. Married her within a month. And he'd really repented at leisure.

Not that he had any intention of getting involved with Amber. Even if she didn't remind him of the biggest mistake of his life, he wasn't looking for a relationship. Not right now, when his life was such a mess. He needed to focus on getting his career back on track. On finding a cure for his loss of smell. He couldn't afford to let his libido get in the way.

'Come and help me with the coffee?' Gina asked.

'Sure.' Amber smiled at her. 'Excuse me, Guy. I enjoyed our chat. Catch you later.'

And then she was gone.

Funny how his little corner of the terrace had suddenly lost its brightness. Guy shook himself. She wasn't his type. And he'd be crazy to let himself think otherwise.

CHAPTER TWO

THE next morning, Amber was awake before the alarm on her mobile phone went off. She had a quick shower and washed her hair, then headed for the kitchen. Allie and Gina were already there, having breakfast; she joined them, then did their nails afterwards and then made them sit to dry their nails properly while she sorted out the washing up.

Next was make-up and hair; and she was intrigued by the differences between a French wedding and an English one. 'So you have two wedding ceremonies—the official one at the *Mairie*, where you wear a business suit, and then at the church, where you have the white dress?' she asked.

'That's right,' Allie confirmed.

'Two weddings. That's just *greedy*,' Amber said, laughing. She stood back to look at her handiwork. 'Oh, Allie—Xav's going to take one look at you and then be desperate to carry you off to his lair.'

'You look stunning,' Gina agreed. 'Radiant.'

Allie flapped a dismissive hand. 'Ah, that's what you're supposed to say to all brides.'

'But it's still true,' Amber said. She pushed back the tiny bit of wistfulness: ridiculous. Right at the moment, she didn't even want to date anyone, let alone get married and settle down.

When Amélie, the flower-girl, arrived, Amber sat on the floor with her and taught her a counting song to make her feel less shy and more at ease, then did her hair, too.

'I look like a princess!' the little girl exclaimed in French when Amber showed her in the mirror.

'You certainly do,' Amber said, giving her a hug. 'Absolutely beautiful. And now I'd better get ready myself. See you all in a bit!'

Guy stared as Amber walked out of the château. Yesterday, in jeans and a T-shirt, she'd been stunning enough. But, dressed up, she was unbelievably gorgeous. As elegant as Audrey Hepburn, in a gold silk dress with spaghetti straps and matching strappy sandals; and her hair was piled on top of her head, secured with pearl-headed pins.

He was glad that he'd offered to drive some of the wedding party to the *Mairie*. At least concentrating on the road would keep his thoughts off Amber. Her smile, warm and bright and yet with a hint of unexpected shyness, made heat coil low in his belly and desire creep all the way up his spine. Worse still, his fingers itched to take the pins out of her hair and tumble her curls over her shoulders. And then he had a thought that really stopped him in his tracks: the idea of her hair tumbled across his pillow.

Oh, hell—he really had to get a grip.

'*Bonjour*, Guy.' Her voice was soft, low-pitched, a little bit on the posh side. Sexy as hell. 'Allie says you're driving us. Thank you.'

'Pleasure,' he responded automatically. 'Grab a seat.'

When she climbed into the front seat next to him, he really wished he'd been more specific and told her to sit in the back. It took all his concentration to drive to the village, knowing that every time he changed gear his hand was only a few centimetres away from her thigh. Especially as the hemline of her dress had already ridden up above her knee to reveal smooth, touchable skin—and she didn't seem in the slightest bit aware of it! She was chatting happily about how this was the first time she'd ever been to a French wedding and she was dying to see the *croquembouche*, the wedding cake made from *choux* buns held together in a pyramid with caramel.

This woman had the power to drive him crazy. Which made her very, very dangerous.

The wedding service at the *Mairie* was short and sweet; while Allie and Xav changed, the rest of the wedding party had a glass of wine in the café in the square, a couple of doors down, while they waited. Amber opted for a coffee rather than wine, wanting to pace herself; although she was chatting with some of the other guests, something made her break off mid-conversation and turn round.

And then she realised why.

Guy had walked into the café, looking stunning in a tailcoat, sky-blue waistcoat and matching cravat. Formal dress really suited him, and Amber wasn't surprised that all the other women in the coffee shop were staring at him, too. Guy Lefèvre was the kind of man who attracted attention, even though he didn't seem to be aware of it. There was just something about him and, when his gaze meshed with hers for a moment, her heart gave an odd little flip.

Oh, this was bad. Even if she wasn't officially being celibate, she couldn't possibly fall for Guy Lefèvre. He might not be one of the rats she usually dated, but she knew it would never work between them; they were from completely different worlds.

Then Allegra and Xavier appeared at the door. Allegra's

wedding dress was simple and elegant, in pure white; she wore a simple tiara in her hair, and carried an exquisite bouquet of white roses. Gina, as chief bridesmaid, was holding Amélie the flower-girl's hand; both wore similar dresses to Allegra's, but in the same sky-blue as Xavier and Guy's waistcoats, and the little girl's dress had a deep blue velvet sash round it.

The whole wedding party walked to the tiny church on the edge of the village, led by the bride and groom; white ribbons were strewn between the hedgerows, blocking their path, until Allegra and Xavier cut them. Clearly this was some kind of French tradition; Amber made a mental note to ask Allie about it later. The church was ancient and pretty, built in pale stone; inside, it was full of light. At the altar there were two red velvet chairs placed beneath a silk canopy—clearly waiting for the bride and groom—and as they walked in Allegra's mother played the violin, a sweet and haunting piece of Bach.

Although the service was conducted entirely in French, Amber could just about follow what was going on. As Allegra and Xavier exchanged rings Amber thought wistfully how lucky Allegra was to have found her one true love. She didn't think she'd ever find one herself.

And then she was cross with herself for letting herself be maudlin. She loved weddings and parties. And, as Allie had claimed that French weddings went on all night and finished at breakfast, Amber had every intention of having a good time.

When the bride and groom had been showered in dried delphinium petals outside the church and had stepped over the laurel leaves strewn on the path, the champagne reception began in the churchyard. The *vin d'honneur*, or the toast to the bride and groom: Amber knew that the whole village was invited to this part. And when Xavier poured a glass of champagne at the base of one of the gravestones and Allegra did the same to what looked like a much newer grave without a headstone, Amber realised it was a way of including those who were no longer with them—obviously Allie's great-uncle, and someone who presumably had been very close to Xav.

Back at the château, a huge marquee had been set up on the lawn, with tables edging a dance-floor. Time for the champagne reception. But what she hadn't expected was the way the champagne was opened. Guy and Xavier were both wielding curved sabres. They held the bottles with the corks pointing away from them, slid the sabres towards the corks and the corks flew out of the bottles with a short burst of champagne.

Amber had never seen anything like it. It was even more impressive than watching someone do a cascade of champagne glasses. If she could persuade Guy to teach her how to do it, it would be so fantastic for next year's midsummer ball.

Her chance to ask him came when she found herself unexpectedly seated next to him for the formal meal.

'That thing you did with the champagne was very impressive,' she said.

He lifted one shoulder. 'The *sabrage*, you mean?'

'It's not something I've seen before,' she said. 'So I take it that it's a traditional French thing?'

'Yes. It's from Napoleonic times—the Hussars celebrated victory by sabring the top off a bottle of champagne while they were still riding their horses at full gallop.'

And she could just imagine Guy in a Hussar officer's uniform. He'd look stunning on horseback. Sexy as hell.

With difficulty, she dragged her mind back to what he'd said. 'That sounds like a recipe for disaster, with glass flying all over the place—doesn't some of the glass get in the champagne?'

'No. The pressure of the champagne takes everything out.'

'How can you be so sure?'

Was she going to question everything he said? Guy wondered. Or was she really interested? To test her, he gave her all the facts and figures. 'It's a matter of holding the bottle at the right angle and hitting the lip of the bottle in the right place—at the seam, where it's weakest. And it's not a sharp sword—it's a champagne sabre, modelled on the design of the Hussars' swords.'

'So, with training, anyone could do it?'

'With training, yes.' And suddenly he realised the hole he'd just dug himself. Surely she wasn't going to ask him to let her have a go?

She smiled. 'Any chance of you teaching me?'

'Why would you want to learn that?' he parried.

'I already told you, I organise parties. And that includes a midsummer ball to raise funds for cancer research. Opening champagne like that at the ball would be spectacular—even better than the cascade of champagne glasses we did this year.'

'Why cancer research?' he asked.

'Because my favourite grandmother had breast cancer.' For a moment, a shadow crossed her face, but then she smiled. 'She's in remission right now, but this is my way of doing something to help.'

'Partying.'

'If you organise parties well and people have a good time, they're prepared to pay a lot of money for the tickets, which means the charity makes more,' she said. 'Sure, I could've done a sponsored walk or sat in a tub of baked beans or what have you, but this is more fun. It's a win-win situation for everyone.' She grimaced. 'And that wasn't meant to be a pun on my name.'

That sounded personal, Guy thought. No doubt the press enjoyed making puns with her name.

'Actually, I might as well be bold,' she said. 'As well as the money I make from the ticket sales, I hold a tombola to raise funds—big things, like a make-over, or a balloon flight, or a spa day, or a portrait by a really good photographer. I've managed to get dinner with a heart-throb in there too, by getting Mum to chat up one of her friends.'

'Your mother being…?'

'Libby Wynne, the actress.'

Oh, so *that* was why she looked familiar. Now he knew, he could see the resemblance. Though if pressed he'd say that Amber was even more beautiful than her mother.

'So, as you're this genius parfumier,' she continued, 'could I put you down for making a personalised scent for someone?'

It was the worst thing she could possibly have asked him.

Four months ago, he would probably have smiled and said yes. Now, he had no idea if he'd actually be able to do it. 'It's not just something you do on a whim,' he said coolly.

She spread her hands. 'Obviously there's more to it than just mixing a couple of oils together.'

'A lot more.'

'If designing a scent is too much to ask, maybe I could ask you for a gift basket instead—a big one?'

He wasn't sure if her chutzpah amused him or terrified him. 'You're utterly shameless, aren't you?'

'If you don't ask, you don't get.' She shrugged. 'What's the problem? I can't expect people to read my mind.'

What's the problem? he thought. My problem is that I'm incredibly attracted to you and I really don't need this. Not right now. 'Whatever,' he drawled. 'Put me down for a basket—just tell Allie nearer the time and I'll sort something out. And I'd better circulate a bit. We have dancing between courses, with this being a French wedding.' And please don't suggest I start dancing with you, he begged inwardly.

She didn't—and then he discovered he was disappointed that she hadn't asked.

Crazy.

He needed his head examined.

Amber recognised the tune of the first dance—'Time After Time.' It seemed to be traditional in France, too, that the newlyweds should start the dancing, followed by the best man and the chief bridesmaid. And such a beautiful song, she thought wistfully, mentally singing the lyrics. Would she ever find someone who'd catch her when she fell, someone who'd wait for her and support her? Judging by her past relationships, probably not; she always managed to pick the complete opposite.

She took a sip of her champagne. Enough of the pity party. This was a wedding, and she was going to have fun. There were loads of people here she hadn't met yet, and a few people who looked shy and a bit left out. One thing she was good at was getting a party going—and that was exactly what she planned to do.

Guy knew exactly where Amber was, even when his back was to her, because he could hear laughter. She was clearly working the party. Asking for more donations for her charity ball? he wondered, and sneaked a look.

No, she was fetching drinks for his great-aunts and

charming his great-uncles, and there was an approving smile on all their faces as she chatted with them. He was beginning to see why she organised parties: she had excellent people skills and the gift of putting people at their ease.

Then she went up to Allie's parents. This would definitely be worth watching, he thought, no longer hiding the fact that he was looking at her. The Beauchamps were notoriously standoffish; they'd been the parents from hell for Allie, and if Amber asked them to come and do a guest number at her ball, for nothing, he knew they'd send her away with a flea in her ear. They might even use it as an excuse to flounce off and fly back to wherever they were next playing a concert.

And then he blinked. Was he seeing things? Emma Beauchamp was actually smiling. Either Amber had met her before—and, even though she was a friend of Allie's, he thought that unlikely—or her people skills were even better than he'd thought. If she could thaw Emma Beauchamp, she could charm anyone.

He couldn't take his eyes off Amber. Clearly deciding that she'd schmoozed enough, she started dancing. But not on her own. And not a sexy, siren-type call to all the men who also couldn't take their eyes off her, either. No, she'd got all the children together in a group, and she was teaching them a simple routine. The girls all seemed thrilled that one of the grown-ups was paying them so much attention, and the boys were all clearly bowled over by her smile and couldn't do enough to please her. And their parents were all watching her with an indulgent smile; as soon as she noticed, she beckoned them to come up and join in. Within ten minutes, all the people who hadn't been dancing were up on their feet, joining in. And when one little girl slipped over, Amber scooped her up, gave her a cuddle to dry her tears and had her smiling again within a minute.

Amber clearly didn't care about grubby finger-marks, despite the fact that her dress was obviously expensive. She was all about *fun*.

Unable to resist the pull any longer, Guy fetched a flute of champagne and took it over to her. 'You look hot,' he said.

She dimpled at him. 'Now, are you saying my face is bright red, Monsieur Lefèvre, or was that an offer to dance with me?'

'Uh, I meant you've been dancing for ages and probably needed a drink, not that you look…' His voice faded and he could feel his own face heating. Especially as the look in her eyes told him that she knew he was lying. The attraction was mutual. He could tell by the way her lips parted, inviting him to kiss her—and it looked like an unconscious reaction rather than a planned seduction. 'All right. Both,' he admitted.

Her grin broadened. 'Well, hey. I did wonder if my dress was a bit too short.'

Above the knee. Yeah. He'd noticed. But her words made him look again.

For a moment, his tongue felt glued to the roof of his mouth. Then he called her bluff. 'Nice knees, Mademoiselle Wynne.'

'Why, thank you, Monsieur Lefèvre. And for the drink.' She took the glass, and it felt like an electric shock going through him when her fingers briefly brushed against his. And he definitely couldn't take his eyes off her mouth as she sipped delicately at the rim.

She had a beautiful mouth.

Irresistible.

And at that second he knew that, at some point tonight,

he was going to kiss her. And he knew that she'd be kissing him right back.

The jazz band switched into a number Amber recognised. The tango from the old Al Pacino film she'd watched with her mother a few months ago and loved. Even though she knew it'd be much more sensible to sit this one out and not bait Guy any further, her mouth wasn't working in sync with her brain. 'Dare you.'

'Dare me?' His eyes were suddenly very, very dark.

Shut up, Amber, shut up *now*, she warned herself. But her mouth was on a roll. 'Or can't you tango?'

'Challenging me, Amber? Isn't that a bit risky?'

Say no. Back off. Sit down, her brain telegraphed urgently.

Her mouth was having none of it. It smiled. Taunted him. 'Bite me, Guy.'

With slow, deliberate movements, he took the glass from her hand and set it down on the table. Then he yanked her into his arms, so his mouth was next to her ear. 'Bite you, hmm?' he drawled, his voice low and incredibly sexy. 'I'm taking that as an offer, *mon ange*.'

Amber was very, very glad that he was holding her up. Because she could imagine his teeth grazing her skin as he explored her all over with his mouth, and the idea sent her weak at the knees. Not to mention sending her pulse rate into overdrive.

It looked as if she'd just unleashed a monster.

There was no going back, because then Guy began to dance with her.

She'd danced with professionals, but it had felt nothing like this. With them, it had been choreography and patience. This was something more elemental, leaving her aware of every beat of blood through her body. Her body was reacting to his closeness, growing more aroused every time he spun her back into his body and wrapped his arms round her midriff, holding her close to him, sliding one leg between hers and encouraging her to do the same to him.

What would've been choreography with anyone else felt like a prelude to sex with Guy. A thigh pressed between hers. Another press, making her wonder what it would feel like to have his bare skin against hers, his legs tangled with hers. A withdrawal, as if he'd pulled out of her body, ready to surge back in as deeply as he could. Her body pressed against his, hip to hip and belly to belly and breast to breast. The scent of his skin, overlaid with a light citrussy fragrance that made her want to taste him.

Nothing existed except Guy and the music. Every nerve-end was concentrated on him—on the way his body touched hers, teasing and enticing and promising all at the same time.

And then she felt the brush of his lips against the bare skin of her shoulder, a feather-light contact that made a pulse beat hard between her legs.

His eyes were dark, a stormy blue in the evening light. Did he feel this same deep throb of desire? Was he thinking about what it would be like to kiss each other properly, hot and wet and urgent?

Bite me, she'd said.

And how she wanted to feel his mouth on her body. Teasing her. Arousing her. Taking her right over the edge.

And then the music came to an abrupt end. Shockingly so.

'Bravo, Mademoiselle Wynne,' Guy whispered in her ear in the final hold.

Amber was even more shocked when people actually clapped them.

Oh, no. Don't say they'd been the only dancers on the floor?

But when she glanced round, the dance-floor was empty.

This was bad. He was going to think she was a total show-off. And although she opened her mouth to speak, to tell him she hadn't meant this to happen, the words just wouldn't come. She didn't have a clue what to say.

Celebrity Life would have a field day with her, because she was behaving just like the airhead they always made her out to be.

'I'm sorry,' she whispered finally.

He drew closer, stooped slightly so that his breath fanned her ear. 'I'm not. That was…enlightening.'

And she was in too deep. Way too deep. 'Could I, um, get a glass of water or something?' she asked.

He raised an eyebrow, as if calling her a coward. 'Sure.' He escorted her over to the bar area, and ordered them both a glass of iced water. 'So where did you learn to dance like that?'

'I had lessons when I was in my teens.'

'And?'

She sighed. 'All right. I've dated a couple of dancers. And, because I organise the balls, I've talked a few professionals into coming and giving a display before the general dancing starts. One of them taught me to tango.'

'Like that?'

She laughed wryly. 'Hardly.' She'd never danced quite like that with anyone before.

'Why not?'

Because the dancer hadn't turned her on, the way Guy Lefèvre did. There hadn't been the chemistry—on either side. 'Let's just say I would've needed a Y chromosome for it to work,' she said drily.

Guy raised an eyebrow. 'Nicely put.'

'Maybe. I'm sorry. My mouth runs away with me. Thank you for the water.'

'Pleasure.' But he didn't move away and start circulating, as she'd expected. He sat down with her.

This should be relaxing. It was the first time she'd sat down since the jazz trio started playing. But it felt as if she were sitting on hot coals. She couldn't stop fidgeting.

'What's the matter, Amber?' he asked softly.

'Nothing.'

'Liar.'

She took a deep breath. 'How many more times do I have to apologise to you?'

'You don't.' He sighed, set his glass down and took her hand, pulling her to her feet. 'Come on.'

'What—you want to dance again?'

'It's noisy in here.' In silence, he shepherded her away from the marquee and the dancing, to the peace of the rose garden.

This was bad, Amber thought. Very bad. Leaving a wedding party before the bride and groom was incredibly rude—unless things were different in France, which she somehow doubted. And if anyone had noticed, it meant she'd have a lot of explaining to do tomorrow.

'Dance with me here,' he said softly.

She could still hear the music from the jazz trio, but here it was muted. Soft and dreamy and incredibly lovely. And the air was filled with the scent of roses. How could she resist stepping into his arms?

One of Guy's hands was splayed across the bare skin between her shoulders. His touch made her skin tingle—and she wanted more. Much more. She found herself moving closer, wrapping her arms tightly round him. His cheek was pressed against hers, and Amber wasn't sure which of them moved, but then his lips were brushing the corner of her mouth. Like gossamer, but it lit a fire deep inside her.

She kissed him back, still keeping it light.

In return, his mouth turned coaxing, drawing a line of tiny, nibbling kisses all the way along her lower lip.

With a small sigh of pleasure, she opened her mouth to let him deepen the kiss. And it was like nothing else she'd ever experienced. Nobody she'd ever kissed before had made her feel literally weak at the knees, making her hold onto him for dear life. Every stroke of his tongue, every touch of his skin against hers, stoked the desire higher and higher. Wanting more, she couldn't help pressing against him, shifting her stance slightly so that he could slide one thigh between hers—just as he'd done when they'd danced the tango, except this time there was no audience. Just the two of them.

Then he pulled back. 'This probably isn't a good idea.'

'No, it isn't,' she agreed.

'Tell me to stop.' He hooked his thumb into the strap of her dress and bared her shoulder before nibbling his way along it.

'I can't.' She undid his cravat, then the top three buttons of his shirt, and pressed her mouth against his throat in a hot, wet, demanding kiss.

'Amber.' His voice was husky. 'Last warning. Tell me to stop.'

She undid his waistcoat, then finished undoing his shirt. 'Go,' she whispered.

In response, Guy scooped her up into his arms and carried her into the house.

CHAPTER THREE

GUY paused at the top of the stairs, set her on her feet, backed her against the wall and kissed her again. Thoroughly. By the time he broke the kiss, Amber's knees felt decidedly weak, and she was forced to cling to the front of his shirt to hold herself up.

His gaze was hot and intense as he touched the backs of his fingers against her cheek. '*Alors, mon ange,*' he said, his voice low and soft and incredibly sexy. 'In the rose garden, I gave you the chance to stop. This really *is* your last warning. If we don't stop now, I'm going to take you to my bed.'

'I'd rather that was a promise than a threat.'

'A promise of what?'

'Pleasure. For both of us. Just for tonight.' She took a deep breath. 'I'm a disaster area when it comes to relationships. But there's a spark between you and me, and the way you danced with me…I can't ignore that.'

'I'm not exactly good at relationships, myself,' Guy told her. 'And I'm not looking to get involved with anyone.'

'Right. So we both know where we stand.' She stood on tiptoe, and pressed her mouth lightly against his. Nibbled his lower lip.

He gave an exclamation of what sounded like mingled

need and frustration, and kissed her back, his mouth hot and sweet and demanding.

Then he took her hand and led her to the end of the corridor. Not to her room, she noticed: he took her to his.

It turned out to be similar to hers, with a huge old-fashioned half-tester bed covered in pure white bed-linen. The walls were painted teal, and the heavy damask curtains were a similar shade, lightened with cream voile; there were rugs scattered across the polished wooden floor, and a landscape painting hung on one wall.

No doubt in some of the rooms there would be portraits of his ancestors—men in eighteenth-century costume who looked exactly like Guy, with those same amazing blue eyes and that sun-kissed hair.

And who knew? Maybe one of them had danced with a woman at a wedding, and the attraction had been so strong that he'd carried her up the stairs to this very same bed…

'Are you still sure you want to do this?' Guy asked softly.

She trailed a forefinger down his chest. He really could've been a model for one of his own perfume ads. Muscular without being overdeveloped, his skin burnished to gold by the sun and beautiful enough to make any woman want to reach out and touch him. 'Absolutely. I had these pictures in my head when you danced the tango with me,' she admitted softly.

His gaze was scorching. 'I hope they're the same pictures that were in mine.'

She did, too. 'There's only one way to find out.'

His response was to kiss her hard.

And then he took the pins from her hair, one by one, and laid them on his dressing table. He combed through her hair with his fingers, and nodded in satisfaction as it fell past her shoulders. 'I like that. And your hair's so soft. So silky.' He wound a strand round his finger, then released it again. *'Ravissante.'*

When he spoke in his own language, it was incredibly sexy. She licked her lower lip, wanting him to kiss her again; but instead he took her clothes off, very, very slowly. So slowly that it made her ache with need and want to push his hands away so she could rip them off, then rip off his own clothes and guide him into her body.

But Guy was being thorough. Methodical. Paying attention to the little details. A tiny mole on her shoulder, the crease of skin on her elbow, the softness of her curves. Almost as if he were learning her shape with his mouth and his hands. He unzipped her dress with incredible slowness and patience—and then let it drop on the floor while he stroked her skin.

'I love this lacy stuff. It's gorgeous. Like you.' He traced the edge of her camisole top with the tip of his forefinger. 'But it has to go, Amber. I need you naked. And I really, really need to be inside you.'

Oh-h-h.

She wanted that, too. So desperately.

He slipped one spaghetti strap down over her shoulder and kissed her bare skin. She closed her eyes and tipped her head back in offering to him; he took the hint and kissed a line across her throat, pausing to tease the spot where her pulse beat crazily, then moved to the other shoulder, nuzzling her skin. His hands rested lightly on her waist, and the heat of his mouth against her skin was driving her mad. By the time he'd stripped her down to just her lacy knickers, she was quivering.

He looked gorgeous, with his shirt and waistcoat open and his cravat undone, but she needed to do more than just look. She needed to touch. To feel. To explore him, the same way he'd just explored her. Curve for curve, touch for touch.

'You're wearing too much,' she said shakily.

'I'm in your hands.'

The waistcoat went first, and then she pushed the soft cotton of his shirt off his shoulders, tracing the line of his collarbone as she did so. His skin felt glorious, soft and smooth, and there was just the right amount of chest hair to be sexy; she couldn't resist trailing her fingers across it.

'You have lovely hands,' he said, his eyes darkening. Giving her permission to go further.

She undid the button at the waistband of his trousers, and ran her fingers across his flat abdomen. 'Very nice.'

'*Merci*, Mademoiselle Wynne.' His voice was full of amusement.

She felt the colour flood into her cheeks. 'I didn't mean to say that aloud.'

'I'm glad you did.' He traced a lazy circle round her navel. 'You feel nice, too. Warm and soft. And I'm so going to enjoy exploring you, Amber.'

She was going to enjoy it, too. Given the way he'd danced with her in public, she had a feeling that his private love-making was likely to blow her mind.

She undid his zip, and gently drew the material down to his thighs; his trousers fell to the floor and he stepped out of them, kicking off his shoes and removing his socks as he did so. His erection was very obvious through the soft jersey of his boxer shorts and her mouth went dry.

'Whatever I said earlier, you can still change your mind, *mon ange*,' he said softly.

She shook her head. 'I want you, Guy. It's just...' Her breath hitched. How could she explain?

'I know, *chérie*. It's the same for me. Unexpected.' He

brushed his mouth gently against hers. 'This is just between you and me. Nothing to do with anyone else. No guilt, no worries—just pleasure.'

Pleasure.

Oh, it would be that, all right. For both of them.

He pushed the duvet aside, lifted her up and settled her against the pillows. The white linen was soft and smooth against her skin—seriously expensive high thread-count, she recognised—and the pillows were decadently soft.

Guy hooked his thumbs into the sides of her lacy knickers and gently drew the material down. Amber lifted her bottom slightly to help him remove them; and then she was completely naked in front of him and shyness washed over her.

'I'm going to look at you, *mon ange*,' Guy murmured, correctly reading her expression, 'because you're beautiful. And then I'm going to taste you. And then…' He gave her a lazy grin. 'Then, I'm going to blow your mind.'

'Is that a promise, rather than a threat?' she asked huskily.

'*Absolument*. And—just so you know—I always keep my promises, Amber.'

He teased her nipples with the pad of his thumb; she could feel them tightening and hardening under his touch. Then he leaned forward and took one into his mouth, sucking hard. His mouth was hot against her flesh, making her arch towards him and slide her fingers in his hair. This was good, but she wanted more. Much, much more.

He kissed his way down over her abdomen, and suddenly Amber forgot how to breathe. Was he going to…?

He shifted to kneel between her legs, rocked back on his haunches and gave her a truly wicked grin, one that sent her pulse rocketing. Then he started at her ankle and kissed all the way up; clearly he was paying attention to what made her arch towards him and what made her catch her breath, because he did the same with the other leg.

By the time his mouth was idling along her thigh, she was practically whimpering, her hands fisted in his hair. 'Guy, please…' The words came out as a needy little moan, but it had been months since she'd last had this kind of relief, and nobody had ever made her feel quite this abandoned before.

She felt the long, slow stroke of his tongue along her sex. He swirled the tip round her clitoris, teasing her, and she pushed hard against him, demanding more. He gave her exactly what she needed, varying the pace and pressure so her arousal coiled tighter and tighter and tighter, until she didn't think she could bear it any more. She was babbling his name when her climax exploded through her, more intense than she'd ever thought possible.

This shouldn't have been so good. Not for a first time. It should've been clumsy and embarrassing and faintly disappointing.

But she had a feeling that Guy Lefèvre was no ordinary man.

He shifted up the bed and drew her into his arms, holding her close. 'Better now, *mon ange*?' he asked softly.

She nodded, not trusting herself to speak.

'Good, but that was only the start. To take the edge off.' His eyes were intense. 'Now, it really begins.'

That definitely sounded like a promise.

And Guy had said he was a man who prided himself on keeping his promises.

Almost shyly, she removed his boxer shorts, then sucked in a breath. 'Guy, you're truly beautiful.'

He actually blushed, to her secret pleasure. 'I think that's the first time anyone's told me that.'

She kissed the corner of his mouth. 'And I really,

really want to make love with you.' She stole another kiss. 'Right now.'

He reached over to the drawer in the table next to his bed and removed a foil packet.

She curled her fingers round his. 'My job, I believe.' Gently, she took the condom from him, unwrapped it and rolled it onto him. In response, Guy kissed her hard—and then rolled so that he was lying on his back. He drew her with him so that she was straddling him, and then fitted the tip of his penis to her entrance with one hand and rested the other on her hip, urging her to bear down on him.

God, this felt good. Really, really good.

She moved over him, seeing his eyes darken with pleasure as she lifted and lowered herself; they darkened even more when she tensed her muscles round him.

'Do you like that?' she whispered.

He gave her a slow, sensual smile. 'What do you think, *mon ange*?'

'I think,' she said, 'I want to blow your mind the way you just blew mine.'

'Then do it,' he said, his voice fierce.

She leaned forward to kiss him, nibbling at his lower lip until he opened his mouth and let her deepen the kiss. And then she began to move again, driving them both hard, slowing down so it was like an exquisite torment, then hard again. She could feel her climax rising again, and it shocked her; she'd never come twice so quickly before. Everything in her body seemed to tighten; and, as she hit the peak, she felt his body tense beneath her hands. He sat up and jammed his mouth over hers, kissing her hard as they both came; she held onto him for dear life as wave after wave of sensation swept through her.

Afterwards, he held her close, stroking her hair. 'You have amazing hair. It's the first thing I noticed about you.'

He tangled his fingers in her curls. 'I love these. So soft and silky. And they're natural, yes?'

She nodded. 'I hated it when I was a teenager; my hair would never do what anyone else's did. I even resorted to ironing it, once.'

'Ironing it?'

'That was in the days before you could buy decent hair straighteners. And I kept it straight for quite a while.'

'I'm glad you don't now. This is too glorious to be reined in.' He kissed her swiftly. 'I'd better deal with the condom.'

Which was her cue to leave. 'And I'd better go.'

'Why?' he asked.

'Because it'll be just my luck that I'll bump into someone as I go back to my room, hair all over the place and lipstick kissed away and clothes all crumpled. It'll be so, so obvious what I've just been doing—and, after the way you danced with me tonight, with whom.'

'And that's a problem?'

'Yes.' He'd called her shameless, but she wasn't a tart. 'Look, I know everyone thinks I'm an airhead party girl, but I don't normally sleep with someone until I've known them for a while. And I definitely don't sleep with someone I'm not even dating.'

'There's a way round that,' he said.

Her heart skipped a beat. Was he going to ask her to start dating him?

'Spend the night with me,' he said. 'And we'll get up earlier than everyone else to avoid them. They'll all be exhausted after partying half the night and will sleep in—and those who aren't won't be in the château anyway. They'll be outside in the marquee, waiting for their onion soup.'

'Onion soup? You have to be kidding.'

'The dancing at French weddings goes on until

dawn—and then we have breakfast. Traditionally, in France, it's onion soup—though Allie says she wants to make it Anglo-French and have the option of bacon sandwiches.'

She stared at him in disbelief. 'This has to be the most surreal conversation I've ever had in my life.'

'If I were a true gentleman, *mon ange*,' he said, 'I'd ask you to start dating me. But my life's complicated, right now—I don't need a relationship to make it worse.'

She lifted her chin. 'I don't need a relationship, either. I wasn't fishing.'

'I know you weren't, and I'm making a mess of this.' He sighed. 'Actually, I was hoping to persuade you to come and have a shower with me.'

'A guided tour of your personal bathroom, hmm?'

'A personal tour.' He stole a kiss. 'Very personal.'

'Just so we're clear about it,' she said, 'this is *just* sex, and it's just for tonight, and then it'll be out of our systems, and nobody has to know about it.' And then hopefully she'd be able to look at him without wanting to rip his clothes off.

'That's *a lot* of sex,' he corrected, 'but the rest of it, agreed. It's between you and me.'

'Good.' She licked her lower lip. 'So show me this fabulous bathroom of yours...'

CHAPTER FOUR

AMBER woke, slightly disoriented for a moment; and then the memories of the previous night slammed back in.

She was in bed. Specifically, in Guy Lefèvre's bed. And right now his body was wrapped round hers.

What an idiot she was, jumping into bed with a man she barely knew. Last night's bravado was all gone; this morning, she felt cheap and nasty.

First things first: she needed to wriggle out of his arms, without waking him; find where her clothes were; tiptoe out of his room, still without waking him; and then have a shower and clean her teeth, before facing him.

And then she'd drive herself to the airport.

She could probably skip the 'facing him' step and leave him a note…but that would be even tackier. No, she had to be brave about this. Face up to her mistakes. And hope that somehow *Celebrity Life* wouldn't find out about it and crow about how Bambi had seduced the best man at her friend's wedding. She didn't want Allie and Xav dragged through the mud next to her—or Guy. That wouldn't be fair.

Slowly, carefully, she moved his fingers away from her waist, and then his palm. She'd just freed herself from his arms and wriggled to the side of the bed when she heard him say, *'Bonjour, mon ange.'*

There was nothing she could do now except brazen it out. She sat up and faced him. And oh, he looked good, still rumpled from sleep and with a faint shadowing of stubble. She damped down the surge of desire, knowing how inappropriate it was: they'd agreed that last night was one night only. 'Good morning, Guy. Sorry. I was trying not to wake you.'

'Running out on me?'

'No.' She frowned. 'I was going to have a shower and then face you.'

'You know where my bathroom is.'

Yes—and the shower in which they'd made love last night. Twice. 'That isn't what I meant.' She sighed, sat up and tucked the duvet carefully round her to cover her breasts.

Guy propped himself up on one elbow, looked up at her and laughed.

'What?'

'I think the modest maiden bit might be a little out of place, after last night.'

She felt the colour rush into her face. 'Last night was last night. This morning's different.' She dragged in a breath. 'OK, let's get it over with. I'm sorry for flinging myself at you. I'm trying to break myself of my unsuitable-man habit.'

'But?'

God, he was relentless. 'You were the most gorgeous man at the wedding, and you know it.'

'Actually, I didn't know it,' he corrected, sitting up. 'But thank you for the compliment.'

'If you'd scowled all evening like you did the first time I met you, I could've resisted you.'

'You started it. "Bite me,"' he quoted.

Amber discovered that it was physically possible to blush harder. 'You provoked me.'

'We could agree that we're both as bad as the other,' he suggested.

She sighed. 'Maybe. But, just so you know, I don't usually jump into bed with someone I don't know very well. In fact, you're the first. And I don't want you thinking I'm some kind of cheap—'

He stopped her words very effectively, by leaning over and kissing her swiftly on the mouth. 'You're not cheap. You're high-maintenance.'

'I can maintain myself, thank you very much,' she said, her eyes narrowing. She didn't like where this was going. 'And if you dare offer me—'

He kissed her again to shut her up. 'Why are we fighting?'

'Because you're laughing at me.'

'I'm not laughing at you.' He sighed. 'Are you one of these people who are a complete nightmare in the mornings until you've had a cup of coffee? Because, if you are, I suggest you curl back up under the duvet and I'll go and get you some coffee. And then you don't talk until the caffeine's kicked in.'

'I—' She wasn't. Her friends were all disgusted that Amber could burn the candle quite happily at both ends with no ill effects. It was just *Guy* making her grouchy and out of sorts. Unsettling her.

'Right. Coffee,' he said, and slid out of bed.

He was still completely naked—and unselfconscious about it. Last night, she'd thought he was beautiful. This morning...she still thought he was the most beautiful man she'd ever met. Perfect.

And he'd just said he was going to fetch coffee. Surely he didn't mean...? 'You can't go downstairs naked.'

He shrugged. 'It's my house.'

'Guy—' Her voice came out as a panicky croak. How had she ever thought she could handle a man like this?

And then he grinned. 'You really do need coffee, *mon ange*. I was teasing you. Of course I'm not going downstairs naked. It would hardly be fair to shock the wedding guests.'

But all he did was pull on his trousers—which were obviously creased, as if he'd removed them in a hurry and hadn't bothered hanging them up. Which was, she thought, exactly what had happened. They'd been in such a rush to go to bed with each other that nothing else had mattered except being skin to skin.

He remained barefoot, his hair was rumpled, his face was covered in stubble and he looked utterly louche. Sexy as hell. Desire surged through her entire body, to the point where she almost slid out of bed and started walking towards him.

'Go back to sleep. Coffee's on its way,' he said, and walked out of the room.

No way could she possibly go back to sleep.

She slid out of bed to retrieve her clothes, and groaned. Her dress was impossibly creased. Even a steam cleaner might have problems getting that lot out. And it was her favourite dress. Cross with herself, she hung it carefully over the back of the chair next to Guy's dressing table. And then there was her underwear. She didn't want to put on the clothes she'd worn the day before, so they were out, too. Hopefully Guy would be kind enough to lend her a T-shirt or something, and then she could make a run for it from his room to hers and cross her fingers that nobody came out into the corridor and realised she was wearing nothing at all underneath the T-shirt.

But she'd learned her lesson about making assumptions,

where Guy was concerned; she wasn't going to raid his wardrobe until she'd asked.

In the meantime, there was one thing she could wear to make herself decent. She went into the bathroom, took a towel off the heated rail and tucked it round herself, sarong-style. A glance in the mirror told her that her hair was wild, way beyond control—she'd have to spend a good half an hour combing the knots out. Not to mention using a whole bottle of detangling lotion. She made one attempt at combing through it with her fingers, and winced as she pulled hair from the roots. Not good.

At the same time as she emerged from the bathroom, Guy walked back in with a tray containing a cafetière, two mugs, a jug of milk and a bowl of sugar. 'Very fetching,' he said drily, setting the tray down on his dressing table.

'I don't exactly have a lot of sartorial choice, right now,' she said, scowling.

'Coffee,' he said. 'Please don't talk any more until you've drunk some coffee. Use sign language.'

She did—very pointedly—but he just laughed and ignored it. 'Milk?'

She nodded, bringing her thumb and first finger together to indicate just a tiny amount.

'Sugar?'

A definite shake of the head.

He poured coffee into two mugs, added milk to both and handed one to her. 'Drink, and don't say a word until you're human again.'

She already *was* human. He was the problem, not her. But she subsided and drank her coffee.

'Better?' he asked when she'd finished.

'Not much,' she said, deciding that coming clean was probably the best policy. 'I hate this morning-after awkwardness. I don't know what to say, other than that I'm embarrassed and I feel lousy.'

'If it helps,' he said, 'you don't look lousy.'

She narrowed her eyes at him. 'I wasn't fishing for a compliment. I know perfectly well that my hair's all over the place—and it'll take ages to get all the knots out.'

'Is that what's bothering you?' He placed his mug on the tray and walked into his bathroom. He came out wielding a comb. 'Right. Come and sit here, and I'll get the knots out for you.'

'Thank you for the offer,' she said politely, 'but I'd rather do it myself.'

'Scared I'm going to rip your hair out by the roots?'

'Since you ask, yes. Curly hair is a nightmare. I'll need a ton of detangler to deal with this.'

'I once knew someone like you,' Guy said. 'She had hair exactly like yours. And I learned very quickly how to get knots out of her hair before she started throwing things.'

Amber blinked. 'I don't throw things.' And then the full force of his words hit her. 'You slept with me last night because I look like someone you once dated?' So much for thinking it wasn't possible to feel any worse. Now she felt third-rate, a poor substitute.

'No. I slept with you because you were dancing with the children.'

She shook her head in disbelief. 'You're seriously screwed up.'

He just laughed and patted the bed next to him. 'Come and sit here. I promise I won't hurt you. And you won't need detangler.'

'Yeah, right,' she muttered, but went and sat next to him.

To her surprise, he was incredibly gentle, and she barely felt the pull as he painstakingly combed out the knots.

'You lit up everyone at the wedding last night,' he said softly. 'I was watching you. You weren't flirting with anyone or expecting anyone to wait on you hand and foot. You were making sure that everyone was having a good time. You spent time with the great-aunts and -uncles, making them feel important, and you spent time with the kids, making them feel part of what was going on. Even the shy ones—you made the effort to sit and chat to them. Your warmth is irresistible. *That's* why I slept with you.'

She couldn't say a word; there was a huge lump in her throat.

'That,' he said, 'and the fact that I couldn't get you out of my head for the whole day. Bearing in mind that I've dealt with a few perfume ad campaigns, in my time, I mean it when I say that you're the most stunning woman I've ever seen. And I wanted you, very badly.'

As much as she'd wanted him. With a desperate hunger that had made her act much more recklessly than she usually did—whatever the press might say about her, she didn't usually leap straight into bed with someone she barely knew. This was a first.

'Just so you know.' He dropped a fleeting kiss on her shoulder, and she had to stop herself turning round and sliding her arms round his neck and pressing a kiss to his mouth. Last night was gone. Today was a new day and a new deal.

'OK, your hair's done.'

She moved away, and then turned to face him. 'Thank you. For looking after me just now. And for what you just said.' She dragged in a breath. 'And I'm sorry I was grouchy.'

'*Ça ne fait rien*. So, what now?'

She shrugged. 'I don't know. We said that last night was a one-off.' Even though she was aware that she'd like it to be more than just one night. Guy Lefèvre was full of surprises. Like being able to get the knots out of her hair without hurting her; like the fact he'd noticed what she was good at. Like the fact he wasn't treating her like a cheap tart.

There was something about him. Something she couldn't define, but something that was different from the men she usually dated. He intrigued her. And she wanted to know more.

'So you're going back to England?'

She spread her hands. 'I was originally planning to spend a few days in St Tropez. But Allie's been telling me how gorgeous it is in the Ardèche, so I thought I might take a look around, do the touristy stuff. So if you have any suggestions about places I should visit and good places to stay, now would be a good time. Otherwise I'll check things out on the Internet, and pick somewhere to stay that takes my fancy as I drive round.'

Guy looked at her. This was his cue to suggest somewhere on the far side of the Ardèche. And for him to drive straight back to Grasse and bury himself in work at the perfume house—to put as much distance between them as he could.

But a mad impulse made him say, 'You could stay here.'

'Given what happened last night,' she said carefully, 'is that a good idea?'

No. It wasn't. 'I meant as a base. Not…' Oh, hell. How could he put this without it sounding insulting?

'Message understood,' she said, surprising him. 'But, if I'm going to be your ho[illegible]'ll let me take you out to din[illegible]ng a host gift.'

'Yes, I do. I'm not a freeloader, you know.'

He blinked. 'I never said you were.'

'Yesterday, you said I was shameless.'

He shrugged. 'You asked me for donations to your charity-ball tombola. How many other people did you ask?'

'That's irrelevant.'

'So you did ask others.'

She lifted her chin. 'It's for a good cause.'

'You're very defensive.'

'Are you surprised?' She sighed. 'Maybe it's not a good idea for me to stay. We'll fight.'

'I'm sorry.'

She looked surprised. 'You're apologising to me?'

He smiled. 'Where we're concerned, it's usually the other way round. Make the most of it.'

'So I can ask you to make it up to me,' she said thoughtfully.

'Name your terms.' He kept his voice light, but his heart rate had speeded up a notch. Was she going to ask for a kiss? And would they end up back between those crumpled sheets, driving each other on to deepest pleasure?

'Could you lend me a T-shirt for about three minutes, please?'

He blinked at the unexpected request. 'A T-shirt?'

She gestured to her dress. 'It's so badly creased, I can't wear it. So, unless you want me to scandalise your guests by running naked from your room to mine, I need something to wear. Look, I'll wash and iron it before I return it, if you like.'

He [illegible] ...ver ironed a thing in your li[illegible]

fingers. 'You helped out in the kitchen, the night of the barbecue. But you don't iron, do you?'

'All right, I use a laundry service. And I have someone come in to clean for me.' She put her hands on her hips and glared at him. 'Satisfied?'

He raised an eyebrow. 'I'm just wondering what a party girl does all day.' Did she spend her days the way that Véra had?

Her eyes narrowed. 'I have lunch with my friends, I go shopping and I giggle while we paint each other's nails.'

'Nope. Apart from the fact that you don't giggle, I think you'd be bored doing just that.'

'So what do you think I do all day?' she challenged.

'I think you spend half the week planning and schmoozing and talking people into doing things for your charity stuff, and the other half going out to lunch, the cinema and the theatre with your friends. Oh, and partying, of course.'

She spread her hands. 'Busted. Though I do like shopping. Especially for shoes,' she added. 'So may I borrow a T-shirt, please?'

'I think seeing you wearing just a T-shirt would put any male around here in heart failure,' Guy said, heading for the bathroom. He took his bathrobe from the back of the door. 'Try this.'

She took it, smiling gratefully at him.

'And you don't have to wash it before you give it back,' he added with a grin.

She gave him a speaking look—then, to his surprise, she stood up, untucked the towel and dropped it.

He was definitely having trouble breathing when she gave him a seriously saucy grin, then shrugged on his bathrobe and tied the belt round her waist. 'That's what you get for being cheeky,' she said.

A surge of desire rendered him temporarily speechless, and by the time he'd thought up a suitable retort she'd kissed him lightly on the cheek, scooped up her clothes and vanished—leaving the towel defiantly on the floor.

He sat back on the bed. Amber Wynne intrigued him and annoyed him in equal measures. She was a party girl and a spoiled media darling—and yet there was more to her than that. And last night had felt like nothing he'd ever known. That mad, hot, sweet intensity, the way she'd responded to his touch, the way she'd explored him and found out just what drove him wild…

If things were different, he'd definitely be dating her. Though he'd be taking it much, much more slowly than they had last night.

He must have been out of his mind, offering to let her stay here. How the hell was he going to sleep, knowing that she was at the other end of the corridor? He didn't even have the comfort of his lab to distract him, right now: only the endless search for someone who could help him fix the problem. A search that he was beginning to think might be fruitless, and the idea that he might never be able to work again at the job he loved so much ripped him to shreds. What use was a parfumier who couldn't smell? He'd have to do something else. Sure, he was capable of turning his hand to something else, but his heart wouldn't be involved any more. So it wouldn't be living: it would be mere existence.

What was that old Chinese curse? *May you live in interesting times.*

The next few days were certainly going to be interesting.

CHAPTER FIVE

WRAPPED in Guy's fluffy navy bathrobe, Amber could smell his citrussy scent all the way to her room; it was as if his arms were wrapped round her and her face were pillowed against his chest, the way it had been last night. Comforting.

And that in itself was scary. Since when did she need a man to comfort her or make her feel protected?

She really couldn't work Guy out. He owned the château and a perfume house, so he was financially on equal terms with the men she usually dated—but he wasn't like them. He didn't have that hard edge. She couldn't pigeonhole him as a financier who liked dancing until dawn or a lawyer who liked the best tables at the best restaurants.

Guy Lefèvre had a lot more facets to him, and maybe that was what was throwing her. What was drawing her to him.

He was a generous lover and he had a huge reservoir of kindness; he'd been patient enough to work all the knots out of her hair this morning without complaint and without hurting her. Yet he was also the man who'd been so angry with her in the rose garden for picking a single rose. The same man who'd made it very clear that he wasn't looking for a relationship; and yet he'd offered to let her stay here while she was looking round the area.

As a base, not…

Yeah, she knew. She was the kind of girl that men wanted to snog but not marry. A good-time party girl. And that was fine, because she didn't particularly want to get married and settle down. Or, if she did, it'd be to someone from her own world. Her parents were a shining example of what not to do: they'd been from totally different worlds and they'd been really unhappy together. But when her father had remarried—to a lawyer, someone who understood the business circles he moved in—he'd become settled and happy. Her mother, who was on her fourth husband, was rather less so; or maybe that was just Hollywood, Amber thought, because celeb marriages were lived so much in the spotlight that they often couldn't handle the strain.

Pushing the thoughts from her head, Amber showered swiftly, moisturised her skin, put her hair back in a pony-tail, and changed into black jeans and a hot-pink strappy top. She had the perfect shoes: shiny, platform-soled sti-lettos in the same colour as her top, with the tiniest strap around her ankle. A spritz of Chanel No 5 and a touch of sheer lipstick, and she was ready to face the world.

And if anyone said anything about her disappearing act last night…well, she'd just give an enigmatic smile. With a smile, you could get through anything.

Guy had said something about breakfast for the wedding guests in the marquee. She still wasn't sure whether he'd been teasing her, but if it turned out that he had she could always bluff it and say she'd wanted some fresh air.

As soon as she rounded the corner of the garden, she knew he'd been telling the truth. About the onion soup, too; several guests were tucking into bowls of the stuff.

Xav and Allie were there, still in their wedding finery; though Amber was relieved to see that neither of them was eating soup.

'We all thought you'd be the last one standing. What happened to you last night?' Allie teased.

The man sitting at your table happened to me, Amber thought; but wild horses wouldn't drag the admission from her. The way Guy was dressed, he looked even more gorgeous than he had the previous night. Faded, soft denims and a black cashmere sweater—and he looked utterly touchable. It was all she could do not to march over and grab him and jam her mouth over his.

'Bambi?' Allie looked worried. 'Are you all right?'

'Bit of a headache.' That was real enough. 'Too much champagne,' she fibbed.

Allie looked relieved. 'Sounds like you need a bacon sandwich.'

'Cake would be better. The best hangover cure ever is cake,' Amber said.

'You're telling me that you eat cake for *breakfast*?' Guy asked, looking shocked.

She wasn't going to let him see that he rattled her. Right now, she was Bambi Wynne, Party Girl, and she was going to do what she did best: she was going to *shine*. 'Leftover pudding is even better. If you haven't had pavlova or chocolate bread-and-butter pudding for breakfast, you haven't lived.'

Guy raised his eyebrow. 'So that makes us all zombies, does it?'

'Speak for yourself, sweetie.' She blew him a kiss. 'I'm going to get myself some coffee.'

'No need. There's a jug here.' To her shock, he shifted over and made room for her.

Sitting next to him would scramble her brains. But refusing to sit there would make everyone else ask questions. Caught between a rock and a hard place, she thought ruefully, and sat next to him.

He took a clean mug from the tray in the middle of the table, and poured coffee into it for her. 'I don't know how you like it,' he said.

Her eyes met his. Liar. He knew exactly how she liked it.

Coffee *and* sex.

Without missing a beat, he added, 'So help yourself to milk.'

'*Merci*, Monsieur Guy,' she said sweetly, and shifted her foot so she could press her heel into his toe.

'That's going to cost you later,' he murmured, *sotto voce*, before adding in a louder tone, 'So you seriously eat pudding for breakfast?'

'She reads menus backwards, too,' Allie said. 'There was one occasion when she met me for lunch—I was trying to persuade her to come and do event management for me, so I went along with what she ordered. Except she ordered two puddings and no main course.'

Amber spread her hands. 'What can I say? I have a sweet tooth.'

'But you don't take sugar in your coffee?' Guy asked. 'That's contradictory.'

'Don't be mean, Guy,' Xavier said. 'Amber, just ignore my little brother. He's a nerdy scientist with no social skills.'

'Says the nerdy vigneron whose wife needs to teach him some social skills,' Guy retorted with a grin.

When the waiter came over with a pile of bacon sandwiches, Guy said something swiftly that Amber couldn't catch to translate. If he'd ordered her a bowl of onion soup, she thought, it'd end up in his lap.

Two minutes later, the waiter reappeared with a bowl of lemon tart and a jug of cream. 'Mademoiselle?' he said with a smile. '*Pour vous.*'

Guy said nothing, though his eyes had crinkled round the corners. And it warmed her that he'd gone to the trouble to ask for this for her.

'*Merci,*' she said to the waiter. 'And thank you, too, Guy.'

He'd been calling her bluff. But she amazed him by eating every scrap, with gusto. His ex-wife had never touched puddings, or anything else containing carbs, and she'd counted every single gram of fat; whereas Amber had poured cream quite happily over the lemon tart.

He really couldn't work Amber out. She appeared dedicated purely to pleasure. She'd even turned down an offer of working with Allie—which he found odd, because event management would've suited Amber very well. Organising things and charming people, with a smiley public face: they were all her strengths. She could've made a fantastic career out of it, and yet she chose to organise events for nothing. For fun. Though she'd admitted to him last night that it was also for a cause very close to her heart, so clearly there was a serious side to her. One that he had a feeling she kept hidden from most people.

And then there were her shoes.

When she'd come strutting round the corner, in those crazy shoes, he'd wanted to leave the table, scoop her up and carry her back to his bed, the way he'd done the previous night.

Having her stay here wasn't going to be good for his blood pressure. Or his peace of mind. If they hadn't been surrounded by wedding guests, he wouldn't have been able to resist bending his head and licking off that tiny smear of cream on the corner of her mouth.

Oh, for pity's sake. Hadn't he learned from his mistakes with Véra? Clearly not, because Amber was from the same world. Celebrity parties, premières, her life lived through the camera lens and splashed across magazines. As a nerdy scientist, Guy hadn't fitted into that scene. At all. He'd loathed the intrusiveness of the gossip pages and the paparazzi—so what was he doing, letting himself dally with someone who was perfectly at home with that kind of attention and probably even courted it?

He needed to put the brakes on, right now.

'That was perfect,' Amber said. She smiled, and leaned back in her chair. 'The perfect pleasure. And life is all about pleasure.'

'That might be a good name for your new perfume, Guy,' Xavier said. 'Pleasure.'

The name of Guy's perfume was still under wraps, even from his brother and his business partner. And how strange that the pet name he'd found himself calling Amber was so close to it. 'I'm still thinking about the name,' Guy said lightly.

'Joy would be good, too,' Amber added.

Guy shook his head. 'That name was taken back in nineteen thirty.'

'Really?' She looked surprised.

'Patou's Joy is one of the most famous, uplifting fragrances ever. It's a great name, but I can't rip it off.'

'Don't argue with him, Amber,' Allie said. 'He has an encyclopaedic memory and can tell you who designed the scent, what all the notes are and probably who designed the bottle.'

'Well, hey. I wouldn't be much of a parfumier if I couldn't.' And he probably wouldn't be one for much longer. Guy forced himself to damp down the fear. Not now, not here. Wait until he was in his lab and wouldn't be disturbed. Then he could check the Internet and see if any new research had turned up in the last two days. See if anyone was running any kind of medical trials, maybe, where he would be a suitable candidate for treatment. There had to be something. Science moved on all the time. He wasn't the only one in the world who'd suffered from anosmia; someone, somewhere, would be investigating the problem and someone, somewhere, would have answers. He just had to find that one person and everything would be all right again.

After breakfast, Allie and Xavier changed and left for Paris; everyone waved them off from the front of the château. During the morning, the rest of the wedding guests drifted away, and workmen came to take down the marquee. Guy had disappeared too, so, after making coffee for herself and the team dealing with the marquee, Amber sat at the table on the terrace overlooking the garden, armed with paper, a pen and her mobile phone, and began looking up local beauty spots on the Internet.

An hour later, Guy emerged from his lab to make himself a coffee. Looking through the kitchen window, he could see Amber ensconced on the terrace, making notes of some kind. Might as well make her a drink at the same time, he thought, and carried a mug out to her.

She was definitely making notes; but what amused him was that she was clearly replying to a stream of texts with her left hand while she wrote notes with her right. Definitely a multi-tasker, then. And he'd just bet that all the texts were from her party-girl friends. And that they'd all be written in textspeak—something he loathed utterly.

Deciding not to disturb her, he placed the mug of coffee next to her in silence; but she looked up and smiled at him, sending a rush of heat through his body.

'Thanks, that's really kind of you,' she said.

'*Ça ne fait rien.* It's possibly a bit too cool to use the pool, but feel free if you want to.'

'Thanks.' She gave him another of those smiles, and he had to stop himself wondering what she'd look like in the pool, with her hair spread out around her. Like a mermaid, probably. Sexy as hell, with that kissable mouth pouting up at him.

He stared at the floor, trying to get his thoughts back under control. Bad move. She was still wearing those ridiculous shoes. They were completely impractical. And he couldn't get them out of his head. Or the thoughts of what her feet looked like out of those shoes. How her legs went on for ever. How her legs had felt, wrapped round his body.

'I'll try not to get in your way while I'm staying here,' she said.

She could try, but he had a nasty feeling that it wouldn't make any difference. And an even nastier feeling that even if she weren't staying at the château, he'd still be thinking about her. There was something about her that drew him, caught his attention. 'What are you doing?'

'Planning where I'm going.' She showed him the list. 'What do you think?'

He read it swiftly. The lake at Issarles, the Pont d'Arc, the gorges and the Ray-Pic waterfall. All favourite tourist spots—and some of the most beautiful places on earth. 'You'll enjoy them.'

'Anything else you can think of? The main produce here is wine, yes?'

'And chestnuts, olives and lavender.'

She scribbled more notes. 'Any local specialty foods I should try? Well, obviously apart from chestnuts?'

'Picodon cheese.'

'Right.' She looked thoughtful. 'That dinner I owe you—can it be somewhere they do local dishes?'

'You don't owe me dinner.'

She flapped a dismissive hand. 'We've already argued that and I won.'

She most definitely hadn't won, but he could see that she was set on it. Arguing would get him nowhere. 'When were you thinking?'

'Tonight.'

And he'd need a long, cold shower first, to make sure he kept his hands off her. Especially if she was wearing those shoes. 'I'll book a table. I have things to do this afternoon.'

'Cool. Meet you at your front door at seven? And I'll drive.'

'I'll drive,' he corrected.

'In your monster four-by-four?' she scoffed. 'My hire car's more fun.'

'The four-by-four was Xav's car. I'll bet you mine's more fun than yours.'

'A bet, hmm? What are the stakes?'

For a second, he couldn't breathe.

A kiss.

And he could see the same thought reflected in her eyes. A kiss. His lips parting hers. His tongue duelling against hers. Her naked body pressed against his. Losing himself in her warm, sweet depths.

'No stakes,' he muttered hoarsely. 'Just saying.'

Her phone rang; she looked at it and smiled. 'I'd better answer that. *Ciao*, babe.' She gave him a tiny dismissive wave and then, with incredible insouciance, pressed a button on her phone and started chatting—as if nothing had happened between them just then.

She was going to drive him crazy.

And he really needed that cold shower.

He needed it even more when he saw his bathrobe folded neatly on his bed. Unable to help himself, he brought the material up to his face. Breathed in, even though he knew damn well that he wouldn't be able to smell her scent.

And he was definitely going crazy, because he could've sworn that he smelled roses. A scent that broke his heart.

Dinner.

It had to be a little black dress, then. Even though this wasn't a date, Amber still intended to dress up for it. The pink shoes? No. Too obvious. In the end, she decided to go for the classic look: the black dress, a pair of plain black stilettos and a black pearl choker. She put her hair up again with the white pearl-headed pins—which she'd rescued from Guy's bedroom when she returned his bathrobe—and added a smudge of charcoal eyeliner and a slick of a slightly darker lipstick, for evening wear. She studied her reflection in the mirror. Excellent. She looked businesslike. And this was business, of a sort. *Not* a date.

When she met Guy in the hall, she had to swallow hard. He was dressed in smart-casual, black trousers teamed with a smoky blue cashmere sweater that really brought out the colour of his eyes. His hair looked slightly rumpled, as if he'd been in his mysterious lab and had raked his hair out of his eyes while he was working; and it made her remember how he'd looked this morning, all rumpled and sexy and wearing only a pair of trousers.

Oh, help.

Last night had been a one-off. She was officially off men.

But she knew that all he'd have to do would be crook his little finger and she'd be wrapped right round him, kissing him until they were both dizzy.

She really had to get a grip.

She blinked when he opened the front door for her and she walked out of the château to see the car parked on the gravel drive. Low-slung, sleek and gorgeous, with a soft top.

'Like it?' Guy asked as he opened the passenger door.

'It's OK.'

'Going to admit it's better than yours?'

She sighed. 'All right. It's better. Though it's a bit flash for you.'

He laughed. 'This is my solitary vice.' Then he gave her a sidelong look as he got into the car. 'Well, one of them. I don't have that many.'

Her mouth went dry. She'd found out what one of them was, last night. Something he was seriously good at. And she wished her dress were made of thicker material when her nipples responded to the memory. He couldn't fail to notice.

Well, two could play at flirting. She fluttered her eyelashes. 'I'm not sure I dare ask what the others are.'

'The car's number one. This—' he switched on the stereo, and loud rock music filled the car '—is number two.'

'Dinosaur rock?' She'd had him pegged as a classical fan.

'And number three is—' he paused, until she met his eyes '—off limits.'

Oh, double help.

He knew exactly what he was doing.

Well, if that was the way he wanted to play it… She shifted in her seat so her hemline rose up a bit. And she knew she'd hit the target when he whacked up the volume on the stereo to hide his intake of breath.

He turned it down again when they were on the road out of the village. 'Sorry. Bad habit, listening to loud music. And I guess it wouldn't be your kind of thing.'

'I don't mind this. You can at least sing along with it,' she said.

'Getting middle-aged?' he teased.

'I'm only four months older than you.'

When he said nothing, she glanced at him. 'What?'

'How do you know how old I am?'

'I looked you up on Google. So I also know that you won a huge award at a ridiculously young age, developed a couple of top-selling perfumes for a big name in the perfume industry and then set up your own perfume house, also at a ridiculously young age.' She paused. It had been niggling her all afternoon. And he had to know that if she'd looked him up on the Internet, his divorce would've been one of the biggest stories about him. So there was no point in pussyfooting round it. 'And that you used to be married to a supermodel.'

'Right.'

'She has straight hair, nowadays. And it's blonde. Nothing like mine.'

'Is it?'

Was he really as unbothered as he sounded? Or was that all an act, as she suspected? She sighed. 'I suppose I should be flattered. Or is that why you don't like me?'

'I didn't say I don't like you.'

'You don't have to *say* it.' The way they ended up sniping at each other, it was all too obvious. 'I guess, from the back, we might have looked a bit alike—that's why you were grouchy with me in your rose garden, isn't it?'

Guy blew out a breath. 'Do we have to have this conversation?'

'Yes. Because, actually, I'm a bit annoyed at the thought that you slept with me because of her.'

'I didn't sleep with you because of her.'

'No?' she said. 'You told me you knew someone with

hair like that and she threw things. That's how you learned how to get knots out of hair without detangler spray.'

'You don't look that much like her, not facially,' Guy said. 'Though you're from the same world as her.'

'Which is why you don't want to date me.'

'One of the reasons, yes. It's not my world. I'm not interested in making small talk, or gossiping about other people's love lives. And I don't enjoy living in a goldfish bowl where everything's out of proportion and the unimportant stuff takes over.'

While he had been married to a supermodel, he would certainly have been a target for the paparazzi, she thought. But there was more to her world than just gossip. Then she realised what he'd said first. 'So what are the other reasons?' she asked, suddenly curious.

'I thought you didn't want to date me, either?'

'I don't, because you'd probably think it's only because I know you're loaded and I'd expect you to shower me with expensive presents.' She lifted her chin. 'Just so you know, I have my own flat in London and a trust fund. I pay my own way. And I don't expect men to shower me with presents. Though, if they want to, vice number four is acceptable.'

'Shoes?'

'Chocolate,' she corrected. 'But it has to be *good* chocolate.'

'Just out of interest,' Guy said, sounding incredibly casual, 'why would you want to date me?'

'Shared vices,' she said. 'Specifically, number one.'

'I would've said number three.' Guy's voice was just that little bit deeper.

Suddenly, there wasn't enough air in the car. And she could still remember how he'd felt inside her. How he'd made her feel. All that power, channelled right in on her, pushing her closer and closer to the edge—and holding her as she fell.

She couldn't cope with this. 'Any chance of having the roof down?' She really hoped he couldn't hear the quiver in her voice.

'On a late-September evening?'

'Yes.' Because it would be cold enough to freeze out the hot surge of desire. And it might blow some common sense back into her head.

'Sure.' He pressed a button, and the top folded up.

Between the noise of the road, the noise of the wind and the sound of his stereo, there was no hope of having a conversation. Which was a good thing, Amber decided. She'd already said way too much for comfort, this evening.

What was it about him that threw her like this?

Guy parked outside an unpromising-looking place, put the hood back up and turned off the stereo. The moment that they walked inside the restaurant and Amber smelled the scent of the food, she knew he'd picked somewhere good. 'This place smells gorgeous,' she said.

Was it her imagination, or did he just flinch?

Her imagination, she decided, because then he shrugged.

'The food's pretty good.' And he'd clearly been here before, because the waiter greeted him by name. 'What would you like to drink, Amber?'

'Something soft, please.'

He spread his hands. 'I'm driving, so it's safe for you to drink.'

'I might be a party girl,' Amber said, 'but I do keep an eye on my liver. Sparkling water is just fine, thank you. With a slice of orange, please.'

'Not lemon or lime?' He looked slightly amused. 'Oh,

wait. You have a sweet tooth. And I bet number four means white chocolate.'

'Don't be smart.'

He grinned. 'It does, doesn't it?'

'Actually,' she told him loftily, 'it's gianduja, praline, for your information. Which, for your information, is better than number three.'

'Is it, now? Interesting theory.'

It was on the tip of her tongue to tell him that she could prove it, but she knew he was waiting for her to say that. Instead, she said sweetly, 'Perhaps you'd be kind enough to ask for the menus as well as the water?'

'There isn't actually a menu here. They serve what the chef feels like cooking.'

'That's fine. I don't mind going with the flow.' She gave him a pointed look. 'I'm not one of these people who makes a fuss about every course and insists that things are changed to make myself feel important.' Though she'd just bet that his ex had. And, given that she came from the same kind of world as her, she'd bet that he was judging her by his ex's standards. Which wasn't fair.

And it was time they changed the subject. In her experience, the best way of drawing someone out was to ask them about themselves. Given that what he did for a living wasn't a run-of-the-mill job, he was bound to open up to her if she asked about his work. 'So what made you choose perfumery as a career?' she asked.

No doubt she was just being polite, Guy thought, but she'd unerringly picked the one subject that could really rattle him. His career. Soon to be ex-career, if he couldn't find a doctor to help him. 'I was always good at chemistry at school—and I'm interested in how scent works, how it can change perceptions and moods.'

'And you're wearing your signature scent tonight—Bergamote Fraîche?'

'Looked that up on Google as well, did you?' he asked.

'No. I noticed it yesterday.' She blushed slightly, and Guy knew exactly where she'd noticed it. On his skin, while she'd been kissing him. His body tightened at the memory.

'Gina said that *Celebrity Life* raved about your citrussy shower gel—' she rolled her eyes '—which has to be about the only nice thing it's done all year. And Allie said it was an extension of the line; it was the first cologne you created for GL Parfums.'

Yes. And he might just have created his very last fragrance. He forced himself not to tense up, and drawled, 'You've done your homework.' Then he thought about what she'd just said. 'What did you mean about being the only nice thing *Celebrity Life* has done all year?'

She flapped a dismissive hand. 'Nothing.'

'The magazine's run stories about you?'

'Which I ignore.'

'You could get an injunction.' He could remember Véra doing that with one particular magazine.

'If I did, they'd report that, too—with glee,' Amber said with a sigh. 'The magazine never tells outright lies, so I can't take them to court. It's the spin they put on the facts.' She shrugged. 'Guess I'll have to live with it. I never read that magazine, anyway. Though the stories end up spreading through the others.'

'Doesn't it bother you?'

'It used to,' she admitted, 'but then I thought about it. When people have had a rough day at work, they can come home and relax with a magazine, read all about the lovely things that their favourite celebs are wearing or have just bought for their home, and find out where they can get the same look for a fraction of the price on the high street. Who am I to stop them having that pleasure?'

He hadn't considered things from that viewpoint. He'd just thought about the intrusiveness; and Véra had been furious when a magazine had taken a picture of her at a party and done exactly that kind of feature on her. She'd always worn very exclusive clothes given to her by designers.

'Do the paparazzi stalk you?' he asked, thinking of the way he'd been doorstepped when news broke of the split between himself and Véra.

'Now and again. And they're going to run a lulu of a story about me this week,' she said, rolling her eyes. 'I went to Venice last week to pick up Allie and Xav's wedding present—these gorgeous Venetian wine glasses. Someone snapped me falling flat on my face as I stepped into the water taxi by the airport and lost my footing. I saw the flash as I hit the floor.' She shrugged. 'Never mind. They got a nice shot of my shoes. And if they do run it, I might ring *What's Hot!* magazine—that's *Celebrity Life*'s biggest rival—and tell them where I got the shoes. One of Gina's friends from art school became a shoe designer, and her shoes are just gorgeous. If they give her a puff, it'll be really good for her sales.'

'And then she'll give you free shoes?' That was the way he remembered it working.

She gave him a scornful look. 'Of course not. If Zaza kept me in free shoes, she'd go bankrupt! I already told you, Guy, I pay my way.'

'I didn't mean to offend you.' But it intrigued him that she saw things in such a different way. 'You're very relaxed about the press.' Even about the prospect of having a photograph of her in less than a flattering light splashed across the magazines. Véra would've stormed round the house in a fury for days. Or was Amber simply putting a brave face on things, the same way that he was right now?

'I used to get uptight, when I was a teenager, but Mum sat me down and said that if you kept smiling, you were the one in control.' She took a sip of her mineral water. 'So that's what I do. I keep smiling. The more the stress, the bigger my smile.'

Amber turned out to be incredibly easy to talk to; Guy found himself talking to her about all kinds of things, from the sort of books he enjoyed reading through to the fact he missed having a dog but it wasn't fair to have one when he spent so much time in his lab, splitting his time between Grasse and the château. And it turned out that she liked dogs, too, but didn't have one as it wouldn't be fair to keep one cooped up in her London flat. He discovered that they liked the same kind of films, too. And she was a fellow foodie; unlike Véra, she didn't nibble on a lettuce leaf or claim she was full after one mouthful. She ate with gusto, commenting on textures and seasonings and how they worked together.

He couldn't quite work her out. Just when he thought he'd pigeonholed her, she said or did something that threw him. One minute, she was the spoiled media darling, working the press to her best advantage; and then she revealed unexpected depths. Then, just when he was beginning to think that there was a lot more to her, she said or did something that reminded him so much of his ex-wife that he almost started grinding his teeth.

But she also intrigued him more than anyone had in years.

What was it about her?

'Allie said she tried to persuade you to do event management for her. Why did you turn her down?' he asked.

'Because I don't want to be tied down to someone else's

schedule. Organising the charity balls and helping friends organise parties is fun. And I can still do what I like, most of the time. I can enjoy having lunch with my friends without having to worry that I'll be late back for work, and I can go and see my mum in LA without having to book time off weeks in advance and then come back to London before I'm really ready to leave. I like my life as it is.' She eyed the remaining chocolate on the plate between them. 'I suppose, as you're my dinner guest, I ought to be nice and offer that to you.'

'As I'm your guest, I'll be polite and refuse so you can have it.' He couldn't resist teasing her. 'Are you sure chocolate's only number four on your list of vices?'

She blushed spectacularly. 'Don't be mean.'

Then she had her revenge. Because she ate the chocolate really *slowly*. Just like the model in one of the confectionary ads that had stirred him as a teenager. Her mouth was practically having sex with the chocolate, and Guy couldn't take his eyes off her. By the time she'd finished, he was near to hyperventilating.

And he knew that she knew exactly what effect she'd had on him, because she gave him the sauciest smile. 'I'll go and pay.'

'No, it's my bill.'

'The deal was,' she corrected crisply, 'that you'd allow me to take you out to dinner as a thank you for letting me stay at the château. But I might need your help if I get stuck on the language. I'll call you over if I do.'

No, she wouldn't need his help, he thought. She'd smile and mime her way through it, and have all the restaurant staff smiling along with her. She charmed everyone she met; the waiter had loved it when she'd made the effort to speak to him in French and complimented him on the meal and the service, even though her grammar and her accent weren't perfect and she had to ask for help with some of the words.

She charmed him, too. Even though he knew he ought to be wary of getting involved with someone from her world, her sunny, bright, super-optimistic outlook was infectious—and he was finding her seriously hard to resist.

He relaxed more on the drive back to the château, this time switching the stereo to a classical station.

'This is more the kind of stuff that I thought you'd listen to,' Amber said.

'I do when I'm working.' He glanced at her. 'Do you want the roof down again?'

'No need. I've had chocolate.'

He couldn't help laughing. 'Number four being a substitute for number three?'

'Don't knock it. There are surveys out there that prove women prefer chocolate to sex. It's all to do with satiation centres in the brain.' When he said nothing, she said, 'OK, so I dropped out of university, but it wasn't because I was thick.'

That was clearly a sore spot. Had people accused her of being an airhead? 'Anyone who talks to you will know you're not stupid. What were you reading?'

'History of art. And, as I didn't want to go and work in a gallery, it all felt a bit pointless. Better that the place went to a student who really wanted to do it,' she said.

'Fair enough.'

'That isn't what Dad said.' She shrugged. 'But he came round in the end. After I threatened to become a model, he stopped nagging me about getting a proper job.'

A model. Like Véra. Guy went cold. 'Did you want to be a model?' he asked carefully.

'And exist on lettuce leaves for years? No chance. I like food.'

'You're slender enough to get away with eating what you like—and I've seen how much pudding you eat.'

'I still wouldn't do it. It's not a nice world—people watch you and wait for you to fail. And there's so much jealousy and backstabbing.' She grimaced. 'No, thanks. That's no fun.'

'And your life's all about fun.'

'Exactly. Not that I expect *you* to get that.'

'Because I'm boring?' he asked, thinking of the accusations that his ex-wife had flung at him.

'No, because you're über-clever. You're a scientist. You're looking for different things out of life.'

She'd hit the nail squarely on the head, he thought. They were from different worlds. In his life with Véra, Guy had hated the media spotlight, the first nights and celeb cocktail parties where he was expected to make small talk with people he had nothing in common with; whereas Amber, like Véra, would thrive on them. She loved parties and meeting new people, and she treated everyone she met as a potential new friend; her warmth wore down any barriers. They were complete opposites; so there was no point in starting something that would never work. No matter how tempting he found her. And they'd agreed that last night was last night.

So it had to end here.

CHAPTER SIX

AMBER excused herself when they got back to the château, saying that she was a bit tired. Guy had a feeling that she wasn't telling the truth, but he didn't call her on it. Instead, he sat up in his lab, checking the Internet for any new developments in the treatment of anosmia, the loss of sense of smell.

Even though his eyes were aching by the time he'd finished, he couldn't settle. He wasn't sure whether it was more because of the fact he hadn't found anything new, or because he knew Amber was asleep upstairs and part of him was regretting that he hadn't taken the chance to change things between them, start seeing her properly. Despite the fact that his life wasn't in the right place for a relationship, something about her made his world feel brighter. Part of him really wanted to take the chance; and yet part of him knew that it would be unfair to use her in that way. It was already bad enough that he'd slept with her last night and let her help him forget his worries. Selfish as hell.

'You're a mess, Lefèvre,' he told himself. 'And you need sleep.' Maybe in the morning everything would seem different.

At the foot of the stairs, he realised that the light was on in the kitchen. He must've left it on, earlier. He walked in, intending to switch it off, and discovered Amber there, hunched over at the table.

'Are you all right?' he asked.

'I couldn't sleep,' she admitted. 'I just made myself some hot milk and cinnamon.'

'Cinnamon.' He couldn't smell it right now, but he could remember the scent. Heady. Like her.

'Sorry, I know I should've asked first. I hope you don't mind that I poked about in your kitchen.'

'Not a problem. Help yourself,' he said.

Her eyes narrowed as she looked at him. 'Are you all right?'

'Yes,' he lied.

'You look as if you've spent too long in front of a computer screen. Your eyes are bloodshot.'

'I couldn't sleep, either,' he admitted.

She handed him the mug. 'Try this.'

He took a sip, more to humour her than anything else; his sense of taste was going along with his sense of smell. 'So why can't you sleep?'

There was a long, long pause. He said nothing, waiting for her to speak; finally, she sighed. 'Number three.'

He was impressed that she'd had the courage to admit it. And fair was fair. 'Me, too,' he said softly. 'Maybe I should call my new perfume that.'

'Is that what your new perfume's about?'

'No.' But he knew exactly what fragrance he wanted to make next. A hypnotic, sensual one with a glossy surface and a hidden depth of sweetness. Like her. And it frustrated him to hell that he couldn't do it. All the notes of the perfume were in his head, and part of him wanted to run to his lab and start creating it: but he knew there was no point. Not until his nose was fixed. Until then, he wouldn't be able to check if the formula needed tweaking.

He couldn't do anything about that, right now. But the other problem—the attraction between himself and Amber—was something he could sort out. 'So what are we going to do about this?' he asked her.

'I don't know. But I don't think it's a good idea for me to stay here with you.' She took the mug back from him and sipped. 'Especially if you're going to wear touchable clothes. Because I'm a bit impulsive and I don't always know when to stop.' She dragged in a breath. 'It's OK for you. You have a sensible job and a sensible life and a sensible outlook.'

'Not always. Especially when the most beautiful woman I've ever met decides to hike her skirt up in my car.' He looked at her. 'Are you wearing anything at all under that silky wrap?' It was hot pink, like her sexy shoes—though right at that moment she was barefoot.

'I don't think I should answer that.'

He groaned. 'I think you just did.'

'It's OK. I'm going upstairs to have a very, very cold shower. And I'm moving out to a hotel tomorrow.'

'No.' He reached out and took her hand, drawing it up to his lips. 'I know this is a seriously bad idea, but I don't think either of us is going to get any sleep at all tonight if we don't do something about this—' he paused, shaking his head in frustration because he couldn't think of the right word '—this *thing* between us.' Even though she was the kind of girl he'd sworn he'd never go near again, he simply couldn't resist her. He needed to taste her. Needed to feel her skin against his. Needed the release that only she could give him.

Her eyes looked absolutely enormous. 'So what are you suggesting? That we have a mad affair?'

'One night didn't get it out of our systems,' he said. 'Maybe it just takes a little longer than that.'

'But it's not going to be serious.'

'Agreed. Exclusive, though,' he warned, remembering his ex.

'Definitely.' She dragged in a breath. 'Starting now?'

'Oh, *Dieu*, yes,' he said, wrapping his arms round her and doing what he'd been thinking about all evening—jamming his mouth over hers. And her mouth was warm and sweet and sexy as hell. So were her hands, sliding under his sweater and stroking his skin.

'My room,' she said as he broke the kiss.

'You're on,' he said, scooping her up and carrying her up the stairs.

When Guy woke in Amber's bed, the following morning, he was slightly disoriented at first; and then disconcerted to find that he was alone in the bed. The coolness of the sheets where she'd lain suggested that he'd been alone for a few minutes. He could see the en suite from the bed, so he knew she wasn't in the shower.

'Amber?'

No reply.

Frowning, he climbed out of bed, pulled on his underpants and trousers, and headed downstairs.

She was back in the kitchen. Barefoot again, and wearing only her silky wrap.

And he knew for a fact that she wore nothing underneath it.

How to make a man's blood pressure spike.

He stood in the doorway, watching her potter about. She was humming to herself as she whisked something in a bowl, completely absorbed in whatever she was making. She looked adorable, and it took a lot of effort for him not to go over to her, turn her round to face him and kiss her until both their heads were spinning.

'Bonjour, mon ange,' he said from the doorway.

She turned round and smiled at him, making his heart skip a beat. '*Bonjour*, Guy. I was going to bring you breakfast in bed but, since you're up, have a seat.' She smiled again. 'I'm making pancakes.'

He blinked. 'You eat crêpes for breakfast in England?'

'No, but my mum does in LA. Anyway, these are American breakfast pancakes. Thicker and fluffier. We're having them with stewed apples and Chantilly cream.'

She'd taken him at his word last night, then, and made herself at home in his kitchen, finding the ingredients and utensils she needed.

But pancakes for breakfast? Considering she'd eaten lemon tart with cream at the wedding breakfast, it seemed that she really was intending to cook pudding for breakfast. 'Sounds interesting,' he said neutrally. 'Shall I make coffee? And I could juice some oranges.'

'Thanks, that'd be great.'

Weird. If anyone had told him six months ago that he'd enjoy something as simple and domesticated as pottering around in a kitchen, while someone else cooked breakfast, he would've laughed. Then again, six months ago, he would already have been in his lab for a couple of hours, trying out ideas he'd woken up with.

How things changed.

Would he ever be able to do that again? In a few months' time, a year even, would things be back to normal? Would he be living his dream again, developing fragrances and feeling glad to be alive when he woke up, instead of feeling useless and a complete failure and desperately trying to hide the truth from everybody?

He pushed the thoughts aside and concentrated on making coffee, juicing oranges and laying the scrubbed pine table while she flipped a batch of pancakes; he set her at the head of the table and himself at the side, at right-angles to her. Companionable. 'Coffee's ready when you are,' he said, pouring it into two mugs and adding milk before setting the mugs next to the glasses of juice.

'Perfect timing. Sit down.' She put a bowl of whipped cream on the table, added another bowl with warm stewed apple and then slid a plate of pancakes between them. 'Help yourself.'

He was pretty sure he couldn't taste them in quite the same way that she did—with scent being such a large part of taste, he could barely make out the flavour of the cinnamon in the apple or the vanilla in the Chantilly cream—but the pancakes were light, fluffy and melted in his mouth, and the texture of the pancakes made a stunning combination with the grainy apple and the light-as-air cream. 'I admit, this is fantastic. You're very good at this,' he said.

'Thank you.' She inclined her head in acknowledgement of the compliment and gave another of those sunny smiles that sent a jolt of desire through him.

'I think you might be right about pudding for breakfast.' Guy helped himself to more. 'From now on, I'll always associate you with apples and vanilla.'

She raised an eyebrow. 'Isn't vanilla meant to be bland?'

Bland was the last word he'd use to describe her. 'No. It's sweet, but it's also amazingly sensual.'

'Why, thank you.'

He grinned. 'You have the cutest dimples. And when you blush like that…it makes me want to make you blush all over.'

'I'll take that as a promise,' she said. 'Later tonight.'

Why not now?

The question must have shown on his face, because she

explained, 'You probably have work to do, and I already have plans for today.'

'Oh?'

'I'm going exploring. You know, the list I made yesterday?'

'Uh-huh.'

Her eyes narrowed. 'What? You're thinking I'm a woman so I can't navigate?'

'I didn't say that. But you don't know the area.'

She folded her arms. 'There is such a thing as satnav.'

'True. But wouldn't it be easier for you if someone else was driving? Someone who does know the area, and can find nice places for lunch?'

'I don't spend my entire time having lunch, you know.'

He raised an eyebrow. 'That's not what you said yesterday.'

'I was cross with you.'

'And you're cross now.'

'Because I know what you're doing. You're trying to get me really cross with you, and then you're planning on having make-up sex with me.'

He laughed outright at that; he loved it when she was forthright. 'Are you calling me shallow?'

She rolled her eyes. 'You only have one X chromosome. *Of course* you're shallow.'

'You're wearing a skimpy bit of hot-pink silk and nothing else. What do you expect?' he fenced back.

'Well, hey, I'm just an airhead party girl.' She drawled it contemptuously, but he could see something in her eyes. He'd just hurt her. And he had no idea what he'd said.

'Amber?'

Her reply was a really, really bright smile. But he remembered what she'd said last night, and he knew that she was smiling to keep herself in control.

He took her hand and drew it to his lips. Kissed her palm, and folded her fingers over it. 'I can see I've just upset you, and I'm sorry for that. I don't know what I said but, believe me, I didn't mean to insult you. If you'd like me to drive you to the places you want to visit, I'm more than happy to do that.'

'Don't you have work to do?'

That was the rub. He did—he just wasn't physically able to do it, right now. At least, when he was with her, his attention was away from that. And her company might stop him brooding about the problem that seemed to be moving further and further away from a solution. 'I can take leave for a day.' He leaned over and stole a kiss. 'Thank you for breakfast, *mon ange*. I'm going to have a shower now—and if we're to have a hope of actually getting out of the château today, I need to have that shower on my own. See you by the front door in an hour?'

She blinked. 'Do you take that long to get ready?'

'No.' But Véra used to, so he had assumed that Amber would need the same amount of time.

'Give me five minutes to clear away here, and ten minutes to shower and change.'

'Seriously?' He was surprised—and impressed. And, because he'd just insulted her, he felt he owed her. 'Skip the clearing up. I'll help you when we get back—considering I ate half of what you made, the least I can do is half the cleaning,' he said.

'OK. Deal.' This time, Guy realised, her smile was genuine. Because it reached her eyes and it was a shade less glittery than her professional smile.

Though in fifteen minutes' time, when she met him at the front door, he looked at her feet and sighed. 'Amber, are you seriously expecting to walk anywhere in those shoes?' At least they weren't the pink ones, but they were very similar, this time in bright turquoise. They looked only suitable for a catwalk.

'I can walk in these. Well, unless you're intending to drag me up a mountain.'

'Which is exactly what I was going to do.' He sighed again. 'Don't you have any walking boots?'

'Living in London, I don't tend to go on long walks in the country at the weekend or what have you,' she said, 'so, no. I don't even *possess* a pair of walking boots.'

'Trainers?' he suggested hopefully.

She looked faintly disgusted. 'The only flat shoes I have are the ones for my dance class. And, apart from the fact that they're in London right now, they're ballet pumps so they wouldn't be any good on a mountain, either.'

Just when he thought she was different, she did something exactly like Véra would've done. Why couldn't he keep it in his head that she was from his ex's world? 'OK. We'll skip the mountain.'

'I'm not trying to be difficult,' she said. 'And I *can* walk in these. All day, if I have to.'

'Right.' He knew that was just bravado.

As if he'd spoken aloud, she lifted her chin. 'Want to bet on it? Because, if you do, I can tell you now that you're going to owe me a box of the best gianduja at the end of today.'

'And if I win?' he asked silkily.

She grinned. 'Then I'll eat it off you.'

There was nothing he could say to that. *Nothing*. Because the picture she'd just put in his head had rendered him temporarily speechless.

'What's the matter, Guy?' she taunted. 'All the blood from your brain just gone south?'

In answer, he pulled her into his arms and plastered her against him.

'Point taken,' she whispered shakily.

Oh, her runaway mouth. Was she ever going to learn? If she carried on like this, he'd despise her. And she really, really wanted to be different.

Knowing that she reminded him of his ex had shaken her. Amber wasn't the diva type, so why did he persist in thinking that about her? She was very aware that Guy disapproved of her world; he'd been there and hated it. But her world wasn't that bad—was it?

Being with him made her look at herself and reassess her life, and she wasn't entirely sure she liked what she saw. Her world was fun—but she had to admit that it was based on gossip and the latest hot trends. She spent her time chatting and shopping and lunching and partying. There was no depth to anything she did. And everything was done in a rush...including the affair she'd started with Guy.

But not everyone could change the world. Not everyone could find a cure for diseases, or be an inspiring teacher to a generation of children, or rescue people from halfway up a mountain. She wasn't special like that: she was simply Amber Wynne, party girl. And she was honest about who she was. She never hurt people intentionally. She made people smile and feel good. That wasn't a bad thing.

And she really had to stop obsessing about the differences between their lives. This was only temporary, so it didn't matter. Did it?

Guy had borrowed Xavier's car again, so clearly he'd meant it about mountains. Well, she'd walk up his wretched mountain in her pretty shoes, even if she had to pay for it with a week's worth of blisters. No way was she backing down.

He took her out to the north of the region, driving through a wild landscape of gorges and scrubby heathland. She noticed that he drove very steadily rather than speeding round the bends—and discovered why, when mountain goats skipped across the road in front of them, heedless of the traffic.

Though the scenery was stunning. And she loved the lake at Issarles, a huge deep crater filled with dark blue water and surrounded by meadows.

'It's prettier in the spring,' he said, 'when all the wild flowers are out. How are your feet?'

'They're fabulous, thank you.' Even if they had been hurting, she wouldn't have admitted it. Not to him. 'And this is pretty. So this is the volcanic part of France?'

'It is indeed—and I'm taking you to the longest lava flow in France, next.' He drove a little further into the Ardèche, through more of the wild, almost lunar landscape.

'La cascade du Ray-Pic.' She read the sign in the car park. 'That's the waterfall.'

'One of the most stunning you'll ever see,' he promised.

They walked through the woods and up some rough-hewn steps; Amber stumbled a couple of times, and was relieved when Guy took her hand.

'Are you going to admit now that your shoes are completely unsuitable?' he asked.

'Never in a million years.' But she didn't let his hand go. Not because she was worried about tripping, but because it was beautiful and romantic out here, and just for a little while she could pretend that they were really dating.

Which they weren't.

And wouldn't be, because they came from different

worlds and it just wouldn't work. This mad, crazy fling was just that—mad and crazy. And temporary.

She could hear the noise of water thundering down, and then suddenly there they were, watching the water streaming down over a striated volcanic rock face and landing in a clear turquoise pool at the bottom. 'That's beautiful,' she breathed.

'Here. Let me take a picture of you here,' he said, getting her to pose for him. And she persuaded him to stand with her so she could take a snap of them together on her mobile phone's camera.

'I had no idea that France could be so—well—wild,' she said.

'What did you think France was?'

She sighed. 'My experience of France—before this week—was Paris and St Tropez. Oh, and I did go skiing once at Val d'Isère.'

'Party girl,' he teased. 'I bet you skied once and spent the rest of the time drinking hot chocolate and admiring the mountain views.'

'Nothing wrong with that.' She laughed. 'Actually, I hated skiing. But the après-ski was fun.'

'Mmm, because even *you* couldn't ski in those shoes.'

'Why do you hate my shoes so much?' she asked.

'I don't. But this is the fourth different pair I've seen in three days. I'm just wondering how many more you have.'

She laughed. 'You really wouldn't want to know.'

'I would.'

'Tell you a secret.' She beckoned him closer, making him stoop so that she could whisper into his ear. 'I have a shoe room.'

He pulled back and stared at her. 'You're kidding me.'

'Nope. Actually, *What's Hot!* does this feature called

"What's in the closet?" and a couple of months ago they did one on my shoe room. The photo shoot was the most fun I've had all year. You can look it up online if you really want to see it.' She spread her hands. 'Hey, I did warn you that you wouldn't want to know.' And she couldn't quite read the expression on his face. Disapproval? He already thought she was shameless. Now he'd think she was a show-off, too. Time to salvage the situation and change the subject. 'Is it lunchtime, yet?'

He laughed. 'Hint taken. Let's go.'

They stopped in a little stone village, perching precariously on the side of a cliff, for lunch; the tiny bistro served fabulous food and Amber enjoyed every second of it. It was the lightest, most melting omelette she'd ever eaten, stuffed with ceps and served with some excellent rustic bread and slices of tomato scattered with basil and bursting with flavour. Guy chose home-cured sausages on a bed of lentils, and insisted on her trying it from his fork.

'Fantastic,' she said.

He coughed, and nodded at her plate. 'Fair's fair.'

'You want a taste?' She smiled, and made him reach for it.

When Guy allowed himself to forget that he was a nerdy scientist, she thought, he was fun to be with. Not to mention sexy as hell.

'Pudding?' he asked.

'There weren't any on the menu. I looked.'

'That's because they're on a separate menu,' he told her.

'Oh, what?' She sighed. 'That's not fair. I think I'm too full.'

'Shame. There's a chestnut pudding on the menu that's to die for.'

'Well, there are two ways we can do this. We can either

wait here for an hour until I have room for pudding—or you can order it and feed me a taste of yours.'

He raised an eyebrow. 'In other words, your feet are sore and you want a rest.'

'They are *not*.' She glared at him, outraged. 'Order the pudding. I can do this.'

The pudding turned out to be *pisadou*, layers of pastry filled with chestnut cream, vanilla seeds and *marrons glacés*.

'This is gorgeous. And I really like these.' She indicated one of the *marrons glacés*.

'Crystallised chestnuts. I have to admit, they're one of my weaknesses,' Guy said.

'Vice number what?'

'That'd be telling.' And his eyes had gone all sensual and hot; her pulse spiked in response. She made a mental note to look up recipes on the Internet for puddings that involved crystallised chestnuts, and make one for him. And they'd eat it in bed.

After lunch, he drove them south to the amazing gorges between Vallon Pont d'Arc and Saint Martin d'Ardèche. 'This is the French equivalent of the Grand Canyon,' he told her.

She could see exactly what he meant. There were incredibly steep drops, and she surreptitiously hung onto the car door handle. In places, the road went down to the water level, but most of the time they had stunning views of the river.

'In the summer, the viewpoints are heaving. But today we have the space to stop,' he said, and parked in a lay-by overlooking a particularly serpentine stretch of river so that she could take more photographs.

They ended up at the Pont d'Arc, a huge natural limestone

arch that stretched across the river. 'We could go shooting the rapids in a kayak, if you like,' Guy suggested.

'I'm up for it.'

He laughed. 'In your pretty shoes?'

'I can take them off. Just for the kayaking.'

'And you've done kayaking before?'

'Well—no,' she admitted. 'But it looks like fun.'

'Maybe another day. Let's chill out, instead,' he suggested.

They sat on the shore for a while, watching people canoeing and kayaking. On the way home, they stopped at another of the cliffside villages, and ate on the terrace of a bistro looking out at the sunset. Again, the food was amazing: a fabulous starter of langoustines with pink grapefruit and sesame seeds, then beef casserole with red wine and more of the chestnuts she was beginning to realise had a huge part on most menus, followed by delicate lavender ice cream and finally cheese and great coffee.

Guy held her hand across the table, and she realised just how easy it would be to fall for him. He was great company, charming and he was different from the men she usually dated—not one of her shallow, heartless liars. If she ever settled down, she'd want a man like this. Someone she knew she could rely on, who'd stop her being completely frivolous and yet who'd let her tease him into having fun. Someone who'd be her other half in all senses of the word.

Though she knew that man couldn't be Guy. He'd made it very clear that this was a fling, nothing more, and she didn't think he was the kind of man who changed his mind very easily.

Don't lose your heart to him, she reminded herself. Don't get involved.

Though a little part of her thought it might already be too late.

CHAPTER SEVEN

OVER the next week, Guy found himself getting closer to Amber. They'd fallen into a routine where she spent the morning reading on the terrace while he caught up with his work. She never interrupted him in his lab; she seemed to realise what a huge part of his life his work was. He knew she was curious, because she'd asked questions—sometimes very intrusive questions; but when he hadn't been forthcoming, she'd backed off. Maybe she knew he was deflecting her—she was certainly sharp enough to work that out—but he appreciated the fact that she'd give him the space he needed.

He usually took her out for lunch, and then they spent the afternoon visiting the tourist attractions. Amber still hadn't worn the same pair of shoes twice, much to his amusement; and he'd secretly looked up the feature on the *What's Hot!* website, curious to know whether she'd been teasing him or not.

She'd been telling the truth. And she'd looked gorgeous in the feature, all long legs and short skirts and glorious hair and kissable mouth. Although her smile had been bright, it hadn't been brittle. She'd clearly loved every second of the photo shoot, and the camera had loved her right back.

And yet here, in France, she'd enjoyed pottering about the château and taking over his kitchen. Which was the real Amber? The media darling or the domesticated angel? He still didn't have a clue. Though he recognised just how much he liked having her around. She made his world a brighter place, with her ready smile and sparkling eyes.

If it weren't for the fact that his sense of smell still hadn't come back and he'd started getting bad headaches—which he was pretty sure was caused by the stress of not being able to sort it out—he thought he'd almost start being happy again.

He checked his email. A pile of things that could wait; one he'd been looking forward to, the first draft of a design from Gina; and one he'd expected but hoped wouldn't materialise, another message from Philippe trying to persuade him to sell to the conglomerate. He sighed, and worked methodically through every single one of his business partner's arguments, chopping them into firewood. And then, just to sweeten the edge, he mentioned that he had the first draft of the design for the new perfume.

But before he pressed send, he opened Gina's file and studied it carefully. What would she have done with the brief for 'Angelique'?

To his delight, she'd captured the dual side of the fragrance: the sweetness of the vanilla base and the rose heart, and the edgy notes of pepper and myrrh. And what she'd come up with was a line drawing of an angel: very simple, with a hint of darkness around the wings. Not an over-pretty cherub, either—this was striking, sensual beauty, reminding him of a painting he'd fallen in love with once at an exhibition: Rossetti's 'Venus Verticordia.'

And then he wished he hadn't thought of that picture, because now he could imagine Amber in that pose. A coronet of golden butterflies round her glorious loose hair, surrounded by full-blown sensual roses and honeysuckle—and naked to the waist.

He really had to get his mind off sex.

And it was just sex, he told himself. He wasn't going to lose his heart to Amber, the way he had to Véra. He didn't want to get seriously involved with another party girl. Even if she did have a sweet, domesticated side that had surprised him.

He sent a quick email to Gina, thanking her for her work and giving her the go-ahead for the next stage; then sent the email to Philippe and logged off. And then he went in search of Amber.

They spent the afternoon wandering around the caves at Chauvet—Amber had mentioned that the cave paintings were the only bit she could remember from her History of Art course—and then headed back to the château. And in the evening Guy settled at the kitchen table, chatting to her as she pottered around the kitchen. Again, he found himself wondering which was the real Amber.

She dished up chicken wrapped in bacon and poached in apple juice, served with steamed green vegetables and a pile of fluffy couscous to soak up the gravy.

'This is fabulous,' he said.

She shrugged. 'I just like messing about in the kitchen. I actually found the recipe online,' she admitted with a smile.

Guy was even more impressed when she took pudding from the fridge. 'Crème brûlée and raspberries.'

'I made it this morning, when you were working.'

'It's my favourite.'

'Are you just saying that? Oh, wait—you said earlier that you loved vanilla.'

'Mmm. Though I also like the scent of amber.'

He realised what he'd said when she blushed to the roots of her hair.

'I'm sorry, *mon ange*, I didn't mean that the way it

sounded. I meant amber as in perfume amber. It's warm and rich and earthy, sensual and yet calming at the same time,' he explained.

'Sounds lovely.'

'It is. To make an amber base, I'd mix it with beeswax, then might add other notes, depending on whether I want it as a spicy or sweet base.'

'Which do you prefer?'

'For a woman's perfume, I like it mixed with vanilla,' he said. 'Which I'm ashamed to say is probably something to do with a lifelong love of *glaces*.'

She laughed. 'So you're an ice-cream fiend?'

'Have you not noticed the contents of my freezer?' he deadpanned.

'I imagine,' she said thoughtfully, 'that you're pretty sensitive to scent. Like a fashion designer seeing someone wearing a colour that doesn't suit them, or a good hairdresser seeing someone whose hairstyle is completely wrong for them—it must drive you crazy when someone's wearing the wrong perfume.'

Yes. It used to. And he'd been able to see people in terms of scent. But right now he couldn't trust his vision because his nose couldn't back it up.

Not wanting to explain all that, he gave a non-committal murmur.

'Oh, come on. You don't have to be polite. You can be honest with me.'

No, he couldn't. He couldn't be honest with anyone about the thing that was eating him from the inside.

She sighed. 'Is that why you're so moody?'

He blinked. 'What do you mean, moody?'

'One minute you're charming, the next you're unapproachable.'

'No, I'm not.'

'Guy, you are. You go all quiet and broody, and it's as if you've stuck a glass wall round yourself. Is this something to do with being a creative genius?'

'I'm not a creative genius.'

'Don't try to flannel me,' she said. 'Everyone says you're a genius. And you wouldn't be doing what you do if you weren't any good.'

That was the whole point. He might not be able to do it any more.

'OK, so that was maybe a bit too personal,' she said with a sigh. 'Either something is really bugging you—'

Oh, hell. Was it that obvious?

'—or you have to be the first person I've ever met who doesn't like talking about himself,' she finished.

Ha. Six months ago, if she'd asked him about his work, he would've talked her ears off. If only she knew. 'Some people don't like talking about themselves,' he said evasively. 'Let's talk about you instead.'

'You know me,' she said cheerfully. 'Shallow as a puddle. But, since you asked... Tell me.' She tipped her head on one side and smiled at him. 'Do I wear the right scent?'

It was a direct question, so he couldn't avoid it. But how could he answer? He could hardly tell her that he had no idea what she wore. 'I think something with amber and vanilla would suit you, maybe with a little bergamot to add some tartness to the mix—definitely warmth and sweetness.'

'You think I'm warm and sweet?' She sounded surprised, as if she hadn't expected that. 'I normally wear Chanel No 5. You know, like Marilyn Monroe—and my mum. So is that the wrong one for me?'

In his view, the 'classic' aldehyde scent would be too cool for her. But he wasn't exactly in a position where he could give her any decent advice. 'If you like the scent and it feels right to you, then it's the right one for you.' It was a completely anodyne answer, and he knew she deserved better. But, without explaining the problem with his nose, platitudes were all he could offer.

'But plenty of people wear clothes they like that don't suit them. They take advice from professionals.'

He didn't like where this was heading. Was she planning to ask him for advice? He couldn't give it to her, not without being able to smell. 'Perfume's more personal than clothes.'

'Is it? People have their colours done,' she mused. 'Having their scent done might be good, too.'

'It's not the same thing at all. People react differently to smells. It's all bound up with associations and memories. And how perfume smells on you depends on your skin—it doesn't smell the same on everyone.'

'Guy—'

He had to sidetrack her. Fast. 'Why don't you try making your own?'

'I thought it took ages to develop a perfume?' She frowned. 'I asked you about making a personal scent before.'

And he'd reacted badly. 'I know. But there's a business line I was thinking about developing, and you'd be the perfect guinea pig.'

'For what?'

'Come with me, and I'll show you.'

'What, you're actually taking me to the bat cave?' she teased.

'The bat cave?' he asked, mystified.

'Your lair. The secret laboratory, Dr.' She frowned. 'Are you Dr Lefèvre?'

'No. And my lab isn't secret.'

'It's certainly not public.'

'Amber—stop talking, will you?' Just to make the point, he kissed her. And by the time he'd stopped kissing her, she was beautifully pink...and mercifully quiet.

Until he took her into his lab.

'Wow. All those bottles,' she said, looking at his desk. 'I take it they're all different scents?'

'Yes. This is called a perfumer's organ,' he explained. 'Partly because it looks like one—' the bottles were set out in tiered rows on the desk, like the keys on an organ '—and partly because each bottle contains a perfume note. And mine is organised as top, middle and bottom notes.'

'The top note being what you smell first, the middle being the heart and the one you smell at the end of the day being the bottom?'

'Spot on,' he said with a smile.

'How do you know which fragrance goes with which?'

'Experience and experimenting,' he said. 'And, as I said before, everyone's taste is different. It's down to personal choice in the end.'

'It all looks really scientific.'

'Perfumery is an art. And you're creative—' at least, she was in the kitchen '—so let's see what you come up with.'

'It's not going to mess up your desk?'

'It's not going to mess up my desk,' he confirmed, touching her cheek with the backs of his fingers in reassurance. Again, she'd surprised him. He'd expected her to just sit down and enjoy being pampered without thinking about anything else. 'Sit down, *mon ange*. I'm going to give you some choices from the different fragrance families, and you're going to sniff them one by one and tell me whether you like it, loathe it, or you're not sure, and we'll build it up from there.'

'Supposing I pick the wrong ones?'

'You won't. As I said, it's a personal choice, so there's no right or wrong answer. This,' Guy said softly, 'is all about *you*.'

Amber was no stranger to pamper days. She had a regular slot for facials and massages. She'd been on pamper weekends with friends—and even for a whole week, once, when her mother was in the mood for a detox and wanted some company. If she was honest about it, Amber knew she'd spent her whole life being pampered.

But Guy was the only one who'd ever made her feel *special*. As if she mattered. As if she was really important. She wasn't used to that; in her world, she was just part of the crowd, another party girl.

Right now Guy was giving her his time. Full attention. And to have a hotshot parfumier helping her to make her signature scent…that was a rare treat. Something to be savoured.

She sat down at his desk, and he picked out a selection of the dark brown bottles from the racks in front of her and added some narrow strips of what looked like cardboard.

'What are these?' she asked, lifting up one of the strips.

'Smelling strips. They're made from perfumer's blotting paper—it means you'll be able to smell the scent but you won't accidentally get it on your hands, where it would start to blend with another fragrance,' he explained.

'And this is how you usually develop perfume?'

'If I want to test out some ideas, I'll put a couple of drops of each perfume base on the same blotter and let them blend. Obviously that's not precise enough for developing a formula, but it's a way of deciding whether I like the effect or not. It's kind of like musicians building up harmonies, trying different notes—except these are for your sense of smell, not your hearing.'

'I get that,' she said, smiling. 'So it's trial and error.'

'More or less. But I know before I start where I'm going. When I was training, I started with a brief—they'd tell me what kind of effect they wanted the fragrance to have, and I'd have to see if I could make the scent that created that effect. I suppose it's a bit like painting,' Guy said. 'Name a colour to an artist, and they'll be able to see it in their head. A trained perfumer sees the name of a fragrance and will be able to smell it in their mind—I know it sounds weird, but that's actually easier than smelling a fragrance and then trying to work out what the scent is. There are subtle differences.'

'That's fascinating,' Amber said, meaning it. And he clearly loved what he did, so why had he been so cagey about it before when she'd asked him? Something wasn't quite right, but she couldn't put her finger on it. If she asked him, she knew he'd deflect her—he'd done that several times already. What was he hiding?

'Before we start, you need to sniff this.' He handed her a small gold organza bag on the table. 'This is the equivalent of a sorbet at dinner, or bread at a wine-tasting.'

'You mean it's like cleansing my palate?' She was mystified. 'How on earth do you cleanse a sense of smell?'

'Just sniff it,' he said.

She did so, and recognised the scent immediately. 'Coffee?' she asked, surprised.

'It's an old parfumier's trick and it works every time.' He smiled at her. 'You'll need to refresh your sense of smell in between fragrances. I'm not going to tell you what any of the blends are called, because I don't want to influence you. Just remember that this is your perfume, so it's what *you* like that's important. And close your eyes when you breathe it in, to let you concentrate on the scent.'

'So what do we start with? The base?'

'No, the middle. These will give you an idea of the type of perfume you'll end up with, as they last for a few hours. Then we'll do the top notes, and finally the base notes to give it depth and solidarity.'

Going through each bottle in turn, he wrote a number on a smelling strip, dipped it into the bottle, then handed it to her to sniff.

'This one's gorgeous,' she said, picking out one of the top notes.

He smiled. 'Fitting. It's amber. One of my favourites, too.'

Heat coiled inside her at the expression on his face. Pure, unadulterated sensuality. 'Oh.' And she couldn't stop staring at his mouth.

He noticed—and stole a kiss. 'Keep going, *mon ange*,' he said.

The next one to go in her absolutely definite pile was one of the base notes. 'I love this. And I recognise it, too—it's vanilla.'

'Like your Chantilly cream. And the crème brûlée.'

'I'm going to end up with a pudding recipe, not perfume,' she warned.

'It's your perfume,' he reminded her. 'If you want to smell like pudding, *mon ange*, then that's fine. Gourmand perfumes are fairly popular.' He stooped and kissed the curve of her neck. 'Though it might make men want to taste you.' Just to labour his point, he nibbled her skin, making her arch back against him.

'Guy…' She shivered. 'I read somewhere that Chanel said you should put perfume where you want to be kissed.'

He laughed. 'Perfume smells better than it tastes. And it depends where you want to be kissed, *mon ange*.'

Her skin heated.

'I'd put you in a perfumed bath,' he said softly, 'so I could kiss you all over.'

'Now would be a good time,' she said, her voice cracking slightly.

'When we've finished.' His eyes held hers.

'What's the quickest you've ever made a perfume?'

'Patience, *mon ange*, is a virtue.'

'It's not one of mine.' She slid one of the straps of her top down her shoulder. 'And I thought you liked it when I wasn't virtuous.'

'Oh, I do.' He responded by sliding the other strap down. 'Now, concentrate.'

'What, when you just did that?'

'Uh-huh. If you want to be a scientist, *mon ange*, you have to ignore distractions.'

The teasing note in his voice warned her that he was planning more distractions. Very pleasurable ones. So she played along, took a sniff of coffee, then tried the next scent and grimaced. 'No. This one's horrible.'

'Oakmoss is meant to be mysterious.'

She shrugged. 'I suppose that makes me a little common then, not appreciating it.'

'No, it makes you honest. There's no point in wearing a scent you don't like. Moss can bring out notes in other scents, but if it doesn't work for you then don't add it in to your perfume, or you'll hate the final version.'

'Supposing I want to be mysterious,' she asked, 'instead of shallow as a puddle?'

'Trust me, *mon ange*, you're far from shallow.'

She hadn't been fishing for compliments, and she really hadn't expected him to say that. He hated her world and everything she stood for. How could he not think she was shallow?

'You have depth. That's in the vanilla,' he said softly. 'Sweet and sensual. Like you.'

'You really think I'm sweet?' He'd surprised her further, seeing things in her that nobody else had ever noticed. Making her look at herself from a different angle.

'And sensual. Let me show you something.' He switched on his laptop, flicked into the Internet and searched for a file. 'You know something about art or you wouldn't even have got a place at university. Do you know this picture?' he asked, showing her the screen.

'No, but from the style and the model, I'd guess it's a Rossetti.'

'Absolument.'

'And she's naked to the waist, Guy.' She folded her arms. 'That's a very Y-chromosome kind of thing.'

'She's as sexy as hell. She's dreaming of her lover.' He paused. 'And that sensual look in her eyes and on her mouth…that reminds me of you.'

'You see me like this?' She raised an eyebrow, but something in his eyes made her want to push him just that little bit further. 'Give me an armful of roses from your garden, and I'll pose for you.' She paused, and gestured towards the picture. 'Like that.'

'Really?'

'Really.'

His breath hissed. 'Stay there. Sniff the samples and keep sorting them into piles. I'll be back in a minute.'

He was going to cut an armful of his precious roses for her?

No, of course not. Apart from the fact that it was dusk, as soon as he walked outside the cool air would bring him back to his senses and he'd stomp back in and be ever so slightly grumpy with her for distracting him and tempting him to pick his roses.

In the meantime, she carried on sniffing the samples and putting them into piles, the way he'd shown her to do.

Though he'd left the laptop as it was. The more she looked at the painting, the more she could see why it affected Guy so much. The model was gorgeous; but, more than that, her eyes were dreamy. Guy was absolutely right in his assessment: Venus was thinking about sex. Remembering a lover's touch. And those memories, combined with the heady scent of rose and honeysuckle…

Guy burst back into the lab with an armful of roses, and her pulse rate spiked at the intense sensuality in his expression.

'I've taken off the thorns,' he said. 'So I'm calling your bluff.'

'Don't I need an apple and an arrow?'

He shrugged. 'Sorry. You'll just have to improvise.'

The heat in his eyes told her that he really wanted her to do this.

And she really wanted to do it, too. Pose for him. Make him weak at the knees. 'OK. Turn your back.'

He'd already seen her naked. But this was different, and all of a sudden she felt shy, near to losing her nerve. 'I'll tell you when you can look.'

He muttered something in French that she didn't catch, rolled his eyes and turned his back, leaving the roses on his desk.

Slowly, she peeled off her strappy top. Unhooked her bra. Folded them neatly and placed them over the back of her chair.

Oh, her big, impulsive mouth. It was going to get her in trouble again.

One of the roses was still a bud. She'd use that as the

arrow, and the bottle of vanilla as the apple. Improvise, he'd said—so she gathered the roses in her left arm and arranged them so they looked a bit like the hedge of honeysuckle. She flicked her hair forward over her left shoulder and back over her right, then transferred the perfume bottle to her left hand and held the rosebud in her right.

And then she thought about Guy, the way he'd made love to her that first time, and lowered her arm just enough to reveal her breasts over the edge of the roses.

'You can look, now,' she whispered.

Guy turned round, and colour slashed across his cheeks. He said something else she couldn't catch in French.

Worry flooded through her. Had she done it wrong?

'*Dieu*, Amber, do you have any idea how incredible you look, like that?' His voice was husky with desire. 'If I could paint…' He licked his lower lip.

'If you could paint?' she prompted.

'Then I'd paint you where I wanted to kiss you.' He took the rosebud from her and held it like a brush. 'Here.' He skimmed the edge of the petals along the curve of her neck. 'And here, where your pulse beats.' He touched the rose to where the blood throbbed. 'And here.' He drew it slowly down along her breastbone. 'And here.' He dusted it along the undercurve of her breast, making her shiver. 'And finally, here.' He teased the hardened tip of her nipple with the rose.

Oh, yes. She shivered. She really needed to feel his mouth on her.

'Guy,' she whispered.

And, the weird thing was, when Guy kissed her, he was sure he could smell roses on her skin. Right where he'd touched her with the rosebud. Of course he couldn't. He knew it wasn't physically possible. But his head was filled with roses as he took the flowers from her and dropped them on his desk.

She tipped her head back, and he kissed a path down the column of her throat. He touched the tip of his tongue to her pulse-point, and heard her give a breathy little sigh of pleasure. And then he followed the movements he'd made with the rose earlier. Between her breasts. Along the soft undercurves. And then finally closing his mouth over her nipple and sucking hard. Her hands were fisted in his hair, urging him on.

Time seemed to blur—and Guy was very, very glad that Amber was wearing a skirt rather than jeans, because he couldn't have waited long enough to take the rest of her clothes off. He needed her right here, right now. Just as he knew she needed him, because her hands were shaking as she undid the zip on his jeans.

'Condom?' she asked.

'In my wallet. Back pocket.' If there wasn't one there, he might just lose his mind.

She reached round to his back pocket, pausing to stroke the curve of his buttocks through the soft denim, then pulled out his wallet and handed it to him.

It was a matter of seconds for him to protect her. And then he was buried in her warm, sweet depths. She'd opened his shirt and his bare skin brushed against hers. Her arms were round his neck, her mouth was jammed over his and his head was full of scent. Vanilla, amber, roses. Things he'd always associate with her, from now on.

She held him tighter, and he pushed deeper into her, harder.

Their shared release, when it came, blew his mind.

And then he realised that they were both still wearing most of their clothes.

'I'm sorry, *mon ange*,' he said softly. 'That wasn't meant

to happen. Talk about no finesse.' He just hadn't been able to stop himself.

'Remind me never to go to an art gallery with you,' she said. 'I think we'd both get arrested.'

'I'd better, um, deal with things.'

She flushed. 'And I'd better get dressed.'

He kissed her. 'This was meant to be showing you how to make your own perfume blend.'

'If that's the kind of personal service you're intending for your clients, Monsieur Lefèvre, you're going to get yourself quite a reputation,' she said, giving him an arch look.

He smiled, and kissed her again. 'You drive me crazy. Do you know that?'

'It's pretty much mutual. I still can't believe you cut those roses for me. You're so precious about your roses.'

'You're worth it. The woman you are...' He stopped dead.

'What?' She frowned. 'What's wrong, Guy?'

'Nothing. That's it.' He could feel some of the clouds shifting away. 'My new perfume. "For the woman you are." That's the perfect strapline.'

'I like that,' she said, looking approving. 'But I'm not going to ask you for a preview, because I know the answer will be no.'

'It's no to everyone, right now. Don't take it personally.' He stole another kiss. 'But you definitely just inspired the strapline. And nobody's ever done that for me before.' He stroked her face. 'Back in a minute.'

When Guy returned, Amber was neatly dressed again, the roses were in a neat stack on his desk, and so were the piles of smelling strips—a small pile of definites, a similar-sized pile of definitely-nots and a larger pile of those she didn't mind.

'So are we going to make this perfume, then?' she asked.

'Sure.' He glanced at her pile of definites. 'You've got a good mix here—you've made a floriental. Amber at the top; vanilla, sandalwood and tonka bean at the base; and middle notes of rose, jasmine and orange blossom.' He fanned the sticks together and handed them to her. 'Wave them up and down in front of your nose, very quickly, and you should get the overall scent of the blend. What do you think?'

'It's nice.'

'But?'

'It feels as if there's something missing,' she said.

'You normally wear one with aldehyde top notes.' Or so she'd told him. One of the classics, though he hadn't been able to smell it on her. He sorted through her 'not sure' pile, fished out one of the sticks and slotted it into the fan. 'Try this.'

She did so, shook her head. 'No. That doesn't feel as if it fits. I don't know why, but it's wrong.'

'Interesting.' Just what he'd thought, then. The perfume she usually wore had the wrong notes. The vetiver would be right for her, and maybe the floral middle, but he would've added something sweeter to the mix, like the vanilla she'd chosen for herself. And something a little spicier. 'Let me try a couple of additions. And remember, this is your perfume, not mine. If you don't like the new notes or something still feels missing, tell me.'

She waved the fanned sticks in front of her nose, and felt her eyes widen in surprise. 'I have no idea what you just did, but that's *lovely*.'

'I added a little spice—cardamom and geranium.'

'It's perfect.' She smiled at him. 'It's got that mysterious note I wanted.'

He kissed the tip of her nose. 'Glad to oblige, *mon ange*. But you need to try it outside, away from any residual scents in here. Sniff the coffee, first, to clear your palate.'

She did so, and followed him outside, where she waved the fan of sticks in front of her nose again. 'Oh, wow. I *really* like that.' She tipped her head on one side and looked at him. 'What do you think?'

He spread his hands. 'Hey, it's your blend, your signature.'

'You helped.'

'Not much. Most of it was you,' he said. 'What are you going to call it?'

Her eyes sparkled with mischief. 'Number Three.'

'Very funny.' But he couldn't resist stealing a kiss.

'So is this the new business thing you were thinking about? Getting people to make their own perfume?'

He nodded. 'I thought I could work out maybe thirty or so blends that go well together and cover the main fragrance families. Then people could do what I've just done with you and make their own signature scent.'

'The ultimate pamper gift, designing your own fragrance? That's a fantastic idea,' she said. 'It's the kind of gift you can give people for special birthdays, Mother's Day and the like.'

'That's what I thought.' He took a pipette full of each of the scents she'd chosen, measured them into a glass bottle and mixed them together. 'Here you go. Number Three.'

'I know you don't like the name. What would you have called it?'

'Verticordia. After the painting.'

She took the bottle from him, and sniffed. 'Thank you. I'm already wearing perfume, so I can't put it on, can I?'

'It'd clash with the fragrance you use now. You'd have to wash yours off, first,' he said.

'Then I'll wear this tonight. After I've had a shower.' She inspected the bottle. 'Were you just going to give people a plain glass bottle, like this?'

'What, you want me to put this in a vintage bottle?'

'No, no, no—this is fine for me.' She flapped a hand. 'But, it's like I said before, little details make it. This bottle's perfectly functional but it's not pretty. It doesn't feel special enough to contain my own special perfume. I think you need to give people a choice of bottles, right from an inexpensive modern flask through to—well, yes, something antique and expensive, so you cater for everyone's needs. And that strapline you were talking about would work even better for this, because the scent's tailor-made for every woman.'

'That's a good thought.'

'And you need it in a box.' She was clearly on a roll, here. 'A plain one is fine, because you don't want to take the focus away from the perfume, but you need a ribbon to tie it. Something that matches a colour note in either the bottle or the tissue paper protecting the bottle.'

'Tissue paper?'

'Because, unless the bottles are all the same size and shape so you can use a custom-made box, you'll need something to protect the bottle inside the box.'

Guy looked at her, surprised. 'You seem to know a lot about packaging.'

'Because I'm one of these annoying people who spend hours wrapping presents,' she explained. 'I like adding all the flim-flam to make people feel special. The bows and the curled ribbons and maybe a sprinkling of confetti inside the wrapping. Details *matter*.'

'Like the candied rose-petals and the sparklers on your pudding.'

'Exactly.' She slid off the stool and kissed him lightly.

'Thank you for helping me make this, Guy. It's really special.'

And so, he was beginning to think, was she.

CHAPTER EIGHT

THE following morning, Guy was making notes about the perfume launch when his email pinged.

Philippe.

And he wanted a meeting. Guy sighed inwardly. He had a feeling that this was going to end with him talking to his bank manager. Though if Philippe really wanted to leave the perfume house, it wasn't fair of him to keep his business partner hanging on. And email wasn't always reliable—especially when it came to making appointments. He picked up the phone and, when Philippe answered, said, 'It's Guy. I'm coming back to Grasse this afternoon. Do you want to meet at the perfume house?'

'Your office, two o'clock?' Philippe suggested.

'*D'accord*. See you then.' He replaced the receiver and went outside in search of Amber, who was reading a magazine and texting her friends at the same time. 'I need to go back to Grasse,' he said.

She raised an eyebrow. 'Problems?'

'No,' he lied.

She reached over and squeezed his hand. 'I wasn't fishing, but you look a bit tense.'

He shrugged. 'Just some things that need sorting out.'

'With your new perfume?' She stopped herself. 'Sorry,

I know I shouldn't ask. My mouth runs away with me sometimes.'

He stole a kiss. 'It's a beautiful mouth.'

'Thank you.' She paused. 'So I guess, if you're heading back to Grasse, this is goodbye, then.'

Ending things between them would be the sensible thing to do, he knew, especially as his life was about to get messy; it wouldn't be fair to drag her into this.

'Can I email you?' she asked.

He blinked. 'Email me?'

'Your idea about designing your own perfume—I've been thinking about that and I have some thoughts about it.'

'Why don't you tell me on the way to Grasse?' The words were out before he could stop them.

She looked surprised. 'You'd take me to Grasse with you?'

Tell her no. Tell her you've changed your mind. But his mouth wasn't listening. 'If you'd like to come with me.'

'I'd love to. I've never been to Grasse. The perfume capital of the world.'

Too late, now. He couldn't back out. Then again, part of him didn't want to. He wasn't quite ready to say goodbye to her.

Then her face turned serious. 'What about my hire car?'

He shrugged. 'We could take it back to the airport this morning. I'll follow you in my car, then we'll go on to Grasse together.'

'Offer accepted.' She smiled. 'So do I get to see the bat cave in Grasse, too?'

He laughed. 'I don't live in a bat cave. And the perfume house isn't a cave, either.' And he must really need his head examined.

* * *

It didn't take Amber long to pack. After she'd dropped off her hire car at the airport in Avignon, Guy drove them to Grasse.

'I've been thinking about this "design your own perfume" thing,' Amber said. 'It's a genius idea. I can see it working as a pamper party type thing—a lot of cosmetics parties have branched out into jewellery, and customised perfume's the obvious next step. We could even do a big launch party to generate more interest in the idea.'

'No.'

'Why not?' And then she thought about it. Of course. It was *obvious*: pride. 'Look, I know you're practically a master parfumier so you won't want to let anyone else make the blends, in case they don't come up to your standards, but if you're in charge of supplying the blends and you hold training days for, I don't know, beauty salon staff or the people who are going to do the pamper party—then that won't be a problem, will it?'

'I keep my launches low-key. Word of mouth. And it's only going to be available in the Grasse shop.'

'Guy, word of mouth is great, but how do you think people find out about things in the first place? They read about it, online or in magazines.'

'Which means intrusive journalists.' He gritted his teeth. 'No.'

'They're not *all* intrusive. Some of them can be a pain, I admit, but the beauty journos are all lovely. Allie's bound to have contacts from her days at the agency. And I have contacts, too. I could help you.'

'It's not how I do things,' Guy said. 'I thought you had some good ideas about the packaging, yesterday, and I'd be very happy to consider those. But absolutely no to the media.'

He really was being ridiculously stubborn about this,

and she couldn't for the life of him see why. 'Guy, what's your problem with the media?'

His problem with the media? Ha. He blew out a breath. 'You know I used to be married to Véra. The press hassled us a fair bit.'

'That goes with the territory, Guy—you have to be realistic about things. If you're a rising star in the business world and you marry a fashion princess, of course the papers are going to want to run the story about you. It's a fairy-tale romance and the public loves that sort of thing. It sells copies.'

'That wasn't the problem.'

'Then what was?'

'Fairy tales are just that—fairy tales. This was real life, and it got messy. And the paparazzi wanted front-row seats as our marriage disintegrated.'

She frowned. 'Didn't your publicist sort it out?'

'I didn't have a publicist.'

'Well, Véra must've had one. I mean—unless you're really good at PR yourself, if you're in the public eye you need someone to help you get the right spin on a story.'

That had never occurred to him before. 'You mean, she deflected the heat off her by setting them onto me instead?'

'I have no idea. I don't know Véra, and I don't know what happened between you because I don't tend to read the gossip pages anyway—well, not unless it's a story about one of my friends and I know I'm going to have to go round with cookies and tissues and sympathy that afternoon. I read features about clothes, make-up and shoes. And recipes, though if you tell anyone that,' she warned, 'I'll deny it and then I'll stick a fork in you where it really hurts.'

He couldn't help smiling at that. 'OK. I promise I won't rat you out to the press.'

She bit her lip. 'Guy, I wasn't prying.'

'I know you weren't.' He sighed. 'Look, if I tell you, then maybe you'll understand why I don't want the press involved and you might stop nagging me.' The memories stuck in his throat for a moment. 'Véra and I should never have got married in the first place. Or, at least, she should never have given up work.'

'She gave up work to be with you?'

'I think she had this idea that I would just go into the parfumerie for an hour or so, dabble around with a couple of essences and delegate everything else so I could go home to her.'

'She didn't know you very well, then,' Amber said. 'Or understand how your job works. But why didn't she do something like developing her own make-up in tandem with your perfume?'

'She wasn't interested.' He shrugged. 'Maybe if we'd lived in Paris, near her friends, it would've been OK. Or Nice, or even Cannes—somewhere that she'd be surrounded by people from her world. She hated being on her own.' He grimaced. 'She drove me crazy at work, ringing me every few minutes—and it was never anything important, just because she was bored and wanted my attention. "High-maintenance" doesn't even begin to describe her.'

'That's what you called me,' Amber said, sounding hurt.

'You're not that much like her. Well, not often,' he said.

'Thank you for the non-compliment,' she said drily.

'It wasn't all her fault. She wanted more attention than I could give her, and I didn't understand that, for her, everything was about being a celebrity and she missed her old life. I thought she was being princessy and demanding—and I did the worst thing possible. I shut myself in my lab for some peace and quiet. She thought I was ignoring her, when really I was just trying to avoid the fights.'

'And stop her throwing things at you?'

He must've looked surprised, because she said drily, 'I remember what you said when you got the knots out of my hair.'

'Yeah, she used to throw things. That's why I moved my perfume bottle collection to the shop. When it was in our house, it'd be the first thing she'd pick up and throw.' He rolled his eyes. 'I lost some of my best examples because of her temper.'

'Ouch,' Amber said. 'That's tough.'

'It got messier after that,' he said. 'It might've been different if she hadn't given up work to be with me, or if I hadn't been trying to get the perfume house up and running and spending too much time at work.' He shrugged. 'But then her agent called and asked her to go back to work. I thought it might help because, if we were both busy, then we'd appreciate our time together. Except she went on a shoot to New York, found a photographer who paid her more attention than I did and decided she wanted a divorce.'

'Hard on you—but probably for the best, since you were making each other unhappy.'

'Yes. I could cope with that.' He sighed. 'What I couldn't deal with was the media. They spotted her canoodling in New York with her photographer, and they refused to accept my statement that we were parting due to irreconcilable differences. They wanted the dirt behind the story. They wanted to know how I felt and they expected me to bleed on their front pages. I hated it, Amber. All the questions and the demands. It was relentless. At home, at the office, in my lab… They were everywhere. That's why I keep all my launches low-key, so I don't have to deal with that kind of thing again. It drives Philippe mad—my business partner thinks the way you do, that I should cosy up to them—but it's not the way I do things. And it's not negotiable. I don't want the press sniffing round.'

Especially because, if they started digging for dirt, the way they had when he and Véra had split up, they could find out that he'd been visiting doctors. They'd start adding up the clues and start speculating until one of them hit on the truth about his anosmia—and then all hell would be let loose. He had to keep the press at bay until he'd found the solution, dealt with it and no damage could be done to the perfume house. Not just for his own sake, but for the people who worked for him, who'd supported him through the tough times and didn't deserve to be let down so badly.

'Not all the press are bad, Guy,' Amber said softly. 'I'm sorry they gave you a hard time. But this wouldn't be that kind of story. This would be one for the features magazines. About how to make people feel special, the kind of one-off treat that would really put sparkle into someone's life. It's a feel-good, positive story.'

'No,' Guy said.

Talk about stubborn. The man was impossible. Surely he could see it would make good business sense? Though admittedly the journos probably would mention that he used to be married to Véra. She could see how that would rub a bit of salt in his wounds.

'Let's change the subject, as we're here,' Guy said. 'Welcome to the perfume capital of the world.'

The town was built on a hill, spreading down to what Amber guessed would be flower fields in the spring and summer; it was dominated by a church and a tower.

'I had no idea it would be so pretty here.'

'Apparently, it was Queen Victoria's favourite winter spot.'

'I can see why. Have you lived here for long?'

'For about seven years, now. Though I still get the same rush when I come home as I did when I first came here as a small child, when my mother brought me here to buy a birthday present for her aunt and took me to see all the old-fashioned lab equipment in the museum.'

'So you were the family's mad scientist even then?' she teased.

He laughed. '*Absolument*. Papa bought me a chemistry set for my birthday, one year, and my mother had kittens that I was going to blow up the château.' He parked in a narrow street. 'I'm afraid this is as near as we can get to my flat because the roads are too narrow for traffic in this part of town. This is the *vielle ville*, the old town. It's quiet and you can go for a stroll and just lose yourself in your thoughts without all the noise and fumes of traffic.'

He helped her out of the car, then took her cases from the back. 'This way.' He led her through winding streets that she could see were way too narrow for cars and were lined with ancient buildings—five-storey houses, painted in red-and-yellow ochre, with narrow doorways and tall, narrow windows with shutters painted in *eau de nil*. Everywhere she looked, there were old-fashioned wrought-iron lamps and hanging baskets filled with scarlet geraniums.

'We need bread and milk,' he said, stopping outside a delicatessen. 'Will you be OK if I leave you here with your cases?' At her nod, he said, 'I'll be two minutes, OK?'

While Amber waited for him, she took in her surroundings. Further ahead, the narrow street became a series of steps, and bistro tables were even perched on the steps outside what she presumed were cafés. Everywhere seemed fresh and vibrant and busy—and yet at the same time there was the slower pace of life she'd come to associate with Guy, people lingering over coffee and pastries and browsing through newspapers. She could see exactly why he loved it here. She could easily fall in love with this part of France herself—even more than she adored Paris.

He emerged from the deli with a baguette and a paper carrier bag. 'Would you mind carrying these for me?' he asked.

'It's OK. I can manage my own luggage,' she said.

'Absolutely not,' he said, and handed her his purchases before picking up her cases.

She could see it would be pointless to argue with him, so she followed him through one of the little narrow archways she'd noticed earlier. It opened up into a pretty square with a fountain and a tree in the middle.

'That's Grasse for you,' he said with a grin as she exclaimed in delight. 'Full of surprises. And this is where I live.' He gestured towards a town house that was painted a sunny yellow colour with grey shutters; the wrought-iron balconies were filled with pots of shrubs.

'This is all yours?' she asked.

'Only one floor of it,' he said. *'Bienvenue.'* He tapped in a code to let them through the front door, then strode up the stairs to the next floor.

Amber wasn't sure what she'd been expecting—something like the château, perhaps?—but his flat was a revelation. Most of it was open-plan: there was a small kitchen with cabinets painted china-blue and cream to one side, then a living room with a comfortable-looking cream leather sofa, a glass-topped table and two wrought-iron chairs set by one window and what looked like a seriously expensive sound system in the corner. The floor was polished wood, with a large Persian rug in shades of ruby, ochre and navy spread across the centre. There were voile curtains and cream drapes at the windows and the French doors, the walls were painted cream and hung with modern watercolours of what she guessed were places in Grasse. Along the mantelpiece, there were framed photographs of Xavier and two older people that looked enough like him and Guy to be their parents, and one of Guy laughing up at the camera with a chocolate Labrador sprawled all over him.

'Your dog?' she asked.

'Noisette,' he confirmed. 'I lost her just over three years ago, and then I moved to my flat.' He shrugged. 'It's just never been the right time to get another dog.'

She remembered the conversation they'd had, the night he'd let her take him out to dinner. He still missed his dog, and she caught the wistfulness in his voice.

'The bathroom's here, if you want to freshen up,' he said, gesturing to one of the two doors leading off the main room, 'and the bedroom's here. I'll make some coffee while you unpack, yes?'

'That'd be wonderful. Thank you.'

He took her cases through into the bedroom and set them on the bed. 'Help yourself to whatever space you need. There should be some spare hangers in the wardrobe.' He glanced at the lighter of her two cases. 'Though I'm afraid I don't quite run to a shoe room.'

'That's OK. The shoes can stay in their case.'

Guy's wardrobe was built-in, and the doors were painted the same colour as the walls. It was such a relaxing room, she thought: as light and airy as the living room, again with a wooden floor and cream walls, but here the curtains were navy blue and toned with the blue oriental rug next to the bed. The bed was king-sized, she noticed, with a wrought-iron headboard and soft-looking pillows and pure white bed-linen. There was a table next to the bed with a lamp, a clock and a book; she couldn't resist taking a look, wondering what he read for pleasure. Although it was in French, she was able to work out from the back cover that it was a biography of Marie Antoinette's parfumier. Guy had already admitted to being a workaholic, so she wasn't too surprised that his idea of a relaxing read was related to his work.

By the time she'd finished unpacking—and it felt strange to have her clothes hanging up next to his in the wardrobe, something she'd never done with any of her former partners—Guy had made coffee and set the table with bread, butter and cheese.

'Thank you,' she said as she sat opposite him. 'I love how you've decorated your flat. And those paintings are beautiful.'

'They're of Grasse,' he said. 'My neighbour downstairs is an artist. I bought them at her last exhibition.'

'I can see why. And they make me want to go out exploring, to see if I can find the places she painted,' she said.

'Maybe you can explore the town a bit this afternoon,' he said, 'while I'm in a meeting.'

She smiled. 'Oh, I have every intention of exploring. *Especially* the shoe shops.'

He eyed her in disbelief. 'You don't have enough shoes with you?'

'A girl can never have too many pairs of shoes,' she said airily.

'I submit.' He fished in his pocket and took a key off the keyring. 'I need to get going, so I'll give you my spare key.' He kissed her swiftly. 'I'll call you when I'm done at the office and I'll carry your new shoes home for you.'

'Excellent—you're well on the way to being trained,' she teased. 'I'll clear up here, first.'

'No. You're my guest.'

'And you have a meeting. I'll handle this.' She shooed him to the door.

He kissed her again. 'Thank you, for being so understanding.'

Amber cleared away their lunch things, then headed out to explore. She browsed round one of the museums, then spent a very satisfying half-hour in one of the shoe shops. And then she realised that the shop next door was GL Parfums; she couldn't resist going in for a look round. The shop was airy and bright, and the perfumes themselves were lovely, but what really caught her attention was the display of antique perfume bottles. They were so beautiful; why on earth had Véra smashed some of them in temper?

She bought some of Guy's posh shower gel for Sheryl, and then wandered through the old town again until she found a café in a pretty square. Despite the fact that it was October, it was still warm enough here to sit outside. Like an Indian summer day in London, she thought. She texted Sheryl to say that she was staying in France for a bit longer, this time in Grasse.

Two minutes later, her phone beeped. *With Guy? Just be careful and don't fall in love with him.*

She texted back, *'Course I won't.* But she knew even as she tapped the keys that she was lying: she was already doing that. For lots of reasons, and not just because the sex was good—she'd finally learned to tell the difference between lust and something deeper. She liked Guy's quick mind, and his ready smile, and the intensity in his gorgeous blue eyes whenever he looked at her. The way he argued with her, even—because it showed that he took her seriously and saw her as more than just a party girl. He thought that her ideas were valid and worth talking about. And he'd asked her to think about packaging for his 'design your own perfume' line.

Being with him made her feel different. He'd shown her a side of life she hadn't seen before—something with a slow pace, something with depth. And it was something she realised now that she wanted more of. That maybe in the past she'd rushed into things because she'd been looking for the place where she'd fit: and, now she'd stopped rushing, she'd found what she'd been looking for. Not where she'd expected to find it, either: with someone who was her complete opposite.

Although they'd said their affair was only temporary, maybe, she thought, if they took it slowly, this might develop into something more. Something with a future.

Could they make a go of it? It would mean compromise—probably more on her part than on his, she thought, because she'd be the one who'd have to move and change to fit in here. But he'd brought her here, to the more serious side of his life: the place where he lived and worked. And he'd let her into his lab at the château. To her, that suggested that he was letting her closer and taking his barriers down.

And maybe, just maybe, they had a chance.

She was still thinking about him when her phone rang.

'*Alors, mon ange*, I'm done. Where are you?'

'I'm sitting in a square, drinking coffee.' She glanced round quickly to find the street name, and couldn't spot it. 'Um, I'm not sure whereabouts exactly.' She named the café. 'And there's a florist's shop next door.'

'I know where you are. I'll come and meet you.' She could almost hear the smile in his voice: slightly amused, indulgent. No doubt most of the cafés in Grasse had a flower shop or a perfume shop nearby.

She'd just finished her coffee when he arrived. He stooped down to kiss her and sat down opposite her. Her heart skipped a beat as he smiled at her; she still couldn't quite believe that he was all hers, even though it was only for a little while.

He set some paper carrier bags on the empty chair between them. At her look of surprise, he said, 'This is dinner. I picked up a few things at the market on the way here.'

'I thought you didn't cook?'

'I'm not completely incompetent in a kitchen.' He shrugged. 'Though I admit I don't normally bother if I'm on my own. So how many million pairs of shoes do I have to carry?'

'Two carrier bags. Though I might have to go back tomorrow because I really should've bought this pretty scarlet pair…'

He groaned. 'You're a shoe-aholic.'

'What, you noticed?' she deadpanned.

When they returned to his flat, he started getting things out in the kitchen area. 'I'm going to make us a casserole. I'm sorry, there are a couple of little admin-type things I need to do while it's cooking, but feel free to take a shower or a bath or what have you.'

'I'll definitely take you up on that.' She blew out a breath. 'I can see why you're so fit, walking uphill all the time. My muscles are already protesting!'

He laughed. 'You get used to it, *mon ange*. Help yourself to whatever you need in the bathroom.'

She thoroughly enjoyed wallowing in a warm, deep bath filled with bubbles—especially as she could smell garlic and tomatoes and herbs, meaning that Guy was cooking something Provençal-style.

And then, a few minutes later, she frowned. She could smell burning. And it was getting stronger.

'Guy? Is everything OK?' she called.

When he didn't answer, she climbed out of the bath, wrapped a towel round herself—more to stop herself trailing water everywhere than for modesty's sake—and opened the bathroom door. She could see straight away what was happening: the heat was set too high and Guy's casserole had caught on the bottom of the pan.

Quickly, she grabbed a tea towel and used it as a makeshift oven glove, moving the pan onto a cold part of the hob. Guy was completely oblivious, working on a laptop on the table, with his back to the kitchen and headphones on. No wonder he hadn't heard her call out to him. But why on earth hadn't he smelled the burning? Even her father, the most focused man she'd ever met, wouldn't have been able to work through that.

She turned off the hob, then walked over to Guy and laid a hand on his shoulder.

He jumped, looked up at her and removed his headphones. 'Sorry, I didn't hear you call me. Is everything OK?'

'No.' She frowned. 'Guy, your fish is ruined.'

He blinked. 'How do you mean?'

'The ring was turned up too high and it caught on the bottom of the pan. Can't you smell it?'

He went white. 'Sorry. I got caught up in work and all my attention was focused elsewhere. I apologise for dragging you out of your bath—and for making dinner inedible. I'll take you out to eat tonight instead. There's a nice restaurant round the corner.'

'Guy, didn't you—?' she began.

'I'll deal with it,' he cut in, his tone making it very clear that he didn't want to discuss it. He'd gone moody on her again, putting up all his glass walls, and she had no idea why. Was this reminding him of some fight he'd had with Véra or something?

'Go back to your bath, if it hasn't got too cold.' He shooed her back to the bathroom.

Hell, hell, hell. This was worse even than he'd imagined it could be, Guy thought as he scraped the fish and the burned Provençal sauce into the bin. How could he not have smelled something so foul and so strong?

And it was obvious that Amber hadn't accepted his excuse that he'd been so focused on work that he'd blocked everything out.

Stupid.

Maybe he should tell her the truth.

But then she'd start to pity him, and he knew he couldn't handle that.

To his relief, she didn't mention it when she emerged from the bedroom, or on the way to the little restaurant in one of the squares near his flat. She kept the conversation light, telling him about where she'd visited in the town—and he knew he was being a lousy host, nodding and smiling at what he hoped were the right points but not offering much to the conversation. The knot of misery in his throat was too tight.

Even though the food was good, Guy could hardly swallow a thing, and ended up pushing his food around the plate.

'Are you all right?' Amber asked.

There was no judgement in her eyes. Only concern. This was the point where he knew he should open up. Tell her that he was far from being all right, and that his world was falling apart. He even opened his mouth to tell her.

But the words that came out weren't what he'd intended.

'I'm fine. It's just another headache.' That bit at least was true; the headache he'd had since that morning still hadn't shifted.

'Guy, if something's worrying you, you know you can talk to me and it won't go any further.' She curled her fingers round his.

'It's just a headache.' Guy forced himself to smile and be charming, and to his relief Amber responded. And when they went back to his flat, they sat on his balcony, sharing a glass of wine and looking out over the lights of the town in companionable silence.

Though he couldn't sleep. Even making love with Amber didn't help him lose himself completely: the worry was still there, at the back of his mind. In the end, he got up—quietly, so as not to disturb her—and closed the bedroom door behind him.

Maybe this time he'd find what he was looking for. Or maybe it was time he tried a specialist outside France. Someone who could help him right now, so he could put his life back together again.

CHAPTER NINE

WHEN Amber woke in the middle of the night, the bed was cold. Where was Guy? She could see a tiny crack of light around the edge of the door; clearly he was doing something in the living room. She climbed out of bed, pulled on her silky wrap, and opened the door. Guy was sitting on the sofa, hunched over his laptop, with his headphones on; he hadn't switched any of the lights on, so clearly the glow from the screen was what she'd seen.

What on earth was he doing on his laptop at this time of night? She couldn't see him as the type who'd mess about with social media, and he didn't strike her as the type who'd spend hours playing games online, either.

As she drew nearer she looked over his shoulder. The website was in French, and the title bar didn't help much: *cause et traitement d'anosmia.*

'Cause' and 'treatment' were easy enough to work out. But anosmia? It wasn't a word she knew.

'Guy?' she said, putting her hand on his shoulder.

He jumped, and nearly dropped his laptop. Hastily, he closed the page, then removed his headphones, closed the laptop and put it on his coffee table. 'Amber? What are you doing here?'

'I woke up and you weren't there. I saw the light, so I

came out to see what you were doing.' She frowned. 'Are you all right?'

'I'm fine.'

'You don't look it.' He looked haunted, and there were lines of strain around his eyes. And she was pretty sure it was to do with whatever he'd been looking at. 'What's anosmia?'

'Nothing. Go back to bed, *mon ange*.'

'I can go onto the Internet and put it through one of those translation websites,' she said, 'but it'd be quicker and easier for you to tell me.'

'I…' He sighed and shook his head. 'I don't want to discuss this. Go back to bed.'

'Guy, I know something's wrong. OK, so I don't know you that well, but over the last few days I've been finding it easier to read you—and right now I can tell that you're really tense.' She took his hand. 'You can talk to me.'

He said nothing.

She sighed. 'Guy, if this is something personal, it's not going any further than me. I promise you. And I always keep my promises.'

He still didn't say a word.

'All right. I'll look it up for myself.'

He closed his eyes. 'It's the inability to smell,' he said, his voice flat.

'But why are you looking at…?' she began—and then it hit her. And lots of things started adding up and making sense. Why he'd avoided her questions about his work. Why he hadn't smelled the fish burning. Why he'd put barriers up. 'You've lost your sense of smell?'

Bile rose in Guy's throat, thin and sour. The words echoed in his head: *you've lost your sense of smell. You've lost your sense of smell.* Slow and deep and monotonous, like a bell tolling. The death-knell of all his dreams.

He pulled his fingers away from hers and buried his face in his hands instead. 'Yes,' he muttered hoarsely. 'God help me, I can't smell anything.'

And then she was next to him on the sofa, wrapping her arms round him and holding him close.

'You need to talk about it, Guy,' she said. 'You can't keep something this big inside you. It'll destroy you.'

He already felt as if he were crumbling, but her arms were round him, shoring him up.

'Talk to me,' she said softly. 'I'm not going anywhere, and I'm not going to tell anyone what you say. This is between you and me. Just talk to me.'

He pulled her onto his lap. And at last, with her arms wrapped round him and his arms wrapped round her, he was able to let the words spill out. 'I had this virus. It must be three or four months ago, now.' He tried to sound casual about it, but he knew down to the minute when he'd first realised that something was wrong. 'I lost my sense of smell. I thought it was just the virus, but then I felt better and I still couldn't smell properly.' He damped down the shudder that racked through him.

'What did your doctor say?' she asked gently.

'He said I had to wait and see. So I bypassed him and went to a specialist. He said the same. And then I got a second opinion. I rang him for the test results, the day before the wedding.' He dragged in a breath. 'I'm sorry, that's part of why I was so rude to you that day.'

'That doesn't matter, now,' she said. 'What did he say?'

'He said that it might take up to three years. And also that I might never be able to smell properly again—there were no guarantees I'd get it all back. Which means my career would be finished.'

'Oh, Guy.' She held him close. 'Have you noticed any change for the better?'

'What do you think? I couldn't even smell the fish burning tonight.'

'But you were absorbed in your work.'

'Any normal person would've smelled it. You did.'

'I was lazing around in the bath. I've burned things before now because I was concentrating on something else.' She stroked his hair back from his forehead. 'Are the headaches you've been getting anything to do with it?'

He closed his eyes and rested his forehead against her shoulder. *Dieu*, he needed her warmth. And if only he could smell her scent. 'It's probably stress. Right now I'm panicking about what the hell I'm going to do if my sense of smell doesn't come back.'

'Have you talked to Xav about it?'

'How could I? The first couple of months, I thought it would all sort itself out. When it didn't… Well, September's harvest, Xav's busiest time of year. He didn't need the extra pressure of worrying about me. And then there was the wedding. It wouldn't have been fair of me to dump this on him and ruin his happiness.' He straightened up and blew out a breath. Enough of being weak and self-indulgent. 'I'm fine. I'll handle it.'

'You're not fine, Guy,' she said softly, stroking his face. 'Don't shut me out. Maybe you're putting yourself under so much pressure here that you're not giving yourself a chance to heal. Is there anyone who could take the heat off you, step into your shoes for a little bit? Your second-in-command at the perfume house, say, or your business partner or someone?'

'Definitely not my business partner.' The idea was so

unthinkable, he nearly laughed. 'Philippe's the last person I'd talk to about this.'

'Why?' She sounded confused. 'Surely he'd be the first?'

'At one time, maybe.' He sighed. 'The thing is, we've had an offer on the perfume house. From a large conglomerate. Our last perfume did quite well, and I suppose it brought us to the attention of the big players. And Philippe thinks we should accept the offer.'

'I take it you don't?'

'No. I like how we do things at GL Parfums. We're like a family. Everyone knows who everyone is, everyone looks out for everyone else. If you put some conglomerate in charge, things will change—it'll start getting faceless, full of paperwork and all about shaving down the costs instead of creating the best perfumes for our customers. We'll have to use the parent company's corporate suppliers because they'll be cheaper than the ones we use now—that, or drive the costs down so far that it'll push our normal suppliers out of business.' He shook his head in disgust. 'These are people I've known for years. People who gave me a chance when I started out, who've put in the hours and been loyal to me—how can I possibly betray them by selling out?'

'So don't sell,' she said. 'Buy Philippe's share of the business.'

'That's pretty much the decision I'd already come to. Buy Philippe's share and keep GL Parfums as it is—either talking the bank into giving me a loan, or finding another partner.' He grimaced. 'Though it'll be practically impossible to find an investor who doesn't want a say in how things are run. Philippe was brilliant until now, but he's bored and wants a new challenge. And it's not fair to make everyone at the perfume house face the same uncertainties with another partner, a couple of years down the line.'

'Why did you go into partnership with him in the first place?' she asked.

'Because I didn't want to wait until I'd made enough money to buy my premises and equipment outright. I was chasing a dream: having my own perfume house, developing scents that would be special to people—scents that were my own ideas, my own creations. There are people who think I wanted too much, too soon.' He shrugged. 'Maybe they were right. But at the time I thought I was doing the right thing. Philippe's the oldest brother of one of my university friends. He was on my wavelength, until now.' He blew out a breath. 'Well, it got a bit sticky six months in, when Véra decided to take me for every euro she could in the divorce settlement, but Xav bailed me out. We've done well enough for me to have paid him back last year.'

'So you can get a loan or find a new partner—that'll get the conglomerate off your back. So what's the problem?'

'People get bored with scents.'

She frowned, obviously not following. 'Chanel No 5's been going for years.'

'There are classics, yes—perfumes that have lasted for more than ten years—but the average lifespan of a new perfume is two years. The perfume market changes that quickly,' he explained. 'Basically, perfume doesn't stand still. You need to keep developing a scent, either introducing new ones or bringing a new twist to your classic lines. And, if I've lost my nose, I can't do that. I can't do my job.'

'Could you get someone to stand in for you until your sense of smell comes back?' she suggested.

'If I'm honest,' he said, 'I'm not sure I could handle that.

I'd hate going to work every day and knowing that it's not my vision or my creativity moving things forward. The new perfume's going to buy me a few months, but that's all.' He blew out a breath. 'I know I've got to find some kind of compromise, but right now I can't see what.'

Amber suddenly remembered how he'd described developing a new scent. 'You said it was like music. Well, Beethoven still composed when he was deaf, and think how fantastic his ninth symphony is. And you said that you smell perfume in your mind just from the name of the scent, so maybe you can still work?'

'The perfume starts off in my mind,' he said softly, 'but it's only once I've mixed it and sampled it that I know whether the formula needs tweaking or if the balance isn't right. So, no—I don't see how I can continue if my sense of smell doesn't come back.'

'Oh, Guy.' She hated seeing the bleakness in his face. 'It will come back. It has to.'

'That's what I've been telling myself.'

And he didn't believe a word of it. That much was obvious.

'OK, let's look at the really darkest side. If it does turn out that your sense of smell won't come back, then you can get someone in to help you so you can keep the perfume house going.'

'I know.' He dragged in a breath. 'But it won't be the same. It won't be my vision any more, my dream.'

'Yes, it will. Nobody can take away the fragrances you've already designed. Plus there's the "design your own perfume" stuff—I bet you already have a good idea which kind of blends you were going to offer. The person you get in to take over your old job can just fine-tune them for you. It'll still be *your* vision. And, after that...'

'That's what I'm most afraid of,' he said.

'Think laterally. Allie said you have an encyclopaedic memory, that you know about practically all the perfumes that were ever invented. You could be a perfume historian, the person the media comes to when it needs an expert quote.'

'Work for one of the museums, you mean?'

'Or set up your own museum. The important thing is, you don't have to shut yourself off from the world of perfume. You have all that knowledge. You could teach, maybe, write books about it. I know it wouldn't be the same as creating new fragrances, but you don't have to lose *everything*.'

'It just feels like it.'

Hating to see him so hurt, and not knowing how else to help, she cupped his face in her hands and brushed her mouth against his. Her lips moved against his, taking tiny nibbling kisses until he opened his mouth and let her deepen the kiss and take the lead.

When she broke the kiss, he was shaking.

'Guy, I don't know how to help you. I can't fix this for you, and I really wish I could.' She stroked his face. 'But I can do one thing for you—I can make you forget it, just for a little while, to give you a little headspace.' She kissed him again, and shifted on his lap so that she was straddling him; she could feel his erection pressing against her and rocked against him.

'Amber, I need to see you,' he said, his voice hoarse. He undid her wrap, letting her breasts spill into his hands. He teased her nipples with the pads of his thumbs until she tipped her head back, then took one nipple into his mouth and sucked, making her gasp.

'You're stunning, Amber, just stunning,' he breathed against her skin. 'And the way you make me feel...'

She held her breath. Did he feel the same way that she did? Was he going to say it?

But he let the sentence trail off, instead concentrating on kissing every inch of her breasts, lingering on the soft undersides until she arched against him, wanting more.

'Guy.' She dragged in a breath and slowly pushed his robe down off his shoulders. 'You're beautiful. Like a perfect sculpture.' She stroked his pectoral muscles, feeling the light dusting of hair tickle her fingertips. 'Except you're warm.' And all hers. Even if it was only for a little while.

He kissed her again, his mouth sweet and yearning. 'Take me to bed, Amber,' he invited.

She slid off his lap, took his hand and drew him to his feet, then led him back to his bedroom. She switched on the bedside light, then stood on tiptoe and kissed him hard. By the time she broke the kiss, his penis was iron-hard and he was quivering with need.

'Condom?' she asked.

'In the drawer.'

She found the foil packet, ripped it open and rolled the condom over his penis. 'All mine,' she said.

Guy was right where he wanted to be, lying back against soft downy pillows with Amber kneeling astride him, her beautiful curls all messy and her mouth looking as if she'd been thoroughly kissed. Somehow she managed to look wanton and regal all at the same time—and he wanted her. Badly. She was right: she could make him lose himself.

And he loved her for doing this. For being so generous with herself—so unlike his ex.

She wrapped her fingers round his shaft to position him where she wanted him, and eased slowly down over him.

'Oh, *Dieu*,' Guy said, completely lost, and her fingers tangled with his.

Pleasure built and built and built, leaving no room for any worries. All he could focus on was Amber: how good she felt wrapped around him, how much he loved the feel of her skin against his and how much he needed her.

And even though he knew he was being selfish, taking everything she offered, he lost himself within her; she was warm and sweet and comforting, pure balm to his soul. He pushed in deeper, wanting more, and she quickened her pace, rocking over him. At last he felt her body begin to tighten round his; as he fell into his own release he sat up and wrapped his arms round her, holding her tightly, as if he'd never let her go.

He never wanted to let her go—and how unfair was that? Right now, he had nothing to offer her except failure.

As if she felt him tense, she shifted and kissed him. 'Don't start thinking again, Guy,' she whispered. 'Just be.'

Oh, he could fall in love with this woman.

Could?

No, it was too late for that. He'd already fallen in love with her. With her sunny smile and her soulful eyes and the sheer unabashed pleasure she took in things. So what if she was a party girl, a media darling like his ex? Somehow that had stopped mattering. She was warm and sweet and like sunshine on a frosty day. And she made his world a better place. Especially right now, when everything felt so dark and constricting that he could hardly breathe.

Gently, he moved her off him and kissed her swiftly.

Afterwards, he climbed back into bed with her and settled with her in his arms, his body curved spoon-style round hers. As he heard her breathing grow deep and regular he brushed his mouth against her shoulder. '*Je t'aime*, Amber,' he whispered. Words it wouldn't be fair to say to her when she was awake, but words he needed to say to her. *'Je t'aime.'*

If only things could be different.

CHAPTER TEN

AMBER woke before Guy, the next morning. In sleep, he looked relaxed, with none of the strain or wariness in his face.

If only I could fix your world for you, she thought. But I can't. I know how important your work is to you. Nothing will be able to take its place and I won't be enough to stop you missing it, no matter how hard I try. I love you—not just because you look gorgeous and you make my knees go weak, but because you're different. You're not like my losers and liars. You're honest and you're clever and you're serious; but you're also witty and fun to be with, and you make me see the world in a different way.

But I also know that my love isn't going to be enough for you. You need more. You need to be able to create your fragrances. Without that, you won't feel that you're yourself: and I don't know how to make you see that yes, your work's important, but there's also more to you than that.

Quietly, she slid out of bed, borrowed his bathrobe—it was too big for her and she needed to wrap the belt round herself twice, but it was warm and comforting and it smelled of him—and went to make them both some coffee.

He was awake when she brought the mugs through. She kissed him gently. 'How's your head?'

'I'm getting used to waking up with a headache,' he said. 'It's OK.'

She almost suggested that he took the day off; but then, the way things were going, he was likely to have more days than he wanted away from his work in the future. Better that he enjoyed whatever time he could at the perfume house. She climbed back into bed with him. 'Anything I can do?'

He kissed her. 'No, but you're lovely—do you know that? You make my world a brighter place.'

She laughed, but his words warmed her deep inside. He made her world a brighter place, too. And, coming from a private man like Guy, it was practically a declaration of his feelings. 'Very smooth, Monsieur Lefèvre. Thank you for the compliment.'

'What are you going to do today?' he asked.

'I assume you're going to be working, so I might wander round town.'

'I do have a pile of meetings,' he admitted. 'And I need to work on the new perfume. Gina's sent me the design, and it's good.'

'Of course it is. She's brilliant. And your new perfume is going to knock everyone's socks off.' She paused. 'Guy, do you have a model in mind?'

He raised an eyebrow. 'Are you offering?'

'No. But I do know someone gorgeous who never does ads for beauty products, even though people are always asking her. And I know she'd make an exception for you, if I asked her.' She lifted her chin. 'My mum. That'd get you tons of publicity—the fact that Libby Wynne's modelling for you.'

'Trying to fix things for me, *mon ange*?'

'In my airhead party-girl way.'

'There's nothing airhead about you, and you know it,' Guy said. He glanced at the clock. 'And I'm going to be late if I don't get a move on. Thank you for the offer—I'll think about it, if you don't mind?'

'Of course.' He was being nice about it, but she knew she'd been pushy. It was just that she so badly wanted to do something to help. To make his world right again.

Sheryl, her best friend, was engaged to a doctor. Hugh worked with children rather than adults, but he was bound to know a specialist in his hospital who dealt with nose problems and might have some suggestions that Guy's doctors hadn't already thought of. After she'd kissed Guy goodbye and waved him off to work, she sent Sheryl a text, explaining the situation and asking her if Hugh could give her any advice. *Obviously this has to stay confidential*, she added—even though she knew she didn't really have to say it. Sheryl was her best friend and she knew the hassles Amber had had with *Celebrity Life*.

She spent the rest of the morning reading up about anosmia on the Internet, and what she read made her heart ache. Guy must be going crazy. Waiting would definitely drive her nuts, and her sense of smell wasn't that important; her career didn't depend on it, the way Guy's did. But she was shocked to discover that loss of smell also caused loss of taste. If she was in Guy's position and knew that she'd never again be able to taste a ripe, freshly picked English strawberry still warm from the sun, or the sharpness of blue cheese on fresh bread, she'd be so miserable.

Please, she begged silently, let Hugh be able to come up with something new. Something that could fix things for Guy.

In the afternoon, Amber explored more of Grasse, wandering round tiny churches and gardens that would no doubt be even prettier in the spring. She could really understand why Guy loved it here. She was falling for the place herself.

When Guy came home, that evening, he looked tired, so she refused his offer of dinner out. 'Put your feet up. I wasn't sure what we were doing tonight so I picked up some fresh pasta, bread and salad at the market, in case you wanted to eat in. It's not as if it'll take more than five minutes to cook.' She didn't want to admit just how much she was enjoying pottering round and being domestic. The people in her usual social set would laugh at her, with the exception of Sheryl; and, although she knew that Guy wasn't like them, she didn't want him to feel pressured. As if she had *expectations*.

'It's really sweet of you,' Guy said, 'but I'm not expecting you to wait on me.'

'I know. If you did, I wouldn't have offered.'

He laughed. 'That's contrary.'

'No. It's because you don't take me for granted that I'm happy to do it.'

'Then thank you, *mon ange*. Pasta, bread and salad would be very nice.'

Though she could still see the strain in his face after they'd had dinner. 'Another headache?' she asked gently.

'Yes. I'll take some paracetamol and it'll be fine.'

'Come and sit with me,' she said. 'Lie with your head in my lap, and I'll massage your scalp. One of my friends taught me how to do Indian head massage, and it's brilliant.'

'Now there's an offer I won't refuse.' He took a headache tablet, then came to sprawl on the sofa with her. He closed his eyes as she slid her fingers into his hair and started to massage his scalp and temples. 'That feels good, *chérie*. Thank you.'

'Pleasure.' She stroked the hair away from his forehead. 'So how was your day?'

'OK. I've given Gina the go-ahead. And I had an appointment at the bank to discuss buying Philippe's share of the perfume house.'

Which was one of the biggest weights on him right now, she knew. And she'd been thinking about how she might be able to help. 'Guy, if you need a business partner, I'm sure my d—'

He reached up to press his fingertip gently against her mouth, stopping her saying any more. 'Thank you for the offer, *mon ange*, but I'm OK. Really. I can sort this for myself. Things might be a bit tight for a while, but the deal's on the table. They're going to tell me their decision first thing tomorrow morning. I've worked out a business plan, and I'm pretty sure they're going to say yes.'

'Of course they will. You're fantastic at what you do and you're just about to launch a new perfume that's going to be the height of cool. You're an excellent risk.'

Though they both knew what she wasn't saying.

He was an excellent risk, provided his sense of smell came back.

And, if it didn't…

Then his future could be very tough indeed.

'Will you ring me when you hear?' she asked, the next morning as he opened the front door to leave.

'Of course, *chérie*.' He kissed her goodbye. 'Wish me luck.'

'Break a leg,' she said, trying to sound bright and cheerful, for his sake.

But she was fidgety all morning, worrying about Guy. The only thing she could think of to keep herself occupied was to do some baking. Luckily there was a grocer's just round the corner where she could buy the ingredients she needed—along with a vanilla pod and chocolate.

Keeping her hands busy helped to calm her down; the scent of vanilla cupcakes and choc-chip cookies helped even more, but it also made her realise just how difficult it was for Guy. Losing a sense, for her, would make her life flat. For him, it was his whole life. The thing that made him himself. If his sense of smell didn't come back, he'd be in hell.

She was halfway through getting the last batch of cookies out of the oven when her phone began to ring and when she saw it was Guy, she almost dropped the tray. She managed to shove it on top of the hob in time, then grabbed her phone—just as the call went through to voicemail.

'No-o-o!' Voicemail wasn't good enough. She needed to talk to him.

She gave it fifteen seconds for him to leave a message and end the call—which felt more like fifteen minutes, the second hand on the clock dragged round so slowly—and rang him. Engaged. She ended the call, pressed redial and kept doing it until at last his phone rang.

'Guy? Sorry, I haven't checked voicemail but I was getting cookies out of the oven when you rang. What happened?'

'You've been baking?'

'It was that or chew my nails off. What did they say?'

'You know how banks are.'

'Guy, I swear, I'm going to smack you over the head with the cookie tray when I see you if you don't tell me *right now.*'

He laughed. 'They said yes, *mon ange.*'

She whooped. 'Brilliant.'

'So I'm playing hooky and taking you to lunch. In fact, we're going to be out all afternoon.'

'Is this a good idea? Don't you have work to do?'

'It can wait. Right now I want to celebrate. With you.'

He was home within fifteen minutes. And he ate three cookies in quick succession after walking through the front door.

'You didn't taste a single one of those, did you?' she asked wryly.

He spread his hands. 'Hey. I had to check.' He gave her the most disarming smile. 'The texture was good, though,' he added.

'Thank you. I think.'

He kissed her swiftly. 'I'm going to change. You're fine as you are—you just need shoes.'

'Funny you should say that. I bought that scarlet pair, yesterday.'

He laughed. 'Now why doesn't that surprise me?'

They walked down the hill to where he'd parked his car, and he drove them south, towards the sea.

'We're going to the beach?' she asked.

'I was actually going to take you to Le Suquet, the old part of Cannes, but if you really want to go and do the touristy thing and walk along La Croisette and put your hand on top of a celebrity handprint, or go shopping in designer boutiques, we can do that.'

'No, that's fine. Though if there's a shoe shop in Le Suquet, I might be forced to go in.'

He laughed. 'Lunch, first, I think.'

Le Suquet turned out to be really pretty, with fantastic views of the old port and the bay. And, after a leisurely lunch at a tiny bistro, Amber enjoyed wandering through the narrow streets with Guy, their arms wrapped round each other. She took pictures over the bay in the late afternoon, when the sun made the water look incredibly enticing. 'This has to be one of the nicest days I've ever spent,' she said.

'Me, too,' he said.

Their eyes met, and for a moment Amber couldn't breathe. Was he going to say it…?

But he simply tucked an errant curl behind her ear. '*Mon ange*,' he said softly.

Angel. It was the loveliest, sweetest endearment. But she so badly wanted to hear the three little words that should go with it.

She could see he was looking at her mouth, so she tipped her head back in offering. He smiled and cupped her face in his hands. 'You're adorable.'

So are you, Amber thought as he kissed her. And I love you. And I want you to love me back.

But now wasn't the time to go all princessy and demanding on him, the way his ex had. He had more than enough to deal with. The best thing she could do was hold his hand, telling him without words that she'd be there for him. And maybe, when this was all sorted out, maybe she could be brave and say it first. And maybe, just maybe, he'd say it back.

Even though Guy hadn't made a declaration, Amber thought he was different with her after that. It felt as if they were closer, and there was an extra depth and sweetness when he smiled at her. And although he hadn't actually asked her to move to France to be with him, he also hadn't suggested that she should go back to England. Which gave her hope.

On the Wednesday morning, she was having breakfast with Guy when her phone rang. Amber checked the display.

She smiled at Guy. 'Do you mind? It's Sheryl.'

'It's fine, *mon ange*. It gives me a chance to catch up with the business news.'

While he immersed himself in the newspaper, Amber went to sprawl on the sofa and chat to Sheryl. When she ended the conversation, she went back to the table and swallowed a cup of coffee in silence.

'What's the matter?' Guy asked.

'I just spoke to Hugh—Sheryl's fiancé. He's a doctor,' Amber said. She dragged in a breath. 'I hope you don't mind, but I asked him about your anosmia.'

'You did what?' Guy's eyes narrowed.

'He's a children's doctor—but most of his friends are doctors, too. And he's bound by confidentiality,' she added hastily, guessing what Guy's real issue would be, 'so he's not going to be talking to anyone. Neither will Sheryl. I'd trust her with my life. And I didn't say it was about you. I said I was asking about someone…someone I knew.' And they both knew that Guy had become more than just an acquaintance.

Guy said nothing, so she ploughed on. 'He's been off duty for a few days, and then the person he knew who works in that area was off duty—but they went out for a drink together last night. Apparently, the most common cause of anosmia is polyps.'

'I know that and I've already had a camera up my nose,' Guy said. 'If there were polyps, surely my specialist would've seen them already?'

'I don't know. I'm not a medic,' Amber said. 'But Hugh said if you're getting headaches, it might be worth going back again and asking them to repeat the test.'

'The headaches are from stress,' Guy said. 'Sure, I can ask them to do the camera thing again, but I know what they're going to say. The same as they've been telling me all along. That I have to wait—' his face tightened with frustration '—and see.'

'Thank you for shooting the messenger,' Amber said drily.

He slid his arms round her and held her close. 'I'm sorry, *mon ange*. I know you were trying to help, and I appreciate that. I shouldn't take out my frustrations on you.'

'I just wish I could wave a magic wand,' she said.

'So do I. But it's not going to happen.' He sighed. 'I can't see that anything will have changed in a month, but I'll make another appointment with my specialist. And thank you for trying.'

'Trying?' Her mouth twisted. 'I didn't exactly do anything useful, did I? You already knew what I told you.'

'You cared enough to talk to someone for me who might've been able to help. And you've been there for me. You've helped me see that if the worst does happen, it's not the end of the world because I can still be involved in the business—just in a different role. You've helped me come to terms with that, which hasn't been easy at all.'

She'd really done that for him?

He stole a kiss. 'And you haven't given me a hard time for getting up at stupid o'clock because I can't sleep, then coming back to bed freezing cold and warming myself up on you.'

'That,' she said with a grin, 'is because you wake me up so nicely, Monsieur Lefèvre.'

'Mmm. And if I didn't have a meeting with Philippe this morning, I'd carry you back to bed right now.' He kissed her again. 'But I'd better go. What are you up to, today?'

'I thought about catching the bus into Nice and seeing what their shoe shops are like.'

He laughed. 'I should've guessed. Don't bother with the bus. Take my car.' He handed her the keys.

'Won't you need it?'

'No. Go and find some nice shoes.' His eyes were full of laughter. 'And some matching underwear might be nice. I'll take you out to dinner tonight, and you can model them for me afterwards.'

'And then you can take them off me.'

'You're the perfect woman, *mon ange*. You can even read my mind,' Guy teased.

She laughed. 'It's not that difficult, Guy. You have a Y chromosome.'

He stole a last kiss. 'I'd better be going.' He paused by the door. 'And, just so you know—it isn't just sex. You and me, I mean.'

Was that his way of telling her that he loved her? That he felt the same way about her as she did about him? Amber wanted to run after him and ask him what he meant, ask him to explain in words of one syllable. Preferably three words.

Did he love her?

Tonight, maybe, he'd tell her.

And that, she thought, would be a moment worth all of her favourite shoe purchases rolled into one. The best moment of her life.

CHAPTER ELEVEN

THOUGH things didn't go quite according to plan. Guy came back from the perfume house in a dark mood, and he was quiet all through dinner. Even modelling her new shoes and underwear for him didn't lighten his mood; in the end, Amber just held him close. 'Guy. It's going to work out. It *has* to.'

Though he clearly didn't believe her. And when she woke in the night, finding his side of the bed empty, she knew exactly where he'd be. Hunched over his laptop, desperately trying to find someone or something that could help him. She pulled on her wrap and padded out to the living room.

He looked up from the laptop. 'I didn't mean to disturb you.'

'Come back to bed, Guy. You'll wear yourself out.'

He said nothing, but to her relief he switched off his laptop and let her take him back to bed. Though it was a long, long time before she could get back to sleep again.

When Guy's mobile shrilled, the next morning, he groaned, rolled over and answered it. 'Lefèvre.'

Amber could hear the person on the other end shouting, though she couldn't make out the exact words. And then Guy jackknifed up to a sitting position. 'What? Uh.' He sighed. 'Yes, it's true. No, Philippe, I wasn't—look, this is pointless. Meet me in the office in half an hour and I'll explain properly.' He ended the call and said something very savage that Amber guessed was a tirade of expletives.

'Guy? What's wrong?' she asked.

'*Dieu*, I really should've seen this coming. What an idiot I am.' He shook his head, looking disgusted. 'So much for trusting your friend with your life. She wasn't exactly careful with mine.'

'What?' What was he talking about? She didn't understand. Frowning, Amber sat up.

'That was Philippe. He's just been contacted by a journalist wanting to know if the story's true—that we're selling GL Parfums because I've lost my nose.'

'What? But—but—' Ice trickled down her spine. How on earth could the press know anything about Guy's problem with his sense of smell? She digested what he'd said. He thought *Sheryl* had told them? She shook her head. 'No, it couldn't possibly have been Sheryl. She'd never do anything like that. She's my best friend. I've known her since I was twelve—for more than half my life,' Amber said. 'It *couldn't* have been her. Or Hugh. He's a doctor.'

'What difference does that make?'

'I know them—*both* of them—and neither of them would deliberately hurt you. Or me.' She shook her head. 'No way would they talk to a journalist.' But if the news had leaked out, it could cause huge disruption. And then a really nasty thought hit her. It might even destroy Guy's business.

Guy had already powered up his laptop and was checking the news sites. '*Merde*. It's everywhere.'

'Maybe it's the conglomerate, trying to drive the price down.'

'Then why didn't they try that months ago? Why now?

Funny how it happened just after your so-called friend discussed it with a colleague.'

'Sheryl and Hugh would never, ever break a confidence like that,' she repeated. To prove it, she grabbed her phone and speed-dialled Sheryl.

The phone was ringing when Guy tapped her on the shoulder and pointed out another story. French Parfumier Seeks English Help.

Oh, no. And it was all about how he'd used an intermediary to get advice from an English doctor, after French doctors couldn't help him. So the leak had to be from Hugh or Sheryl. But how? She couldn't imagine either of them betraying her like that. She just *couldn't.*

'Bambi?' Sheryl was crying as she answered the phone. 'Oh, Bambi, I'm so sorry. This is such a mess.'

Amber realised that her friend must have heard the stories spreading through the press. 'I know, we've had calls already.'

'I didn't say a word to anyone—only to Hugh, like you asked me to.' Sheryl's breath hitched. 'We had a huge fight about it this morning because I accused him of selling you out. He's so angry with me. I think he's going to move out.'

'Oh, honey—hang in there, he'll calm down.'

But whether Guy would ever forgive her… She couldn't see that happening. The way things were going, it was highly likely that he'd lose the perfume house. All his dreams, everything he'd worked so hard for. *Because of her.* She could see that he was on the phone again, and he was looking grim. Which left her torn. She needed to support her best friend—but, right now, she had a feeling that Guy needed her more. 'I'll call you later, OK? Don't worry, honey. It'll work out.'

And she'd do whatever it took to fix this.

'That was the bank.' Guy put down the receiver very coolly and calmly, and it was somehow worse than if he'd slammed it down in anger, because it meant he'd gone past the point of rage into pure coldness. 'They're scrapping the deal.'

Amber caught her breath in shock. 'But they can't.'

'Oh, but they can, *mon ange*,' he said bitterly. 'Because I didn't give them all the pertinent information in the business plan. I didn't tell them that I couldn't smell any more, so I can't do my job. Which makes me a complete no-no in terms of risk—and I'm the one who breached the contract terms, so I can't do a thing about it.'

'It wasn't Sheryl who leaked the story,' she said to Guy. 'And I don't think it was Hugh, either.'

'Then who was it? Mr Invisible?' He raked a hand through his hair. 'Oh, *Dieu*. I need to go to the perfume house. I need to call everyone in, to reassure them that the perfume house isn't going under, they're not going to lose their jobs and we're going to get through this. Somehow. And then I need a meeting with Philippe to see if I can buy some time to find another source of finance.'

Guilt flooded through her. The story wasn't just going to affect Guy. It was going to affect everyone who worked for him, too. She stared at him, stricken. She'd always thought the gossip magazines irritating but basically harmless; but now she was witnessing firsthand what they could do to people's lives.

Destroy them.

If he needed another source of finance, she could definitely do something about that. Either ask her father for help, or talk to the trustees to see if they'd release money from the fund she lived off. 'Guy—'

'Save it. I don't want to hear,' he said, and headed for the shower.

He was ready to go in less than ten minutes. 'I don't know when I'll be back,' he said, and walked out.

And although she could understand why he didn't kiss her goodbye, it hurt. Hurt like hell. Surely he must know that she would never have betrayed him like that? She would never have done anything to hurt him. The world felt as if it were crumbling beneath her feet. This couldn't be happening. It just couldn't.

But the story was all over the Internet. No doubt it would be in the local press, too. And, to her horror, she discovered that *Celebrity Life* was even running a poll on how long it would take her to dump Guy now that he was losing his business. What? She'd had no idea they even knew that she was seeing him. And now this… Did people *really* think she was so shallow that she'd desert her man the second that things got tough? That hurt so much that, for a moment, she couldn't breathe.

Guy's landline started ringing. Should she answer it, or would it be the press? She let it go through to the answering machine, and heard a voice she recognised as Xavier's. Guy's brother sounded furious. He was talking so rapidly that Amber didn't have a hope of translating it, but she could guess what he was saying—something along the lines of 'what the hell's going on?' She desperately wanted to pick up the phone and explain, but it wasn't her place—and, anyway, how could she explain?

Hell, hell, hell.

She'd wrecked Guy's life—and now she had to fix it.

Grim-faced, Amber picked up the phone. This was definitely a time when she needed help from her mother—and, even though she knew it would be a ridiculous time in LA, Libby would forgive her. Because this was important.

* * *

Guy was bone-deep tired by the end of the business day, and he knew it wasn't going to end here. He still had to get through the paparazzi, who were staked outside the perfume house and would no doubt be outside his flat, too. Amber had probably been trapped there all day. And he had to face her, too.

This was just like Véra all over again. If he hadn't let his heart overrule his head and got involved with her, this would never have happened.

How could he have been so stupid?

By the time he closed his front door, having ignored the cameras thrust in his face and the babbled questions of the journalists, he was in serious need of coffee and a sugar fix. He'd hated all the fuss when he'd split up with Véra, and he hated this even more. Because this time it wasn't just his personal life: it was his business. Everything he'd worked so hard to build.

'Guy?' Amber was sitting on the sofa, looking wary.

'I hate being doorstepped.' He raked a hand through his hair.

'I'm sorry.' She dragged in a breath. 'I know this whole thing has hurt you badly, hurt people you're close to, and I swear I never meant this to happen.'

He knew that. Of course she hadn't intended it. But it had still happened. And his life was sliding into the abyss.

'Guy, I… Look, I had a word with Mum's publicist this afternoon. We can fix this.'

'We?' He narrowed his eyes at her.

'I'm the reason you're in this mess in the first place. I got you in it, so I'm going to help get you out of it.'

He shook his head. 'I know you weren't the leak. It was your friend.'

'No. I already told you, she'd never do that. She's as

upset as I am, and she's found out what happened. She rang me back this afternoon.' She dragged in a breath. 'When Hugh went for that drink with his colleague, another colleague was there as well, with his girlfriend. Hugh accidentally mentioned my name and she put two and two together—I didn't see it, but apparently there were rumours in *Celebrity Life* last week that we were dating.'

'So this girlfriend told the press about me?' Guy really didn't get it. 'But I don't even know her. Why would she do that?'

Amber squirmed. 'I dated her boyfriend a couple of times—a year before he started seeing her, I might add, and it was over after the second date—and apparently she's a bit jealous. For some stupid reason, she got it into her head that I might be trying to get him back, so she decided to leak stuff to the press to make life hard for me and keep me away from her man. He's dumped her because of it, but…oh, it's just a mess.' She sighed. 'Bottom line, it's my fault—if I hadn't interfered and asked Hugh for advice, this wouldn't have happened. At least, not right now.'

Guy frowned. 'How do you mean, not right now?'

She bit her lip. 'I know you're angry with me, and I don't blame you. But, Guy, you couldn't keep a secret like that for ever. It was always going to come out.'

'Maybe. But not until after I'd fixed it.'

She took a deep breath. 'I know you don't want to hear this, but you need to face up to it. You've been searching for months and you haven't found a doctor who can help you. You might not be able to fix this, Guy. How long were you planning to follow the doctor's advice to wait and see?'

His face was expressionless. 'As long as it takes.'

'Which is what? A year? Five years? Guy, you said yourself that a perfume lasts for only two years. Which means you have, I don't know, maybe a year before you need to start developing the next one to replace the one you're about to launch. And if your sense of smell hasn't come back by then, you're going to need a contingency plan.'

'Become a business guru now, have you?' he asked, an edge to his voice.

She flinched. 'No. It's common sense. And, in the meantime, you can't just ignore the media.'

'Can't I? You're the one who says you can smile your way through everything.'

'Not with this, you can't. You have to talk to them, or they'll speculate and come up with even wilder theories.'

'And?'

'Just talk to the press, Guy. Tell them what you told me, about how you develop perfumes.'

He felt his lip curl. 'So they can dig around even more?'

'No, so they can see it from another side. If they see you as the underdog fighting hard to beat this thing, they'll be right behind you and they'll back you. Mum's publicist said she'd email me some ideas, but you need to work with them, Guy...'

'You forget,' he said, 'I've been here before. They dig and dig and dig and they never give up.'

'So the way round it is to give the press a story instead of making them work for it. Give them things they can work with. Make it easy for them, and they'll concentrate on the story you want them to tell. Make it hard, and they'll go for the jugular.'

'Right now,' Guy said, 'I'm too tired to think straight, let alone do anything.'

'Sit down. Let me make you some coffee, something to eat.'

'I'm not hungry.'

'Then can I run you a bubble bath or something?'

He shook his head. 'Amber, my career's going down the drain and you think a bubble bath is going to make everything all right?'

'No, but what do you expect me to do? Just walk out and leave you to it?' And then a nasty thought struck her. 'Is that what you want me to do? Go?'

'Right now, I don't know what I want,' he said.

Which made it pretty clear that he didn't want her, otherwise he'd have no doubts.

'But I doubt you'd get a flight to London until tomorrow,' he continued, 'and there's no point in fighting your way through the paparazzi only to sit in the airport all night, so you might as well stay.'

'I'll sleep on the sofa,' she said, 'so I don't disturb you.'

'You're my guest. *I'll* sleep on the sofa,' he said.

'Guy, I don't want to throw you out of your bed.' She wanted to share it with him. Hold him, let him know that she was going to support him and together they'd get through this mess.

'I'll sleep on the sofa,' he repeated tonelessly.

It looked as if he was going to keep her at arm's length. And there wasn't a thing she could do about it. So much for thinking that he was going to tell her he loved her. Right now, he loathed her—and she could understand why. Because of her, his whole life was in disarray. He was going to lose everything he'd worked so hard for.

Amber slept badly, that night. She knew Guy did, too, because she could see the faint glow from his laptop screen through the gap in the doorframe. She longed to go out there, put her arms round him and tell him she was going to make everything all right—but it would be an empty promise, because she couldn't fix the biggest problem for him. And if she pushed him the way Véra had, made him feel that she was demanding attention, it would only drive more of a wedge between them.

She just had to hope that if she gave him space, time to think, then he might forgive her—and give her the chance to help him fix as much of the damage as she could.

Guy felt like hell, the next morning. He could see dark circles under Amber's eyes when she emerged from the bedroom, and guessed she felt the same; obviously she'd slept as little as he had, the previous night.

He wished he hadn't been so stubborn. He was too tall to sleep comfortably on his sofa, and his back ached. Not that he would've slept properly in bed—he'd been too angry and miserable and frustrated to sleep—but he would at least have been lying in comfort. And with her in his arms.

'How are you?' she asked, her voice sounding scratchy from lack of sleep.

There was no point in pretending. They'd gone beyond that. 'Not good.' He paused. 'You?'

'Not good, either,' she whispered. 'I'm so sorry, Guy.'

He shrugged. 'You can't change the past.'

'If there's anything I can do—anything at all—'

'No,' he said.

He could see her blinking back the tears at his rejection. It really hadn't been her fault. He'd thought about it all night; and, although he was still angry at her friends for their carelessness, he knew she'd had the best of intentions. And, until everything had exploded yesterday, he'd actually been happy with her. 'Look, I have to go to work. We'll talk tonight,' he said, and walked over to the front door.

'Guy.'

'What?' He stopped with his fingers wrapped round the door handle.

'If you have dark glasses, wear them.' She drew a finger along the dark circles under her own eyes, the gesture telling him exactly why he needed to hide his eyes. 'And smile. The worse you feel, the harder you have to smile.'

'That sounds like experience talking.'

She nodded, clearly not trusting herself to speak.

He rummaged in a drawer and found his sunglasses. 'Thank you,' he said.

'You're welcome.'

And she looked so miserable that he couldn't resist touching her cheek with the backs of his fingers. 'We'll talk tonight,' he said softly, and left.

The paparazzi were waiting for him outside. And he took Amber's advice, lifted his chin and smiled. Smiled until his face hurt, all the way to the perfume house. His phone was already ringing as he walked in, and he spent the morning fielding calls at the same time as answering emails, persuading financiers and soothing concerned clients. It was utterly relentless, and he was near to breaking point when Simone, his secretary, brought in a pile of messages.

'Just bin them,' he said. The only people he wanted to talk to had already spoken to him or he was waiting for emails. 'I'm not talking to the press.'

'You might want to call this one back, Guy.' She looked sympathetically at him as she handed him the note.

Professor Pascal Marchand in Paris. It wasn't a name he'd come across before.

'He's a doctor,' Simone added helpfully.

A doctor? Why would a doctor be calling him? Unless... Hope surged through him. Was this the answer he'd been trying so hard to find? 'OK. I'll call him now.'

Please, please, let this be good news, he begged silently. Let this be someone who could help him. Let the professor be there and not tied up with patients for the rest of the day.

To his relief, the doctor's secretary put him through straight away.

'I'm doing a trial on anosmia,' Professor Marchand told him. 'I read about your case in the papers. I might be able to help you, if you're interested in taking part.'

Interested?

He could've kissed the man.

'I'm definitely interested,' Guy said. 'Thank you.'

'Would you be able to come to Paris for a discussion and some tests?'

'Absolutely,' Guy said. 'Just tell me where and when.'

By the end of the call, they'd arranged a meeting for Monday afternoon; and it felt as if the clouds had suddenly parted and let some sunlight in. Maybe, just maybe, this was going to work out.

He took his phone off the hook for a moment while he checked his emails. There was one from Amber, obviously forwarded from someone—her mother's publicist, he supposed. Advice on dealing with the media.

Now he'd had time to think about it, he knew that Amber had a point. He did have to deal with the media. And, given that talking to the press wasn't his favourite thing, he knew it made sense to take advice from a specialist in the field. Someone who knew what they were doing and could stop him repeating the kind of mistakes he'd made in the past.

He skim-read the email, and discovered that the publicist was incredibly down-to-earth and focused; everything he read was perfectly sensible rather than just a piece of fluff. He reread it and worked through the points more slowly, jotting notes on a pad as he did so. Half an hour later, he had a plan of campaign sorted and a phone interview booked with *What's Hot!*

By the end of the afternoon, there were still a lot of rough edges and things to sort out, but damage limitation was well under way. He had a new source of finance so he could buy Philippe's share of the perfume house, he had an appointment with the professor and now he knew exactly where he was going.

Which left one area of his life to sort out.

Amber.

They really, really needed to have that talk.

CHAPTER TWELVE

AMBER was just finishing packing when Guy walked in.

'What are you doing?' he asked.

'Getting out of your hair,' she said. 'Though I wasn't going to just leave you a note and run away, before you start thinking that. I was going to say goodbye to you myself. And to tell you how sorry I am that you've ended up hurt because of me.'

'You're leaving?'

He looked shocked. Not relieved. So did that mean he wanted her to stay? Dared she hope? 'Isn't that what you want?' she asked carefully.

'I…' He shrugged and spread his hands. 'Yes. And no.'

'That's not helpful, Guy.'

'I know,' he said. 'My head is saying yes, leave—because once you're out of the equation the press will see I'm just another boring businessman and ignore me. Just like they did when Véra and I finally split up.'

His head was telling him to make her leave. But he'd said yes *and* no. Which gave her some hope. 'So which bit of you is saying no?' she asked.

'Part of me that I can't trust. It led me wrong, the last time I followed it,' he said.

She frowned. 'I'm not with you.'

'My heart,' he explained. 'You and me, it's all been a rush. Just like it was with Véra.'

'I'm not Véra.'

'I know that,' he said softly, 'but there are an awful lot of parallels.'

'Like how?'

'I met her when she worked on the campaign for my last perfume for my old company. We had lunch together; she was charming, witty and incredibly beautiful, and I fell for her straight away. You know how you see someone for the first time and this zing goes straight through you?'

Just as it had when she'd first met him. She knew exactly what he was talking about.

'I asked her to have dinner with me that night.' He blew out a breath. 'It's not tactful, telling you this, and I apologise for that, but I need to be honest. It was intense as hell. We ended up in bed that night and stayed there all weekend.'

Again, very close to what had happened between them. Had it not been for the wedding breakfast, there was a very good chance that she and Guy wouldn't have got out of bed that morning. Or for the rest of the day, except to shower and maybe grab something from the kitchen.

'I asked her to marry me a week later. She said yes, and I thought she felt the same way about me as I did about her. We decided not to wait to get married—we did it as soon as we could sort out the paperwork, even though we'd barely known each other a month. Xav warned me not to rush into it and to give our relationship more time, but I didn't listen.' He shrugged. 'I was head over heels in love with her, and I thought it would be enough.'

He'd already told Amber about his divorce. 'But it wasn't,' she said softly.

'No. I nearly lost the perfume house over it, and I vowed

then I'd never allow myself to fall for anyone like her again. That I'd never let my heart rule my head.'

'So you're judging me on the same terms as your ex-wife? That's not fair. I'm not like her,' Amber said, more calmly than she felt. 'Yes, I'm from the same world, and I've made plenty of mistakes in my life, but I'm *not* like Véra.'

'I know. But, when I met you, there was that same immediate attraction.'

'So you think that means I'm going to be the same as her?' She shook her head in mingled sadness and annoyance. 'Then maybe it's just as well that I've packed.'

'You're not like her,' Guy said. 'And I don't want you to go.' He sighed. 'Hell, I'm making a mess of this. But right now, the way things are, I'm scared that I'm making the wrong choice, the way I did last time. You're from her world. I wasn't enough for her—and that was when I was starting up the perfume house and had the whole world at my feet. Now everything's hanging in the balance and I can't guarantee what's going to happen in the future, even though I think I'm on the way to fixing things.'

'What?' She stared at him in disbelief. 'You think it's all about money or status? Are you crazy? First of all, let me just remind you that I pay my own way. I'm not looking for a man to support me financially. God, the last thing I'd want is to have to account to a man for every single penny I spend on shoes, or my phone bill. It's up to me how I spend my money, and that's the way I like it.' She grimaced. 'This is the twenty-first century, not the nineteenth.'

Dull colour flooded his face. 'I didn't mean—'

Amber interrupted him. 'Do you want to know what I'm looking for? Before I came to France, I didn't know. But I do now. Being with you has shown me exactly what I want.' She lifted her chin. 'I want an equal partnership.

With someone I like being with, and who likes being with me. With someone who wants to be with me, but not every single second of the day. I want to do girly things with my friends, and I want my man to do his own things, too. It's our differences that'll make us interesting.' And then she stopped. 'My mouth's running away with me again. You haven't actually asked me for a relationship. And you've as good as said that I'm not what you're looking for.'

'We're from different worlds,' Guy said. 'You enjoy the spotlight.'

'Not all of it,' she said. 'But I like having fun and throwing parties and seeing my friends.'

'That's not me. I'm a nerdy scientist who leads a very quiet life.'

'Never the twain shall meet, hmm?' she said. 'This thing between us—it was only ever meant to be temporary. Hot sex.'

'And getting it out of our systems.' He looked at her. 'Is it out of yours, yet?'

'I don't know if I'm brave enough to answer that.' She bit her lip. 'How about you answer it first?'

'You're not out of my system, not by a long way. I like having you around. You've made me smile at a time of my life when it felt as if the world was about to end. You've made me see that, even if I never find a doctor to help me, my life's still got a lot going for it. I admit, my heart's panicking that you're a lot like Véra—but my head knows you're not.'

'And you trust your head.'

He nodded. 'You understand my work and I think you understand what makes me tick. But things aren't going to be easy. If my sense of smell comes back, I'm going to be working long hours at the parfumerie to keep my business plan on track,' he warned. 'And if it doesn't, I'm going to be hell to live with until I come to terms with it completely—and that might take me a while.'

'In any relationship, you take the rough with the smooth.' Amber paused. 'You said you didn't want a relationship.'

'So did you.' He met her gaze. 'What do you want?'

Crunch time.

'That's a hard one to answer,' she said.

'Why?'

'Because if I tell you that I want a proper relationship with you, that I want you to date me and for the world to know that you're my man, you'll think I'm needy like Véra, and it'll make you back off. And if I tell you that I'm fine with a temporary fling and hot sex, you'll think I'm shallow and I'll get bored, like your ex. Either way, I lose.' She sighed. 'What do I want? I want a man who's going to accept me—*love* me—as I am. Who's not going to try to pigeonhole me or control me or change me. Who can accept that I like parties and that I also like pottering around at home.'

'That you're the media darling and an angel of domesticity?'

'I'm no angel,' she said drily. 'I'm just me. Yes, I'm a fluffy socialite, and an airhead party girl. But you're the one who showed me I have depth.'

He nodded. 'And you're not an airhead. I guess it's possible to be more than one thing at the same time.'

'It is.' She paused. 'So let me ask you the same thing. What do you want?'

'You're right, that's hard to answer,' he said slowly. 'I want someone who understands me. Someone who understands that sometimes I'm going to be distracted and living in my head, when I'm creating a perfume, and who won't complain and expect me to drop everything for her. Someone who isn't going to mind that I don't want to live in Paris or New York or Rome—someone who's happy to split her time between the château and the perfume house, as I do.'

So what was he saying? That they didn't have a future? That he wouldn't compromise at all?

'But I also want someone,' he said softly, 'who knows how to have fun. Who'll stop me being too nerdy and serious. Someone who's impulsive and crazy enough to pose like one of my favourite paintings for me. Someone who has a different pair of high heels for every day of—well, at least a month, but I'd guess more like a year. Someone who believes that you can smile your way through almost anything and come out on top.'

Hope rushed through her. Everything he'd just said—that was her. And the way he'd put it, he wasn't going to try to change her or control her or pigeonhole her. 'So you'd take a chance on someone who has a bad track record when it comes to relationships?'

'If she'd do the same for me.' He paused. 'And I'm rather hoping that she's planning to cancel her flight, unpack her suitcase and put her stuff back in my wardrobe.'

'You're sure that's what you want?' There was one thing she knew was a huge issue between them. Something he'd find hard to accept. 'You can cope with the media hanging around us for a bit?'

'Being with you means being in the public eye, at least for some of the time.' He shrugged. 'I'll get used to it. But what I need—really need, right now—is you back in my arms.'

She smiled. 'I thought you'd never ask.'

Half a second later, his arms were wrapped round her and his mouth was jammed over hers. And he was kissing her as if his whole life depended on it.

'I'm sorry I've given you such a hard time,' he said, when he finally broke the kiss.

'It's OK. I understand why,' she said. 'In your shoes, I would've probably done the same.'

'That's more than I deserve.'

She laughed. 'I have ideas about how you can make it up to me.'

'And I'll look forward to hearing them,' he said. 'But there are some things I need to say to you, first.' He stroked her face. 'I love you, Amber—I really, *really* love you. You make my world a brighter place.'

'I love you, too.' She stroked his face. 'I think I fell for you the night of your brother's wedding, when you danced with me. Nobody had ever made me feel that hot and bothered before. I told myself it was just sex, but it wasn't.'

'No. It's a hell of a lot more. But, since you mentioned the *s*-word…'

A long, satisfying time later, Amber lay curled in Guy's arms.

'Something else I meant to tell you,' Guy said. 'Before you distracted me. I had a phone call today.'

She winced. 'Press?'

'A doctor. In Paris. He's running a trial on treating anosmia. I have an appointment with him on Monday afternoon, to see if I'm suitable for the trial.'

'That's brilliant news.' Amber brightened. 'I mean, I know there are no guarantees, but he's the first one who's said anything positive. That's a start.'

'A very good start,' he said.

'I, um, could go with you, if you like,' she offered. 'You know, for moral support and that.' She bit her lip. 'Actually, I'd probably better not. The press might hassle us.'

'They're already hassling me,' Guy pointed out. 'It's not going to make any difference whether they follow us to Paris or not. And yes, I'd like you to come with me. I could do with the moral support. Just in case—'

She pressed her finger to his lips to stop him. 'Don't borrow trouble. Wait and see what he says.' She raised an eyebrow. 'Clearly I'm going to have to distract you all weekend…'

Professor Marchand turned out to be in his late fifties, distinguished-looking and with a ready smile. He was relaxed about Amber staying with Guy for moral support, and she held Guy's hand through all the questions and the uncomfortable-looking procedure of having a tube up his nose with a camera. She had to stay in the waiting area while Guy had a CT scan, but then it was time to go back and see the professor for the verdict.

Guy's stomach was roiling and it was as much as he could do to put one foot in front of the other and rap on the doctor's open door.

But Professor Marchand was smiling as he looked up from the desk. 'Sit down,' he said.

Guy sat in silence, and felt the pressure of Amber's fingers against his.

'I'm afraid you're not going to be suitable for my trial,' he said.

Guy couldn't breathe, and he had no idea what the doctor said next. He'd hoped so much that the new treatment would be the answer. But now it seemed that he was going to have to live with it.

'Guy. *Guy.*' Amber nudged him. 'Did you hear what the professor said?'

'I'm looking for people with true anosmia,' Professor Marchand said, switching to English. 'And yours is fixable.'

Guy looked at him, shocked beyond belief. 'It is?'

'It's caused by a polyp in your sinus—so the tissue at the top of your nose, the one that affects your ability to smell, is fine. I think what happened is that the virus gave you sinusitis and a polyp developed. Your sense of smell got gradually worse since the virus, yes?'

Guy nodded. 'It's practically non-existent now.'

'Polyps are easy to fix.'

Guy couldn't take it in. 'But the last two specialists I saw—they couldn't find a thing.'

'You saw them, what, a month ago, two months?' Professor Marchand said. 'Maybe they were so small that they missed them. Or maybe, because your work is so sensitive, you reacted more strongly than the average person's nose would, out of proportion to the size of the polyps, so they thought there was another cause of the problem instead of seeing the obvious.'

It was fixable. Guy's heart was hammering so hard, he couldn't speak.

'The even better news,' Professor Marchand continued, 'is that the first-line treatment is a simple steroid spray to shrink the polyp. If this doesn't work, there are other treatments we can try, but the most important thing is that your sense of smell will definitely come back—even though I should warn you that it might take a while until it's back completely.'

Guy felt the blood thudding through his veins.

Everything was going to be all right.

'Thank God,' Amber breathed, still holding his hand tightly.

But he still had one burning question. 'Will the polyp come back?'

'If the medication doesn't work, or if the polyp comes back, we can try steroid tablets, or I can operate to remove it. The main thing is, it's fixable. You can stop worrying.

It's a shame for me that you're not suitable for my trial, because a man in your line of work would be an interesting case study—but I'm glad for you that you're not.'

'Thank you.' Guy shook the older man's hand, relief flooding through him. 'I can't say what this means to me. It's…' He was too choked to say any more.

'I'm glad I could help,' Professor Marchand said with a smile. He wrote a prescription. 'You need to take these daily—and you need to take them properly,' he said in English.

'Thank you.' Guy took the prescription.

'Call me if you're worried about anything.'

Guy smiled. 'I will.'

After they'd picked up the prescription and were back at the hotel, he enveloped Amber in a hug. 'It's going to be all right.' He blinked back the tears. 'I feel as if someone's taken the whole universe off my shoulders. And it's all because of you. If the story hadn't blown up in the media, Professor Marchand wouldn't have contacted me. And I would still be thinking that it wasn't fixable. My life would still be a mess.'

'I'm so glad it's worked out. That you're not going to have to live a nightmare any more.'

'No. I'm going back to living the dream. And I want to live it with you, Amber.' He paused, his eyes dark with sincerity. 'As my wife.'

No. He couldn't mean that. And what he'd just said: without her, he'd still be in a mess. He wasn't asking her because he couldn't live without her. 'You don't have to feel obliged to me. Or grateful. That's completely the wrong reason to propose to someone.'

'It's not the reason. I mean, of course I'm grateful to you—but I want to marry you because I want to be with you, Amber. You bring another dimension to everything.

Without you, nothing feels right. The whole heart of my world's missing. It's like a perfume with only a top and bottom note, nothing in between, and everything feels out of balance.'

He really felt like that about her?

Then again, that was the way he'd felt about Véra, and that had ended up badly, too.

'No,' she said. 'I'm still not going to marry you.'

He frowned. 'Why not? I love you, and you said that you loved me.'

'I do.'

'So what's the problem?'

'You married Véra in a rush and you regretted it. I don't want that to happen to us.'

'It won't happen to us.' He drew her hand up to his mouth and kissed it. 'And I know that because you're not like her and I was stupid ever to have thought you were. You come from the same world, yes, but you see things in a different way. We're both going to have to compromise to make this work, but I think we could do it.'

Compromise. That was the word she'd been looking for. 'All right, then, we'll compromise. If you're still sure in six months' time, ask me again and I'll say yes. But not until then.'

He frowned. 'So you don't believe we can make it?'

'Actually, I do,' she said, 'but I need to prove to both of us that it's not going to be like your last marriage. We're not going to rush into it, this time. We'll use our heads as well as our hearts. Besides, I still have things to do in England. I have a Christmas ball organised, and there will be things I need to sort out the week before—things I can't expect other people to pick up for me, because I'm the one who has all the notes and contact details.'

'Of course,' he said. 'I'm not expecting you to give up everything for me.'

'So what are you expecting?' she asked.

'To share my life with you,' he said simply. 'I have my work, you have your fundraising and your friends. But we'll have dinner together and ask each other about our day. Sometimes we'll go to parties. Sometimes we'll have quiet nights in at home.' He paused. 'And sometimes we'll be on the beach, making sandcastles with our children.'

She stared at him, not quite believing what she'd heard. 'You want children?'

'A family,' he said. 'With you, when we're both ready.'

He wanted to make a family with her. A family where she'd be loved for who she was. She had to blink back the tears. 'Oh, Guy. Six months,' she said, 'and then I want a *really* romantic proposal.'

He laughed. 'That's a deal.' And he kissed her, to prove it.

EPILOGUE

Six months later

'GUY, it's not even light yet,' Amber said, snuggling under the duvet. 'Go back to sleep for a little while.'

'Some of us have been up for half an hour already,' Guy said.

She opened her eyes and frowned. 'Why? Is something wrong?'

'No, but you need to get up, have a quick shower and get dressed. Don't ask questions, just trust me,' he added swiftly.

Amber gave up. 'OK, OK. Are you going to be fussy about what I wear, too?'

He indicated the dress hanging up on the door. 'That one.'

It was a shift dress in deep scarlet; Amber could see by looking at it that it was silk. And she'd never seen it before. And then she noticed that he was wearing a formal suit—something he never did for work. 'Guy?'

'No questions,' he reminded her. 'Oh, and no scent.'

'No scent?' She didn't have a clue why, but she'd learned over the last six months that when Guy was enthusiastic about something, it saved a lot of time to go along with him.

She showered, cleaned her teeth, brushed her hair and applied the bare minimum of make-up—just mascara and a slick of rose-coloured lipstick—then tried on the dress. It fitted perfectly; and Guy had left her the most gorgeous pair of shoes in the same colour, in the softest leather.

Wondering quite what he was planning, she headed downstairs. Guy came out of the kitchen, and smiled. 'Perfect. Come into the drawing room.'

She did as he said.

'Stay here—for, oh, two minutes, at most—and no peeping.'

'You're starting to get really annoying, do you know that?'

He simply laughed. 'In three minutes, you'll forgive me, *mon ange*.'

She wasn't so sure, but she stayed put until he came to fetch her. He led her through the French doors in the library through to the gardens at the back of the house, and then to the rose garden. She blinked in surprise as she saw a wrought-iron table set for two; it was lit with a dozen tiny tealight candles. There was a posy of roses in the middle—freshly cut from the garden, and still studded with silvery dew—next to a silver wine-cooler containing a bottle of champagne. And there was a basket of French pastries, still warm from the bakery.

Guy held her chair for her, then sat opposite. 'Now. Breakfast. A little later than the crack of dawn. Any second now…'

And the sun began to rise, casting a pinkish light over the roses.

'Good morning, *mon ange*,' he said with a smile.

She couldn't help smiling back. 'Guy, this is lovely.'

'So you forgive me for making you wake up so early,

now you know I wanted to have breakfast with you at sunrise?'

'Yes. Though I still don't understand why you wanted me to dress up.' She frowned. 'Or why you're wearing a suit.'

'That's the next bit.' He handed her a box, beautifully wrapped in white tissue paper with a gold chiffon ribbon. 'For you, *mon ange*.'

'For me? But, Guy, it's not my birthday for another two months.'

He rolled his eyes. 'I know. Just open it and put me out of my misery, will you?'

The box was way too big to contain a ring. Besides, he hadn't actually asked her to marry him…and that made her realise just how much she did want him to ask her. They'd agreed to give it six months, to see how things went, and every day she spent with Guy—whether it was in England, at Grasse or at the château—had made her happier and happier. She'd become involved in the perfume house, working on the new 'design your own scent' line and dealing with queries from the women's and lifestyle magazines, and she loved every second of her work. And Guy came with her to the glitzy parties, although she barely accepted half of the invitations nowadays, enjoying quiet nights in with her man as well.

It had worked out better than either of them had dreamed.

She undid the wrappings of the parcel, to reveal a plain white box with the GL Parfums logo.

And when she removed the lid, inside was a perfume flask—hand-blown amethyst-coloured glass, in the shape of a heart. 'Guy, this is beautiful.'

'That's the back, *mon ange*. Take a look at the other side.'

She turned the bottle over and there was an outline of a heart inscribed in amber-coloured gold on the glass. Inside, in a flowing script, were the words 'Amber of my heart.'

Her heart skipped a beat. 'What's this, a sneak preview of your new perfume?' The one she knew he'd been working on since the wildly successful launch of Angelique, and he'd gone all secretive and refused to let even her in his lab.

And he'd named it after her?

'It's what it says on the bottle.' He smiled at her. 'And no, this isn't for production. I had the flask designed by a new local craftsman, and it's exclusive. The perfume's a one-off, too. Like you.'

She couldn't quite take it in. 'You designed this for me.'

'Every bit of it is how I feel about you,' Guy said. 'I never told you this, *mon ange*, but I used to be able to see people in terms of scent. I lost that ability for a while, but you were instrumental in bringing it back to me. And this, to me, is you.'

'I…' She blinked back the tears. 'I don't know what to say.'

'Try it,' he invited. 'Tell me what you think it is.'

Now she knew why he'd told her not to wear scent. When she removed the glass stopper—coloured the same gold as the heart—there was an atomiser. She sprayed a little on her left wrist, and sniffed. 'This is lovely. An amber top note, right?'

'Absolutely. Give it ten minutes and you'll start to smell the roses—the very roses I was picking the same day I met you.' He indicated the roses around them. 'Which is why I wanted to give this to you, here. They're for your sweetness.'

She caught her breath.

'And your sensuality.' He grinned. 'I'm thinking of a certain Rossetti picture.'

She blushed, remembering the day she'd posed semi-naked for him in his lab with an armful of roses.

'And there's a base of tonka bean and vanilla; it reminds me of chocolate, the depth in the colour of your eyes and the silkiness of your hair. There are other layers in there, too, because you're complex—vetiver for sexiness and strength, citron for luminosity and cranberries because you're bright and sharp.' He ended his litany with a kiss. 'And I love you very, very much.'

It was a love letter in scent, and it rendered her temporarily speechless.

When she'd recovered herself enough to speak, she said, 'I love you, too, Guy. *Je t'aime. Toujours.*' She stroked the bottle. 'I can't believe you've called this by an English name, not French.'

'Because you're English—and anyway, as I told you, this isn't for production. This is exclusive. It's yours. Just like I am.' His eyes were utterly sincere. 'Always.'

'Guy, that's the nicest thing anyone's ever done for me,' she whispered.

He kissed away the single tear that slid down her cheek. 'Don't cry, *mon ange*. Not now. Because today's going to be a very special day. I hope.' Still holding her hand, he dropped down to one knee. He took a box from his pocket with his other hand, and opened it to reveal a perfect solitaire diamond. 'Amber Wynne—Amber of my heart—will you make me the happiest man in the world and do me the honour of becoming my wife?'

She cupped his face and lowered her mouth to kiss him lightly. 'Yes—oh, yes, *please*.'

He kissed her finger, then slid the ring onto it. It was a perfect fit, just as she knew it would be. Just as she and Guy were—and would be, for the rest of their days.

AT THE FRENCH BARON'S BIDDING

BY

FIONA HOOD-STEWART

Scottish author **Fiona Hood-Stewart** draws on her own experiences in the world of old money, big business and the international jet set for inspiration in creating her books. She lives in Europe with her two sons, with whom she shares her life. Fiona also writes longer fiction for Harlequin® MIRA® books, and has received rave reviews for her vivid characters and deeply emotional, sophisticated, multi-layered stories. Look out for her latest title—coming soon!

CHAPTER ONE

IT WASN'T that she didn't want to go back to France, for in truth she did. But as the chauffeur-driven car drove sedately through the gates of the Manoir that she remembered only vaguely from early childhood, Natasha de Saugure experienced a rush of mixed emotions: she really should have responded to her grandmother's summons sooner.

Yet the past hung between them, and had impeded her from doing so. Now, Natasha hoped that it wouldn't be too late. Her grandmother had sounded so frail over the phone. But taking leave from her job with a humanitarian organisation in Africa wasn't easy. She had, in the short space of time she'd been employed, acquired a post of much responsibility. She owed it to the starving mothers and children they were so desperately trying to save to be there.

Still, after the car had crunched across the gravel driveway and come to a stop, Natasha stepped out and breathed a unique fragrance that she recognized as fresh lavender and thyme; she knew she'd been right to come.

'Voilà, mademoiselle.' The driver smiled at her over his shoulder before jumping out and solicitously opening the car door.

'Merci.' Natasha smiled back. In a quick movement she straightened her long ash-blonde hair and glanced up at the ancient stone façade of the Manoir: its rounded turrets at each corner, the lead-tiled roof, the ivy that weaved over its centuries-old stone walls. Making her way towards the stately front door past grand stone pots filled with well-trimmed shrubs, Natasha sighed. It was many years since

she'd last seen her grandmother—after the irreparable rift between the old lady and Natasha's father when he'd married out of his set.

All at once the ancient front door creaked, opened, and an old, white-haired man in uniform appeared on the steps.

'Bienvenue, mademoiselle,' he said, his face breaking into a wrinkled smile. '*Madame* will be so pleased.'

'*Bonjour*, Henri,' she said; she'd heard her mother talk about the old retainer. She stepped inside the flagstoned hall and gazed about her at the high ceilings and doorways leading this way and that into the warren of passages and rooms beyond. Little by little vague memories unfurled as long-forgotten images jumped forth to greet her.

But the question that still tugged at her as she entered the Manoir was why, after all these years of silence, had her grandmother insisted she come? There had been little in the letter she'd received to indicate her reasons; little in her imperative tone on the phone to suggest she'd unbent after all this time.

Yet insist she had.

And, despite her first inclination to refuse, Natasha had known she had to come. After all, notwithstanding the past, now that both her parents were dead Natasha was the old lady's only living relative.

After Henri had exclaimed, with a tear in his eye, at seeing her again, all grown up, thrilled that she'd remembered his name, Natasha followed him up the stone staircase, amazed at how much she recognized. Over twenty years had elapsed since her last visit to Normandy, but so much felt familiar: the scents, the light pouring through the tall windows and bathing the muted walls, the echo of her heels resonating on the well-trodden steps. And something else that she couldn't quite identify.

'*Madame* is waiting for you upstairs in the small salon,' Henri pronounced in stentorian tones.

'Then I had better go to her at once.' Natasha smiled again, her green eyes sparkling with amusement. The situation was so dreadfully formal, as though she'd walked into another time and place.

With a small bow the butler led the way slowly up the wide staircase. Natasha realized that he suffered from arthritis and found the climb difficult. She was about to suggest that he simply tell her where the salon was and she would find it herself when she realized that would be a grave breach of etiquette. Henri, who had worked here all his life, would not take kindly to any deviation from the rigorous habits her grandmother kept.

Soon they stopped before a white and gold door. Henri knocked, then gently opened it. 'She awaits you,' he pronounced in a hushed tone.

Natasha swallowed. Suddenly this didn't seem quite as simple as she'd imagined it would when she was back in Khartoum. She was a compassionate person by nature, but the drastic way her grandmother had cut her own son out of her life had made Natasha distrustful of the older woman, whom she barely recalled.

Then, knowing she must get on with it, Natasha gathered up her courage and stepped through the door that Henri was holding open and into the high-ceilinged, shaded room. It took a moment or two for her eyes to adjust to the half-light. Then she gazed over at the tiny white-haired figure shrouded under a silk coverlet on an antique pink-velvet day-bed under the window.

'Ah, *mon enfant*, finally you have arrived.'

The voice was a thin whisper and, despite her initial instinctive desire to hold back, Natasha's natural empathy asserted itself. Instead of the grandmother who'd rejected her and her family for most of her life, she saw instead a feeble old lady in need of help. Quickly she approached.

'Yes, Grandmère. I am here.'

'At last.' The old lady turned her once beautiful, fine-boned features towards Natasha, the pale blue eyes searching. 'Come here, child, and sit next to me. I have waited so long for you to come.'

'I know. But I couldn't get away before. We have a humanitarian crisis on our hands right now,' she explained, perching her tall, slim figure gingerly on the edge of a spindly gilded chair.

'Never mind. The main thing is that you are here now. Henri.' The querulous voice had not lost its authoritarian tone. *'Le thé, s'il-vous-plaît.'*

'Tout de suite, madame.'

With another little bow Henri retired, closing the door behind him.

'Are you sure he can manage?' Natasha asked, glancing doubtfully at the closed door.

'Manage? Of course Henri can manage,' the old lady responded peremptorily, straightening herself against the cushions with determination. 'He has been managing since before the war, when he came here as assistant *aide de cuisine*. But enough of that.' The old lady waved a delicate white bejewelled hand. 'Tell me about yourself, child. It has been too long. Far too long.' She let out a tremulous sigh. 'I am to blame for that, I know. But it is too late for regrets.' Her eyes rested on Natasha as though assessing her. Even though she was physically fragile, there was nothing weak about the old lady. Clearly she had all her faculties about her.

'Well, there's nothing much to tell. When I finished school I went to university. But when my parents died three years ago in the car crash, I just wanted to get away as far as I could, so I dropped out. That's when the job in Africa came up.' She shrugged, bit her lip. 'It seemed the right thing to do.'

'And are you happy in your work?' Her grandmother eyed her piercingly.

'Yes. I am. It's very exhausting, and emotionally harrowing, but it's also terribly rewarding.'

The old lady nodded. 'You are a good and compassionate person. Unlike me,' she added with a bitter laugh. 'I was always more concerned about my own well-being than that of others. Now I've paid the price for my selfish behaviour.' She let out another long sigh and closed her eyes.

Natasha hesitated. Part of her was still reticent, remembering her father's sorrow and her mother's sense of guilt at having estranged the man she loved from his family. There was no denying that it was hard to shove a lifetime's grievances under the carpet and pretend that all was well. Still, she didn't want the past to affect the future.

'Grandmère, we all make mistakes in life.'

'That we do.' The old lady nodded. 'I wonder, is it possible for you to forgive me for all the harm I have done to your family, Natasha? I wish so deeply now that I had been more enlightened, that I had not estranged my dearest Hubert as I did.'

Natasha hesitated, saw the flicker of hope in the elderly woman's eyes, and her heart went out to her. 'Of course, Grandmère. Let's look towards the future, and not into the past.'

'Ah.' The old lady rested her hand on Natasha's and smiled a frail yet gentle smile. 'I was right to have you come. Very right indeed.' She laid her fingers over Natasha's and two women sat thus for several minutes, a new bond forming between them.

Then a knock at the door announced Henri with the tea,

and the spell was broken. Natasha jumped up to open the door while her grandmother issued imperative orders regarding the placement of the tea tray. She might be old, Natasha realized, a smile hovering, but she had all her wits about her and her authority still stood strong.

An hour later they had sipped tea, exchanged stories, and the old lady was obviously very tired.

'I'll leave you and unpack,' Natasha said, rising.

'Yes, *mon enfant*. That is a good idea. I'm afraid I won't join you for dinner, but Henri will see to you. Come and say goodnight, won't you?'

'Very well.' Natasha bent down and dropped a light kiss on her grandmother's withered cheek. 'I'll see you later.'

'Yes, my child. I shall be waiting.'

After undoing her case and placing her clothes inside the beautiful lavender-scented armoire in the faded yet elegant blue satin-draped bedroom she had been allotted, Natasha moved to the window and gazed out over the lush green countryside. In the distance she could see a medieval castle, its ramparts etched against the translucent sky. Shading her eyes, she distinguished a pennant flying from the turret. She thought of William the Conqueror, of the Norman invasion. Perhaps it was a historical monument that she could visit.

It was late spring. Flowers bloomed as though they'd constantly burst forth from one day to the next, their rich hues framing a weathered stone fountain; flowerbeds dotted with lupins and roses surrounded the velvet-smooth lawn. It was peaceful and lovely, as though caught in a time warp. Natasha glanced at her watch and wondered if she'd have time for a wander before dinner.

Deciding that she did, she slipped on a pair of sneakers and went downstairs. There was no one in the hall so she stepped out of the front door and began walking, tilting her face up towards the fast-moving cloud, enjoying the wind mussing her hair.

Soon she had wandered well beyond the lawn and the garden perimeter, and was walking across a field, enjoying the fresh breeze and the exercise. Suddenly she heard the sound of hooves. Stopping abruptly, she turned to find out who it might be, surprised to see a tall dark man in jeans and riding boots astride a nervous chestnut horse. The stranger reined in abruptly. He did not, Natasha realized, somewhat taken aback, look too pleased.

'Who are you?' he threw at her in French, in the tone of one unused to being thwarted.

Natasha glanced up at him, stiffening. 'I don't see what it has to do with you who I am,' she retorted in fluent French.

'It has everything to do with me as I am the owner of this land.'

'Well, if you are, I'm sorry I trespassed. I had no ill intention,' she replied in a haughty tone, damned if she was going to be ordered about by this obnoxious man.

'Very well,' he snapped. 'See that it doesn't happen again.'

On that peremptory note he swung the horse around and galloped off, leaving Natasha fuming, her fists balled in anger.

The nerve of the man. Why, he was the rudest creature she'd ever encountered.

It was later than she'd thought and deciding that if she really had stepped onto someone else's land she'd better make her way back to the Manoir, she walked fast. As she approached the stately building she stopped and gazed at it, bathed now in the glow of the setting sun, copper drain-pipes glinting on the roof. Natasha drank in the sight, determined to banish the image of the dark and odious horseman. Still, as she entered the hall and made her way quickly up to her room, she couldn't help wondering who the ignominious rider could be.

Obviously a neighbour if he owned the land. Come to think of it, if he'd had a pleasanter expression she might even have thought him good-looking, she conceded, remembering the dark scowling features and the black hair swept back from his autocratic brow. Not that it was any of her business, she reminded herself. Still, she'd ask her grandmother who he was.

At eight o'clock sharp Natasha, dressed in a dark blue silk dress she thought her grandmother would approve of, glided gracefully down the main stairway and was met by Henri, who immediately guided her into the formal dinning room. Natasha sighed. She had no desire to sit alone at a table big enough to seat sixteen. But she said nothing. This was the way things were—she'd heard it often enough from her father's stories about his boyhood. There was little use saying she'd rather have a tray in the sitting room, as it wasn't going to happen.

After the meal she got up, relieved to have finished, and made her way upstairs to her grandmother's bedroom. She'd say goodnight before it was too late, then go to her room, have a bath in the huge antique tub, and curl up in the blue satin-swathed four-poster and read.

After three unanswered knocks she decided to open the door and peer inside. She smiled when she saw the old lady sleeping. Perhaps she shouldn't disturb her. Yet something pushed her to stay, and she moved towards the bed and gazed down at her grandmother. The Comtesse de Saugure lay perfectly still, her expression peaceful. Then all at once Natasha gasped, leaned forward, and felt for the older woman's pulse.

But there was none.

Heart trembling, Natasha tried to wake her.

'Grandmère,' she murmured, gently touching her shoulder. 'Please wake up.' But she met with only silence. Horrified, her hands shaking, Natasha stood straighter and allowed the truth to sink in.

Her grandmother was dead.

CHAPTER TWO

THE early Norman chapel was filled with mourners, both local and foreign. Old retainers who had worked for the Comtesse for most of their lives lined the narrow road as the hearse made its way through the countryside. Natasha followed in the ancient Rolls, driven by Henri.

Now, as she stood alone in the front pew, dressed in black, listening to the priest read the funeral service, Natasha felt both sad and bewildered. She knew no one except for Henri and his wife Mathilde, standing respectfully in the pew behind her. Part of her shock was caused by the meeting she'd had this morning with the local notary who'd come to read her grandmother's will. To her astonishment Natasha had learned that she was her grandmother's sole beneficiary. She had inherited not only the château in Normandy, but the Comtesse's sumptuous flat in the *16ième arrondissement* in Paris, and her villa on the Côte d'Azur.

Natasha had gathered her thoughts and prepared to follow the coffin down the aisle when all at once she looked up and saw the man she'd encountered in the field, seated in the opposite pew. He looked different dressed in a dark suit and tie, with his hair groomed. Their eyes met and once more Natasha wondered who he was.

Then, turning away, she followed the pallbearers out of the church to the graveyard where the Comtesse would end her life's journey, laid to rest among the ancient crooked headstones, many of which bore the name of Saugure upon them. As the coffin was lowered into the earth and the priest spoke the words she'd heard not that long ago when her parents were buried, Natasha experienced a moment of deep sadness and solitude.

Now she had no one left. Not even the estranged grandmother whom she'd hoped to get to know. Now she had only herself to count on.

Raoul d'Argentan stood a few steps away from the mourners, eyes fixed on the young woman standing next to the grave. Who was this granddaughter of the Comtesse de Saugure who had appeared out of nowhere on the day of her death? He knew, of course, that Marie Louise de Saugure had been estranged from her only son. But that all went back a long way. This, he supposed, must be his daughter. But what a strange coincidence that she should have returned only for her grandmother to die. Well, it was none of his business. The Saugures and the Argentans had been neighbours for several centuries and knew each other well. But their history had not always been pleasant. There were instances dating back a few hundred years, grievances that still rankled. Not that he cared. He had his own affairs to contend with: his auction house in Paris, which dealt in some of Europe's finest art, and, of course, the estate to run.

As he walked back to his car Raoul supposed that he should pay his respects before his departure for Paris the next morning. It was only polite, after all, to offer his condolences. Though it seemed cynical when the girl obviously barely knew the woman who had left her a fortune.

As he drove off down the hill Raoul cast a quick glance in the rearview mirror. The mourners were leaving the graveyard and he glimpsed the woman once more. Whatever else she was, she was damn lovely, that was for sure.

Telling himself to stop being ridiculous—the last thing

he needed was to find himself attracted to a Saugure—he pressed his foot on the accelerator and made his way back to his estate, determined not to think about the lovely wan face and that pair of limpid green eyes, which, despite every instinct, he'd felt strangely attracted to. He consoled himself with the fact that she was unattractively dressed, had no chic at all. In fact, he would go as far as saying she looked frumpy. With a shake of his head he headed back to his château and thought about the upcoming telephone call to New York that he needed to make.

'Mademoiselle?'

'Yes, Henri?' Natasha looked up from the desk where she was going through some of her grandmother's papers and smiled.

'The Baron d'Argentan is here to offer his condolences.'

'Right.' She sighed, laying down the missive. Rising, she straightened her one black dress, realizing she simply must go into Deauville and acquire some suitable clothes. This was not the first neighbour come to pay their respects and satisfy their curiosity regarding the new owner of the Manoir, and she needed to dress accordingly. Better get used to it, she realized, following Henri across the hall to the formal drawing room where the butler liked to install the guests.

But, on stepping inside the room, Natasha felt her pulse leap when she recognized the tall figure silhouetted against the window. She was about to speak, then stopped, and swallowed.

'I come to present my condolences,' he said, in a haughty, rich baritone that seemed to resonate through the elegant room. Then he stepped forward and, raising Natasha's fingers to his lips, bent his head towards them.

'Thank you,' she murmured, feeling her pulse pick up

speed. His fingers felt strangely vibrant, as though an electric current were coursing through them. 'Uh, do sit down,' she said hurriedly, taking a step back and indicating the Louis Quinze chair opposite.

'Thank you.' He waited for her to sit, then followed suit. Natasha was relieved when the door opened and Henri entered with a bottle of champagne, which he proceeded to open.

'I have not had the pleasure of your acquaintance,' the Baron remarked, placing one leg over the other. 'I wasn't aware that the Comtesse had a granddaughter.' He raised a quizzical black brow at her, as though questioning her authenticity. 'I don't seem to recall meeting you in the past.'

Natasha bristled and felt her cheeks flush, a flash of anger take hold. 'That is because I haven't been here for many years,' she said coldly.

'Aha. That would explain it.'

'Yes.'

Natasha felt irritated with herself. Why was she allowing this stranger to make her feel ill at ease? She was, after all, in her own house now, for whatever that was worth.

They each accepted a glass of champagne from Henri and the Baron raised his. 'To a very great lady. The Comtesse will be sorely missed in the region—won't she, Henri?' he said, addressing the butler.

'Ah, *oui*, Monsieur le Baron, she most certainly will.' Henri nodded in agreement. 'But of course we are blessed to have *mademoiselle*,' he added quickly.

'Very true. This has come as rather a surprise to the community.' The Baron twiddled his flute and studied her lazily.

'I hope not an unwelcome one?' Natasha retorted, her chin tilting upwards, anger at his high-handed manners and the idle way his eyes coursed over her increasing by the moment.

'Unwelcome? Not at all. In fact, quite the opposite. You will be a breath of fresh air. That is if you plan to stay here?' Again the brow flew up. It was as though he were searching for something amiss, something untoward.

'It is far too soon for me to decide what to do. I haven't made up my mind yet,' she responded, hoping her tone would dampen any other questions. Yet part of her wanted him to believe her, resented that he should find anything suspicious about her. For it was true. She hadn't decided what to do with her new inheritance. Part of her wanted to run back to Africa, to the safety of her job. Yet another part, a part she hadn't known existed before, was struck by a new sense of loyalty to her lineage and the duties that came with the inheritance. It was her grandmother's personal letter to her that had struck a chord. *You are the only Saugure left to continue the line…* Incredibly, the old lady had expected her to assume all her responsibilities.

The Baron stayed for several more minutes, making polite small talk, then rose. 'If there is anything I can help you with, Henri has my numbers. As you've probably gathered,' he said, a sudden wicked smile curving his well-defined lips, 'I am your neighbour.'

'That much became pretty obvious the other day,' she muttered dryly, smiling despite her initial desire to dislike him.

'Yes, well, I'm sorry for the way I greeted you that day. It was rude and bad-mannered. I'm hoping that, to make up for it, you might come and dine with me one day. Perhaps I can bring you up to speed on the area.' He took her hand and squeezed it in his, holding it slightly longer than necessary, and again Natasha experienced that same pulsating tingle.

'That would be very nice,' she accepted, surprising herself as she extricated her fingers from his.

'Good. Then I'll expect you tomorrow.' He gave a satisfied nod.

'I—I haven't got my schedule here,' she mumbled.

'Oh? Your timetable is already very booked up?' He smiled down at her, his dark eyes brimming with mirth.

Natasha blushed once more. 'That's not what I meant.'

'Then in that case I'll expect you at eight tomorrow evening. Henri will drive you.' With a quick nod he turned on his heel and left the room.

'Well,' Natasha exclaimed under her breath as she walked to the window and let out a long huff. The man certainly didn't lack nerve. Why, he was impossibly authoritarian. And, since she hadn't refused, she was now stuck with having dinner with him. Which reminded her of her desperate need to buy some clothes. Not that it mattered what she looked like, she qualified hastily; he was just a neighbour, and quite a rude one at that. But still, for some inexplicable reason she wanted to look her best. Perhaps it was part of her new-found duty to her name. After all, she must keep up the family reputation.

What on earth had caused him to invite this dowdy-looking Englishwoman to dinner when he'd had every intention of leaving for Paris immediately? Raoul wondered as he drove down the driveway and out onto the country road beyond. It was nonsensical and stupid to delay his return to town. Particularly to dine with someone as un-chic as his new neighbour. The woman's hair looked as if it hadn't seen a hairdresser in years, and her clothes didn't bear mentioning!

Perhaps, he concluded, shaking his head as he entered the castle gates, it was because he didn't want to go back to Paris, where he would have to deal with another of Clothilde's jealous rages.

Slowing the car to a halt in front of his massive oak front door, Raoul glanced at his mobile. Just as he'd thought, there were several missed calls from her. He rolled his eyes and huffed, passing a hand thoughtfully over his bronzed chin. He really must bring this relationship to an end. Apparently staying away for longer periods of time than he usually did wasn't doing the trick. Raoul sighed and alighted from the car. Like most men, he hated facing disagreeable situations. And Clothilde was certainly that, with her hysterical scenes and childish moods. Why, he wondered, had he got involved with her in the first place?

Stepping into the morning breeze, Raoul watched as the stable boys led two of his favourite horses across the cobblestoned yard, then stood for a moment on the edge of the well, dropping a pebble inside. Why not admit to himself that he'd succumbed to Clothilde's charm for the same reason he had all the others: because it was easier to date top models who shimmied in and out of his life than commit to anything more serious. At thirty-six he was a confirmed bachelor, and had no intention of changing his single status. Much to the disappointment of several mothers of suitable candidates to become the future Baroness d'Argentan.

His mouth took on a cynical twist. Women were ambitious gold-diggers, as he'd found out to his cost several years earlier. He would not repeat the mistake of falling for one again. And, speaking of gold-diggers, he reflected, making his way towards the medieval castle that had been in his family for centuries, perhaps Natasha de Saugure was yet another one. After all, this sudden arrival of hers was too damned coincidental to be mere fluke. He just hoped she hadn't frightened her grandmother into having a heart attack.

But as he walked through the great hall Raoul realized with a smile that this was probably a foolish thought. He had known Marie Louise de Saugure since he was a child. If anyone had done the terrifying it could have been her. Still, he felt wary of Natasha. As he would be of any Saugure. Which was obviously why he'd felt the need to ask her to dine: to delve deeper into her motives for coming here in the first place. The more he could glean about her, the better; for the past had taught every member of his family to be wary of Saugure women.

And he was no exception.

CHAPTER THREE

NATASHA tilted her head and took another satisfied look at herself in the gilded three-way mirror. It was a long time since she'd bothered about clothes and looking nice. The last few years, tucked away in the African bush with two pairs of jeans and a few faded T-shirts, had not helped her improve her fashion skills. Still, she'd spent time in Deauville that afternoon and taken the advice of a charming shop assistant who, seeing her in doubt, had helped her select a number of items, discarding others with a disparaging wave of her well-manicured hands, saying that beige did not favour *mademoiselle*.

Now, as she looked at her reflection, Natasha had to admit that the woman had been right. Everything she'd chosen—from the pretty pink tweed Chanel suit to the sleek trousers and the attractive cream dress she now wore—spelled chic, smart, and made her look very different from the girl who'd stepped off the plane a few days before. Suddenly she'd been transformed from average to head-turning, thanks to the make-over that Martine, the shop assistant, had insisted on. Upon her excellent advice, Natasha had gone to the top hairdresser in town and had her long hair shaped, washed and blow-dried. The effect, combined with the new outrageously expensive outfit, was staring her right in the face, and she was finding it hard to reconcile the woman in the mirror with who she was inside.

Oh, well, she conceded with a shrug, surely she could get used to improvement? Plus, she was damned if she was going to dine at Raoul d'Argentan's castle looking like something the cat had brought in on a bad day. Which made her wonder uncomfortably, as she turned away from the mirror and stepped into the bathroom to put on some make-up, why he'd asked her over in the first place. Perhaps it was curiosity. After all, everyone must be wondering who she was and why she was here. Although no doubt Monsieur Dubois, the notary, had dropped hints in his various clients' ears. She could imagine just how intriguing it must be for a small community such as this to have her as the new châtelaine.

Which in turn brought her back to the problem of what she was going to do. Was she really prepared to turn her life around one hundred and eighty degrees and come and live in Normandy, away from the world she knew, to pick up a legacy left to her by a woman who'd denied her that same legacy all her life?

Glancing at the ormolu clock on the pink marble mantelpiece, Natasha realized it was getting late and wasn't the moment for soul-searching. She'd think about her life later. Right now she needed to get downstairs, where Henri would be waiting to drive her over to the Baron's.

After a last peek in the mirror, she picked up a smart evening purse and stepped into her new, amazingly comfortable high heels. She took a few tentative steps. Not bad, considering she'd only worn sandals and sneakers for the past three years.

Hoping she wouldn't totter too badly, Natasha made her way to the grand stairway and accomplished her descent without mishap, glad to see Henri waiting for her in the hall.

As the car drew up at the floodlit drawbridge Natasha caught her breath. The Baron's château was amazing. Her grandmother's Manoir was beautiful, but it was also stiff and formal. This place, in contrast, was a maze of twelfth-century turrets, built of heavy stone and obviously impregnable. The men who'd built it were not to be tampered with, was the message it conveyed. All at once she shuddered and wondered about its present owner.

'It is very *impressionnant*, is it not?' Henri said, seeing her gaze up at the ramparts.

'It certainly is. It must be very old.'

'The Argentan family has lived here since before William departed to conquer England,' he relayed proudly. 'The Baron is a descendant of a long line of warriors. They fought many battles and have made many friends and not a few enemies. The first Baron was also named Raoul.'

He drove the car slowly across the drawbridge, which creaked ominously.

'Enemies?' Natasha asked, her brows knitting.

'Yes. There are many tales in the region of the Baron's ancestors, in particular one Regis d'Argentan.'

'Oh?'

'Yes. But I must not go on. All that is in the past and better left buried there. Here we are, *mademoiselle*.' He drew up in the courtyard and quickly stepped out of the car to help her alight before she could ask any further questions.

Minutes later Natasha was being conducted by a wizened butler up an ancient stone stairway illuminated by torches. Had he put on the full show for her, she wondered, or was there no electricity? The place felt strangely eerie, and an odd sense of *déjà vu* assailed her. But she shrugged it off and, holding her head high as she passed ancient tapestries, braced herself for the evening ahead.

Just as she was wondering where he'd got to, Raoul stepped out of the shadows.

'Good evening,' he said, once more raising her hand to his lips. A curious gleam lit his eyes and he took a step back. 'Excuse me if I seem rude, but I barely recognize you.'

'Is that a compliment?' she asked suspiciously, a laugh hovering.

'I would like to think of it as one,' he confirmed, gallantly steering her into a huge hall with an imposing stone hearth, around which several high-backed velvet chairs were arranged. The fire was burning. Here the lighting seemed at least to be improved. In fact, she realized, it was terribly subtle, with ultra-modern halogens slipped behind the heavy oak beams, pinpointing tapestries and coats of arms which adorned the stone walls.

'Your home is quite amazing,' she said sincerely, aware of his hand at her elbow.

'Thank you, *mademoiselle*—it is *mademoiselle* and not *madame*, I take it?' he enquired smoothly.

'Yes. Of course. I'm not married,' she returned, surprised.

'You object to marriage?'

'It's not something I think about.'

'Really? Well, that is surprising. I thought most women did. How old are you?'

'Twenty-three.'

'Well, that is not a very great age, I admit, but I know a number of girls your age who have several children already.'

'Really?' Natasha tossed her head defiantly. 'I thought women were marrying much later nowadays, and having children in their mid-thirties.'

'Is that what you plan to do?' he asked, that same quizzical brow shooting up, this time with an air of disapproval.

'I have no idea,' she responded tartly. This was not a subject she wished to enlarge upon.

'Ah, so no fiancé dying to drag you to the altar?' he quizzed, motioning to one of the chairs.

'Don't be silly,' she replied with an embarrassed laugh. Thank God he couldn't possibly know about Paul, and all the shame and embarrassment she'd been through at the age of barely nineteen, when he'd dumped her a week before their wedding.

'Very well. Enough about marriage. How about champagne instead?'

'Please.' She sat demurely in the high-backed chair and crossed her legs elegantly. It felt strange to feel so beautifully dressed and feminine, to feel Raoul's eyes devouring her not with the mere curiosity of a neighbour but with patent admiration. And all at once Natasha realized that for the past few years, since her disastrous engagement, she'd been afraid of looking attractive, of facing another relationship, in case she was faced with another misadventure. Well, she was older now, and more mature, she reflected, taking the champagne flute with a smile. She could deal with a little attraction without getting burned or involved.

Raoul settled in the chair opposite. He looked devastatingly handsome tonight, in black pants and a burgundy jacket, his raven hair swept back, his profile caught in the firelight. For an instant Natasha thought he looked just as she would have imagined a Norman Baron must look in his lair.

'So, you are Mademoiselle de Saugure,' he murmured thoughtfully. 'At the risk of sounding nosy, were you expecting to become Marie Louise's heir?'

'Actually, I had no idea. It never occurred to me. I hadn't seen my grandmother in ages. She—she and my father had a falling-out a few years ago,' she finished, not prepared to get into intimate details regarding her family.

'I remember. The Comtesse didn't accept his marriage

to your mother. Very foolish, since it made her into a lonely old lady. But understandable.'

'You think so?' Natasha's hackles rose immediately. Her mother's background was something she defended tooth and nail.

'Yes. Your father would have had problems whoever he married. Unless, of course, it had been someone of the Comtesse's own choosing. She was nothing if not authoritative. Liked getting her own way. We had a few tussles ourselves.' He smiled wryly and their eyes met, locking in the candlelight for a few interminable seconds.

'You and my grandmother?'

'Yes. Ever since my parents' demise several years ago I have been Lord of the Manor, so to speak. The Comtesse deemed it her duty to tell me how to run my estate. When I didn't follow her advice to the letter we had a few tiffs. But we got over them and remained fast friends. Strange that you should have arrived so suddenly and that her death should have ensued in such a precipitate manner.'

'If you think it was my fault I can assure you it wasn't,' Natasha replied coolly, hating herself for justifying something she'd had nothing to do with.

'Of course it wasn't. Perhaps she was waiting for you to come before she let go. She's been fairly ill for a while. Did she tell you about the will?'

'No. I only found out when the notary—look, I really don't see what business it is of yours,' she said, suddenly clamming up.

'Pardon,' he said, with a smile that was anything but apologetic. 'You must excuse my curiosity. But you must admit that the circumstances are somewhat unexpected.'

'They are. Which is why I haven't taken any decisions regarding the future, and don't plan to for a while.'

'Very wise.' He nodded, aware that he'd pushed her too

far. So the little English girl had fangs under that smooth bland exterior. Interesting. Raoul felt an inner stirring which he immediately recognized as lust. Banishing it at once, aware that a quick hot affair with this woman would hardly be conducive to good neighbourly relations, he rose and extended his hand. 'Let us proceed to dinner,' he said, taking her arm in his. 'I hope you will like what's on the menu.'

'And what is that?' Natasha asked archly. She was finding her feet in this game of light flirtation more easily than she would have believed.

'Oh, *ris de veau*. A speciality my chef loves to prepare.' His eyes sparkled with laughter.

Natasha hesitated, swallowed. 'Isn't that brain?' she asked warily.

'When it is prepared by Alphonse you will not think at all about its origin,' he assured her, leading the way into a vast baronial dining room, where liveried footmen stood behind two chairs at the long table.

'Is everything always so formal?' she asked impulsively as they stood in the entrance. 'I don't think I could live as you do and Grandmère did on an everyday basis. I think it would drive me mad.'

'You prefer a more casual lifestyle?' he asked, looking down at her from his six foot two.

'Yes. I've lived in Africa with refugees in the desert for the past three years. It makes one focus on the essentials in life.'

'I can believe that,' he said as they sat down, and he watched her, intrigued. So she was not some dull little secretary from a provincial backwater but rather a woman who sought adventure in her life. The thought was alluring, gave her an extra aura, and as the candlelight flickered and she unfolded her napkin he took a good look at her face, aware now of just how perfect her features were, and how lithe and attractive her body. Would it be pliant and lithe in bed? he wondered, a sudden image of her lying naked among the sheets causing him to divert his thoughts quickly to avoid any embarrassing consequences.

'Tell me about Africa,' he requested, truly interested in learning more about his intriguing neighbour. Perhaps he'd underestimated her.

Dinner went smoothly. Comfortable talking about a place she was familiar with, a culture which she'd taken the trouble to study, and the humanitarian crisis that she felt so strongly about, Natasha relaxed and became her true self. By the time they'd had coffee and after-dinner drinks, it was close to midnight.

'Gosh, it's getting awfully late. I'd better go home…to the Manoir, I mean. Could I call a taxi?' she enquired, glancing at him across the fireplace.

'Out of the question. I'll drive you.'

'That's very kind, but I don't want to be a nuisance.'

'A beautiful woman is never a nuisance. In fact, *ma chère*, it is a pleasure,' Raoul replied smoothly, executing a small formal bow, his lips curved in a half-smile.

Despite her new desire to be cool and sophisticated, Natasha swallowed. The man was positively devastating when he smiled, she realized, and she was still unused to compliments. To her annoyance the earlier flush returned to her cheeks. Still, letting him drive her home was hardly a big deal.

Once downstairs, they stepped outside into the courtyard and Raoul opened the door of his sleek red Ferrari, clearly amused.

A woman who blushed.

That was an interesting concept—one he hadn't come across in a while. For an instant Clothilde flashed across his mind. He doubted she'd blushed at twelve, let alone now. The thought of the other woman reminded him that tomorrow he would have to go back to Paris and deal with her. For some strange reason it all seemed rather further away than it had earlier in the day, as though his evening with Natasha had somehow obliterated any vestiges of feeling he might have had.

Soon they were driving down dark country lanes before heading into the drive of the Manoir.

'I suppose our families have been neighbours for ever,' Natasha remarked as the wheels crunched the gravel and the vehicle drew up at the front door.

'We have, in effect, been neighbours for going on approximately six hundred years.'

'Who was your ancestor—Regis?' she asked suddenly, remembering Henri's words and turning to try and distinguish his expression in the half-light coming from the outside lamps.

She saw him stiffen. 'Who told you about Regis?' he asked warily.

'Oh, somebody mentioned him. I can't remember who,' she lied, sensing there was more to this story than met the eye. More that she definitely planned to find out.

'Regis was a rather flamboyant character. All families have them, I suppose—a sort of black sheep, in a way. I'll tell you about him some time. It would take too long tonight, *ma chère*.'

'All right.' Natasha pretended not to be intrigued by the story. Someone else could surely tell it. Which made her suddenly determined to become better acquainted with the people on the estate and in the village. Perhaps she could glean some interesting details from them, learn all sorts of things about the past.

Then, when she least expected it, Raoul leaned over and

in one smooth, swift movement slipped his hand under her chin and drew her mouth to his.

She should protest, should stop him, should do something, Natasha realized. But it was impossible. For the next thing she knew Raoul's firm lips were parting hers, forcing them to surrender to his will. His arms came about her and her breast cleaved to his hard chest. It was crazy, but all she could do was succumb, allow his probing tongue to wander, seek, explore, and try to ignore the delicious tautness of her nipples, to control the myriad sensations coursing through her body from head to toe. When finally he withdrew his mouth, and stayed staring down at her, she pulled out of his arms, breathless, her pulse racing.

'I'll be back at the end of the week,' he murmured, his voice husky with undisguised desire, 'then we can pick up where we've left off, *ma belle*. I look forward to it already.'

'We will do nothing of the sort,' she retorted, regaining some measure of composure. 'And I'll thank you to leave me alone. I have no need or desire for your attentions. Keep your kisses for your own kind. I have no wish for them.' With that she flung out of the car and, stumbling on the gravel in her high heels, reached the front door.

Henri had given her a heavy key before dinner. Now she inserted it in the lock, her fingers struggling nervously to undo it. 'Oh, bother,' she exclaimed, when it wouldn't turn.

'May I?' Raoul, composed and gentlemanly once more, stepped forward.

'Oh, just go away and leave me alone,' Natasha exclaimed crossly, her nerves still jangling from their unexpected encounter.

'But you'll be stuck out here in the night,' he remarked matter-of-factly. 'Let's be reasonable about this, *ma chère*, after all it was only a kiss.'

With an annoyed huff Natasha stepped back and let

Raoul take over. After one expert twist the key turned. '*Voilà,*' he said, smiling down at her with that same mischievous twinkle which had the effect of making her melt inside. '*Bonne nuit*, lovely lady. May you have sweet dreams.' Then he turned abruptly, just as he had the other day. And the next thing she knew he was driving off down the drive as she let herself into the dimly lit hall.

Sleep was impossible. She simply must pull herself together. Instinctively Natasha walked to the library and switched on a lamp. Perhaps another drink would do her good—a nightcap. Or maybe that was the problem. She wasn't used to much alcohol, and, although it hadn't seemed much at the time, over the course of the evening she must have consumed quite a bit. Perhaps a book might do the trick—distract her from the evening's adventure.

But, as she skimmed the packed shelves of classics, Natasha could still feel the touch of Raoul's lips on hers, the tingling sensation that caused her breasts to peak even now, and a strange delicious throbbing travelling through her. It was ridiculous, she reasoned. Outrageous that a man she barely knew could cause such havoc. Why, she hadn't had a boyfriend since Paul, and even then she'd been hesitant to sleep with him, as though something deep down inside had warned her of his future behaviour. But she had. And it hadn't been a success. She'd been afraid, unexcited, but determined to do what she had to. Never in the two years they'd gone out together had she felt anything close to the extreme rush of pleasure she'd derived in those few minutes with Raoul in the car.

'Absurd,' she muttered, glancing at the rows of titles, determined to find something to distract her. All at once her eyes fell upon a large leatherbound volume. *A Concise History of the Famille d'Argentan*, she read. Extracting the large volume from its slot, where it had obviously remained for many years, she brushed off some dust. There was nothing concise about it, she reflected with a grimace, carrying the enormous book over to the sofa.

Wrapping herself in a rug, Natasha opened the stiff cover and began curiously to turn the pages. There was a long detailed family tree. Suddenly her eye fell upon Regis. His dates were interesting. 1768 to 1832. So he had been a young man during the French Revolution. Then, to her amazement, she read a name that was all too familiar: Natasha de Saugure.

The name was not printed, in the manner of a wife's, but inscribed as a handwritten side-note. A shiver ran down her spine. So she had been named after an ancestor. Her father had never mentioned the fact. Avidly she glanced at Natasha's dates. 1775 to 1860. The woman had lived to a ripe old age. But what had been her relationship to Regis? There were no details. Just the scribbled note. How strange, she thought, flicking through the pages, that her namesake should be inscribed next to the name of the man nobody seemed to want to talk about.

After a while perusing the book, she felt sleep begin to press upon her, and, laying the volume down on an ornate table, she rose and yawned. Time to go upstairs and rest. Tomorrow she would seek further information.

As she wandered up the grand stairway Natasha glanced up at the portraits on the wall. A lovely grey-eyed girl in a stiff brocade dress with a revealing décolleté—as had been the fashion in the late eighteenth century—stared down at her from one of them. Natasha held her breath as her eyes went to the tiny bronze plaque on the frame. As she'd supposed, it was Natasha de Saugure. Who had she married and had she been happy? she wondered suddenly. Her eyes in the portrait looked bright and filled with hope.

But there was something else, a mysterious melancholic twist to the smile.

Natasha glanced at the painting a moment longer, then, letting out a sigh, she climbed the rest of the stairs and headed to her room.

CHAPTER FOUR

A WEEK passed and still Natasha hadn't taken any definite decision regarding her future. To her annoyance she experienced a moment's disappointment when there was no sign of Raoul at the end of the week. But she shook it off, reminding herself that it was for the best. He'd obviously seen the light, realized how embarrassing any involvement would be. After all, they might be neighbours for the next half-century for all she knew.

Neither had she had time to further her investigation into the lives of Regis d'Argentan and her ancestor Natasha, for Monsieur Dubois had appeared at the château the morning following her evening with Raoul, armed with heavy manila files overflowing with documents needing to be signed and filed, and others she needed to read to become familiar with her grandmother's estate.

'And you should visit your grandmother's apartment in Paris immediately,' the *notaire* had admonished in his precise legal tone.

So now here she was, a week later, sitting on a train headed to Paris.

Except for an old schoolfriend, she knew no one in that city. But, despite this somewhat daunting fact, Natasha was excited. Here she was, going to Paris to stay in her very own apartment. It seemed incredible. It was a long time since she'd visited the city with her parents, and the thought of rediscovering such exciting places as the Louvre and the Centre Pompidou, and ambling down the Champs Elysées, stopped her being anxious for long. Perhaps she would even hit Avenue Montaigne, now that she'd discovered the novel and intriguing delight of creating a new wardrobe.

As the train drew up to the platform at the Gare du Nord, Natasha stepped down with her practical roll-on case. She was about to follow the crowd down the platform towards the main station entrance when she heard her name called.

'Oh, my God,' she exclaimed as Raoul stood looming over her, his dark features stark in the afternoon sun. 'You gave me such a fright.'

'Forgive me. It was not my intention.'

'How did you know I was here?' she asked haughtily, hastily regaining her composure.

'I rang the Manoir to talk to you and Henri told me you'd be on the four-fifty, so I came to pick you up,' he replied matter-of-factly.

'Well, that's very nice of you,' she said, hoping her tone was dampening enough, and willing her pulse not to beat quite so hard, 'but Henri had no business telling you my whereabouts.' Another time she'd leave specific instructions not to reveal her plans.

'I think he assumed you would like to be picked up,' he said mildly, taking her case and slipping his hand protectively about her shoulders as two heavily laden backpackers nearly collided with her on the crowded platform. 'I believe you are not very familiar with Paris?'

'No, I'm not,' she acknowledged crossly, wishing she could calm the agitation that being next to him caused. Then, as they began walking down the platform, she saw Raoul signal to an older man in a grey suit and tie.

'May I introduce Pierre?' Raoul said smoothly, as they reached him. 'He drives for me. We shall be taking *mademoiselle* to the Saugure apartment in the Place François Premier, Pierre.' His tone was polite, yet there was no doubt that the words were an order. Natasha felt strangely exhilarated and annoyed. How dared he swan into her life and simply take over? What if she'd wanted to go somewhere else rather than the apartment?

She was about to protest when by chance her eyes fell on the large queue waiting for taxis. It went against the grain, but she swallowed her words. It was really much simpler and more agreeable to be driven, even though Raoul's manner was intolerably high-handed. Of course she'd have to make it very plain indeed that she was not going to be herded around Paris at his pleasure, she reflected, climbing into the Bentley that had materialized as though by magic. She had her own plans for her Parisian stay, and they did not include Raoul d'Argentan.

Or at least they hadn't up until now.

'I thought you'd enjoy dining here,' Raoul said a few hours later as they glanced at their menus over the candlelit dinner table.

Natasha wasn't quite certain how she'd ended up at Laurent's with Raoul. It had all happened in such a natural manner that she'd barely noticed the time go by. First she'd been enchanted by the apartment, situated in one of Paris's loveliest squares. It was ample, elegant, and beautifully decorated. Very different from the stiff formality of the Manoir, as though another hand had been at work here. The housekeeper, Madame Duvallier, a large middle-aged woman with a warm smile and an efficient manner, who had worked with the old Comtesse for many years, had made her most welcome. She'd also greeted Raoul warmly, and it had been plain to Natasha that he was an *habitué*.

Now, as they sat at the candlelit table, she decided to question him. 'Have you come often to Grandmère's apartment?' she asked, after they'd ordered and the menus had been removed.

'Quite frequently. My parents and she were friends. So, yes, I've been in and out over the years. Lately the Comtesse had asked me for some advice about her affairs. In fact, I'm quite surprised she never told me that you were to be her heir,' he added, with that same critical stare that left her feeling as though he was suspicious of her.

Natasha bristled. 'I don't see why she should have. After all, I didn't know myself.'

'No, but—' He cut off his words, shook his head and smiled. 'It is of no importance. Do not let us spoil such a pleasant evening by conjecturing over things which we cannot alter in any case.'

The logic of his argument struck home. There was little use in trying to figure out the old Comtesse's motives. She might as well do as he said, and enjoy the lovely atmosphere of the restaurant.

'Do you plan to make a long stay in Paris?' Raoul enquired as they sipped champagne, and Natasha felt a delicious headiness take hold of her.

'I really don't know. But very soon I'll have to decide whether or not I'm returning to my job. I took two months off. But after that I'll need to make a definite decision as to the future.'

'Do you enjoy your job?' he asked curiously, his eyes boring into hers.

'I do enjoy it, yes. It has been very fulfilling. But…' She hesitated, something stopping her from confiding in him.

'But?' He prodded gently, determined to get her to tell him what was on her mind.

'Well, it's just that all this has been so unexpected. I mean, how could I have imagined when I left Khartoum that my life would take such a strange turn?'

'No, you couldn't, could you?' he murmured, still sizing

her up while accepting the caviar the waiter had placed before them. 'Now things seem very different?'

'Yes.' She hesitated, then decided to risk it and tell him how she felt. Expressing it might help her understand better herself. 'Now it's as though I have a new path that I must follow. Not that I'm certain yet,' she added hastily. 'It's too soon for me to take such a radical decision. The thing is that if I don't remain here—or at least at the Manoir—I'll probably have to sell it.'

'Sell the Manoir?' Raoul's cup hit the saucer with a crack. 'You can't sell the Manoir. It has been in the Saugure family for almost three centuries. The original house much longer than that. It's unthinkable.' His voice cut the air like a knife and his dark eyes flashed with anger.

'I know that. But all things have to move on at some point,' she reasoned thoughtfully.

'That is a ridiculous statement,' he bit back. 'Selling the Manoir is out of the question.'

'Might I remind you,' she said, drawing herself up, 'that it really is none of your business what I do with my property.'

'You can remind me as much as you like,' he answered, his burning eyes meeting hers full on in a clash of wills, 'but I assure you, *mademoiselle*, that I will personally make your life as difficult as possible should you even contemplate such an action. *Mon Dieu.* What would Marie Louise do if she could hear you? She must be turning in her grave at this very instant.' He sent her a withering look across the table and signalled the waiter for the bill.

'I don't see how you can stop me if I do decide to sell,' Natasha challenged, furious at his meddling. 'I have every right to do whatever I like with all three properties. Neither you nor anyone can stop me.'

'Technically I may not be able to stop you,' he replied

in a low, menacing voice as the waiter approached, 'but I assure you that you would regret it if you so much as thought about selling the Manoir.'

'Are you threatening me?' Her chin jutted out and she faced him head on.

'Merely warning you that you are on shaky ground when it comes to selling. You have inherited a duty to your name and your lineage,' he threw, his tone as biting as it was derisive. 'Surely even an Englishwoman like you can understand that? Doesn't your bloodline mean anything to you?'

'You are insupportable,' Natasha hissed, throwing down her napkin on the table and getting up while the waiter hovered anxiously. 'I'll do whatever I like with my property, and I'll thank you to leave me alone. I need neither your assistance nor your advice. Goodnight.' On that dramatic note she swept regally from the table and made her way to the entrance of the restaurant.

When the doorman asked her if she wanted a cab she acquiesced gladly, still fuming from the altercation while desperately trying to ignore the needling truth that Raoul's words had brought home: she did feel a link to the past, and to her name and to all she owed it. But she was damned if she would admit that to him, she reflected savagely, letting out a cross huff as she waited impatiently for the cab.

So she had a temper. Well, he liked her all the better for it. But he was damned if he was going to let her get all sorts of ridiculous ideas into that pretty head of hers. Sell the Manoir indeed. Absurd. Plus, that might lead to the divulging of past history much better left buried.

Having settled the bill, Raoul made his way to the entrance of the restaurant, where he could see Natasha's back stiffly etched in the doorway. A smile hovered about his lips. She was turning out to be quite a handful, the drab little English miss. Not only had she been transformed into a raving beauty, but her character was proving more and more intriguing by the moment.

Signalling the doorman, he murmured to him to cancel the cab and approached Natasha.

'*Excusez-moi, mademoiselle*, if I said anything to offend you,' he murmured in a conciliatory tone, 'but the truth must be faced.'

She whirled around, eyes blazing. 'I've had just about enough of you for one evening, Raoul d'Argentan. Now, please leave me alone. I've ordered a cab and I can find my way back to the apartment perfectly well on my own.'

'But the doorman has just indicated to me that there are no taxis available in Paris at this hour,' he said, sounding much more French than he had before, and raising his hand in a very Gallic manner while shaking his head, eyes twinkling.

'Really? That wasn't the case five minutes ago,' she replied coldly.

'No? Well, things can change very fast in Paris. Transport is unreliable.' He slipped an arm into hers and began walking. 'Much better to let me accompany you—which, I might add, I do with pleasure.' The slight lilt of a French accent thickened and his eyes sparkled. 'Really, Natasha, there is no need to be upset. It is only a ride home, *après tout*, and you are only cross because I pointed out something that I have a funny feeling you already know deep down inside yourself.'

Natasha swallowed, bereft of words. How did he know? And how could she deny the truth? She glanced back at the doorman, who sent her an apologetic look. Anger still seethed inside her at the way she'd been so accurately read and cleverly manipulated. But, she realized, letting out a sigh, it was unlikely that the doorman would order her a cab now that the Baron had imposed his wretched will, and the best she could do, without causing an embarrassing scene, was to concede gracefully.

Several minutes later they drove alongside the Seine, past famous bridges, with the lights from the barges and *bateaux mouches* shimmering. On the Isle Saint-Louis she heard the chime of the bells at Nôtre Dame. It was impossible to be here, in this the loveliest of cities, and not surrender to its charm and enchantment.

'How about a drink before we turn in?' Raoul asked, taking a sidelong glance at her as he kept the car steady in the flow of traffic. She looked calmer, more composed. And he had no intention of letting her go home right now. She looked too beautiful in that silk dress, her hair flowing like golden wheat over her shoulders. Plus, he'd finally dispatched Clothilde and was therefore free as the wind. Added to all these valid reasons was the fact that the kiss they'd shared the other night in the car had remained strangely imprinted in his mind.

'I suggest we pop over to the bar of the Plaza Athénée. If you haven't been there before you'll find the decoration amusing.' He pulled his mobile out of his pocket, and before Natasha had a chance to agree or refuse he was reserving a table in quick French.

'Raoul, I never said I was going,' she said when he'd finished.

'Do you always have to protest against every good idea?' he countered with a shrug, a wicked smile breaking on his handsome face. 'Just relax—*voyons*—and go with the flow, as they say in America. After all, you're in Paris. Enjoy it.'

She sighed, realizing she was beaten and that actually she rather wanted to go for a drink. Plus, there really could be no possible harm in joining him in the bar of one of Paris's best hotels, she justified.

Soon they were seated in the corner of the dimly lit bar and Raoul ordered a bottle of Dom Perignon. The atmosphere was fun and young, and Natasha eyed the bar counter—a replica of a huge slab of ice, internally illuminated—intrigued.

'Like it?' Raoul asked, following her gaze. 'It's fun, isn't it? I like coming here.'

It was only then that he saw a slim familiar figure silhouetted across the room, seated with friends by the window, and his heart sank. Clothilde sat, sylphlike and languorously elegant, dressed as always in the latest Dior fashions. Her dark-eyed gaze fulminated as it rested upon him. Raoul glanced away. Why hadn't he remembered that she'd probably be here tonight? Hopefully she would be too proud to make a scene.

But his hopes were dashed when two minutes later Clothilde snaked between the tables, her slim hips swaying, then stood before him, her long black hair shrouding her face, a cigarette waving in her nervous fingers.

'Monsieur le Baron,' she threw sarcastically, 'to what do we owe the pleasure of your presence here tonight? I thought you were ruralizing for a while.'

'Good evening, Clothilde. May I introduce an English friend of mine, Natasha de Saugure?'

'Non!' Clothilde exclaimed. 'I'm not interested in your friends or your lies,' she spat venomously, sending Natasha a scathing look. 'You're a liar and a cheat, Raoul d'Argentan, and I'll make sure all of Paris knows it. Be careful of him,' she added, addressing Natasha, 'he's the biggest bastard in town.' Then, tossing her head, she turned on her spiky high heels and stalked back to her table, where her cohorts sat watching approvingly.

Raoul sighed and shook his head. 'Sorry about that,' he murmured. 'I'm afraid Clothilde is rather theatrical.'

'Who is she? Your girlfriend?'

'Ex-girlfriend. If you can call her that. I dated her for a while and she thought it was more serious than it ever was. Why is it that women always fall into that trap?' he enquired, brows knit. 'I don't understand why they can't just accept the *status quo* and enjoy it. It always amazes me how they complicate life.' He shook his head and let out a sigh.

'Perhaps the women you run into have a deeper sense of commitment than you do,' she replied, tongue in cheek, before taking a sip of chilled champagne.

'Maybe. But no commitment ever existed in the first place. Not on my side anyway. I made that abundantly plain from the outset.'

'But things can start out as casual in life and then become deeper as time goes on,' Natasha argued.

He shrugged in what she considered to be a very French gesture. 'I never make promises that I might break. And I never offered marriage or even an in-house living arrangement to Clothilde. I really don't see why she's so upset.'

'Well, *she* seems to think she has a ton of reasons,' Natasha remarked tartly.

'You see?' He turned and threw his hands up. 'That is exactly what I mean. Women are all the same—always filling in the blanks with all sorts of reasons and justifications for getting their own way. I will never understand them.'

Natasha smothered a smile and decided there was little point in pursuing the subject. But Clothilde's burst of anger had left her thinking. It was clear that Raoul was a seasoned playboy, used to getting his own way. Perhaps she should take the other woman's warning seriously. After all, she knew nothing about him except that he was her neighbour in Normandy.

Later, as they drove back to the apartment through the quiet streets of the city, she determined to keep her distance from this man. She'd learned her lesson with Paul, hadn't she? The minute you trusted you could also be betrayed. And, frankly, she had very few reasons to trust Raoul.

When they reached the imposing building he stopped the car and parked. 'How about inviting me in for a nightcap?' he said with a grin.

'I don't think so. I'm quite tired tonight. I have a long day tomorrow—meetings with my grandmother's lawyers and so on.'

'Ah, you're meeting with Perret, I take it.' He nodded. 'He's quite a good man on the whole, but I told Marie Louise she might want to consider a change of legal counsel.'

'And why is that?'

'Oh, I'll tell you some other time, when you have more time on your hands,' he answered affably.

Natasha could have kicked herself for falling into the trap.

'Right—well, I'd better be going.' She began opening the door, but he leaned quickly across her and held it closed.

'Not so fast, *ma belle*,' he murmured, his voice turning husky. 'You can't be in that much of a hurry.'

'I—' Natasha felt her body click into overdrive. What was it about this man that left her mesmerized, unable to react as she should? When his hand slipped behind her neck and he drew her close, his lips dropping a trail of deliciously feathery kisses on her cheek, down past her lips, her throat, then slipped to her breast, instead of repulsing him she let out a pent-up sigh of longing.

It was as though her mind had blurred and her normal functions simply didn't work. She knew she should react, knew it was ridiculous to allow him this liberty, but as his fingers expertly caressed her taut nipples and his lips ravaged her mouth with such intense desire it was impossible to resist. Inside she felt a new and strange sensation, the same as she'd felt the other night, as though he'd pressed an invisible button over which he had complete control. His fingers slipped under her top and she gasped as skin met skin and his skilled fingers taunted further, making her writhe, leaving her conscious of a deeper yearning, a need for further fulfilment, that left her aching and damp, longing to throw caution to the winds and let him have his way.

But finally reason asserted itself and she withdrew reluctantly from his embrace. Righting her clothes, Natasha said in a shaky voice, 'I think it's better if we don't see each other any more. This—this shouldn't be happening. I—we're neighbours. We shouldn't— What I mean is—'

Raoul laid his hand over hers and leaned back in the soft cream leather seat. 'Are you afraid, Natasha?'

'I—I don't know. It's all too fast. Too much has happened to me in the past few days. I can't keep up.'

'You mean you're scared of enjoying yourself?' he queried, a subtle knowing smile hovering about his lips. 'My dear, what is wrong with seeking pleasure?'

'Look, I can't handle this, okay?' she said, suddenly upset, tears of frustration and confusion burning as she grappled for the car door handle. 'I want to go.'

'Then of course you shall,' he said quietly, eyeing her, a slight frown entering his eyes. He had not expected this reaction from her.

Quickly Raoul stepped out of the vehicle and opened the door. 'I'll say goodnight and *au revoir*, then, but not goodbye. We will see each other, and if you don't want me to kiss you then I won't,' he said, touching her cheek in a tender gesture. 'But don't get upset. It was just a nice interlude for both of us. *Sans plus,*' he added lightly.

'Right.' Natasha swallowed and took a deep breath.

'I'll give you a call. Maybe I can take you to see some of the sights you may want to enjoy. We could go out to the country for lunch one day.'

This was said in a firm, friendly tone, and Natasha wondered if she'd been dreaming. Had this same man who was now casually saying goodnight held her in his arms so passionately only moments before?

Once inside the building Natasha entered the elevator, sank against the wall, and let out a relieved sigh. Yet it was impossible to deny the internal havoc she was experiencing, the molten desire still throbbing in places she had never before been wholly conscious of. She really must get away from Raoul before she made a complete fool of herself, she reflected, biting her lower lip. Perhaps after the meetings tomorrow she would head down to the South of France and visit her grandmother's villa, near the village of Eze, above Monte Carlo. That would give her time to breathe, to understand better all that had occurred over the past few days, help her to take the decisions that eventually must be faced.

On reaching her floor, she entered the apartment and closed the door carefully behind her. So much had happened so fast and it was hard to keep up. And the roiling feelings caused by the moments spent in Raoul's arms were as perturbing as all the rest.

If not more so.

CHAPTER FIVE

THE meeting with Monsieur Perret proved to be long and rather boring. He went over and over several deeds and papers, leaving Natasha wondering if perhaps Raoul wasn't right, and that more efficient legal counsel might be found. But for now all she wanted was to escape Paris and the proximity of the dangerous Baron. It was most degrading to think that he merely had to touch her to cause her to react as though she'd been lit by a damned match, that a mere kiss and a flick of his skilled fingers could make her quiver like a jelly. It was shaming. Made her wonder just what kind of a woman she was.

But even as she packed her bag, determined to get on the TGV as soon as possible, Natasha found herself unable to banish the previous evening as summarily as she would have liked. She simply must exercise more control over herself, she reflected, zipping the suitcase. Imagine if this happened to her the minute any man touched her! Yet why had it never occurred with Paul? she wondered as she entered a taxi and made her way through the busy Parisian streets to the station.

Once on the train, Natasha sat next to the window and read the paper, determined not to allow Raoul and his magnetic aura to occupy her thoughts. She was dealing with so many new factors in her life. The last thing she needed was to be distracted by silly nonsense.

Several hours later the train arrived in Nice, and she took a taxi up to the medieval village of Eze. The stunning Mediterranean villa stood on a small plateau, caught between sea and mountain. It was spectacular, and had maintained all of its original character, and Natasha knew at once that this was one spot she would not let go of easily. It was as if she immediately identified with the place.

Madame Bursin, the housekeeper, had prepared a lovely room, decorated in pale blues and whites. And all at once time rolled back and Natasha recalled her father telling her of wonderful summers spent here in his youth. She experienced a rush of nostalgia. What a pity it was that her grandmother had banished them so definitively from her life. They could have spent such wonderful times here together.

But there was little use regretting the past, and instead she changed into a brief white bikini and headed out towards the cerulean pool that overlooked the glistening Mediterranean below, dotted with yachts and small craft. It was a sight she knew she would never tire of.

Lying down on a *chaise-longue*, Natasha sighed and smiled. She felt better now, more in control. And even proud of herself. She'd escaped Raoul's clutches and could go back to being her own person. Now all she had to do was relax, think about her life and how it was going to shape up, and she'd be well on her way.

'What do you mean she left?' Raoul asked crossly.

'I'm afraid she's gone, Monsieur le Baron. She left this morning after her meetings with Monsieur Perret.'

'And did she say where she was going?' Raoul drummed irritated fingers on the sleek teak desk of his Paris office and cradled the phone against his shoulder. This was not going according to plan.

'No. I'm afraid *mademoiselle* didn't say.'

'Thank you.' He hung up abruptly and swung around in the black leather chair, his expression foreboding. She was running away from him. The thought both annoyed and intrigued him. Women never ran away from him. Rather they invented pathetic excuses to see him again. Raoul stopped swinging and sat up straight. He must find out where she was. Though why the hell it mattered he hadn't fathomed yet. Perhaps it was just the fact that he didn't like being thwarted. And, although he knew it was not strictly wise, he knew he had every intention of having an affair with Natasha. Or at least taking her to bed a few times to satisfy his desire for her. He had the feeling they would both enjoy that. And she knew it. He *knew* that she knew it. Could tell by her reactions, the way she moved in his arms, the way her body turned pliant and receptive the minute he grazed her breast. So why run? Why not stay and enjoy it?

He let out a long huff and shook his head. Women were, as he'd remarked only last night after Clothilde's little display of hysterics, incomprehensible. But that didn't help him.

As the morning drifted by he felt increasingly frustrated that there was no phone call, no indication at all of Natasha's whereabouts. By midday he was impatiently ringing the Manoir, where he met with another negative.

So she hadn't gone back there.

Had she returned to England? he wondered, glancing at his watch, aware that he was expected at the Relais Plaza in half an hour, for lunch with his cousin Madeleine.

Precisely on time, he entered the restaurant and was greeted by name by the head waiter, who immediately showed him to a table by the window on the banquette. Two minutes later Madeleine, a chic, attractive Parisian woman of his own age, entered the restaurant and he rose to greet her. Soon they were settled and sipping champagne.

'So, *mon vieux*, how is life treating you?' she asked, sending him an amused smile across the table.

'Not too bad. That is to say, did you hear of the death of Marie Louise de Saugure?'

'Actually, yes. I read the obituary. I meant to come up for the funeral but I got caught up with Frederic's exams. Tell me about it.'

'Oh, very impressive—old retainers lining the road as the hearse went by. Just as it should have been.'

'God, you're so medieval,' she remarked, shaking her head and sighing gustily. 'Just like our ancestor Regis, I'll bet, and just as wicked.'

'That is pure speculation.'

'Is it? I wonder if his lover thought so,' she mused.

'The beautiful Natasha?'

'Yes. I've always wondered why those two never married. It always struck me as so silly. All because of false pride. Men are so stupid.'

'What rubbish you talk, Madeleine.'

'Maybe, but the legend has always intrigued me. She was very beautiful, if the portrait at the Manoir is anything to go by. She should have used that to snare him.'

'What an idea. He would never have conceded.' Raoul suddenly remembered the portrait and his eyes narrowed. Damned if it didn't resemble the present Natasha.

'I shall miss Marie Louise and her acerbic remarks,' Madeleine said with a sigh as she glanced through the menu. 'She was a wonderful old lady—although I remember when I used to quake in my shoes whenever we went over to the Manoir when we were children. Now, tell me, who inherits?'

'An English granddaughter,' he replied blandly. 'How about some *foie gras*?'

'You don't say? I'd forgotten the Comtesse had a son she disinherited.'

'She did. He was considerably older than us, which is why we don't remember him well. He married unsuitably. An Englishwoman of no consequence. The Comtesse was very *fâchée*.'

'And cut him out of her will?'

'Exactly. He was disinherited. But apparently she changed her mind shortly before her death. And now the granddaughter, who never even knew her and arrived for a visit only hours before her death, has inherited everything.'

'Well. What a story. And what is her name?'

'Natasha.'

'Excuse me?' Madeleine put her glass down with a snap and their eyes met. 'You can't be serious. Natasha? But surely no one in that family would adopt the name after—well, after what happened.'

'I wouldn't have thought so.' He shrugged. 'Either Hubert de Saugure had a warped sense of humour or he wanted to thwart his mother.'

'Natasha,' Madeleine mused thoughtfully. 'I've often wondered why she did what she did, damaging both our families so completely. She must have loved Regis very much. It all happened so long ago, yet the shadow of her ghost seems to linger, doesn't it?'

'Frankly, I've never considered the matter.'

'How typical. Still, it has to be more than a coincidence.'

'A surprising course of events, I admit, but don't let's stretch our imaginations too far.'

'Tell me, what's she like, this English girl?' Madeleine asked, intrigued. 'How old is she?'

'Young. About twenty-three. She is an interesting young woman who has spent the past few years in Africa doing humanitarian work.'

'Goodness.' Madeleine's brows flickered. 'That sounds dreadfully righteous.'

'Not at all. I get the impression of an intelligent and sensitive human being.' He couldn't explain why, but it annoyed him that his cousin should dismiss Natasha in such a callous manner.

'Oh? So you've talked to her in depth?' A mischievous smile similar to his own curved Madeleine's expressive lips. 'Already smitten, *mon cousin*?'

'Rubbish. But I have had occasion to speak with her, yes. Naturally I went over there to offer my condolences.'

'Naturally.' She nodded, her flashing eyes belying her words. 'Raoul, *chéri*, this is *me* you're talking to—your old devoted playmate who knows you like the back of her hand. And all I have to say is that it would be the first time in history that you went to see any young woman unless she was minimally attractive.'

'Really, Madeleine,' he murmured, his lips quivering, 'you underestimate me.'

'So I presume,' she continued, ignoring him, 'that your new neighbour is at the very least gorgeous?' She quirked a brow and waited.

'She's attractive,' he conceded, reluctant to say more lest Madeleine make the wrong assumptions. 'Frankly, at first I thought she was a dowd. But she seems to have had some sort of make-over. Quite surprising, really. Now, why don't we order?' he said picking up the menu and signalling the waiter. 'I hear the *filets de sole meunière* are excellent today.'

Madeleine opened her mouth, about to say more, then decided against it. Something told her that perhaps she shouldn't meddle this time. So with good grace she picked up the menu and made her choice.

* * *

When by that evening Raoul still had no news of Natasha—and to his annoyance found it hard to concentrate on anything else—he decided he must take measures to ensure his comfort. He was damned if he was going to let her disturb his equilibrium in this manner. He wanted her—wanted to bed her. And that was exactly what he intended to do.

It was only next morning when he woke up that he remembered Marie Louise's villa in Eze and sat up in bed with a start. *'Voilà,'* he exclaimed, snapping his fingers. 'I'll bet that's where she's hiding out.

Minutes later he was up and packing an overnight bag. After a quick croissant and *café au lait* at the brasserie on the corner of his street he jumped in the car and headed south on the autoroute. It would take several hours to reach Eze, but he wasn't in a hurry. He had advised his office that he would be absent for a couple of days, and only to contact him on his mobile in case of an emergency.

Raoul loved a good chase, and this was certainly turning into one. A better one than he'd been offered in a while. Of late his women seemed to comply all too boringly with his every wish. And thus they bored him.

But Natasha certainly didn't do that.

She felt deliciously calm here at the Villa Le Caprice, Natasha decided, letting out a long, delighted sigh. Even though it wasn't that hot as yet, she found lying by the pool relaxing, reading or simply thinking about the future, an ideal occupation. It allowed her to put into perspective everything that lay before her. She must, she realized, find out more about her family's history. It intrigued her now. As though part of her had been missing all these years. She particularly wanted to learn the tale of Regis d'Argentan and how he was connected to the Saugures. There appeared to be a mystery connected to him and her family, and she had every intention of finding out what that mystery was. She wished now that instead of letting herself go all gooey in Raoul's arms she'd spent the time more productively, finding out about her ancestry.

The thought of Raoul—who, if she was truthful, was never far from her mind—made her swallow. What a good thing she'd taken the decision to leave Paris. Thank God she was sensible at heart. Feeling a slight sense of pride at having exercised self-control, despite the longing images that flashed regularly before her at the mere thought of him, Natasha decided that today she would wander further afield. Her grandmother had a wonderful 1960s convertible Rolls, and she couldn't resist the temptation of taking it out for a spin. Madame Bursin and her husband Jacques were everything that was kind and helpful, and the car had been taken to the garage to make sure it was in excellent working order. Now she couldn't wait.

The day was perfect, with a blue cloudless sky and sparkling sea below. Having donned a pair of white capri pants and a pretty matching top, Natasha put on her sunglasses and tied back her hair, feeling positively like a fifties movie star. Tossing her large handbag on the passenger seat, she was about to get into the vehicle when she heard the rumble of an engine.

Standing up straighter, she stiffened. Surely it couldn't be him. Yet there he was, cruising up her drive in that damn sports car of his, as cool as you please. She should have left orders not to let him in. But, she realized, as the vehicle drew up and Jacques hastened towards it, he probably had this lot under his thumb as well.

Knowing she could not make a scene in front of the servants, Natasha pulled herself together and tried to look dignified.

'Well,' she remarked, ignoring her racing pulse once

he'd exited the car, 'what are you doing here?' She hoped to God she looked more poised and sophisticated than she felt.

'I think you know exactly why I'm here,' he answered in a low husky voice as he leaned over to peck her cheek, leaving her no option but to submit to this form of address.

The attractive sight of him dressed in designer trousers, a loose sports shirt and loafers with a navy jersey casually thrown over his shoulders, had not escaped her, and she swallowed bravely, determined not to let him faze her.

'I can't think what can have brought you here,' she replied in what she hoped was a nonchalant tone. 'In fact, you're very lucky to have caught me as I was about to go for a spin.'

'But please don't let me stop you,' he insisted, stepping around the car and opening the door for her. 'It will be my pleasure to be your guide.'

'I wasn't aware I needed one.'

'Oh, but surely, *ma chère*, you don't imagine I would abandon you. It would be too callous of me to allow a young woman on her own—the granddaughter of an old family friend, I might add—to venture alone onto the Riviera without my assistance.' He demurred, eyes sparkling with mischief, as he held the door.

'Oh, do stop talking such rot and rubbish,' she exclaimed, caught between amusement and irritation and the chills coursing down her spine. 'I'm perfectly capable of taking care of myself, I'll have you know. I don't need a chaperon.'

'Ah, but that is where you are wrong. All women need a chaperon—especially beautiful wealthy ones. There are always unscrupulous young men out to make a buck.' He tut-tutted, grinned devastatingly at her and held out his hand. 'Let's call a truce, fair Natasha. I shan't bother you, merely try to be a friend? Okay? You agree?' He smiled winningly now, leaving her no alternative but to shrug and slide behind the wheel with as much grace as she could muster.

CHAPTER SIX

IT WAS impossible not to melt, impossible not to surrender to the enchantment of enjoying the South of France with such a handsome, suave escort.

Raoul knew everything and everybody. They were received in restaurants by name, accompanied by obsequious head waiters to the best tables, and attended to in the best possible manner. How, Natasha wondered dolefully as they returned on their third evening to the villa, could she simply go back to her old life and pick up where she'd left off?

And all at once she knew that it would be impossible.

Sad as it made her feel, she could not go back to Africa.

That part of her life was over and a new chapter was opening before her. For a moment she glanced through the shadows at Raoul, then concentrated on driving up the Corniche back to the villa. He had not, she reflected ruefully, so much as tried to kiss her again. In fact, he'd been so platonic she almost wished he would. Somehow staving him off was a lot more satisfying than wondering why he hadn't made the attempt.

As she drew the car up on the gravel Raoul leaned coolly back into the corner of the passenger seat and watched her. He would let her stew just a little longer, he decided, an amused smile curving his lips through the darkness. She was delightful, his little English miss, but he wanted her on his terms: wanting him. To the point where he could twist his little finger and put into practice some of the many fantasies that had crossed his mind during the past few nights. If truth be told, sleep had come with difficulty. It was not until the early hours that Raoul had encountered peace on his pillow. Now he had no desire for peace. Rather, he wished he could give vent to the strong longing coursing through him. But it was too soon. He needed her to give him that subtle, undefined signal which meant he'd won.

And to his utter annoyance it hadn't come.

When was the last time he'd waited three whole days for a woman to submit to his advances? He couldn't even recall. It was absurd, ridiculous, and he was very nearly losing his patience. But wait he must, or she would have the upper hand. And that, he realized ruefully, he couldn't allow. And then, too, there was something about Natasha herself that stopped him from taking the action he would normally—something he had rarely encountered before in a woman. Not obstinacy, not petulance or selfish desire, which were traits of many of the women he'd dated, but rather a sense of purpose to her life that he found intriguing. They had spent several hours talking about the future, about her plans. He'd sensed her initial reluctance to stay in France, her doubts about whether she should go back to her job or stay in what would be a comfortable and easy lifestyle. And knew from the start that she was seeking something more.

A woman with a purpose in her life.

This was definitely a new breed of female he had rarely encountered. Oh, he'd met enough ambition in his time to recognize that—the calculating style of women determined to claw their way up the social or professional ladder at whatever cost. But Natasha had no such intention. It was as though she was seeking a deeper motivation to make her decision. As though she needed to know what her purpose in France was before she could choose it.

Raoul opened the car door and got out. He felt strangely

confused, annoyed with himself and suddenly with her for placing him on this new untrodden territory. He didn't like being on unfamiliar terrain. Perhaps it was time to leave, shake off this strange spell Natasha had cast over him and return to Paris.

He watched as she stepped out of the vehicle, then together they made their way back into the silent villa and moved towards the terrace.

'A nightcap?' he suggested casually.

'No, thanks.' She shook her head and headed towards the French windows and the terrace. The moon shone full and bright over the shimmering waters of the Mediterranean; the lights of the gin palaces twinkled merrily. Natasha sat on the balustrade and gazed down at them, trying to sum up the past few days, to escape the awareness of Raoul's physical presence: so close, so tempting, so alluring. She was dying to give in to him, to submit to his intense male allure, to all the feelings throbbing inside her. But something stopped her.

She looked up as he came to join her, a snifter of cognac in his hand.

'I shall be returning to Paris tomorrow,' he remarked in that languid tone that left her no clue as to what he felt. She felt a stab and swallowed. How was it possible that in these few short days she'd grown so used to his presence?

'Of course,' she replied, hiding her dismay. What would it be like to be here alone? It was almost as if France and Raoul had become synonymous. Which was ridiculous, she chided herself. She simply must pull herself together and face reality. She had decisions to make. Life-changing decisions. And she needed all her wits about her to make them.

'You don't mind?' He quirked an eyebrow in her direction. 'I had the impression we were getting on rather well, you and I.' He poised a loafered foot on the balustrade and swirled his cognac thoughtfully.

'I think we've spent a very pleasant time,' she said, her voice non-committal lest she betray any feelings.

'A pleasant time?' he remarked, letting out a laugh. 'That is so cool, so very British. I would rather say that we have spent *des moments formidables*. But then I'm French.' He looked down at her speculatively. 'Are you sure this was nothing but a *pleasant time*, Natasha? Are you really able to deny the intense attraction we feel for one another?'

'I—' She clasped her hands, confused by his direct attack.

'You what?' He slipped onto the balustrade next to her, his proximity leaving her in intense turmoil.

'I don't know. I just think, well, that—'

'Stop thinking. One of your problems is that you think too much, *ma chère*. This is about feeling, not thinking.'

The glass was abandoned and his arms closed about her as he drew her up to standing position and folded her in them. 'Stop thinking, Natasha,' he growled into her ear. 'Just feel—feel everything I have to give you.'

She stood stiffly for a moment, then, unable to resist, gave way as his mouth found hers. The kiss was long and sensuous, his tongue investigating her mouth slowly while his hand slipped down her back and cupped her bottom, pressing her against him firmly, so that she felt the hardness of him pressed temptingly against her. Her breasts felt suddenly taut and aching, that strange new tingle throbbing between her thighs so strong and so compelling that instinctively she pressed herself harder against him. Then Raoul's expert fingers trailed down her throat and reached the tip of her aching breast. Natasha threw her head back and let out a sigh of contentment as his fingers grazed the taut peaks, taunting her tender nipples, before reaching further down, down, until he slipped beneath her panties and penetrated the warm, damp softness.

'No, Raoul, please,' she begged weakly. She mustn't let him do this—could not let herself be dominated by this man and her own uncontrolled desire. But she had never experienced anything like it before. She was swooped into a new, terrifying landscape that both frightened and enthralled her.

'Just relax, *chérie*,' he whispered, his fingers caressing her now, causing tiny gasps to escape her lips as his thumb grazed and his fingers penetrated. 'Ah, you are delicious, my Natasha, as delicious as I thought you would be.'

'Raoul,' she whispered, between a plea and a protest. Then, when she least expected it, something extraordinary happened. The tight, anxious throbbing and the incredibly tense build-up that she'd thought she could stand no more gave way, and she let out a long gasp of sheer satisfaction, laced with utter amazement.

It was staggering.

Blissful.

Incredible.

As though a window had opened in her life.

And as she leaned against him, caught in the throes of her first orgasm, Raoul smiled and held her close, pride and triumph rushing through him as he sensed her utter surprise. So she had never experienced this before. He leaned her head against his chest and held her close, feeling the fast throbbing of her heart, quelling his own intense desire as he gazed out over the sea, breathed in the scent of lavender and listened to the crickets' endless chorus filling the night.

'Come,' he said softly, when he felt she'd regained her equilibrium. 'We must finish this off properly, *ma mie*.' He slipped his arms under her and swept her into them.

'But Raoul, please—this isn't—I mean, I don't want—'

He stopped a moment, looked at her with eyes brimming with humour. 'Are you seriously telling me you don't want me, Natasha?' he asked, gazing down at her amused.

'I—it's not that I don't want you,' she whispered hoarsely. 'I just don't feel ready to.'

How she'd managed to retain enough sanity to utter those words she had no idea. But somewhere in the back of her mind a little voice told her that were she to allow Raoul to make love to her tonight it would in some way destroy her.

He hesitated a moment. 'You are talking nonsense,' he said, holding her firmly in his arms. 'Why can't you just close your eyes and enjoy all the pleasure I can give you? Surely you have not had such a bad time this evening?' he coaxed, the knowing smile still playing about his lips.

'Please. Let me down.' It was impossible to reason with him being held in his arms.

Reluctantly Raoul conceded. Once she was standing, Natasha raked trembling fingers through her hair and tried to regain some composure. 'Raoul, I can't. It's not that I don't want to. It's just that I don't feel confident enough.'

'Leave that to me, *chérie*. I realize that you are new at this game, that you have little experience in matters of love. But have no fear, *ma belle*. I have enough for both of us.'

'That's exactly what bothers me,' she retorted, suddenly recovering some of her lost poise. 'I don't plan to be an amusing pastime for you. I'm well aware that it must be intriguing for you to come across an inexperienced bumpkin like me. It may even amuse you to teach me a few things. For a while.'

'And what is wrong with that?' he asked, dropping his hands possessively on her shoulders. 'Think of it as part of furthering your education. Learning the art of lovemaking can be deliciously satisfying, and it will serve you well in the future,' he replied confidently.

'Really?' Natasha pulled away, suddenly clear in her mind as to why she did not want things to go any further. 'Surprising though this may seem to you, Raoul, I don't think of lovemaking either as an art-form or a game. You said you were leaving for Paris tomorrow. I think it's a good thing that you are. We obviously have far less in common than our conversations of the past few days have led us to believe. Now, if you'll excuse me, I'll say goodnight.'

Before he could stop her Natasha had turned on her heel and hastened up the stairs, head high, leaving Raoul fuming in the hall, wondering how what had appeared to be developing into a deliciously seductive evening had so suddenly turned sour.

'Damn her,' he muttered, returning to the terrace, where he downed the rest of his cognac. 'Damn all women.'

And this one was nothing but a little teaser.

Well, he'd had enough. Had wasted too much time on her already. He had a life to live, a business and an estate to run, didn't he? It was high time he got back in gear and stopped fooling around like a raw teenager.

In a few masterful strides he marched to his bedroom on the ground floor, threw his belongings into his Vuitton luggage and, closing the door behind him, made his way to his Ferrari. He would leave not tomorrow morning but right now. He'd had enough of Mademoiselle de Saugure and her silly infantile games, thank you very much.

Natasha sat trembling on the edge of the large canopied bed. Her head shot up when she heard the sound of the engine and the crunch of wheels on the gravel.

So he'd left.

Her hands dropped in her lap and she let out a sigh of mixed relief and regret. But it was better like this, she argued, and she was right to have held back. No good could come of a hot, passionate affair with Raoul. He'd become bored with her as quickly as he'd become attracted. Clothilde's words still lingered in her ears. 'He's the biggest bastard in town.' She had no doubt that Clothilde was right. So why, when she should be feeling nothing but relief at her escape, was she feeling so down?

Probably because they'd got on so well these past few days, she justified, slipping off her dress and underwear and reaching for her nightgown. Still, as she lay between the cool linen sheets it was impossible not to recall the overwhelming sensations she'd experienced. Natasha sighed, turned on her side, and tried to sleep. But her dreams were fraught with images of a tall dark man on a chestnut horse, swooping her up into the saddle, his hand poised possessively on her breast.

And her sleep was troubled.

CHAPTER SEVEN

'So, as I was telling you, Monsieur Dubois, I have decided to remain here in France and assume my grandmother's responsibilities.'

'This is wonderful news, *mademoiselle*,' Monsieur Dubois replied, beaming. 'The people on the estate will be thrilled to know that they will not be dealing with an absentee landowner.'

'No, they won't. I plan to learn as much about the estate as possible,' Natasha supplied with a smile as, seated behind the large desk in the Manoir's office, she flipped through some papers. 'And I also want to learn as much as possible about the history of the place. It is, after all, my heritage. I feel I should be familiar with every aspect of it, both historical and practical.'

'But of course, of course, *chère mademoiselle*. We shall be only too glad to inform you. I personally can tell you about the legal ramifications of the estate, but you must meet with Evreux, the factor. He will be able to fill you in on the happenings on the land. And as for history—well, I can think of no one better than Monsieur le Curé, down in the village. He is a very learned man, and a historian as well as a priest. He has spent thirty-five years in our parish and knows more about the place than anyone I know. Excluding Madame Blanchard, of course.'

'Madame Blanchard?' Natasha asked curiously, the name seeming familiar.

'Yes. She is the housekeeper over at Argentan. She works for the Baron, you know. Has done so all her life. I believe she went as a young kitchen maid before the war. She knows all the anecdotes there are to know. Particularly about yours and the Baron's families.'

'Why is that?' Natasha asked, frowning.

'Well, it is said…' Monsieur Dubois looked furtively about, then lowered his voice as though the walls might hear what he was about to say, 'that *madame*'s father was the issue of an affair between the Baron's grandfather and a village girl. So in some way she is related to the Argentans, and rather proud of it.'

'I see.' And she did—only too well. The Argentans certainly didn't waste their time, she reflected dryly, thankful for her moment's sanity in Eze, which had stopped her from falling victim to the present Baron's ploys. 'I shall look forward to meeting all these people. But first we must go over the details you have prepared for me.'

'Avec plaisir, mademoiselle.' Monsieur Dubois smiled broadly and took out a thick sheaf of papers, and Natasha prepared to begin her first lesson in how to run an estate.

So she'd decided to stay in France after all.

Raoul felt both elated and annoyed. Her presence represented both a challenge and a source of failure. He was surprised that she had assumed her role as châtelaine of the Manoir. After all, she'd appeared very hesitant. But he was fast learning—to his exasperation—that there was a hell of a lot more to Natasha de Saugure than met the eye.

Well, so much the better. At least he'd learned in time. By now Raoul was thoroughly convinced that it was *he* who had extracted himself from Natasha's wiles. The fact that she had summarily dismissed him had been relegated to the confines of his brain, where it remained safely secluded and could not damage his ego. Still, the thought that he was driving back to Argentan this weekend, and would spend the whole three days there without knowing what she was up to, was profoundly irritating.

Never mind, he reflected, banishing the thought, he had the races to attend this weekend. After all, it was mid-August, and the Prix Morny was being run in Deauville on Sunday. He had other fish to fry instead of worrying about Mademoiselle de Saugure. And he had a horse running. A pretty serious contender, too, for that matter. He just hoped the terrain wouldn't be too soft, as it had rained most of the week. Perhaps he should invite someone to attend the races with him in his box.

For several minutes Raoul sat behind his desk and flipped pensively through a small black address book. But none of the names he studied held any appeal. Better, he decided, to go back to the Château d'Argentan and ring his local friends when he arrived. Plus, Madeleine and her husband might be staying in their lovely property near Falaise. He would pop over and visit them. Perhaps they would like to join him in his box on Sunday.

Several hours later Raoul drew up into the medieval courtyard where Jean, the butler, was moving forward to greet him.

'Hello, Jean,' he said, as the butler picked his bag off the leather seat in the back of the Range Rover.

'*Bienvenu*, Monsieur le Baron.'

'So. How are things? Anything to report?' he asked as they made their way to the huge oak front door.

'Nothing much, *monsieur*, except the latest news that has the whole village in a buzz.'

'What's that?'

'Mademoiselle de Saugure has come to live at the Manoir.'

'I'd heard,' he responded shortly.

'Yes. It is exciting, isn't it? All the people on the estate are very happy about it. Apparently *mademoiselle* has taken a great interest in their lives. She has visited all the families personally and is already implementing a number of measures which they've been trying unsuccessfully to get the old Comtesse to put into practice for years.' Jean smiled broadly, glad to be the bearer of good tidings.

'Well, isn't that interesting?' Raoul mused. 'So she plans to make this her permanent home, I gather?'

'Apparently so, *monsieur*. I met Monsieur le Curé at the village tobacconist yesterday and he was singing her praises. Apparently she is most interested in local history and has asked him to fill her in. You know how the Curé loves to go on about the past. He is delighted. He even asked when you were coming as he wants to borrow some old documents from your library.'

'Really?' Raoul's brows flew up and his face closed. 'I shall have to call him, then, won't I?'

Without another word he swung through the door and marched straight to his study, leaving Jean wondering what he had said to provoke his master's ill humour. With a shrug he made his way upstairs, shaking his head. There was just no understanding the aristocracy.

It was both exciting and confusing, and it was a lot to absorb in such a short time. But now that she'd taken the definite decision to stay Natasha had thrown herself wholeheartedly into the task of learning her new role. Not an easy one, she'd realized after studying all that needed to be repaired, listening to complaints and hopes for the future, trying to understand some of the trials that working a thirty-five-hour week implied, and becoming familiar with French employment laws. Of course Monsieur Dubois and the factor, Evreux, took care of most of these aspects of the running of the property, but she was determined to familiarize herself with the details and not be dependent only on the knowledge of others.

That Friday evening she was glad to soak in a bath, slip on a comfy tracksuit and curl in front of the fire in the *petit salon*—the one place in the house that was remotely homey—and watch television. As she glanced about her Natasha realized that her next task would be to undertake some redecorating. She simply could not survive surrounded by such stiff formality, and she already had a better idea of how she'd like the place to look. When she had some time she would pop down to Paris and meet with a couple of designers to see who would be most suited to the task.

Not that time was something she had much of. Meetings and work seemed never-ending now that she'd plunged into the thick of it. Also there were social calls to be paid. The neighbours—excepting Raoul, who hadn't shown any sign of life since her return—were charming. In fact Philippe, son of the Comte de Morrieux, a rather pasty-faced, stiff young man, with sandy hair and very precise speech, had asked her to accompany him and his parents to the races this weekend. At first she'd been inclined to refuse. But then she'd realized that not only would it be fun to go to the famous races in Deauville, but that it might seem churlish and rude to refuse the kind invitation. She just hoped she had something suitable to wear among her new acquisitions. She'd been relieved when she'd learned that she wouldn't be expected to wear a hat.

As she flipped through the TV channels Natasha mentally summed up her first few weeks as châtelaine of the Manoir. It was all so new and so unexpected, yet she'd slipped into the role with far greater ease than she would have believed possible a few weeks earlier. It was as if this new job had been waiting for her all her life. She loved meeting the people on the estate, and learning about their problems. And they, instinctively sensing her genuine interest, responded as they might not have done had she not benefited from her experience in humanitarian work. It all seemed to make sense now, she realized. Often she'd asked herself what the purpose of her job in Africa truly was, apart from the obvious. Now it was plain to her. As though a bigger plan had been underway, preparing her for the task up ahead.

Glancing at the time, Natasha realized it was getting on and that she was hungry. Henri and his wife Mathilde were off this evening, so, leaving the remote control next to the sofa, Natasha made her way through the hall and into the immense, old-fashioned kitchen to fix herself a sandwich, having refused *madame*'s offer of a meal left in the oven. She needed to retain something of her former independence, she realized ruefully, even if it was only making a sandwich on her own and not having it presented on a silver platter.

But as she spread butter onto a crispy baguette she thought she heard a noise. Her head flew up and she listened carefully. It was easy to imagine hearing things in an old mansion like this one. After listening carefully, and realizing she must be mistaken, Natasha finished preparing her meal, added a glass of chocolate milk to the tray and headed back towards the *petit salon*.

It was then, as she was crossing the hall, that she caught sight of a shadow in the doorway. Her heart missed a beat and she nearly dropped the tray. Stopping dead in her tracks, she stared astonished at the outline of a young woman in eighteenth-century dress, her hair done up in ringlets, the expression on her face sad. Then, as quickly as it had appeared, the image faded, leaving her wondering if she'd imagined it. Quickly turning on the three-tier chandelier lights, she stared about the hall. But there was no vestige of the woman she could have sworn had stood there only instants earlier.

She must be dreaming, she decided, moving back into the salon and sitting down on the sofa. Still, the feeling lingered. And later, as she wandered up the main stairway on her way to bed, she stopped before Natasha de Saugure's portrait and shivered.

She'd be willing to swear the shadow she'd seen was the woman in the picture.

CHAPTER EIGHT

SATURDAY dawned reasonably fair, with a scattering of cloud. The Morrieux had insisted Natasha join them for dinner at Le Cercle, an exclusive club situated on the front at Deauville where, every year, a dinner was given to celebrate the end of the season's races, and a mock Battle of Waterloo was re-enacted between the British and French guests. As far as she could gather it was all very aristocratic, and to be a member you had to be able to trace your ancestry back over several generations.

Amused by the entire concept, Natasha had agreed to attend, and, as she didn't want to drive home late after having a drink, had booked herself into a room at the Normandy Hotel for the night, prepared to enjoy herself.

At seven o'clock the punctilious Philippe was waiting for her in the crowded lobby of the hotel, and together they walked the few hundred yards along the seafront to Le Cercle, where they were to meet the Comte and Comtesse and their friends for dinner.

But as they entered Natasha was amazed to see that the charming old building was falling apart. She glanced up uneasily at the cracked plaster in the ceiling, hoping it wouldn't collapse on top of her. The place was, in fact, as stately and yet as decrepit as the appearance of some of its ancient members, rigged out in black tie. But there was also an elegance and old-world nostalgia here, and as she observed all the Légions d'Honneur and Croix de Guerre sewn into the buttonholes of many of the more elderly members' lapels she was reminded of just how brave and gallant so many of these gentlemen were. They represented the courageous generation who'd fought in World War II—the reason why, today, people like herself were free to live in a democratic Europe.

As they entered the bar, and she shook hands with her hosts, Natasha was touched by this maintaining of old customs fast being replaced by other less gratifying practices.

Soon she was sipping a glass of champagne and conversing with the Comte de Morrieux, who was thrilled to learn of her interest in the history of their region. Then, when she least expected it, a familiar voice spoke at her side.

'Good evening, *mademoiselle*.' Raoul executed a small bow before he nodded to the Comte and Philippe hovering close by.

'Good evening,' Natasha murmured, trying not to appear flustered, livid that her pulse was fluttering once more. Surely she could be more controlled than this?

'So. You are being initiated into the customs of our society, I see.' His tone barely hid the irony.

'Yes,' she replied blithely, temper coming to her rescue. 'Philippe very kindly asked me to join him and his family here tonight, and tomorrow at the races. So kind,' she added, twirling around and bestowing a dazzling smile on the dumbstruck Philippe.

'Well, well. You must be the most envied man in the room tonight, Philippe,' Raoul murmured, his lips twisting in a thin sardonic smile.

'Uh, yes, of course. I am very happy to accompany Mademoiselle de Saugure—I mean Natasha.' He blushed, straightened his bow tie and tried not to let Raoul fluster him. It was always so. Raoul would walk in and take the floor. But at least tonight, Philippe reflected with a touch of pride, he'd made it to the winning post first and invited Natasha before any of his contemporaries had the chance.

Raoul was now complimenting the beaky-nosed Comtesse de Morrieux on her appearance, and Natasha noticed crossly that she was, of course, wreathed in smiles. 'I have asked Raoul to join us at our table,' she told her husband, who nodded approvingly.

'Very good, *mon vieux*, we don't see enough of you around here any more now that you spend so much time in Paris.'

Raoul threw Natasha a triumphant glance, read her annoyance at the invitation and felt a rush of satisfaction. So she was trying to set herself up in her own fashion in the region, was she? Had Philippe de Morrieux dangling after her too, did she? Well, he'd make short shrift of that little plan, he reflected, offering his arm to the Comtesse as they prepared to enter the dining room.

'Have you told Natasha about the Battle of Waterloo?' he enquired of Philippe, once they were all installed at table.

'Yes, after a fashion.'

'You'll enjoy that,' Raoul said, smiling benignly at Natasha. 'We have two teams, the English against the French. As you can see there are many of your compatriots here tonight—racing adepts, trainers. And then the big sales begin tomorrow, right after the last race. Many are here to acquire horses.'

'Fascinating,' Natasha murmured, turning her attention back to Philippe, determined not to give Raoul any quarter, while she desperately blinked away the images of their past encounter and tried to eclipse the physical sensation that just seeing him caused. She felt her nipples go taut under her evening dress and a troubling awareness haunted her. It was as though, when his eyes flew over her in that dark, possessive, disturbing manner, he were undressing her, stripping her of the protective sheath of silk and baring her for his pleasure.

She tried to pay attention to Philippe's stilted conversation. Surely Raoul couldn't tell how she was feeling? But when she took a fleeting sidelong glance in his direction and he smiled knowingly at her, she felt her cheeks burn with embarrassment.

He knew, damn him.

Of course he knew.

He had this whole game down to an art, knew exactly what he made a woman feel.

Taking a deep breath, and a few rather larger gulps of champagne than she'd intended, Natasha donned a glittering smile and continued to converse with the other members of the table. By the time the *ragout de Homard* was eaten and dessert served she was wilting under the strain, and sincerely wishing that she'd stayed at home and not exposed herself. Of all people the last person she would have imagined here tonight was Raoul, she thought as they sipped coffee. Yet deep down she knew that wasn't strictly true. Had she, in fact, come here secretly hoping that she would see him?

The thought sent another shudder and another rush of intimate sensations tingling through her pelvis. Damn Raoul. Why couldn't he just get up and leave instead of sitting there talking in that deep seductive voice, bringing her into the conversation whenever he could and being generally odious under the pretended solicitude?

Soon they were rising from the table and entering the room next door, where the Battle of Waterloo was already being prepared.

'We have another lady for the English team,' Raoul

called out to the organizer, a short, busy Frenchman whom the others referred to as '*le général*'.

'Oh, no, please, I'd much rather watch,' Natasha said quickly. She had no desire to participate.

'What? You shrink from playing for your country? Come, come, Natasha, I thought better of you than this.'

'Please, Raoul, just leave me alone,' she muttered.

But Philippe was at her elbow now, leading her across the room towards the general. She looked back at Raoul, who was standing with his arms crossed and a broad grin on his face. He shrugged, letting her know he had no intention of saving her from her fate.

With a sigh, Natasha joined the other English ladies preparing to participate in the game. This really wasn't her thing. But what could she do? Without appearing disagreeable it would be hard to refuse.

'So, *mademoiselle*, here is a glass of champagne.' The general handed her a glass. 'You must drink it *à cul sec*—that means in one go—and then place the glass on your head. Then the next lady in line will do the same. Come on, try it. The team that finishes quickest wins. Now, try.'

'In one go?' Natasha queried, glancing uneasily at the glass.

'Yes. Have a go.'

'Okay.' Taking a deep breath, Natasha threw back the glass of champagne, spluttering as the liquid rushed into her mouth.

'Very good, very good.' The general smiled approvingly and refilled her glass. 'Now, ready to begin, everyone?

The two teams stood in line, side by side, and a good atmosphere reigned. The champagne, downed so quickly, was beginning to take effect, and Natasha felt somewhat light-headed. When it came to her turn she tried to down the next glass under the encouragement of her team mates and ended up spluttering her way to the end and placing the glass on her head. She was positively dizzy now, and wished she could get away.

Then all at once Raoul was at her side, holding her elbow, steering her away. Somewhere in the surrounding haze she realized she'd said goodbye to the Comte and Comtesse and Philippe, and that she was being walked along the pavement held up by Raoul's strong arm.

'Why did you make me do that?' she asked, trying not to stumble.

'Careful, *ma belle*, you're not too steady on your pins. Lean on my arm. There, that's better.'

'Raoul, I don't think that was fair. You should have stopped them. I'm not used to all that champagne.' She gulped and hiccupped, and he laughed.

'Never mind. I'll give you a couple of Alka Seltzers back at the hotel, and after a good sleep you'll feel fine.'

'God,' she groaned, 'I don't want to think of what I'll feel like tomorrow morning.'

'You'll be fine. I guarantee it. Now, here we are at the Normandy. I'll take you to your suite. Have you got the key?'

She fumbled in her evening purse as they went to the lift and handed it to him while her head dropped on his shoulder. It felt so nice to lie against him; the scent of his aftershave smelled good. She felt his arm close firmly around her shoulders as they exited the elevator and made their way along the wide corridor to her suite.

Soon they were inside and Raoul closed the door behind them. 'Now, come and lie down,' he ordered.

'I don't want to lie down. I feel much better now,' Natasha said, giggling.

'Natasha, you've had a lot of champagne. I think it's better you rest.'

'Rest? I don't want to rest. Let's go out and dance. Let's have some more champagne.' She leaned against him and lifted her lips for his kiss. When it didn't come she made a moue and frowned. 'Don't you want to k-kiss me?' She gulped. 'I thought you seemed rather keen on it the other night.'

'You are not in a state to be kissed,' he answered firmly, taking her arm and leading her to the bedroom.

'That's not fair,' she said, shaking her head as she collapsed onto the bed, pouting. 'When *you* want to it's okay, but when I want...' Her voice trailed off and her eyes closed.

Raoul looked down at her and smiled. He shouldn't have put her forward for the game. It had been unfair of him and he knew it. In a quick, matter-of-fact manner he set about undressing her and slipped a nightgown over her head. As he was doing so Natasha's eyes opened. She smiled beatifically at him, then slipped her arms around his neck, pulling him down onto the bed.

'Natasha, this is not a good idea,' he muttered, trying to keep his physical reaction in check.

'Yes, it is,' she slurred, taking his hand and placing it on her breast. 'Mmmm. That feels so nice,' she mumbled as, unable to resist, he grazed her nipple.

'Natasha, you'll regret this in the morning,' he told her, trying to withstand the temptation of her lovely body while letting his other hand slip between her thighs. He was jolted by how wet and wanting she was.

But, instead of protesting, all Natasha did was sigh and surrender to his caresses. Raoul was tempted to undress and take her here and now. But something stopped him. An innate sense of honour. This would be tantamount to rape. He doubted he'd ever exercised such will-power, but exercise it he would. Instead of taking his pleasure he caressed her gently, his fingers penetrating her, following the writhing of her body as she arched up to him, pleading for more, then sighing when she came, before falling prostrate among the pillows, where she immediately fell into a deep and exhausted sleep.

Raoul rose, straightened his clothes and, after taking a long breath, tucked Natasha in. As he left the room he wondered what on earth had got in to him. With a shrug he returned to his own suite, and after a large brandy got ready for bed. He really must bed Natasha or get her out of his system once and for all, he decided firmly as he switched the light off.

One thing was for sure. He couldn't play this game much longer.

CHAPTER NINE

HAD she been dreaming or had Raoul carried her into the room last night and laid her on the bed? And had the rest of what she vaguely remembered been a figment of her fertile imagination, or had he once again made her feel the most incredible sensations she'd ever experienced?

Rubbing her eyes and letting out a long yawn, Natasha sat up and glanced at her watch. My God, it was almost eleven-thirty, and she was due to meet the Morrieux for drinks in the courtyard at twelve-fifteen.

As she entered the bathroom everything came back to her in quick succession, and a wave of embarrassment encompassed her. She really had Raoul to thank for removing her so promptly and efficiently from the scene. All she could hope for was that the Morrieux had not realized how tipsy she'd become after knocking back several glasses of champagne.

The mere thought of the stuff made her grimace. No more of that, she decided firmly, allowing the hot shower spray to soothe her tired body. And what about Raoul? she wondered, her thoughts lingering as she soaped herself. Where was he and what had prompted him to be so nice to her? It was really rather decent of him to have acted as he had. And, she realized ruefully, as her memory jolted, not to have taken advantage of her weakness and vulnerability.

Again her cheeks flamed at the thought of her wanton behaviour of the night before. She had practically—no, she *had*, let's be honest—invited him to make love to her.

As she wrapped herself in a large white terry towel, Natasha realized that there was little she could do except try and carry things off with as much dignity as possible. Though, knowing Raoul as she was beginning to, she doubted he would forego any chance of reminding her.

But there she was wrong.

Several hours later, when their paths crossed at the races, Raoul gave no knowing sign of recollection. In fact, he was very punctilious. And, as Natasha squirmed for several uneasy minutes, he simply made light conversation with the Morrieux, gave the Comte a tip on the horse he considered would win the next race, and asked her if she'd like to back the horse too.

After a while, she felt easier, and was able to enjoy the elegant, amusing atmosphere of the racecourse. Several ladies were dressed to the nines, others like herself, were discreetly elegant. All in all, she reflected, it had—apart from last night's embarrassing interlude—been a very agreeable stay-over. And even the interlude, she reflected ruefully, had been delicious.

Giving herself a quick jolt, Natasha refused to allow her mind to linger on Raoul's fingers gently caressing her. But all too often during the afternoon his kisses and his caresses coloured her thoughts. She would look at him from afar, unable to deny how very male and handsome he was, how devastatingly attractive. She couldn't prevent herself from experiencing a rush of something akin to jealousy when she saw him deep in conversation with a pretty and very chic blonde woman.

This simply must stop, she protested silently, turning her head and entering into an animated conversation with the staid Philippe, who was only too enchanted to be taken notice of by his lovely new neighbour. His parents looked on approvingly. A match between the Morrieux heir and the heir to the Saugure properties would be no mean feat.

The proximity of the two young people had not gone unnoticed by another member of the local community. All the while he was carrying on a flirtatious conversation with his cousin, Raoul had one eye on Natasha. Philippe de Morrieux—a rival! Why, the notion was laughable. Yet she did seem very open to being courted by that young man. A rush of anger overcame him. The little flirt had been writhing in his arms only a few hours ago. Was he perhaps wrong about her character? What sort of game was she playing?

He considered the thought as he approached the betting window and placed a solid bet on an outsider in the up-coming race. He glanced back at her and his lips twisted into a smile before he glanced once more at the list, then made another bet. Then slowly he approached the table in the paddock restaurant, where Natasha was seated with the Morrieux. The Comte welcomed him and told him to sit down.

'I can't, I'm afraid. I'm off to see the next race.'

'Did your horse win?' Philippe asked.

'I'm afraid not. It came in third, though, which wasn't too bad. By the way, I placed a bet for you in the next race,' he said, casually addressing Natasha. 'Would you like to come with me to the box and see if we are in luck?'

She hesitated. His eyes were boring into hers with a determination that was hard to resist. She glanced at the Comtesse, who was engaged in conversation with another elegant, bejewelled older lady.

'Why not?' she said with a shrug and a smile. 'Philippe, will you come too?'

'Oh? Yes, yes, of course—*avec plaisir.*' He grinned

broadly and jumped up from his chair, ready to escort Natasha.

This was not the way he'd planned matters, and the presence of this innocuous young man annoyed Raoul profoundly. But there was nothing for it but to put a good face on it, so he smiled, and together the three of them walked across the paddock and over towards the building where Raoul had his box.

Soon they were watching the horses move towards the starting gates.

'See the jockey with the blue and white shirt over there?' he said, pointing.

'Yes.'

'That's our man.'

'What's the name of the horse?' she asked, eyeing the program.

'I Want You.'

'Excuse me?' She looked up and their eyes met.

'You asked me the horse's name.'

'Yes, I did.'

'Well, that's it. The horse is called *I Want You*.'

'Oh, I see.' She looked away, flustered, her colour rising once more, for the look in his eyes told her there was a not-so-subtle *double entendre* to his words that had nothing to do with the race.

'Maybe we'll get lucky,' Raoul added, glancing at her wickedly before lifting his racing glasses. 'Here, take these. You'll see the race better.'

'Thank you.' She accepted the glasses, glad of an excuse to have something to do other than feel his eyes upon her.

Philippe was studiously reading the programme, and began weighing up the pros and cons of several animals with Raoul. Placing the two men side by side was really rather unfair, Natasha realized ruefully, a spark of humour flashing. Raoul might not have been pleased that she'd asked him to join them, but in reality he should be happy if what he wanted was to promote himself. Next to the stiff, pasty Philippe, he shone like a diamond of the first degree.

Then the race began and all eyes focused on the galloping horses making their way along the straight. Natasha watched through the glasses, excited. She'd never had a bet on a horse before. Now she peered keenly, excitement mounting as *I Want You* edged to the forefront of the race. The crowd rose from their seats, crying encouragement. When in the last few seconds *I Want You* tore ahead by a length to win the race, Natasha was as excited as the rest.

'He did it!' She turned excitedly to Raoul. 'Isn't that wonderful? I can't believe he won. How clever of you to bet on him.'

'It was obvious that he had to win,' Raoul replied with a mischievous grin.

'Really? I thought you said he was an outsider with twenty to one odds.'

'He was.'

'So?' She raised her brow, truly curious as to the reason he'd been so sure. 'How were you so sure he'd win?'

'Because I want you,' he whispered in a lowered voice, his hand slipping over hers and squeezing it in an imperceptible yet intimate gesture.

Confused, Natasha drew away. It was all happening too quickly. She was so attracted to Raoul, yet she sensed the danger she would get into should she surrender to her desire for him. He was so sophisticated and worldly, and once more Clothilde's words of warning rang in her ears.

'I'm going back to my place after collecting our winnings,' he remarked in a very different tone, as though he hadn't noticed that she'd not answered.

'Ah, yes. Well, I must be getting back, too.'

'Why don't you come by and have a drink? Or rather, upon reflection, why don't we stop off for dinner somewhere? There is a very lovely little restaurant in Beaumont that you simply must discover.'

'Raoul, I need to get back, I have my car waiting, I—'

'Just a moment,' he instructed, lifting his index finger authoritatively. He pulled out his mobile and before she could stop him was making arrangements to have her car delivered back to the Manoir.

'Raoul, I never said I was coming with you,' she protested, exasperated. The man was far too sure of himself, she concluded, wishing she had the strength to refuse him point-blank, but knowing instead that she had every intention of going.

The restaurant turned out to be as charming as he'd predicted, with low beams and dried flowers, pristine tablecloths and attentive service. The food was undeniably delicious, and his company, she admitted reluctantly, was delightful.

Raoul went out of his way to put her at ease and to make her feel good in his company. He didn't quite understand why he was bothering to go to all this effort, though being pleasant to women came naturally to him. Still, something in Natasha compelled him.

'Raoul, I want to ask you a question.' She laid her forearms on the table and clasped her hands.

'Go right ahead, *ma chère*,' he invited, taking a sip of the excellent claret he'd ordered.

'It's about your ancestor, Regis d'Argentan. What exactly happened to him and Natasha? Why is everyone so secretive about them?'

The raised glass poised in mid-air. 'Why are you so curious about the past?' he asked, swirling the wine.

'Because it fascinates me. I want to know all about the history of the place. After all, I've decided to make it my home. I know that Natasha de Saugure and Regis were in some way connected.' She hesitated, then decided to tell him. 'You know, a funny thing happened the other night.' She glanced at him, swallowed, wondered if she should divulge her experience.

'Go on,' he urged, looking at her eyes narrowed. 'What happened?' He laid his glass down, giving her his full attention.

'Well, you'll probably think I'm mad, but I could have sworn that I saw her, standing in the doorway of the salon.'

'Saw who?' His brows met in a thick ridge above his patrician nose.

'Natasha de Saugure. I—well, this all sounds so silly, but—' She raised her hands and looked embarrassed.

'There is nothing silly about seeing a ghost,' he remarked, as though it were an everyday occurrence.

'You mean, you think it actually could be her?'

'Why not? It is not uncommon for strange things to be seen in ancient *demeures*. Whether they are real or not can be debated. But there are those who claim to have seen them.'

'Have you seen ghosts at your castle?' she enquired, brows shooting up.

'I wouldn't go so far as to put it in the plural.' He laughed. 'But there have apparently been sightings at certain times. Not that I give much credibility to such stories,' he added, eyeing her again, as though he were about to say more but then thought better of it.

'Raoul, do tell me—please.' She reached her hand across the table and placed it on his forearm. Raoul looked down, felt his arm tingle at the touch of her fingers, and restrained a sudden urge to take the hand in his and hold it.

'It all happened a long time ago,' he said reluctantly as she removed her fingers. 'Regis was a young man at the start of the French Revolution. He fought for the *aristos* and got himself involved in complicated doings.'

'Oh? Such as?'

'He was not wise in his choice of friends,' Raoul answered shortly. 'Now, shall we choose dessert? The strawberries should be excellent at this time of year.'

'Raoul, please don't fob me off. I want to know.'

'I'm sure Monsieur le Curé can give you a better and more balanced account of the past than I.'

'But why? It's just a story of something that happened over two centuries ago. Surely it's not that important?'

'Apparently important enough for it to still haunt the present. You told me you believe you saw Natasha. How do you know it was her?'

'Because she looked the same as the girl in the portrait on the stairs. I'm certain.'

'You know why Natasha was called Natasha?' he asked, changing the subject subtly.

'No, actually, I don't. I didn't even know it was a family name until I came here. My father never mentioned it. I just thought my parents liked the name.'

'Natasha's mother came from a noble Russian family. That is why she named her daughter thus.'

'And Regis fell in love with her?' She looked him straight in the eye.

'Yes,' he said slowly. 'Regis fell in love with her.'

'But?'

'How do you know there was a "but"?' he queried.

'Because of the way you said it. Because in the family book of the Argentans she appears as nothing more than a hand-scribbled note in the margin. Not as his wife.'

'Natasha played fast and loose with him,' he retorted

sharply. 'She played with his feelings and his safety. It was a difficult and dangerous time. He took extraordinary risks for her sake and she—well, she did something unforgivable.'

'I see. So the family never got over their hurt pride.'

'That is ridiculous,' he scoffed, snapping the menu shut. 'Hurt pride, indeed. We are talking of honour, *mademoiselle*. Natasha had no honour. She pledged her word to Regis and then flew into the arms of a revolutionary.'

'I see.'

'No, you don't. Few people today understand those times. She prostituted herself with a traitor.'

'Was there a reason for her action? Didn't she love Regis?'

'So she claimed,' he said witheringly. 'But she was all too happy to spread her legs for the local revolutionary leader. It caused a rift between the Argentans and the Saugures for several generations. But thankfully that is all in the past, and the two families maintain friendly relations once again.'

'I see.' Seeing the anger in his eyes, and the taut expression, Natasha realized she'd do better to change the subject. At least now that she knew a part of the story she could get the Curé to tell her more. 'I think strawberries would be an excellent choice,' she said, smiling winningly, glad to see his features relax.

'With cream?'

'Why not? Though I've eaten so much these past few days I must be putting on pounds.'

'You certainly don't look any heavier to me,' he responded, his eyes giving her a quick, all-encompassing scrutiny that left her swallowing and wondering how, in the flick of an instant, he could make her feel as though he'd undressed her. When his eyes rested a moment longer on her breasts she felt her nipples stiffen and ache longingly against her thin cotton bra. How could she be so brazen? How could this man leave her so vulnerable, so needy?

As though he could read her every thought, Raoul smiled and reached his hand across the table. 'Natasha, let me tell you something.'

'What's that?' she asked warily.

'To *want* is not a sin. It is a natural, healthy reaction. And don't pretend you don't know what I mean, because you do. Very well. Last night proved that to me.'

'Last night was—was an aberration,' she muttered, trying to resist the delicious sensation of his finger caressing the inside of her bare forearm in what was turning into a dangerously erotic motion.

'Last night was the proof that you want to make love with me,' he murmured huskily. 'In fact, I have already made love to you. Only not fully. The rest is still to come.'

'I—'

'Shush...' he ordered, slipping a finger over her lips. 'No more words. Just allow things to take their course. But, please, don't resist what we both know must occur between us.'

To her relief the waiter appeared with the strawberries and Raoul immediately returned to his former self. It was so hard to know what to do, she reflected, savouring the delectable fruit on her tongue, unaware of how sexy she looked as she bit into the fruit's red texture. Part of her admitted he was right. That sooner or later the fire must be consumed for it to burn out. Another part told her to take care, to beware, not to give in to him so easily, even though he knew perfectly well what her feelings were.

CHAPTER TEN

BY THE time they'd finished dinner and returned to the Ferrari it was dark. A near full moon lit the inky sky, illuminating the pretty Norman village with its hanging flower baskets, neat cobbled streets and crooked Tudor-style houses. She sighed. If anyone had told her a few weeks ago that she was going to be driving through a Norman village in a Ferrari, next to one of the handsomest men she'd ever met whose sexual advances she was finding it hard to resist, she would have laughed outright. Yet now the thought of spending a whole night in Raoul's arms enticed more than it frightened.

'There is somewhere I would like to show you before I take you home,' he said, taking a turning on the country road bordered by shadowy hedgerows.

'What's that?' she clasped her hands nervously.

'A place I think you may find intriguing.' He kept his eyes on the road and said no more until they'd turned off down a country lane, at the end of which stood a small yet well-kept cottage.

'What is this?' she asked, her heart missing a beat.

'It is the cottage where Natasha and Regis used to meet in secret in the days of the Terror and after,' he replied quietly. 'It was here they made love for the first time.'

Her head flew round and she looked at him, not knowing what to say. It was obvious that he'd brought her here for a reason. But why, when he seemed so angry about these ancestors, would he want to bring her to the very spot where they'd come together?

'I brought you here because I thought it might be nice for you to see the cottage,' he said, his tone non-committal as he got out of the vehicle.

Two minutes later they were walking towards the front door. Raoul produced a large, ancient, heavy-looking key and inserted it in the lock. Soon the door creaked open.

'How come you have the key to this place?' she asked, stepping inside.

'Because I own it. It is part of the Argentan estate.' He switched on the light and Natasha looked about her, amazed at how little must have changed since the days when the two lovers had met here in secret.

'It must have looked just like this when they were here,' she whispered, allowing her fingers to trail over the ancient velvet settee.

'Yes, I believe very little has changed. My grandmother had the furniture re-upholstered, and some of the pieces restored. Also she had bathrooms and electricity installed. But come,' he said, reaching for her hand and leading her towards the stairs.

And suddenly she knew why they were here.

This was it, Natasha realized, overwhelmed by the significance of being in this place. Was it a trick? A way of getting her to submit to his desire for her? Or was there more to his sudden decision to bring her here?

As they climbed the ancient crooked stairs Natasha's pulse leapt and her skin tingled with anticipation. When they reached the door of the bedroom and he opened it she hesitated.

'This is where they made love,' he said quietly, drawing her inside, 'and this is where I shall make love to you,' he murmured, moving inside and lighting two candelabra perched on the stone mantel over the fireplace.

Natasha looked about her at the four-poster bed, draped

in ancient tapestries, noting that it had been made up with fresh linen, as though awaiting them. There were flowers on the windowsill. The room glowed softly under the flickering flames of the candles and all she could do was imagine the two young people of long ago, entwined on that same bed.

But before her imagination could reach any further back in time Raoul was fixing her in the present. He moved across the room and placed his hands on her shoulders. Their eyes locked as though mesmerized, caught in the magic of the moment. When he began slowly unzipping her dress and unhooking her bra she made no protest, merely waited for his lips to touch hers, to feel what was fast becoming a familiar delicious exchange of sensations. Before the kiss was over, his tongue teasing expertly, her clothes were lying strewn about her on the floor and she stood naked before him.

Drawing his head away, Raoul took a step back and studied her. 'Beautiful,' he said, his voice husky, 'Just as I knew you would be. Come.'

Unable to do more than surrender to his command, Natasha took his hand and allowed him to lay her on the bed.

He was extraordinarily tender, not the fierce lover she'd imagined, and as she lay among the lavender-scented sheets all she could do was close her eyes and feel, bask in the delight of his ever more intimate caresses, feeling his lips lightly graze the tips of her nipples, his fingers slipping gently between her thighs, languorously discovering each tiny secret spot of pleasure until she could bear it no more. Arching towards him, Natasha let out a small cry as at last he brought her to satisfaction.

Raoul gazed down at her, eyes gleaming. She was wondrous, deliciously wondrous. But he had only just begun.

In several quick movements he had divested himself of his clothes and was lying next to her, naked. She had no experience of men, he realized as his hands resumed their wanderings, and to his surprise he discovered that he liked it that way. Part of her was hesitant and stiff, and he sensed there must be a story behind it. All at once he felt angry with whoever the man was in her past, who'd made love to her incompetently. But he would remedy that, he vowed, reaching over and placing himself above her.

'I am going to make love to you, *chérie*,' he murmured, opening her thighs with his knee. 'Just lie back and enjoy it.'

Natasha could do no more than let out a long sigh and obey. When she felt him thrust firmly inside her a little gasp escaped her. Then her muscles relaxed and she let him enter deep inside, each thrust bringing him closer to her core. Then, without realizing it, she picked up his rhythm. Her hips arched and moved with him as their bodies intertwined. Finally, when neither could bear it any longer, they came together, hurtling over the edge, exploding with pleasure before tumbling among the sheets and lying saturated in each other's arms.

He had expected a pleasurable experience, but nothing like this, Raoul reflected once he was able to think straight. He had not made love to a woman like this in years, had not met with such reciprocated passion—ever.

The shock of the truth of this last statement hit him like an inside curve ball. *Mon Dieu*, this could become dangerous. Already was. He had never allowed anyone to reach into the confines of his heart. Not since Janine. Not since he'd suffered rejection. Once was quite enough, and he'd vowed at the early age of nineteen never to subject himself again to such raw humiliation.

But as he looked down at Natasha's sleeping form, her lovely golden mane strewn carelessly over the pillow, glistening in the moonlight, he felt something he hadn't thought he still possessed: a feeling of deep tenderness.

Quickly he rose from the bed and, slipping on an ancient silk dressing gown that hung behind the door, he moved towards the window, where he perched on the ledge. What had incited him to bring Natasha to this place? It had been a foolish decision, he realized in retrospect. For, although this night had been very near perfect, the spot held other connotations. Deep implications for both their families. And, since he had no intention of pursuing an affair with her, it was dangerous. Now he'd bedded her he must consider himself satisfied and be off to Paris first thing. There was no use hanging around and letting her believe he was prepared to get involved, for he wasn't. As he'd remarked several times, women had a disagreeable tendency to mistake a good night's sex for love. And he'd be willing to bet that Natasha was no exception.

He sighed. Why did it have to be like this? Why couldn't it all be simple? He would love to have another few nights like this, with no strings attached. But he had the nasty feeling that wasn't going to be possible.

Just then Natasha opened her eyes sleepily and stretched. So it had finally happened. She had let Raoul make love to her. All at once she came to, and realized she was alone in the bed. Fully awake now, she let her eyes wander across the room and she saw him, silhouetted in the moonlight. She experienced a wave of tenderness. How wonderful it had been, how simple and unimaginably perfect.

Natasha's eyes rested on Raoul and her pulse beat faster. He had made love to her, here in the very bed where their ancestors had joined, in this nest of forbidden passion. But common sense prevailed and she quickly told herself not to set too much store by this. She'd had a feeling Raoul might use whatever lures he thought necessary to break down her resistance.

And he had.

She had fallen for the bait, if bait it had been. Perhaps she was being cynical. Perhaps for now she would let herself believe that he too had sensed the shadow of the past hovering over them, and that something inexplicable had compelled him to bring her here rather than just lust.

Slipping from the bed, Natasha tiptoed across the ancient wooden floor. 'Awake?' she whispered.

Raoul turned, startled by her unexpected approach.

'I'm enjoying the night,' he said, slipping an arm about her and drawing her close. 'Look at that moon. It shines so clear and so bright.'

'I wonder if they ever had a night like this,' she murmured.

'You mean Regis and Natasha?' he queried, stiffening.

'No. I meant the local cats, Raoul. You know perfectly well I meant our ancestors. And I don't know why you're so loath to talk about them. After all, you're the one who brought me here,' she added, cross with him for pretending to misunderstand.

'I know. And I have been regretting it for the past half-hour. It was a silly notion.'

A stab of hot pain pierced her soul.

So she'd been right. It had been nothing but a clever ploy, a manner in which to pierce her shield and reach her at her most vulnerable. Swallowing the lump in her throat, she moved from the curve of his arm.

'I think we'd better get back. I have a lot to do tomorrow,' she muttered in as firm a voice as she could muster. It was hard to swallow, hard to think, hard to hold back the tears burning her eyes. But she was determined that

Raoul wouldn't see how deeply the experience had affected her. Let him think that, like him, she had merely taken pleasure in an enjoyable bout of sex and now she was ready to move on.

'Very well,' he answered, lifting his brows. A strange feeling of emptiness gripped him as he watched her move towards the bathroom—a modern addition his grandmother had insisted on. He hadn't expected her to react quite like this. Perhaps he'd been too brusque. But he didn't want to get into a whole diatribe about Regis and the former Natasha. Particularly now that he'd decided to cool things down a tad.

Hadn't he?

Raoul swung off the windowsill and stood a moment in the darkness. Then with an impatient gesture he grabbed his clothes from the floor and began to dress. He couldn't analyze all this right now. He would think about it some time tomorrow. If at all. The best thing was exactly what was occurring. And the sooner he dropped Natasha at home the better it would be for both of them.

Half an hour later they were driving in silence through the cool Normandy night. Soon they had reached the gates of the Manoir and were rolling up the drive.

It was five in the morning, Natasha realized, suddenly embarrassed at what Henri and the servants might think of her appearing home in the middle of the night with Raoul. But, after all, they'd been away, which made it simpler to explain.

When the car rolled up to the front door, she summoned up her courage and prepared to bid him a cool, disinterested goodbye, but was impeded from saying it when he slipped from the car and took her case out of the back. Reluctantly Natasha followed suit and exited the vehicle.

'Thank you for a very pleasant dinner,' she said coolly as he deposited the case on the large stone step.

'You're very welcome,' he answered, eyeing her closely as she fiddled in her bag for her key. Soon it was inserted in the lock and she turned it.

This was it, Natasha realized, gathering all her dignity. 'Well, goodnight, Raoul. I'm sure I'll see you around some time. Our paths will inevitably cross, I imagine.'

'Natasha—' He cut himself short, taken aback by her coolness, the way she was brushing him off. It was unheard of. Nobody brushed off the Baron d'Argentan in this off-hand manner.

'Goodnight,' she said again brightly, picking up her case and standing with her hand on the door, clearly meaning to close it.

'Goodnight,' he muttered finally, unable to decide whether to kiss her or not. As the door closed firmly on him Raoul swore under his breath. Never, in the course of his active life, had any woman closed the door in his face. Except in a flaming row. But that was different, he reflected, gunning the engine and heading off angrily down the drive. Flying crockery and slamming doors were fine when you were in the middle of a passionate row that would likely end up horizontally.

But this… This was unheard of.

Grinding his teeth, he swerved onto the country road, barely missing a milk van.

He would teach Natasha a lesson, he vowed. Damned if he would take her impertinence lying down.

Leaning back against the front door, Natasha let her head drop and sighed shakily. It had taken all her courage to act the way she had. But there was no doubt inside her that it was for the best. Raoul was history. And although part of her regretted tonight's tryst—for that was what it had been, if truth be told—at least she'd know what it was like to feel truly wonderful in a man's arms.

But at what cost? she wondered, picking her case up and making her way silently up the large staircase. When she reached Natasha's portrait she stopped for a moment and peered up at her in the half-light. Had she too experienced similar sensations in the arms of Raoul's ancestor? And what had happened to make Raoul so loath to talk about them? For a moment she lingered, then proceeded on to her bedroom. She simply must unravel the mystery, find out why Raoul felt so strongly about her ancestor. Something very serious must have happened for it still to affect someone of his generation.

Tomorrow, she vowed, undressing, her fingers smoothing her skin softly, recalling his touch and the scent of him, she would call the Curé and try to discover more.

But for now she must try, despite her pain and her agitation, to get some sleep.

CHAPTER ELEVEN

'*MADEMOISELLE*, you have a visitor,' Henri announced as she sat, several days later, going through the household accounts.

'Oh? Right. Who is it?' She brushed her hand through her hair and wondered why the numbers never tallied. Arithmetic wasn't her best subject.

'It is Monsieur le Maire,' Henri said proudly. 'He was away on holiday all this time, visiting his relations in America. But now he has returned and has come to pay his respects.'

'Good. Well, show him into the *salon*,' she said with a smile, aware that another morning was blown. Not that she really cared. In fact, quite the opposite. Lately it had been hard to concentrate on her duties, and any excuse to avoid them was welcome.

She glanced in the mirror. It was impossible to hide the wan look on her face, however hard she tried. Eating had been somewhat difficult of late. And she couldn't help her pulse leaping every time the phone rang.

Just in case it was Raoul.

But of course it never was.

It was over, and the sooner she got the message the better.

Moving across the hall, Natasha entered the *salon*, surprised to see a young, handsome Frenchman standing before her wearing corduroys, a cashmere jersey and a blazer. She'd expected someone bald and middle-aged.

'Mademoiselle de Saugure—what a pleasure. I'm so

sorry I was absent all this time. May I present myself? Gaston Mallard at your service.' He bowed over her hand, then smiled a handsome open smile that Natasha immediately took to.

'It's a pleasure to meet you too,' she said, smiling back and inviting him to sit down. 'Would you like some coffee? Or something stronger, perhaps?' She glanced at her watch. It was almost midday. 'I think we could allow ourselves a glass of wine, don't you?'

'I would be delighted.'

'Then, Henri, please bring some white wine.'

'Très bien, mademoiselle.' Henri closed the door discreetly behind him while Natasha took the opportunity of studying her guest more closely. He was extremely good-looking, with chestnut hair and blue eyes, of medium height and well dressed. Most of all there was something frank and inviting about him. To Natasha, living in the aftermath of her unfortunate night with Raoul, he came as a breath of fresh air.

'So, you've been *maire* of the village for a while?' she asked, sitting opposite him.

'Two years. It was almost an inherited post,' he added, laughing. 'My father and grandfather were *maire* before me, back to the days of the Revolution, and so I suppose it was my turn to take over.' He laughed again and shrugged. 'I run a calvados business near here. We like to think that this old family tradition is very unique and that we make the best and oldest calvados in Normandy.'

'And do you?' she queried, her face breaking into a small laugh at his open demeanour.

'The truth?'

'Absolutely.'

'Well, I think we make excellent calvados, but whether it is the best or not I couldn't say.' He frowned jokingly.

'But you must vow on your life that if you come across my grandfather or father you will never say that. They would disinherit me in the same instant.'

'Goodness. I would hate for that to happen,' she exclaimed, laughing, relaxing for the first time in days.

By the time they'd had a glass of wine and chatted some more Natasha felt very pleased to have made a new friend. Gaston was charming, friendly, and surprisingly unflirtatious—which, coming from a Frenchman, was something.

'Why don't you stay for lunch?' she asked, on the spur of the moment.

'I would love to,' he responded regretfully, 'but unfortunately I have a committee meeting early this afternoon. But…' he hesitated.

'Yes?' she prompted.

'I was going to suggest that, should you like, we could dine together. Perhaps tomorrow night?'

'That would be very nice,' she agreed happily. This man's company would do her good, and help get Raoul out of her mind and system.

'Good. Then I shall pick you up around seven-forty-five tomorrow. There is a very nice little restaurant in Beaumont that I think—'

'Oh, no,' she cut in, before she could stop herself.

'You don't like Beaumont? You already know it?'

'Yes—no. What I mean is that perhaps it would be fun to try something else. I've already been to Beaumont.' She rescued herself hastily. 'I'd love to discover some of the other places around.'

'Very well.' Gaston opened his hands in a gesture of accord. 'Then I shall think of somewhere I am certain you have not visited previously. Goodbye, *mademoiselle*.' He lifted her hand gallantly to his lips.

'Please, call me Natasha. It makes me feel as if I'm a hundred when everyone treats me so formally.'

'*Très bien*, then Natasha it shall be. And you shall call me Gaston.'

They smiled in a friendly manner and Natasha accompanied him to the front door. What a charming man, she concluded, closing it after him. How nice that she'd met someone fun and engaging; someone, she reflected glumly, who could take her mind off Raoul's silence.

After a light lunch, determined not to fall into the dumps—a frequent occurrence of late—she stepped out into the garden, where André the gardener was busy clipping the hedge. She took a deep breath and lifted her face towards the sky, watching the fast-moving cloud, the patches of blue interspersed with grey announcing possible rain later in the day. Perhaps she should take a walk down to the village and pass by the Curé's house—a plan she'd promised herself to carry out but still hadn't found the time to execute.

Stepping back inside, Natasha picked up a jacket in the hall, that was fast becoming less formal than her grandmother would ever have deemed proper, and slipped outside. She began walking at a good pace towards the village, waving across a field at Rolland Hervier, one of the tenant farmers on her land, riding the knew combi-harvester that the estate had invested in. She liked seeing the people happy and busy, knowing that her actions were causing the place to become more productive. And she felt a deep sense of belonging.

As she stepped into the cobblestoned village street several people smiled and said hello. Madame Blanc from the bakery, Rémy from behind the bar at the café, Monsieur Lenoir at the *tabac*, who now ordered the English newspapers for her.

'A nice day, *mademoiselle*,' he commented as she stepped inside the small cluttered shop.

'Yes. It is. Did *The Times* arrive?'

'I'm afraid only yesterday's. It's all due to this silly new distribution system they've implemented. Everything comes from Paris now.' He shook his grey head disapprovingly. 'But one can't do anything about it, I'm afraid. It's the way of the world. Change. Always change.' He shook his head again. 'I was saying to my wife only the other night that we are really quite lucky. Not much here has changed. Though of course when the Baron gets married things will probably take a turn. The new Baroness will want things her own way, no doubt.' He sniffed, and Natasha swallowed.

'You mean the Baron d'Argentan?'

'Of course. When we refer to the Baron here we mean him. The Marquise de Longueville, who lives over in Falaise, has been spreading the news around. Apparently the Baron has become very attentive to her only daughter, Camille. Though between you and me I can't see what he sees in her,' he added, leaning conspiratorially across the chocolate bars.

'Well, I'm sure she's a very nice girl,' Natasha said weakly, trying to rid herself of a sudden dizziness that made her light-headed.

'No doubt. And it may all be a figment of the Marquise's imagination. She's been trying to fob that girl off on someone for the past ten years. Of course the Baron would be a great catch.' He nodded sagely. 'A great catch indeed.'

'I'm sure.' Natasha braced herself. 'Well, if the papers haven't arrived I'd better be on my way. Goodbye, Monsieur Lenoir, *à bientôt*.' Hastily she retired from the shop, glad to be outside once more, afraid her sudden rush of emotion might show. So she was right. He'd merely wanted to bed her to prove to himself that he could. Well, he'd done a pretty good job, she recognized bitterly as she hurried down the street, anxious not to get caught in another round of conversation she didn't feel up to. Her mind was in turmoil, and her heart felt a strange stab of hurt. Which was ridiculous, of course, since there was nothing between her and Raoul except a strong physical attraction.

'You look in a hurry.'

She spun around to see Gaston crossing the road to greet her. Mustering a smile, she responded.

'Hello, Gaston. How are you?'

'Fine.' He took his hand in hers and studied her closely. 'But you, *ma chère* Natasha, do not look so fine.' His brows met. 'Is something the matter?'

'No, no, I'm all right,' she protested, shocked that she could be so transparent. 'I just—' She stopped short, not knowing what to say.

'Why don't we have a coffee and a brandy?' he suggested in a comforting tone. 'And you can tell me—or not, as you wish—what is wrong. It must be quite lonely for you to find yourself in a new community. I can perhaps be a friend?' He raised a brow and smiled that warm, friendly smile she'd felt so drawn to at their meeting earlier in the day.

'Okay,' she said, smiling back. Together they walked back up the street to the café, where they settled at one of the small round tables on the pavement and Gaston ordered two *cafés filtres* and two brandies.

'Now. Will you consider me nosy if I ask what is troubling you? I barely know you, but friendship doesn't necessarily need time to develop.'

This last was true. Natasha had made many good friends on her African travels, some of them in little more than a moment.

'It's nothing. Just a piece of news that's left me a little off keel, that's all. But it's not important in the least.'

'You're certain? It didn't seem that way a few minutes ago. In fact, I felt you'd been hit over the head with a baseball bat, as the Americans say.'

'Not that bad.' She laughed, cheering up and feeling more her old self. 'Nothing to worry about.' She smiled, raised her brandy snifter, and they clinked glasses.

They chatted a while, and Gaston tactfully dropped the matter of what was ailing her. But just as they were finishing their drinks a familiar vehicle in the form of Raoul's black Range Rover drew up and parked on the opposite side of the street.

'Ah. There's Raoul. I think he was in Paris this past two weeks,' Gaston remarked, waving.

Natasha watched, heart sinking, as Raoul, dressed in jeans and a loose navy sweater, made his way lazily across the street. She felt her cheeks burn and her pulse jolt. Why did he have such an effect on her, damn it? Surely she could keep these feelings under control? It was ridiculous—shaming. The man had made it clear he wanted nothing more to do with her. Surely she'd got the message loud and clear?

Determined not to lower herself by showing any of these thoughts, Natasha plastered on a social smile.

'Gaston. Natasha. I see you two have met.' His eyes flashed over her. God, she was beautiful—though a little pale and flushed now that he looked closer. So Gaston had discovered the new local beauty. Well, well, well.

'Why don't you join us? We were just having *café* and cognac.'

'Good idea.' He drew up a chair and sat down between the two, his presence immediately dominating. 'So, you two are getting to know each other?'

Natasha caught the inflection behind the statement, the

fleeting exchange between the two men, and wondered what was going on.

'Yes. I had the pleasure of meeting Natasha this morning. As you know, I've been away for a while and wasn't able to attend the funeral.'

Why did he need to justify his visit to the Manoir to Raoul? she wondered, annoyed at his high-handed air of owning the place. And there was Rémy, coming out solicitously from behind the bar to shake hands. She could have slapped Raoul at that moment for being so odiously larger than life.

'I think it's time I was going,' she remarked. She was damned if she was going to sit here being surveyed as though she were under a damn microscope. He'd made it plain he didn't want her, hadn't he? She pushed back her chair.

'So soon?' Raoul's brow rose and an amused smile hovered about his lips. Again the urge to slap him made her clench her fists into two tight balls.

'Actually, I have some things to do. Including stopping by Monsieur le Curé's,' she said sweetly. 'He's going to tell me some of the history of these parts. Like how our ancestors interacted. Things like that.' She sent him a bright, brittle smile and rose.

'I see. How about dinner tomorrow night?' he asked suddenly, his eyes boring into hers.

'That's very kind, but I'm otherwise engaged.' Natasha turned, flapping her eyelashes provocatively at the surprised Gaston. 'Thanks for the refreshment. And *à demain*.' She waved her fingers and, turning on her heel, made her way down the pavement, letting out a triumphant sigh of relief. *Serve you damn well right, Raoul d'Argentan.* That should put him in his place. At least now he'd know that he wasn't the last Coca Cola in the desert. That she'd been invited out by someone else. And someone not to be sneezed at. Gaston was handsome, self-assured, and he held a position of importance in the area.

With a determined nod she stepped past the church and moved towards the *cure*—the rectory—where she hoped to find the priest at home.

CHAPTER TWELVE

'SO YOU'VE met Natasha. What do you think of her?'

The question was delivered in a short, matter-of-fact manner that left Gaston in no doubt of Raoul's meaning.

'Yes, I have, and I like her,' he replied immediately, swirling his brandy thoughtfully and taking a quick oblique glance at his friend. Even though they came from very different backgrounds, Raoul and he had played together as boys, had been given a similar education, and had courted the village girls as they'd grown up. Even after Raoul had taken his place in Paris society and Gaston had remained in the village where he belonged, their friendship had flourished. 'Do I get the drift that you're interested in Mademoiselle de Saugure?' he threw out casually, taking a sip of brandy.

'Me? Interested? Why should I be interested in her? What an idea,' Raoul scoffed. 'I find her *sympathique*, at most. No.' He shook his head. 'I'm not interested in anybody right now.'

'Really? There's a rumour going about that you might ask for the Longueville girl's hand in marriage.' Gaston grimaced. 'Rather you than me, *mon vieux*.'

'What rubbish. I've known Camille all my life. God, I'd rather marry a jockey than marry her. All she can talk about is horses. Plus, she's hardly what I would think of as attractive. No, but I've been over there quite often lately, looking at some horseflesh.'

'Natasha is certainly attractive,' Gaston countered. 'And I'm glad to know you've no interest in that area.' He took a last swig and rose. 'Because I find her delightful. Really rather alluring. *Au revoir, mon ami. A bientôt.*'

Gaston nodded briefly, then turned on his heel and ambled up the street, a smile hovering as he made his way thoughtfully towards the Town Hall. Was his old friend Raoul more smitten than he cared to let on? Why, that would be something. Particularly in view of his family history. Of course it was to be hoped that if he did fall for Natasha the outcome would be more satisfactory than his ancestor's.

Gaston stopped a moment in the Plâce du Village. It was here, in the 1790s, where the guillotine had been erected on which his ancestor, Benoît, had nearly managed to have the Baron Regis d'Argentan beheaded. It always sent a weird sensation coursing through him to think of it. And it was the famous Natasha who had saved the two men from one another. He shook his head. What women did for the sake of a man they loved. And how stupidly men interpreted their actions, he reflected ruefully.

With a shrug and a sigh he turned and made his way into the Town Hall. All that was ancient history. Had nothing to do with today's world. Yet a funny feeling told him that history was repeating itself in a different manner.

But one which could prove just as fascinating.

Natasha paused at the door of the Rectory, then, lifting her right hand, banged the knocker several times.

Soon she heard shuffling footsteps in the corridor beyond and the door opened.

'Ah, *mon enfant*, it is you.' The old Curé, his white mane gleaming, beamed at her. 'Come in, come in, my dear. It is a pleasure to have you in my home.'

'Thank you so much. I hope I'm not disturbing you at a bad time?'

'Not at all. I was just trying to come up with an idea for Sunday's sermon. Perhaps you will inspire me.' He winked and smiled, and ushered her down a tiled corridor into a long beamed room that looked out over an attractive orchard.

'What a pretty room,' she remarked, gazing out of the window, enchanted. 'This is a very special house.'

'Yes, it is,' the Curé agreed, motioning to the sofa. 'Sit down, my dear, and let me order a cup of tea for us from Madame Sarasin.'

'Thank you.' Natasha didn't like to say that she'd just had coffee and cognac with the *maire.*

'So. You have come to discover more about your family. That is good. I'm glad to see what an interest you are taking in your inheritance. Such a shame that your father was unable to assume his duties as Comte. But we must not regret the past. It is God's will that things should have happened in this way.' He shrugged in a Gallic manner and came to sit opposite her. 'Now, tell me, my dear. What exactly would you like to know? There is so much—so many stories. Perhaps you should be specific.'

'Well.' Natasha clasped her hands, suddenly nervous. 'I wondered if you knew something of what happened to Regis d'Argentan and Natasha de Saugure, after whom I believe I must be named?'

The Curé's fingers steepled and he looked thoughtful. 'That is most interesting. And why, I wonder, would you be so intrigued by their story?'

'Oh, just general interest,' Natasha prevaricated.

'I see.'

Natasha got the feeling that this man saw a lot more than he made out, and she hastily continued, 'I am, of course, interested because of my name.'

'Why, naturally. And then you know Raoul. I heard you have been seen together dining, and at the races.'

A dull flush rose to her cheeks. 'Yes. Well—actually, we were. I went to the races with the Morrieux, but then—'

The Curé raised his hand in a peremptory gesture.

'You have no need to furnish me with any kind of explanation. It is not my business who you see or don't see. Raoul is a good young man, if somewhat lost. He suffered a bad experience in his youth, you know.'

'No, actually I didn't.'

'Yes, it was a shame. When he was nineteen he met a girl who played fast and loose with his heart and his hopes. Raoul was very fond of her. But she—well, she had a liking for adventure and wealth. She left him for an Arab sheikh. I don't think his pride has ever quite recovered.'

'I see.'

'I thought you would. Now, as for your Natasha—well, let me see. She began her career as any young aristocrat of her time would have. But that was cut short by the Revolution. They were terrible times that affected everyone's lives. Nothing would ever be quite the same again.'

'I can imagine that it must have been awful.'

'Yes. I believe it was. There were many rivalries settled in a dishonest fashion. Love affairs were avenged, jealousy and pain assuaged by the elimination of a rival.' The Curé folded his hands and sighed sadly.

'You mean that someone took revenge on Natasha?'

'Not on Natasha herself. But Benoît Mallard was in love with her. He knew she was out of his reach, she being an aristocrat and he a revolutionary. She'd been promised since childhood to Regis d'Argentan, with whom she was in love. But he was a flighty one. He had many mistresses and enjoyed life.'

'But weren't he and Natasha in love? I thought—'

'Yes. I believe that deep down they were. But they were two proud young people, caught up by events. Natasha didn't want to be one more notch on Regis's belt. And his wife, to boot. She knew Benoît loved her passionately. And frankly, from all I can gather, she encouraged him to believe that she would look favourably upon his suit simply to provoke Regis's wrath. Now, you can imagine how that must have affected the poor young man. Here he was, a simple merchant, with no hope of aspiring to the hand of such a wealthy noble lady as Natasha. And all of a sudden she lures him on, and the revolutionaries tell him that everyone is now equal.'

'Go on,' Natasha urged when he paused.

'Well, during the Revolution Mallard was given a position of power in the Nouveau Régime. It was too tempting not to use it. He had d'Argentan tried for treason, imprisoned, and sentenced to the guillotine.'

'So he was guillotined?'

'No. He escaped.'

'My goodness, how?' Natasha sat on the edge of her chair as history unwound before her.

'It was Natasha who saved him. But at a price.'

'What do you mean?'

'She slept with the enemy, so to speak.'

'You mean with Benoît?'

'Yes. Realizing that even now he still had no chance of marrying her, and that what would most hurt Regis would be to dishonour her, Benoît offered Natasha a pact: her virginity for Regis's life.'

'And she agreed?'

'Yes, she agreed.' The Curé nodded, raised his hands and sighed.

'And what happened?'

'Regis escaped with his head but never forgave her. He

would have rather have lost it than see the woman he was promised to sullied by another. Particularly one he considered his enemy.'

'You mean he rejected her after all she'd done for him?'

'I'm sad to say that, yes, he did. Outwardly, that is. The two of them escaped to England together, but he refused to marry her, considering her a traitor to France and to the Royalist regime.'

'But that's absurd,' Natasha exclaimed angrily. 'She gave up what at that time was a most precious part of her life.'

'I know. But Regis was young and proud and stupid. He died an angry, bitter old man. Oh, they were able to return after the Revolution. Napoleon gave them back their lands and their castles. But they lived side by side for sixty years, married to other people without ever talking to one another again publicly.'

'Goodness, what a story.' Natasha swallowed and shook her head. No wonder the young girl in the portrait looked sad. She had given up everything for the man she loved and this was what she'd received in return. 'Was the Mallard in question Gaston Mallard's ancestor?'

'Yes. He was.'

'Yet Gaston and Raoul seem to be good friends.'

'Well, let us be thankful for the healing of time,' the Curé said benignly. 'After all, over two hundred years have elapsed since the events we speak of.'

'True. But tell me, there is a cottage I've heard about somewhere in the countryside where Natasha and Regis met.'

'Ah, so you've heard about that,' the Curé said, looking at her curiously. 'Not many people know that version of the story. I wonder— But, no—forgive me, that is none of my business.' He waved a hand. 'It is said that despite their public rejection of one another the lovers did in fact meet secretly in that cottage. It is on the Argentan estate, you know. The old Baroness, Raoul's grandmother, had things tidied up, but kept the original furnishings. It is said that the bed there is the same one the couple slept in. She apparently found the tale most romantic.'

'It is. Very.' Natasha swallowed. 'Well, I've taken enough of your time, *mon père*. I had better be on my way.'

'What? No tea?'

'No, thanks. Another time, with pleasure, but I think I'd better be getting back to the Manoir.'

'Very well.' The old gentleman rose and, taking her hand in his, held it a moment. 'You know, history need not necessarily repeat itself,' he murmured, in a low gentle tone. 'Raoul is a good man, despite his blindness. Maybe some day he will wake up.'

Then, before she could answer, he turned and conducted her back to the front door, and after a quick and warm goodbye Natasha was on her way.

CHAPTER THIRTEEN

IT WAS high time he returned to Paris, Raoul realized, staring in annoyance out of the mullioned window at the rain, pouring steadily as it had all day. But although he'd been tempted to get in the car, drive off and forget the whole matter, Raoul found himself incapable of blotting out the image of Natasha and Gaston cosily ensconced at the Café des Sports, chit-chatting very comfortably.

And perhaps more.

It was this *perhaps more* that was the crux of the matter. He didn't mind her dining with his old pal, not in the least, he told himself repeatedly. But the idea that she might submit to his caresses as she had to his was infinitely more disturbing.

He glanced at his watch. Five o'clock. In a couple of hours Gaston would be picking Natasha up to drive her over to Honfleur for dinner. Or perhaps they'd changed plans since the weather was so rotten and were staying closer to home. Worse, maybe Gaston had invited her to dinner in his extremely charming low-beamed thatched farmhouse, which was, Raoul realized, eyes narrowing, an ideally romantic spot for seduction.

'Bon sang!' he exclaimed, bringing his fist down on the ancient stone parapet against which he'd been leaning. He would not allow this to happen—wouldn't let her slip through his fingers. He'd been a gentleman, hadn't he? Had not taken advantage of her inebriated state the other night, which he quite easily could have. Instead he'd respected her, waited for the right moment. Now she should jolly well

respect him too. And anyway, what business did she have going to dine with another man? A man who, although he was his friend, was the descendant of one who had already sullied the family reputation. No, he decided, walking determinedly down the ancient worn steps to the Baronial Hall, he would not allow this to happen just like that.

Grabbing his Barbour jacket in the hall, Raoul banged the heavy front door behind him and, ducking from the rain, hurried to the Range Rover. It was time to take action. Before things got out of hand, he reflected, gunning the engine.

Time to show her he meant business.

Curled up in the *petit salon*, Natasha was enjoying the end of a riveting novel which had helped take her mind off the images of Raoul that lingered, however determinedly she set them aside. It seemed that however hard she tried to banish him from her thoughts he kept creeping back in, the impression of his dark, windswept countenance hard to shake off. But the good news was that she was having dinner with Gaston, she reminded herself, laying the book down and staring into the flames. Gaston was charming and handsome, gallant and gracious. The perfect antidote to Raoul, who was arrogant, selfish, autocratic and odious.

Bracing herself, and for the hundredth time telling herself she was well rid of him, Natasha glanced at the ormolu clock on the mantelpiece. It was five-thirty. Soon she needed to go upstairs, have a bath with some of the delicious lavender bath essence she'd bought the other day in Deauville, and prepare for the evening's outing.

As she prepared to unfurl her long legs from under her Natasha heard the sound of a car in the drive. Who on earth could it be? Someone to see Henri, perhaps?

But her heart stood still when, stepping over to the window, she spied the familiar figure of Raoul getting out of the vehicle. Natasha swallowed and closed her eyes for a second. She should get Henri to say she wasn't at home. But as the doorbell clanged she knew she was not capable of doing that: the desire to see him, speak with him, feel him close was too tempting to resist.

'Stop it,' she admonished herself out loud. She was acting like a gooey teenager when she was a grown-up woman. Just because he was the first man to make her feel those wondrous sensations she'd experienced in his arms it didn't mean she was spineless.

Pulling herself together, Natasha marched out into the hall, determined to give him a set-down. Henri had already let him in and he was taking off his jacket.

'Ah. Natasha. I'm glad I found you at home. I have a problem I wish to discuss with you.' He sounded friendly and businesslike, and she wondered suddenly if she'd misread his sudden visit.

'Right. Well, I haven't much time.' She glanced pointedly at her watch. 'I have a dinner engagement.'

'This won't take very long. But I need to have your agreement,' he said, moving towards her and taking her hand in his.

Again the deadly tingling magic coursed up her arm and throughout her body. She swallowed and smiled coolly, despite her inner turmoil.

'We'd better go into the office,' she murmured, hoping that the austere atmosphere of this workspace would help her regain control.

'You mean you aren't going to offer me a drink on a filthy evening like this?' he cajoled, eyes meeting hers full-on.

'Uh, well, yes—of course. Henri, could you bring a bottle of wine to the *petit salon*, please?' she said, turning quickly and leading the way to the room she had just abandoned, hoping he couldn't read her mind, that the desire churning inside her was hers and hers alone to witness.

'Ah, it is good to be inside on such a miserable evening,' Raoul said, rubbing his hands and approaching the unlit fireplace. 'I hope Henri has seen to it that you have wood in for the winter. You'll need it. It gets quite chilly in these parts, and the central heating in this place isn't the most modern. Your grandmother refused to have a new unit installed. Said that anyone who was cold could damn well put on another sweater.' He rose and stood over her, eyes laughing. 'So, Natasha, *ma belle*, you look put out. Have I done something I shouldn't?'

'Not at all,' she dismissed coolly, perching on the arm of the sofa and crossing her legs protectively. 'But perhaps you'd like to state your business. I don't have much time.'

'Of course. But let's wait until Henri has brought the wine.'

'Very well. Do sit down,' she added formally, glad that her voice sounded chilly even to her own ears. 'How was Paris?'

'Fine, I imagine.' He shrugged and sat comfortably on the armchair opposite, slinging one corduroy-clad leg over the other while his arm rested elegantly over the back of the cushion.

He was too damn at ease, Natasha thought, quelling the images of him that night in the abandoned cottage, too damned at home for his own good. She simply had to put an end to these ridiculous fantasies.

A knock on the door announced Henri and the wine. Soon it was uncorked and Raoul was handing her a glass. When the door closed behind the manservant Natasha peered at Raoul over the rim of her glass.

'So. What brings you here this evening?' she asked frostily.

'Ah, yes, the reason for my visit. Well, you see, there is a fence that divides our properties on the southern boundary. There is some slight damage. I want to have it repaired but need your consent to do so.'

Natasha frowned. It sounded rather a weak excuse, and she wondered suddenly, her pulse picking up, if he'd come because he wanted to see her.

'I'm sure there isn't any problem. Is the fence my responsibility or yours?'

'Mine.'

'Then why would you need my permission to repair it?' she queried, her chin coming up. 'I really don't know why you bothered to come out on a rainy night to tell me this, Raoul. Surely our factors could have dealt with it?'

'Bien sûr,' he agreed smoothly. 'But as it is the first time that something has come up between the properties since you've become mistress, and because you left the other day in perhaps not the best of moods…' his brow rose and a smile twitched around his well-shaped lips '…I thought it would be more courteous to come personally.'

'Very thoughtful,' she answered dryly. She would not let him get the better of her. She could feel the tentacles of his influence reaching out, creeping around her, pulling her towards him in that mesmerizing manner she found so hard to resist. 'Well,' she continued, letting out a deep breath she'd been holding, 'that's fine. Do whatever has to be done. I really don't mind. But I'm afraid I'm going to have to ask you to leave soon. Gaston's picking me up in forty-five minutes.'

'So soon?'

'Yes.'

'I see. Well, let us finish this glass of wine and then I shall leave you to prepare for your date.'

Despite her nervousness Natasha caught the edge to his voice and her heart leapt once more.

He was angry.

Serve him right.

Let him stew in his own juice for a while. She would not succumb to him to be abandoned, thrown out like an old rag, or treated like her ancestor. The mere thought of what the previous Natasha had sacrificed for his forefather only to be humiliated for the rest of her life was warning enough, surely?

'I shall be going to England for a few days soon,' she remarked. 'I have a number of loose ends to tie up and friends to see. Everyone is very surprised at my decision to stay in France.'

'I'm sure they must be. I was surprised myself. I think it is very courageous of you,' he added, his expression changing to one of admiration. 'It takes guts to walk into a situation like this and not shy off like a frightened filly. But you're not a frightened filly, are you, Natasha?' He rose, and before she could move was drawing her into his arms. 'You're not frightened, just inexperienced,' he murmured, his hand slipping into the small of her back and pressing her body to his. 'You know that I want you just as I know you want me. Why bother to deny it? You enjoyed the other night as much as I did. Admit it.' He gazed down arrogantly at the top of her head.

'I—' Natasha stared at his chest and clenched her fists. 'I'm not in the habit of simply scratching an itch,' she replied through gritted teeth. 'I think what happened between us was a mistake. One that should not be repeated.'

They were the hardest words she'd ever spoken to him,

but despite the scent of him, the temptation to lift her lips and receive his kiss, Natasha stood firm.

Raoul stiffened. 'What do you mean a mistake?' His hold on her tightened. 'You call this a mistake?' In one swift movement his hand slipped under her chin and he tilted her face up. Then, before she could react, his lips came down firmly on hers, parting them, forcing her to open up to him, to allow him in where she'd vowed she wouldn't.

She could feel the hardness of his arousal against her abdomen, felt herself go liquid inside, felt her nipples ache against his chest, was yearning for that feathery caress, an easing of the tightness that was spiralling within her.

'This is no mistake,' Raoul growled, lifting his mouth from hers and staring deep into her eyes while his fingers found her breast, 'and neither is this,' he muttered, slipping his hand deftly below her sweater, a triumphant smile breaking as he felt her braless nipple peak under his grazing thumb. 'I will teach you how to recognize a mistake, *mademoiselle*,' he whispered, taunting further, making sure she felt him as his other hand slipped under the elastic of her sweatpants. The smile turned into an arrogant grin as he realized she wore no panties, and his hand roamed freely.

Natasha flushed, felt his fingers come into contact with the delicious welcoming wetness between her thighs and tried to resist, to protest. But once again his lips were on hers. She felt drunk on emotion, high on sensations spiralling, curling within her, felt his expert touch caressing each needy spot inside her until she was gasping in his arms, begging for fulfilment.

'Not so fast, *chérie*,' he muttered, taking it slowly, prolonging the delight. 'Not so fast. When you come I want you to be damn certain that this is no mistake.'

Then when she could bear it no more his fingers quickened their pace, bringing her over the edge, making her cling to him, dizzy with pleasure, unable to do more than lean her head against his broad chest and allow him to take her in his arms and sit her on his knee on the sofa.

Before she had time to recover he'd slipped off her pants and was quickly undressing himself.

'Raoul,' she begged weakly, 'this is crazy. Someone could come in. I—'

'Shush,' he ordered, lying on top of her and easing himself inside.

'Ahh.' Natasha sighed as he entered her, feeling him fill her and knowing it felt so right. For a moment Raoul lay thus, staring down at her, their bodies as one. Then with slow methodical thrusts he had her gasping again, raising her hips to his as together they discovered a new and wonderful rhythm that she wished would go on and on for ever. She forgot where she was, the time and place, simply gave way to the delight of his lovemaking, drawing him further and further within her until at last they came in a frenzied rush and Raoul sank on top of her.

They lay, spent, hearing the beat of each other's heart. But after a few minutes reality began to sink in and Natasha took stock of her situation. Here she was, half-naked, lying in the arms of one man while expecting another to take her to dinner at any minute.

'Raoul,' she whispered, touching his shoulder.

'Mmm,' he grunted.

'Raoul, we must get dressed. Gaston will arrive at any moment and I'm not even ready.'

She felt him stiffen, then raise himself. His dark hair was tousled and his eyes turbulent as he stared down her.

'You mean you still intend to go out with Mallard after what just occurred here?' he bit out, eyes blazing.

'I have to. I accepted his invitation. It would be very rude to cry off at the last minute.'

There was a moment's silence before he withdrew himself in one quick movement and rose. 'I should have expected this,' he exclaimed jeeringly. 'They say like mother like daughter. In your case,' he said bitterly, pulling on his clothes, 'I should say like ancestor like descendant. It is obviously not just Natasha's name you inherited, but her nature as well.' With that he dragged his fingers through his hair and, sending her one last fulminating glance, marched from the room.

Bewildered, Natasha hastily pulled on her clothes as the sound of his car engine disappeared into the night. This was all too crazy, too ridiculous for words. Here she was being accused of…what? What exactly was he accusing her of?

She ran upstairs to her room and hastened to the shower. Gaston would be here any minute.

How could she possibly face him after what had just happened?

Oh, Lord.

This was all so confusing, so unsettling. Hadn't she promised herself not to submit to Raoul's advances again? Yet at the first opportunity she'd faltered. And now he was accusing her of being like her ancestor. Well, he could be easy on that score, she reflected with a sniff, letting the hot jet of water soothe her satisfied body. She would not let what had happened to her ancestor happen to her. Would not be despised and humiliated, however hard he tried.

With a determined huff Natasha dried herself with a large terry towel and, grabbing a pair of jeans and a silk shirt from her closet, pulled them on just as a flash of headlights illuminated the night.

Gaston was here.

Oh, God.

She would have to use all her British *sang froid* to keep her cool tonight, she realized, taking a deep breath. Too bad if Raoul was upset that she was dining with Gaston. He was being ridiculous. Surely he must realize she would be incapable of doing anything with another man? The realization hit her hard and she swallowed.

Was she really that badly smitten?

CHAPTER FOURTEEN

RAOUL drove back to the Château in a towering rage.

How dared she flout him like this? How dared she go from his arms to the company of another man? He should have known. Hadn't history warned him enough? Weren't the circumstances recounted to him since childhood sufficient warning to keep him away from her?

'Bon sang!' he exclaimed, ramming his foot on the accelerator angrily. That he, a seasoned womanizer, should get caught in a trap like this. Destiny surely had something to do with it. And she'd said she'd seen Natasha's ghost. Perhaps there was more to it than met the eye. Perhaps the old Natasha had come to take revenge on his ancestor through him.

He shook his head and told himself to stop being ridiculous. This was the twenty-first century, after all. He must simply bring an end to this damn nonsense and leave for Paris immediately. Perhaps he should just marry Camille de Longueville, whose mother had been pushing her at him for the past months, and have a traditional French marriage with several mistresses on the side and be done with it.

Right now, he reckoned, furious, anything would be better than this.

'You seem tired tonight,' Gaston remarked as they finished dessert.

'Oh, just a little,' she evaded, mustering a smile. Where was Raoul? On his way to Paris by now, probably.

'Well, maybe it's the sudden change in temperature,'

Gaston replied blandly. 'It has become quite cold for the season.'

'Yes. I suppose it has,' she answered vaguely. What if he'd left in anger and had an accident on the road? It would be all her fault.

'Natasha?' Gaston leaned across the table and touched her hand. 'You seem very far away. Is something troubling you?'

'I'm so sorry,' she said, blushing, realizing how rude she must appear. 'I was just distracted by something.'

'Some*thing* or some*one*?'

Her eyes flew up. 'I—'

'You don't need to explain,' he said, squeezing her hand. 'I caught the vibes between you and Raoul yesterday. It is quite obvious that the two of you are very attracted to one another.'

'Is it?' She looked squarely at him now, her eyes big with wonder. 'I didn't realize that other people were aware.'

'My dear, this is France,' he replied, with laughter in his eyes. 'Romance is in the air. It is the first thing we sense between a man and a woman.'

'Oh, gosh. It's all so difficult.' Her shoulders slumped.

'Why? Or rather, why don't you tell me about it?' Gaston sat back and smiled at her. 'I am your friend, Natasha, I'm here to help. I am also Raoul's friend, and I get the feeling that something isn't right between you two.'

'You're only too right. It isn't.' She sighed, leaned her elbows on the table and steepled her fingers.

'Then let me order a couple of calvados and you shall tell me about it.' He raised a finger and beckoned the waiter.

'There's nothing much to tell, really. We met, and we—

I—well, we sort of ended up attracted to one another,' she mumbled, not knowing what else to say.

'And then? You made love?'

Colour flew to her cheeks. 'How did you know?'

'It's written all over you. You made love, and now part of you regrets it because Raoul is a selfish bastard who has no desire to commit to anything. You, on the other hand, are a loyal and trustworthy woman who would not have made love with him were you not emotionally involved. Am I right?' His blue eyes penetrated hers, filled with warmth and understanding.

'That just about sums it up.' She nodded glumly. 'I don't know why I let myself get involved with a man like that. It's crazy. It never should have happened.'

'Why not? It is the unusual in life that attracts us, not the banal. Or not people like you and Raoul anyway.'

'Raoul is obsessed with the past. He seems to have some fixation about that story between Regis and my namesake. It's almost as if it haunts him.'

'Perhaps it does,' Gaston responded thoughtfully, picking up the glass of calvados and taking a sip. 'You know, the Argentans are a very proud and noble family. They never forgave my ancestor for taking the lovely Natasha's virginity for Regis's life. To them, it constituted the ultimate humiliation. Raoul still thinks of it thus. We used to talk about it some years back, about how funny it was that we could be such good friends when our ancestors had been mortal enemies.'

'Well, just be careful he doesn't become your mortal enemy now. He knows we're dining together tonight,' she said, with a humourless laugh.

'And was not pleased?'

'That's putting it mildly.' She rolled her eyes heavenwards. 'He was furious, and left in a rage saying I was just like the first Natasha,' she ended, deflated.

'I see. Well...' Gaston pondered a moment, then smiled, 'I wouldn't set too much store by Raoul's temper. It flares up, then subsides just as quickly. And I'm a big boy. I can deal with Raoul's tantrums. Also, it won't do him any harm to realize he's not the only kid on the block.'

Despite her anxiety and nervousness Natasha laughed. 'It's so funny hearing you use American expressions,' she said, smiling, more relaxed now that she had opened up to this man whom she was fast considering to be a good friend.

'I like them. They are most descriptive. But, coming back to the subject at hand, *chère amie*, I would not be surprised if Raoul isn't angry because he has stronger feelings for you than he intended.'

'Do you really think so?' Natasha looked across at him doubtfully. Raoul's behaviour hadn't led her to believe anything except that he wanted his cake and to eat it.

'I cannot be certain, but I think there's a good chance.'

'Well, whatever it is will have to wait,' she said, gazing down into her glass. 'I'm off to England for a few days. I need to settle my affairs there if I'm coming to live permanently in France.'

'Of course you must. Also, getting away will allow you to get a better perspective of the situation.'

'Gaston, there is no situation. Just a hot and heavy physical attraction that got out of hand. I think the sooner I realize that the better it will be for all concerned.'

Gaston shrugged. 'As you wish. Of course only time will tell, *ma chère*.'

That night, as she lay tucked under the covers listening to the wind and rain buffeting the Manoir's solid stone walls, Natasha thought back to every incident she'd experienced since coming to France: her first meeting with Raoul in the field, followed by her grandmother's sudden death—and her new life. It was all very bewildering that, in the space of a few days, her life had taken such a radical change of direction.

She sighed, letting her mind rest for just a moment on the incredible lovemaking of earlier this evening. They could so easily have been caught *in flagrante*. She smiled in the dark, wondering what Henri would have said and done had he walked in on them. Then, turning on her side, she closed her eyes and tried not to wonder where Raoul was precisely at this moment and go to sleep instead.

It was odd walking into her old flat in South Kensington, for now it formed part of another era of her existence. She had contacted the offices of the organization she'd worked for in Africa and regretfully handed in her resignation several days previously, but there were still a number of issues to be dealt with.

As she flipped through the post lying on the floor behind the front door Natasha realized that she felt no nostalgia. Not that she'd ever spent much time here, she admitted, sitting down at the small dining table and depositing the pile of envelopes there while she glanced around the place. It had been more of a *pied à terre* than anything else—a place to drop off stuff, and pick up mail.

An address, but never a home.

She had sold the home near Oxford that had belonged to her parents shortly after the accident, knowing she couldn't bear to live there among the memories. Now she realized that everything that had occurred had conspired to prepare her for the huge change that was about to set her life into a tailspin. Even the lease on this flat was practically up, as though it too was ready to move on and fit in with her new life and plans.

Tonight she would stay home and answer some of the mail, and then she'd begin clearing out the apartment, Natasha decided, pulling her hair back into a ponytail. Then later she would pop down the road to the small Italian restaurant that she'd used to frequent whenever she was in town and say hello to Mamma Gina, the owner. Surprisingly, the restaurant was one of the few things she'd truly miss, she realized, opening the hall cupboard and grimacing at the mess inside: old backpacks, sandals, windbreakers and sunhats—all the stuff she'd needed in her previous life which now seemed so remote. Perhaps she should make up a big parcel and send it all to the Salvation Army.

Bracing herself for an afternoon of sorting, Natasha entered the kitchen and took out two large plastic rubbish bags.

'Better get on with it,' she muttered to herself, rolling up her sleeves. No time like the present.

'What do you mean, she's left?' Raoul snapped down the phone.

'Just as I said, Monsieur le Baron,' Henri answered patiently. '*Mademoiselle* said that she was leaving for a few days.'

'Did she say where she was going?' There was a moment's hesitation. 'Well? Come on, man,' he urged impatiently, 'where is she?'

'I am not at liberty to say.'

'Not at— What on earth do you mean, Henri? This is *me* you are talking to you, not some stranger.'

'I know, Monsieur le Baron,' Henri replied uncomfortably. 'But *mademoiselle* gave special orders not to disclose her whereabouts.'

'I quite understand. Quite right. Can't have strangers knowing all one's moves. So where is she?'

'Monsieur le Baron, I have just told you that I am not permitted to say.'

All at once the penny dropped, and Raoul sat up straighter behind the desk. 'Are you saying,' he asked deliberately, 'that *mademoiselle* left specific orders not to tell *me* where she was going?'

'That's it, sir.' Henri was obviously relieved that Raoul had finally understood. 'She was quite adamant about it.'

'She was, was she? Thank you, Henri.'

He laid the phone back in its cradle, leaned back thoughtfully in the deep leather office chair and twiddled his Mont Blanc pen. So she was running away. Had had the nerve to give orders not to disclose her whereabouts.

'Ha!' He let out a harsh humourless laugh. As if he was interested in her damn whereabouts. The woman had a nerve. Hadn't he immediately left for Paris after her abominable behaviour the other day? Hadn't he made it clear when he'd departed that he wanted nothing more to do with her?

Perhaps, he admitted, letting the chair swing back to its normal position, but it still didn't explain why he couldn't get the wretched creature out of his mind. Her image haunted him. And to make matters worse he'd been out with three different girls, each one prettier than the other, and had deposited all three of them on their doorsteps by eleven in the evening, aware that he had no desire to make love with any of them.

Things were bad when it came to such a pass.

And something must be done.

Urgently.

As far as he was concerned there was only one way of dealing with these *affaires de coeur*. Once you were bitten you had to live it out. He needed to find Natasha, persuade her to go off with him—say to the Caribbean for a couple of weeks—and make love to her endlessly to satisfy the yearning he was experiencing. After that, once he'd had her in every way he'd been imagining for the past few days and nights, he would be over it and would be able to resume his existence without further disturbance.

The only problem with this most laudable plan was that A: he had to get Natasha to co-operate—though he didn't doubt that with a little persuading he could manage that—and B: he hadn't a clue where to locate her.

'Merde alors!' he exclaimed, rising and pacing the large high-ceilinged office like a caged leopard. Imagine disappearing in this unusual manner and then having the nerve to leave specific instructions not to inform him. *Him!* It was unheard of. No sooner had he turned his back on her than she was up to something. Well, not for long, he vowed, an idea shaping in his fertile brain.

Stopping in front of the desk, he picked up the phone and dialled.

'Hello, Gaston, *comment vas-tu*?'

'Very well. And you? Are you here?'

'No, I'm in Paris. But I'll be back at the Château in a few hours. Doing anything tonight?'

'Nothing special.'

'Then how about a bite of dinner?'

'Sounds good, *mon ami*. Where?'

'At my place,' Raoul responded, taking a sudden decision. He wanted to be on home turf for the conversation he was going to have later that evening.

Of that he had no doubt.

CHAPTER FIFTEEN

'WELL, well— Santa Maria, that is an amazing tale you just told me.' Mamma Gina wiped her hands on her red and white checkered apron, took a sip of the wine she'd brought to the table and shook her head, her black and grey curls bobbing.

'I'll miss you, Mamma Gina. In fact, you and the restaurant are the only things I'll miss. London was never my home. None of my friends are here—or not permanently anyway.'

'But of course you are correct to go back to your family's rightful home,' Mamma Gina exclaimed, shocked that Natasha could have doubted for a moment that she had taken the right decision. 'It is your blood—*la sangue*. It is more important than anything. The rest—bah! That is unimportant. Now all you need is to find a good man and settle down in this nice home your grandmother left you and have lots of *bambini*.'

Natasha laughed and shook her head. 'I don't think that's likely to happen any time soon, Mamma Gina,' she replied, smiling.

'But why not? Are these Frenchemen blind as well as crazy? Look at you, *una bella ragazza*, in the flower of youth, ready for marriage. Why, of course you will find a husband soon.'

'Frankly, I'm not looking for one.'

'You say that because you are still angry about Mr Paul,' Mamma Gina said, eyes narrowed and shaking her head wisely. 'He was no good for you.' She gave a demonstrative wave of her hand, relegating the infamous Paul to the past. 'I never like him. He very, very selfish. Not good for you. But you must keep open your heart, Natasha.'

'That's not easy when all the men I meet merely want to go to bed with me and then drop me like a hot potato,' she said with a touch of bitterness, her mind racing back to Raoul and his insupportable behaviour.

'Ah.' Mamma Gina nodded wisely and wagged her finger. 'So there is someone after all.'

'No, there isn't,' she responded, a little too quickly.

'*Eh, va bene.* As you wish.' Mamma Gina rolled her eyes and sighed gustily. 'I don't ask any more questions. When you're ready to tell me you will tell me.' Then she got up and grinned widely. 'Now, you will eat some of Mamma Gina's pasta, *sì*? You look too thin. I think they don't feed you properly in France.'

She bustled off to the kitchen to see to the preparation of the pasta and Natasha leaned back in the booth and sipped her wine, remembering Gaston's words at dinner. It was true that being out of a situation allowed one to view it more clearly. And it was becoming abundantly clear to her that, however painful, she simply must cut Raoul out of her life before he hurt her too badly. The realization that her feelings for him were far stronger than she had at first imagined came as a shock. How had it happened? How had this whole episode transformed from mere attraction into…?

Love?

Natasha set her glass down so sharply that a few drops of wine spilled on to the checkered tablecloth. Surely she must be imagining this. The feelings she had for Raoul were tempestuous, and they ranged from anger to deep attraction to wondering whether he'd got over the slight cold he'd had when they'd last met. But surely that didn't mean…?

She must definitely banish him once and for all from her existence, she realized, relieved that she'd left Henri instructions not to divulge her whereabouts. She needed time to think, to decide exactly how she would act. But that was almost impossible since Raoul was so erratic.

The main thing, Natasha reflected anxiously, hastily composing her features as Mamma Gina came out of the kitchen door with a plate piled high with spaghetti Carbonara, was to avoid him at all costs. That way, whatever damage had already been done to her heart would be limited.

She hoped.

'Was there a specific reason for you inviting me here to dine?' Gaston asked, coming directly to the point as he accepted a whisky from Raoul and sat in the deep sofa opposite the fire.

'Why would you imagine that?' Raoul queried, eyes narrowed as he leaned against the huge stone mantel.

'Just a gut feeling. I know you very well, *mon ami*. Remember, we've been through a lot together since we were children. I know how you operate.'

'Operate?'

'Exactly. Let's not beat about the bush, Raoul. You invited me here tonight because you don't know where Natasha is and it's driving you crazy.'

'Rubbish.' Raoul stood straighter to disguise his discomfort at his friend's astute summing-up of his motives for inviting him over.

'Isn't that it? Come, come, *cher ami*, this is you and I talking. No need to keep up the façade between old friends.'

'Old friends,' Raoul mused, staring into his glass. 'Yes, we are, aren't we? Yet our ancestors were mortal enemies. All because of another Natasha, to whom this one is related.' His eyes met his friend's full-on. 'I would hate for our friendship to end up in a similar manner. All because of a woman.'

'Are you implying that I'm trying to court Natasha?' Gaston said, an edge to his voice.

'Why not? You've taken her out to dinner; she's a very attractive woman. You know that I'm not interested.'

'Do I?' he challenged. 'Or do you, the Baron, still expect me, the mayor, to ask for your permission to court a woman he considers his? In other words, it's all right if you don't want her any more? I thought *droit de seigneur* went out of fashion with the Revolution.'

'Don't be absurd, and stop pokering up in that ridiculous manner,' Raoul muttered, realizing he'd insulted his friend. 'I meant nothing of the sort. I know you're not the kind of man to undermine his friends.'

'In that case you should know very well that I would never court Natasha, and this conversation shouldn't be taking place,' Gaston said, slightly appeased. 'But you are the one being ridiculous. You are crazy about her, and guess what?' he murmured smugly, taking a long sip. 'I know where she is.'

'Damn it, why did she disappear like that all of a sudden?' Raoul burst out. 'She won't tell me where she's gone. I can't make head nor tail of it. Women,' he exclaimed, rolling his eyes and shaking his head. 'Always complicating what is perfectly simple.'

'I fail to see how Natasha's leaving for a few days complicates anything. Besides, as she pointed out, it's really none of your business.'

Raoul stiffened. 'She said that?'

'Loud and clear.'

'Well, *ça alors*,' he huffed. 'None of my business, indeed. What does she mean by that?'

'Exactly what she said.'

'But I'm her neighbour. I might have a problem between the estates which could require me getting in touch with her urgently. I might—'

'Raoul, are you listening to what you're saying?'

Raoul stopped suddenly, realizing that what he was saying was indeed absurd. Shaking his head, he raised his hands with a shrug and gave in. 'Okay, I admit I've missed her, wondered where she is.'

'Ah, that's better. And, for the record, having deeper feelings for a woman isn't a crime.'

'Who says I have deeper feelings for Natasha? I don't. Remember, she's a Saugure. They betrayed my family once already.'

'If you call giving up your virginity to save the man you love more than life a betrayal,' Gaston remarked sardonically. 'Personally, I would rather have thought of it as heroism. But there, of course, we differ.'

'Because it was *your* ancestor she slept with,' Raoul retorted, casting Gaston a dark look from under his thick brows.

'Raoul, grow up, for goodness' sake. We live in the twenty-first century, not in the midst of the French Revolution. Times were different then. Surely you can understand what was really behind the way those two men interacted?'

'Well, yes, of course I can. Regis was a fool in part, I suppose.'

'A complete fool, who threw away his and Natasha's happiness out of misplaced pride. Just as my ancestor was a bastard who should never have taken advantage of a desperate woman in such a manner. But let's stay in the present. What are your intentions towards the present Natasha?'

'My intentions?' Raoul looked up, surprised. 'What intentions? I like her a lot, that's all. *Ni plus ni moins.*' He shrugged.

'Strange, I had the impression that perhaps you felt more for her than you wish to admit.'

'Put it this way,' Raoul said carefully, swirling his whisky before taking a long sip. 'I'm interested enough to want to know where she is and with whom.'

'*Where* I may be able to help you with. *With whom* I have no idea. Probably on her own, from what I gathered.'

'I see. Did she prohibit you from enlightening me about her destination?' There was a glint in Raoul's eyes as he spoke.

'Not at all. She is in London, tying up some details from her former life and closing her flat.' Gaston threw his arm over the back of the sofa and observed his friend. He could read the conflict, the antagonistic war of pride and emotion. Ah, Raoul. When would he forget the past and wake up to the present?

'Thank you, *mon ami*. I feel relieved to know she is safe. Do you have her address and number, by any chance?'

'Since I was pretty sure that this was why you asked me here tonight, I went to the trouble of writing it down.' Gaston's eyes were filled with understanding mischief as he took a slip of paper from his breast pocket and handed it over. '*Voiçi, mon ami.* Make good use of it.'

Raoul accepted the paper and glanced at it a moment. 'Be sure that I will. *Merci.*'

CHAPTER SIXTEEN

STARING at the pile of boxes filling the small living room, Natasha leaned against the bookcase and took stock of her handiwork. Practically all her former possessions were packed away. She glanced at her watch. The storage company she'd hired would be here to take them away in half an hour. After that there would be little left to do except give the place a final go-over and hand the keys back to the estate agents.

As she was about to put the last items inside the one remaining open box, the doorbell rang. Gosh, the movers had come early.

She hastened to open the door, and a quick gasp escaped her.

'Paul,' she exclaimed, bewildered. 'What on earth are you doing here?' She took an instinctive step backwards.

'Hi. I was in the area and thought I'd drop in, see what you're up to these days.'

'Well, I'm fine,' she responded warily. 'Actually, I'm in the middle of moving.'

'Leaving this place, are you?' He leaned casually against the doorjamb and smiled cheekily at her. He looked unkempt and scruffy, and not for the first time Natasha asked herself what she'd seen in him.

'Paul, I really don't know what you're doing here or why you bothered to come,' she said pulling herself together. 'You left fast enough last time, if I remember rightly.'

'Still sore about that, are you?' He reached up and tweaked her hair.

Natasha pulled back abruptly. 'Look, I'm afraid you'll have to leave now. I have the movers coming in a few minutes.'

'Hoity-toity. Back to our aristocratic little self, are we? Always thought you were better than everyone else at uni, didn't you?'

'Paul, don't be ridiculous. Just go away and leave me alone. I'm busy, and we really have nothing left to say to each other.'

'Says who?' He stood straighter. Suddenly he was looming over her, leering down at her, and Natasha realized he was drunk. Fear shot through her. She was here alone. What if—?

At that moment Paul reached down and yanked her towards him.

'Stop it!' she cried, pushing her hands against his chest. 'Leave me alone and go away. You have no right to come here.'

'Now, now, don't get snotty with me, Miss Smarty-pants. I'll show you who's in charge here.' He forced her against him and his mouth clamped down on hers.

Natasha fought vainly, the futility of her plight all too clear. For although Paul was thin and lanky he was also strong and wiry, and there was little she could do to prevent his attack.

Raoul stood at the bottom of the stairwell and glanced at the piece of paper. Second floor.

It was only as he was climbing the stairs that he heard a scuffle and a muffled cry from above. Hastening his step, he took the stairs three at a time. When he came across Natasha struggling in a man's arms his reaction was quick and thorough. He grabbed the man by the scruff of his T-shirt collar and yanked him off her so fast that Paul didn't know what had hit him. In another swift and accurate move he sent him rolling down the stairs.

'Didn't you hear the lady?' Raoul enquired icily of the whimpering creature lying prostrate on the landing below. 'Now, get out, and don't ever come back—*salop*.'

Then he turned and eyed Natasha, who stood shaking in the doorway. She looked very young and vulnerable in an old T-shirt and faded jeans, tennis socks and a ponytail. 'Are you okay?' Raoul asked, frowning. He wanted to move forward, take her in his arms and make sure she was all right, but something stopped him. 'Who is that bastard?' he demanded.

'My old boyfriend,' she whispered.

'Ah.' Raoul nodded, came inside and, taking her arm, led her into the living room where he sat her down on the sofa. 'I'll get you a drink. Do you have anything here?'

'No, just water.'

'Right.' He moved quickly towards the kitchen and poured her a glass.

'Drink this,' he commanded.

Too shocked to do otherwise, Natasha did as she was told. The water soothed her. 'I don't know why he turned up here today. I haven't seen him for years, and then suddenly out of the blue, on the day I'm moving, he appears.'

'In France we say that bad grass—*les mauvaises herbes*—has a habit of popping up when least wanted,' he answered dryly, looking down at her, his eyes filled with concern. So this was the bastard who'd hurt her. Now he wished he'd taught him even more of a lesson.

Sitting next to her, Raoul slipped an arm around Natasha's shoulders. 'Now, calm down, *ma petite*. It's all over. He won't be back any time soon.'

'No. Thanks to you, I don't think he will,' she agreed, a shy smile hovering as she turned and looked at him.

'Thanks for what you did. But how did you know I was here?' She frowned, remembering her instructions to Henri.

'Oh, I have my ways and means of finding things out when necessary,' he said, touching her cheek and smiling down at her. 'Now, tell me, what is all this packing?'

'I'm leaving this flat and the movers should be here any minute.'

'And where do you plan to go tonight?' he enquired, interested.

'I don't know. Actually, I hadn't really thought about it. I—'

Raoul pulled out his cellphone and rose to his feet, punching in numbers as he did so. 'Is that the Berkeley? Peter—good afternoon. I'll need you to reserve a suite on the same floor as mine. It's for Mademoiselle de Saugure. Yes, we'll be arriving in a couple of hours. You do have one available? Perfect.' He ended the call. 'Well, that's settled. No need to worry about accommodation.'

'Raoul, I never said I wanted to go to the Berkeley,' she protested, torn between annoyance and amusement at his high-handed manner.

'Why not? It's a perfectly respectable establishment, I assure you.'

'I'm very well aware that it's a perfectly respectable establishment, but that's not the point—'

'Then what is?' he asked, eyes dark as he drew her up into his arms. 'Is there somewhere else you'd prefer to go? If so, tell me and I shall cancel everything, *chérie*. Your wish is my command.'

'I give up,' Natasha exclaimed, rolling her eyes and glancing again at the boxes. 'Raoul, I really have to get this finished.'

'Fine. Then I shall sit here and watch you.'

'Couldn't I just meet you later? I'll grab a cab when they've gone.'

'And risk having that creep return? *Non, non.* No way can I permit that. I shall stay, whether you like it or not. I'm afraid you're stuck with me.'

'Oh, very well.' Natasha let out a sigh and, realizing she must finish off quickly, got down to the task of checking every last drawer, nook and cranny where some item might have been forgotten. She was conscious of Raoul in the room, conscious of how physical he made her feel. How was it that just the feeling of Paul close to her had caused nothing but repugnance and disgust, yet Raoul's closeness sent delicious shivers running through her?

Several minutes later two burly men arrived from the moving company, and soon there was nothing left in the apartment but a few memories, most of which she had no regrets at leaving behind.

'Right. I'm ready to go,' Natasha said, turning to Raoul.

'Are you sure? No regrets at leaving this part of your life behind you?'

'Actually, no. It was time.'

'Good. Then let's get going.'

Placing his hand lightly at her elbow, and picking up her duffle bag in the other, Raoul steered her out, and she locked the door behind her for the last time.

CHAPTER SEVENTEEN

HARRY'S BAR was packed that evening, but of course Raoul had been kept one of the best tables in the corner, from where they had a full view of the restaurant.

Natasha noticed several notables, one famous rock star and two royals, seated not far from them. It amused her how everyone treated Raoul so deferentially. No wonder he was so sure of himself. He took it all for granted, as though it was his right. Perhaps he wasn't so different from Regis after all, she reflected, hiding a half-smile as she studied him from behind the menu while a little voice inside told her to take heed of this last thought. Regis had deprived her ancestor of true happiness, thanks to his insufferable pride. It would be too easy for his descendant to do the same.

Telling herself not to imagine things, Natasha concentrated on the choice of dishes, deciding on potted shrimp followed by Dover sole. A bit fishy, perhaps, but two things she loved and would not be having in France. Not that she planned to abandon England; in fact, the thought of acquiring a small flat here had occurred to her.

But not now. Later, maybe.

Right now she needed to focus on getting the estate into good order and enjoying the flat in Paris and the villa in Eze that her grandmother had bequeathed her.

Once they had ordered Raoul seemed more relaxed, as though he'd dealt with an important issue and could now focus on her. She noted that whatever or whoever he focused on was given his full attention. She was, Natasha realized ruefully, taking an awful lot of notice of Raoul d'Argentan's habits.

'So. You like Harry's Bar?' he asked, slipping his hand proprietorially over hers.

'I think it's delightful. I've never been here before. My father and I always used to go to the Savoy Grill together.'

'Ah, an excellent choice. But without your father it is not as charming as it used to be?'

'No. I decided not to go back. I'd rather keep the memories intact.'

'You are right. It is always better so. *Le passé* is the *passé* and should stay that way.'

'You haven't ever spoken to me of your past,' she remarked, discreetly removing her hand from his.

'You mean my childhood?' He raised his brow and smiled, that same intense smile that left her swallowing and taking a quick sip of the delicious Pouilly-Montrachet that the sommelier had poured them.

'Yes. What was it like growing up in a fortress?'

'No different than growing up anywhere else, I imagine.'

'Surely it must have been. Not many people have that opportunity. It's a very different life, after all.'

'Different from what? How would I know the difference? I never lived anywhere else,' he said with a nonchalant shrug.

'No. I don't suppose you would see the difference,' she said dryly, thinking of all the children she'd looked after in Africa and their deprived backgrounds.

As though reading her thoughts, he responded, 'That does not mean that I am not aware that I have been very privileged to be born with—what is it you call it in English?—a silver spoon in my mouth?'

'Something like that.'

'My mother was very conscious of making me aware of

my good fortune. That is why I have many friends in the village. People like Gaston, for instance. We went to the village school together until we were twelve.'

'What happened after that?'

'I went to L'Ecole des Roches. It is a prestigious boarding school. The equivalent of your Eton.'

'And Gaston?'

'He came too.'

'Really?'

'My parents insisted that we both have a similar opportunity in life. My father paid his school fees.'

'That was nice of him.'

'Nice? I don't know about nice. It was the right thing to do. Gaston was a far better student than I ever was. He deserved the opportunity. He is a very bright man. But apparently you know that, as you have seen quite a lot of one another, *n'est-ce-pas*?'

'I wouldn't say a lot, but some,' she demurred, realizing he was fishing and determined not to fall into the trap.

'Don't you find him charming?' Raoul's eyes bored through her as though he were searching her soul.

'I find him a very nice man. I think he's a good friend. Well, you should know that.'

'Yes, he is. But there is no friendship where a woman is concerned.'

'What do you mean?' She stiffened.

'Merely that when a man and a woman are interested in one another, friendship often falls by the wayside.' He drank, peered at her over the rim of his glass, studying her closely.

'Is that what you think?'

'Yes. It is.'

'Perhaps you should be more trusting,' she replied coldly, 'and not underestimate people. And if you're implying that Gaston made a pass at me you'd be making a big mistake. Not that it's any of your business,' she added, taking a deep breath and looking stonily at her plate. Gosh, the man had a way of getting on her wrong side.

'Now, now, *ma chère* Natasha, don't get upset with me. I wasn't implying anything at all.' His hand strayed towards hers once more but she slipped it neatly under the table. 'Are you cross with me?' He tilted his head with a disarming smile.

'I'm not cross, Raoul, just fed up with you always trying to manipulate people and situations.'

'*Moi?* Manipulate?' He looked honestly shocked and she could have laughed out loud at his outraged expression.

'Yes. You like to organize everyone and everything around you like pawns on a chessboard.'

'*Vraiment!* That is ridiculous. I am the most tolerant of persons. Why, I am all for liberty and—'

'Fraternity and equality?' she teased, laughing, unable to stop herself. 'Why, Raoul, don't you think it's time you did a reality check?'

'Now you tease me,' he said, seeing her eyes filled with mirth. Why, this woman was not only lovely and sexy and delicious, she was intelligent too. The thought was somewhat discomforting. He avoided intelligent women on principle. Janine, he recalled, echoes of the past hovering, had been highly intelligent. And much good it had done him.

'Sorry, just having a little fun at your expense.'

'Be my guest, *ma chère*, I have a sense of humour.'

'Yes, you do.' And it's one of the things I so like about you, she thought regretfully as the waiter placed the potted shrimp and buttered brown bread on the table.

'I don't know how you eat those things,' Raoul remarked as he cut a morsel of warm *foie gras*.

'It's typically English and I won't get much of it in France, I suppose.'

'Natasha, should you desire it I will have a shipment delivered immediately to the Manoir.' He reached for her hand and raised her fingers to his lips.

'I don't think I'm that desperate for potted shrimp,' she replied, laughing. The atmosphere, the companionship and the smooth wine were all setting her more at ease than she ever could have imagined.

The dinner progressed in this same vein, with light banter and amusing small talk, the comings and goings of elegant fellow diners, the bustle of efficient waiters and waitresses serving one delicious dish after the other. Soon they had finished dessert and were ready for coffee.

'How about having coffee and an after-dinner drink back in one of our suites?' he said, suddenly smiling.

'Why not?' she replied, liking the idea.

Moments later, as Raoul summoned the waiter for the bill, she began having second thoughts. Perhaps it wasn't a good idea. She was asking for trouble. She should avoid situations that—

All of a sudden Natasha pulled herself up with a jolt.

Damn all her sensible reasoning. Who was she trying to fool? She wanted the man, didn't she? Was more than half-way in love with him. And if the truth be told she knew that she would spend tonight in his arms. It would be the last time she allowed herself to do so. Forget rational thinking for tonight, she ordered herself, and enjoy it.

If only for a while.

CHAPTER EIGHTEEN

AS THEY stepped out of the car at the hotel the night air felt cool against her skin, and for a moment Natasha shivered. What she was about to do was unlike anything she'd ever done before. Except with Raoul, she admitted, remembering their time at the cottage. But she'd never *consciously* decided to make love with a man. Particularly knowing that it was not a serious relationship; that there was no commitment.

'Are you cold?' he asked, slipping his arm protectively around her shoulders as they entered the lobby and walked up the few stairs to the elevator.

'I'm fine,' she answered, wishing it was true. All at once her stomach felt odd and her head dizzy. The scent of him so close, the feel of his arm around her and the protective aura of his presence seemed suddenly all too much. She was foolish to have allowed herself to get into this position again. For in the end she was the one who was going to get hurt. And the deeper she got in, the harder the fall and the more intense the pain would be.

As the elevator climbed to their floor Raoul looked down at her, sensing the tension. There was no pretence between them tonight. They both knew what they were about to do. And he liked it that way, liked the fact that he now controlled the situation, and that they understood one another.

Game-playing was over.

It made matters so very much easier. Yet he felt something in her being that was not in entire accord with her decision. And, despite his desire to pay no attention, it bothered him.

'Is something wrong?' he asked finally as they walked down the corridor to his suite.

'No, everything's fine,' she lied.

'I don't think you're telling the truth, Natasha. Something bothers you.' He stopped, looked at her hard. 'If you are not happy, tell me,' he ordered, in that autocratic manner that made her smile.

'I'm fine, really.' She mustered a bright smile. After all it was she who had given the signal, she who had made up her mind. It was silly to spoil what she herself had opted for.

'Good.' He looked her over once more, then smiled back, banishing any doubt and concentrating on slipping the card key in the lock.

'Shall we skip coffee and have a drink?' he suggested, taking off his jacket and slipping it over the back of a chair.

'Great.' Natasha sat down on the sofa, slipping off her pashmina, determined to feel at ease and sophisticated, as though she did this all the time. She thought fleetingly of her friend Melina, who dated different men constantly and had no problem enjoying sex with them. Why couldn't she just think of it like that? As a moment of pleasure.

But as she watched him prepare two brandies, she had to force herself not to experience a rush of something so deep and so intense that it made her feel faint. She swallowed. How had this man managed to captivate her as she was sure he had so many others—women he then dropped as soon as he'd had his fill of them?

Stop it.

Angry with herself, Natasha forced another bright smile and patted the sofa invitingly.

He didn't need to be asked twice.

Raoul sat next to her and, after placing the brandies on the coffee table before them, wasted no time in taking her into his arms.

Ah, she was delicious, he reflected, lowering his lips slowly to hers, nibbling them, allowing his fingers to travel down her swan-like throat, trail lightly over the curve of her small yet full breasts, determined to enjoy the extent of what she was offering. Slipping his other hand into the small of her back, Raoul worked on her zipper and then the hook of her bra. When it gave way he let out a satisfied growl, and, slipping the dress off her shoulders, drew back to view his handiwork.

'*Ravissante,*' he muttered, enjoying the sight of her peaking breasts awaiting his attentions, her lips so sensual, just parted, her eyes full of expectation and that slight hesitation he found so terribly tantalizing. He leaned forward and gently pushed her back among the cushions, where she lay, hair splayed over crimson velvet. 'You are too beautiful, *chérie*,' he murmured, lowering his lips to her right breast, taking the nipple delicately between his teeth, satisfied when he heard her quick intake of breath. Tonight he was going to love her fully, as he'd be willing to bet she'd never been loved before.

Drawing back, he lifted a brandy snifter and, tilting it, allowed a few drops to fall on her breast. Then his tongue followed, flicking there. 'Delicious,' he murmured, reaching his fingers towards her other nipple, which he played with, using index finger, thumb and his tongue to drive her wild. He could feel her begin to writhe underneath him, feel the spiral of tension rising within her, knew she must be aching now between her thighs. And he continued slowly, patiently, determining the rhythm, allowing her no choice but to submit entirely to his whim.

'Ahh.' Natasha let out a small cry of pleasure as his

tongue and fingers worked magic. And this was just the beginning. She wasn't even fully undressed. He was just ravishing her breasts as though they alone were the pivotal point of his attention. When she could bear it no more, feeling the rush of damp heat burst between her thighs, an involuntary gasp escaped her and she clung to him, her nails digging into the back of his shoulders as though holding on for dear life, an indescribable pleasure ripping through her like a flash of hot lightning. Then, just as quickly, it eased, leaving ripples in its wake. But when she was about to sink back into the cushions she felt him slip her dress and stockings over her thighs. Soon she was lying naked before him.

'Ah, *ma* Natasha,' he murmured, his dark eyes filled with an expression so intense it affected her as much as his fingers. 'Look at you, how lovely, how beautifully you give yourself.' His fingers trailed over the soft white surface of her naked thighs, temptingly close but not quite touching the spot she was dying for him to reach. It was like a delicious torture, a taunting that she wanted to beg him to end yet delighted in. Then to her utter surprise he was kneeling on the floor, and instead of his fingers he lowered his lips to her.

Hands lacing his hair, Natasha cried out as his tongue found her, flicked her most vulnerable sensitive spot as cleverly he discovered her. Then, just as she thought this was more than she could bear, his fingers penetrated, bringing her to such unutterable completion that she shook, her whole body racked with indescribable bliss, her gratification such that all she could do was collapse, her fingers raking his hair, gasping.

Raoul rose and, sitting back on the sofa, took her into his arms.

'Ah, Natasha, you are so beautiful, so lovely, such a

complete woman. You were made to be loved by a man who can satisfy your desires. How is it that you waited so long to fulfil them?'

Unable to answer, she lay in his arms, basking in contentment, happy just to savour the moment and not think of anything except the delightful fulfilment she was experiencing. Never in her wildest dreams had she ever thought making love could be anything like this. Nothing, she realized, turning her face into his chest as a rush of tears came over her, could have prepared her for this.

'Are you all right, *ma chérie*?' he asked, stroking her hair with one hand while unbuttoning his shirt with the other.

She nodded silently, unable to speak, too afraid that if she did the spell would break and she would wake up from this wondrous dream.

Soon Raoul was naked too. She could feel his growing desire hard and tense against her thigh, and a new and intense stirring began. Was it possible that after all she'd just experienced she could feel the spiralling excitement quivering once again?

As though reading her thoughts, Raoul rose and lifted her in his arms. 'Time for the real thing,' he said, smiling down at her as he entered the dimmed bedroom and laid her on the large bed, its covers turned down.

Natasha knew it was her turn, that she should pleasure him as he had her. But Raoul didn't give her the chance. When she attempted to reach for him he removed her hand.

'Another time,' he whispered, placing himself on top of her. Parting her thighs, he braced his hands on each side of her and in one quick deep thrust entered her.

Again Natasha gasped, her hips reaching up to meet his. And once again he smiled down at her. 'Not so fast, *mon amour*. Lie back and enjoy. There is time enough for you to join me.' Then, as though by some miracle of witchcraft, he began making love to her slowly, rhythmically, determinedly, easing himself within her, seeking that crucial spot deep inside as though he knew every secret place within her. And Natasha obeyed him, lay back and allowed him to take her on a new incredible journey of discovery.

But suddenly she could bear it no more and, reaching up, she pulled him down on top of her, thighs curling about his hips, crying out for him as they joined in a frenzied, perfect coupling that intensified until all at once, together, they tumbled over the edge of a ragged cliff, gasping, crying with joy as they fell, limp and satisfied, in each other's arms among the rumpled sheets.

Several minutes passed before Raoul opened his eyes and realized he had Natasha pinned beneath him. He was finding it hard to digest the experience. Never in all these years and with all the women he'd been with—and God knew there had been a few—had he experienced anything quite like this. It was fantastic, but also troubling, and he sat up, withdrawing his arm and pulling the sheet over them.

'Are you cold?' he asked, for something to say to restore normality to a situation that, had he not been a down-to-earth, sensible man, he might have believed was magical.

'No,' she murmured, turning on her side, opening her eyes and looking at him in a way that left his already fast-beating pulse leaping.

This was ridiculous.

Absurd.

Usually once he'd made love with a woman he made an excuse to get into the shower and then leave. Yet here he was, unable to stop himself from leaning down and kissing her, stroking her hair, sinking back into the pillows and surrounding her with his arms, curling up against her and holding her close. 'Go to sleep, *ma mie*,' he murmured, giving way to temptation and breathing in the soft, enticing scent of her hair. 'Make sweet dreams.'

Natasha smiled sleepily into the pillow and slipped her hand over the one that was covering her breast. It felt so right, so warm, so wonderful.

And she wished it could last for ever.

CHAPTER NINETEEN

IT WAS autumn now and a panoply of multicoloured leaves carpeted the wide stone terrace that led from the front façade of the Manoir to the lawn.

Natasha stared out of the study window, unable to pin her thoughts down, unable to concentrate on the bills and accounts she'd had lying on the desk for several days now but which she seemed incapable of addressing.

There had been not a word from Raoul after their return from London. Then all at once he'd phoned and said he wanted to dine with her. Knowing she'd be signing her own death warrant if she accepted, Natasha had forced herself to refuse. She'd been off-hand, almost bored on the phone, leading him to believe that she was very busy and had little interest in his company.

But nothing could have been further from the truth. Not an hour passed without something sparking her memory, reminding her of the passion they'd shared, making her want to rush to the phone and say that she'd changed her mind. When he'd phoned her again, two days later, and asked if she'd like to join him in Paris for the Prix de l'Arc de Triomphe race at Longchamps, she'd wavered. Surely it wouldn't be so bad just to see him? After all, it was a day event, with other people. Surely she could handle that?

Now, with dusk gathering, she rose and went into the hall. Henri and his wife were out for the day and the house was empty. Natasha switched on the hall lights. She really must do something about the lighting in this place. The electricity was dicey at best. As though divining her thoughts, two bulbs on the immense chandelier looming over her suddenly popped. She sighed and headed for the stairs, lit by the glow of the picture lamps. As she placed her foot on the first step Natasha stared towards the top of the stairs and drew in her breath.

Surely she must be dreaming.

There, descending the stairs and coming towards her, was the same delicate outlined image she'd seen once before. But this time it was clear. She could distinguish the pale blue hue of the satin dress, the sparkle of something at the woman's throat. It was as if her ancestor was trying to speak to her, to convey some important message. But what?

Natasha stood in a trance for what felt like minutes, and when her thoughts cleared she stared intently up at her namesake's image, straining to hear her thoughts across the centuries. She looked closer at the portrait and it was as if the woman smiled down at her, encouraging her to listen to a message Natasha couldn't hear.

It made no sense, Raoul reasoned. Hadn't they made love incredibly that night in London? Hadn't they slept together for the rest of the night? Breakfasted together next morning? Then what was the matter with the woman? It was a pity he had been so damn busy, having to make a quick trip to New York and then spend some time in Paris, or he would have already gone over to the Manoir to demand an explanation from Natasha as to why she was behaving so oddly.

Surely they now had an affair going on? One, he admitted, that had both its conveniences and inconveniences. On the one hand it was good to know that she was cloistered at the Manoir, unlikely to be going out with anyone else.

On the other, she was still his neighbour and the whole thing must be dealt with in a manner which would allow them to extract themselves from the relationship when the time came without too much long-term collateral damage.

Now, as he drove thoughtfully up the motorway, Raoul reflected hard on these matters. She still hadn't said if she was coming with him to the Prix de l'Arc de Triomphe or not. Which gave him a perfect excuse to pop over in a friendly manner to enquire. Yes, he decided as he headed down a country road, that was what he would do. He wouldn't phone, but would go over personally instead tomorrow and test the terrain.

Satisfied that he'd come up with the optimal solution, Raoul drove into the courtyard of his Château, realizing that he was hungry and looking forward to dinner. For an instant as he slipped out of the car he felt a sense of loneliness. There was never anyone special to receive him when he got home at night. Not that this fact had ever bothered him in the past. He shook his head, frowned, and waved to Jean, hurrying towards him.

'*Bonsoir*, Jean.'

'*Bonsoir*, Monsieur le Baron. Did you have a good drive from Paris?'

'*Oui, merci,* Jean. Everything is fine. Any news around here?'

'Well, nothing much.' Jean rubbed his forehead thoughtfully. 'Oh, there was the inauguration of the new organ in the church, of course.'

'New organ? In the church? But how is that possible?' He stopped in his tracks.

'Mademoiselle de Saugure gave the church a new organ in memory of her grandmother, sir. There was a ceremony and a fête in the village. Everybody went.'

Raoul stood still, completely taken aback, then experienced a moment's anger. He had received no invitation to any inauguration, either from the Curé or Natasha. Plus, the Argentans always dealt with church matters.

'Right,' he said, heading towards the door and entering his domain. What the hell was she playing at?

He entered his office, switched on the desk lamp and flipped through his mail absently. The third envelope was an invitation. He opened it. There it was. An invitation to the inauguration. Sent as though he was some *inconnu*, some unknown. She should have personally telephoned him, told him of her plan, found out if it was suitable for her to take such action and gone to the trouble of seeking him out, making sure he was part of the activity. Instead she was treating him in this high-handed manner, as though she owned the damn church.

Well, he wasn't having it.

Turning abruptly on his heel Raoul grabbed an old jacket lying on the chair and marched purposefully back towards the car. Minutes later he was entering the gates of the Manoir and heading up the drive.

When the doorbell clanged Natasha was upstairs, still pondering her strange sensations in front of her ancestor's portrait. Suddenly she became conscious of the ringing bell. Who on earth could it be at this time? She glanced at her watch. It was actually only seven-thirty, but because it got dark much quicker now she was less conscious of the hour.

Making her way down the main stairway, Natasha cast a quick glance up at the portrait. But that was all it was now. A static picture of a late-eighteenth-century woman.

In the hall she reached for the big lock and pulled it back, realizing too late that perhaps she should have found out first who was out there. After all, she was alone in the house. But it was too late for that now.

'Raoul,' she exclaimed in surprise, her pulse leaping.

'Yes. As you see.'

His thunderous expression made her wonder what had upset him. 'Well, I suppose you'd better come in,' she said.

'If it wouldn't be too much trouble,' he replied sardonically.

'I didn't know you were back,' she murmured, letting him past.

'I got back a few minutes ago.'

'I see. Then you must be in need of a drink.'

Raoul ground his teeth and watched her. She seemed calm, cool and collected, and very sure of herself. Not like the woman he'd held quivering in his arms a few weeks ago.

'Yes, a drink would be most acceptable,' he muttered, removing his jacket and flinging it on one of the hall chairs.

'Good, then we'll go to the *petit salon*. I find it's the warmest place in the house. The weather has become quite chilly lately, don't you find?' she commented politely, leading the way into the sitting room.

'Natasha, I did not come here to talk about the damn weather,' Raoul exploded from the doorway.

'No? Then what exactly did you come to talk about, Raoul?' Natasha'a brow flew up in a manner that he was unused to.

'I came here to talk about this—this inauguration in the church that you had the nerve to go ahead with without my authority.'

'Excuse me?' Natasha stood her ground and crossed her arms. 'Did you say *authority*?'

'Yes. You had the impertinence to arrange the inauguration of a new organ to the church, something that has been an Argentan tradition for centuries, without so much as a by-your-leave.'

'Well, if it's an Argentan tradition to help with the

church organ, you haven't been attending to it,' she said simply. 'The organ was in an appalling state of disrepair. The poor organist could barely squeeze out a decent hymn.'

'Then it was up to the Curé to tell me.'

'Apparently he's tried several times. But you were always too busy or away. And, as you rarely attend any services in the church, you haven't had the opportunity to hear for yourself,' she responded sweetly. 'Whisky?'

'Yes,' he snapped. 'But that has nothing to do with—'

'Ice?' she interrupted in the same tone.

'No, damn it, water.'

'Good. Because I would have had to fetch the ice from the kitchen, since Henri has the day off,' she said conversationally.

'Natasha, will you stop these witless remarks and listen to what I have to say?' Raoul demanded, his high cheekbones flushed with anger.

'Sorry, I thought I was. Now, you were telling me—or rather were about to tell me—why you had not been upholding your family's tradition properly, weren't you?'

He took two quick steps across the room and before she could stop him pulled her roughly into his arms. 'Stop it,' he ordered.

'Why?' She glared up at him, eyes blazing. 'Because Monsieur le Baron says so?'

'Yes, damn it. You have no right to come here and flaunt our customs. To—to—agh! I don't know how you say it in English.' He turned, threw his hands up and muttered something under his breath in French.

'Why don't you have your whisky and calm down?' Natasha said softly. 'There's no need for all this to-do, Raoul. If I've done something to offend you, I'm sorry. It wasn't my intention. But the organ was in desperate need of renewal and past repair. It seemed to make sense to give the church a new one that would be in place in time for the choir to practise its Christmas repertoire,' she said simply.

The logic of her words sank in. And all at once Raoul realized that he was acting in an inappropriate manner.

He turned, straightening his shoulders. 'It is the duty of the Baroness d'Argentan to attend to such matters,' he said haughtily, accepting the whisky from her. 'My mother was very attentive to such things.'

'I'm sure she was. Unfortunately she is not among us any more, or I'm sure there would have been no need for me to take this measure.'

'Well, I suppose *à la longue* it is for the best,' he muttered grudgingly. 'But I still want to pay for half the organ.'

'I'm sorry, but I've already dealt with it.'

'You cannot deny me that right. It would be a dishonour to the Argentan family if I was not known to have participated in the cost of the instrument. I—'

'Raoul, will you stop thinking that you live in the Middle Ages? Frankly, nobody could care less who paid for the organ. The parish is merely pleased to have the problem solved. The choirmaster is thrilled and Mademoiselle Boisier, who plays the organ, is delighted. I really don't see what you're making such a fuss about. And as for the cost—I can well afford it, thanks to my grandmother's generosity.'

'That is not the point. You don't understand,' he said, taking a long gulp of whisky and shaking his head. 'I told you earlier that you were usurping the place of the Baroness d'Argentan.'

'Really?' She crossed her arms and looked at him, her eyes steady.

'Yes. My mother, and my grandmother before her, were always in charge of attending to these church matters. It was their role. Now you come, a Saugure, and want to take over.'

'I have no such ambition,' she replied coldly, 'and as you are not attending properly to your duties then it is for me to do so.'

'No. It's not,' he snapped back. 'That is the duty of my wife.'

'I wasn't aware that you were married,' she retorted, turning to pour herself a glass of wine, her hand quivering.

Suddenly Raoul stopped dead in his tracks and realized what he'd just said.

My wife.

He'd never thought of having a wife. The idea of Camille de Longueville was nothing but a joke. He raised his eyes, watched Natasha carefully pouring the wine, and blinked.

Impossible.

He must be dreaming.

Of course he was.

Pulling himself together, Raoul stepped over to where she stood. 'Let me do that,' he said in a friendlier tone.

'Don't worry, it's done, thank you.' Natasha turned around and, avoiding him, went to sit down in the armchair, where there was no chance he could join her.

'I'm sorry if I lost my temper,' he said stiffly.

'Oh, that's fine.' She smiled briefly. 'I can see that it must be difficult to come to terms with several centuries worth of high-handedness, even though we do live in the twenty-first century.'

'I am not high-handed,' he replied deliberately. 'I merely carry out what is expected of me.'

'Quite so,' Natasha replied, hiding her smile behind her glass.

'And there is no need to snicker,' he reprimanded, seating himself opposite.

'I wasn't snickering. I merely find your attitudes amusing.'

'I am glad that I provide you with amusement, *mademoiselle*,' he said sardonically.

'Oh, Raoul, stop taking yourself so seriously,' she exclaimed, laughing despite an attempt to stay solemn. 'If you could see yourself, all pokered up and stiff! Why, I'll bet you look just like your ancestor Regis.'

Raoul looked across at her curiously. 'What prompted you to say that?' he asked, eyeing her closely.

'Nothing.' She shrugged her shoulders. She did not intend to share her recent strange, almost ghostly experience with him. 'Just the way you looked, I suppose, so proud and autocratic. It reminded me of what your ancestors must have been like.'

'I suppose they must have. After all, we have the same blood.'

'Precisely,' she murmured with a sigh. 'So, how long are you here for?'

'I don't know. I haven't made up my mind yet.'

Then, to her surprise, he rose, snapped the glass down on the small Louis Quinze table to his right and faced her. 'I have to go. I'll be in touch.'

With that he marched from the room before Natasha could react, and was out of the door with his jacket before she could do more than step into the hall.

'Well!' she exclaimed, standing with her glass as the front door reverberated behind him. 'If that doesn't beat all.'

CHAPTER TWENTY

RAOUL drove back to the Château at a furious pace. He was too stunned by the thought which had crossed his mind only minutes earlier. In fact, he'd nearly choked on his whisky it was so outrageous.

Marriage.

To think that he could even imagine such a thing as Natasha becoming his wife—when the whole world knew that Argentans and Saugures would never be joined by marriage after what had occurred two centuries earlier. It was so unimaginable as to leave him in shock. Something he had never before experienced.

On arrival at the Château he waved away Jean's offer of dinner, having lost his appetite, and headed back into his office. There he threw himself down on an ancient leather couch before the freshly built fire and stared doggedly into the flames. Then, almost surreptitiously, his eyes rose above the great stone mantel and he stared at the handsome portrait of Regis d'Argentan, standing stiff and proud in a wig and pearl satin, which had been there for as long as he could remember.

'This is all your fault,' he muttered, standing up and facing the painting.

'Yes, it is.'

Raoul stared ahead, but the portrait was exactly the same. Yet he could have sworn that a voice had answered him.

Spinning around, Raoul saw the deep burgundy velvet curtains flutter. The curtains never fluttered; they were too heavy.

'Who is there?' he said, wishing he was armed and realizing that he didn't have a revolver in the desk drawer, even if he could make it over there in time.

Raoul stood rooted to the spot, stunned. Surely he must be dreaming and this must be a figment of his imagination. Ever since he was a child he'd heard stories of the occasional apparition of his ancestors in the Château, but had never given them credence, always believed they were part of the folklore of the place. All good castles needed a ghost, after all.

Sitting down abruptly in an old tapestry chair by the fire, Raoul stared up at the portrait. Then he got up slowly from the chair and went and stood by the window. As his eyes adjusted to the dark he could distinguish the turret where the pennant flew. His family's colours and coat of arms. Was the spirit of Regis trying to tell him something? That it was time to bury the hatchet with the Saugures and finally unite the two families?

He turned back into the room and shook his head, thinking about Natasha, about the nights spent in her arms, about the extraordinary closeness and fulfilment he'd experienced with her, such as he had never known before.

At the thought of her his senses became aroused. Never had he shared such moments with any other woman. Perhaps Regis was right and he mustn't let her go. But still. He was his own master and would make his own decisions.

He was damned if he would be dictated to by a ghost.

CHAPTER TWENTY-ONE

THE racecourse at Longchamps was packed with everything from exotic hats in the private boxes to people in jeans and T-shirts come to bet on one of the biggest races of the year.

Natasha hadn't seen Raoul since the evening when he'd come over and departed so abruptly, and in the meantime she had taken the time to think.

However much it hurt, she must not accept less than everything. For that, she realized, was what she truly wanted from this man. Halfway measures just weren't enough. She wanted to be his wife and bear his children, never mind how odious he could be.

And that, she knew—had understood again from Gaston one evening over a drink—was impossible. The dice had been thrown all those years ago, and the same pride still haunted their lives today. So why had she accepted his invitation to come to the races? Because, as she'd told herself before, there was no danger here of them being on their own?

Probably that was the reason. After all, they were here in his box, with Gaston and his pretty new girlfriend, Victoire, and Raoul's charming cousin Madeleine and her husband Gerard.

'Do look at that amazing hat,' Madeleine said, nudging Natasha. The two women had immediately hit it off and were exchanging an amusing conversation together.

Natasha glanced at Raoul, who had raised his racing glasses the better to see the horses that were coming out for the next race, and thought how sad it was that the past prevented them sharing a future. Not that he'd ever indicated he wanted one, she was hasty to remind herself with a little sigh. He looked so divinely handsome in a dark grey double-breasted suit, his hair swept back in that nonchalant manner she had learned to love, his skin still bronzed from the summer sun, and those hands… Her eyes stopped there for a moment, her heart lurched, and again that warm tingling sensation gripped her. God, when she thought about the magic those hands were capable of arousing she shivered.

Quickly glancing the other way, she caught Madeleine peering carefully at her.

'Be careful of that one,' she murmured, smiling in the direction of her cousin. 'He's a wonderful man, and I love him dearly, but don't get caught in his web. It's too tricky.'

Natasha mumbled something incomprehensible and felt the colour rising to her cheeks just as Raoul turned and offered her his glasses. 'Look over there—the jockey in the green and pink shirt. That's number six, *Grand Amour*, the horse you bet on.'

'Is it really Grand Amour?' Madeleine whispered to him softly, for only him to hear.

Raoul turned and looked at her. 'Shut up, Madeleine, and stop talking rubbish.'

'Now, now, don't get snotty on me—I'm your cousin; I have a right to tease you whenever I feel like it.'

To his relief, Natasha, who was adjusting the glasses, did not overhear the interchange. But Madeleine's words left him troubled.

For several days now—in fact two weeks, to be exact—Raoul had been in a quandary. Never before had he experienced anything similar. Any other woman would have fallen at his feet at the drop of a hat, only too glad to be invited here, yet Natasha had left him dangling. At first he'd been annoyed, and had thought of ringing her and demanding an immediate response. Then he'd changed his mind and decided to bide his time. This was the first time he'd ever needed time to consider a situation with a woman.

His vision of Regis, and the message he'd sensed from his ancestor, had left its mark. But he was still damned if he would let a ghost dictate his future. He needed to follow his own instincts. Now, as he watched her standing next to him in the box, he suddenly wondered what it would be like to be without her. It was months since he'd broken up with Clothilde, and he hadn't had another steady relationship since. For some strange reason he hadn't wanted one.

Forcing his eyes back to the course, Raoul concentrated on the race that was about to begin. *Grand Amour* was well placed. Seconds later they were following the galloping horses, glad to be distracted.

It was a difficult concept to accept, Raoul admitted to himself later, after spending the better part of the night pacing his library. Difficult to come to terms with. But, like it or not, he must: he couldn't live without her.

It bothered him profoundly to know that he could have become so attached to another human being, so dependent. On the other hand, the knowledge that he could conceive of a lifelong commitment with any woman was so surprising it left him flabbergasted.

What he still didn't know—hadn't allowed himself to ponder too closely—was how Natasha felt about him. Oh, he knew she was attracted to him; that much was obvious. But what about the rest? It was, of course, an honour for any woman to be considered as a prospective candidate for the role of Baroness d'Argentan, he reminded himself. But was Natasha fully aware of precisely what an honour he was planning on bestowing upon her?

After several more minutes' debate Raoul decided there was only one way to find out. He would drive over to the Manoir and explain, carefully and methodically, so that she was fully aware of the facts, what was expected of her. Satisfied that he had come up with a well-thought-out, rational solution, Raoul went on his way.

She had no expectation of seeing him any time soon, Natasha reflected as she stepped out onto the terrace after breakfast for a breath of air. Autumn was here to stay now, the leaves red and golden, the air crisp and cool. She pulled her cardigan about her and moved towards the lawn, where she wandered for a few minutes. There was a lot to do this morning—correspondence to catch up with, and so many other little tasks that needed attending to. Her daily life had filled quickly, with so many different activities it was hard to keep up. Yet even though she was constantly doing, she still found it hard to banish Raoul from her mind, to accept that it was not to be and that it was for the best in the long run.

She let out a long sigh and stuffed her hands in her pockets. Then she looked up and to her utter surprise saw Raoul's tall, determined figure moving towards her across the lawn.

Her breath caught and she smothered the desire to run and throw herself into his strong arms. That was all in the past now.

Raoul was approaching, and she pulled herself together and plastered on a little smile. 'Good morning, Raoul. What brings you here so early in the day?' Her tone was casual and pleasant, nothing more.

'I have something I wish to speak to you about,' he said, taking her hand and lifting it perfunctorily to his lips.

'Oh? Should we step into the office?'

'No. That won't be necessary.' Raoul cleared his throat and looked her over thoughtfully. 'I need you to pay close attention to what I am about to say, Natasha,' he continued in an authoritative tone.

'Very well,' she responded, mystified at the seriousness of his demeanour. 'Is something wrong, Raoul?'

'Uh, no. Not exactly. *Enfin*, in a way there is.'

'And how can I help you?' she said patiently, wondering when he would come to the point.

Standing to his full height, Raoul looked down at her. 'Natasha, I have come to ask you to do me the honour of becoming my wife.'

'Excuse me?' She blinked up at him in amazement.

'I understand your surprise. In truth I am surprised myself.' He smiled self-deprecatingly. 'I had no notion that such a thing would come to pass. Particularly with a woman like you.'

'A woman like me?' Now that the surprise was waning, and she understood the full import of his message, Natasha experienced a mixture of amusement at his arrogance, anger at his nerve, and cool detachment.

'Yes. I had no intention of entering the marital state, but I find I cannot be without you. I am profoundly disturbed by your absence. As you can imagine, this is most unsettling. Not only does it affect my business acumen, but it also disturbs my sleep pattern, not to mention several other things.'

'Really?' she murmured dryly. 'I'm very sorry to hear that.'

'Yes, well, I hope that soon all that will be in the past,' he said with his winning smile. 'I think we shall deal very well, you and I, despite your being a Saugure.'

Natasha avoided his outstretched hand and took a step back. She straightened her shoulders and eyed him askance.

'Frankly, I find it quite amazing that someone with your strong ties to the past and your family reputation would even consider asking me to marry him,' she said, controlling her temper.

'Well, yes,' he replied ruefully. 'As I just said to you, it wasn't an easy decision to take. I had to overcome quite a few qualms.'

'I see. And how did you overcome them, may I know?' she asked sweetly.

'That is another long story, which I will share with you in due course. Suffice it to say that I have decided this to be the best course of action.'

'For whom?'

'Why, for me, of course. And I—'

Natasha's colour heightened and her chin went up. 'Is this supposed to be a compliment?'

'Well, I think that any woman would be honoured. After all, I have one of the oldest names and titles in France,' he replied modestly.

'And you wish me to give you an answer?' She tilted her head, amused now at the sheer arrogance of the man, the utter disregard for anything but his own comfort.

'Well?' He smiled down at her confidently.

'Well, here is my answer,' she said, shoving her hands further into her pockets and looking him up and down scathingly. 'I thank you for thinking of me as a possible—though I gather somewhat unsuitable—candidate for the job of becoming your wife. Unfortunately, I do not find the post alluring. So my answer is a resounding no!'

'Excuse me?'

'Exactly what you heard, Raoul. I have absolutely no desire to marry a man who is not only full of his own self-importance but considers that he is doing me a favour by asking me to marry him. For your information, I'm very happy the way I am. I don't need you, and I can think of nothing worse than becoming your chattel. And, let's face it, that's basically what you consider your wife should become. Someone ready to hop, skip and jump every time you snap your aristocratic fingers, to be there when it suits you, and to efface herself when it does not.'

'But—'

'I haven't finished.' She raised her hand like a traffic cop, allowing him no chance to speak. 'I imagine that you would also expect me to accept with a blind eye all your affairs and to be thankful for the rest of my days. Not to mention having to be eternally grateful that the Baron d'Argentan would even *consider* me as worthy enough of being offered marriage.'

'Natasha, you are taking this in completely the wrong light. I had no intention of—'

'Insulting me?' she retorted. 'Well, guess what? Not only am I insulted, but I must ask you not to set foot on my property ever again. Is that understood? I think after a few hundred years we Saugures have had just about enough of you. Good day.'

With that she turned around and marched back to the house, slamming the French door behind her.

'Ce n'est pas possible,' Raoul muttered, aghast, staring at her retreating figure, trying to assimilate all that had just taken place. Natasha must be mad.

Angrily he marched around the Manoir, got back into his Ferrari and drove off towards the village. Driving slowly down the main street, he saw Gaston seated outside the café and immediately pulled over.

'I need to talk to you,' he said, his mind still bursting with surprised outrage.

'Fine. I'll order you a coffee.'

'Make it a double,' Raoul muttered between gritted teeth as he parked the Ferrari and jumped out.

'So?' Gaston looked him over and raised a brow. 'What's left you in this foul mood?'

'*Who* do you think?' Raoul threw out, dropping onto the basketwork chair and flinging an arm on the small bistro table.

'I haven't the slightest notion.'

'Well, let me put you in the picture.'

'Go ahead,' Gaston said, agog with curiosity.

'I have just—against my better judgement, mark you—asked Natasha to marry me.'

'*Mon Dieu.* Are congratulations in order?'

'No, they are not. She refused me.'

'Ah.' Gaston nodded sagely.

'What? You are not surprised? I just told you that she refused my offer of marriage. It is *incroyable*.'

'Yes. Well, I had a feeling that might happen one of these days,' Gaston replied in a conversational tone.

'Excuse me? I seem to be missing something here.' Raoul sat up straighter and stared his friend in the eye. 'Why the hell did you think anything of the sort? Is my offer not good enough? Why, I have offered her one of the oldest names in France and she refuses!'

'That's where the problem lies,' Gaston answered patiently. 'You see, Raoul, Natasha doesn't give a damn about your noble name.'

'That is ridiculous,' he spluttered, accepting his coffee from the waiter.

'No, it's not. In fact, you should be very flattered.'

'I can't imagine why.'

'Because it is *you* Natasha cares for. Raoul the man. Not the Baron, not the spoiled odious brat, but the sometimes great guy who lies beneath that aristocratic veneer.'

'This is a ridiculous conversation,' Raoul demurred, a cold feeling gripping his gut. Had he got it wrong? Had he missed the boat completely?

'It is not ridiculous, and you know it. For once, my friend, listen to the counsel of one who knows better than you. You are a proud, selfish, egotistical son-of-a-bitch.'

'Merci.'

'But you are also my very good friend,' Gaston continued, ignoring the sardonic interruption. 'One I would very much like to see happy. Has it never occurred to you that you should be *begging* that woman to become your wife? That she is the best thing that has happened to you in the last twenty years? Or are you too stupid, too full of aristocratic nonsense, to see what any other man would already have understood a long time ago?' Gaston's eyes blazed into his.

Raoul hesitated, then, placing his coffee cup back in the saucer, leaned forward. 'You really think this, don't you?'

'Yes, I do,' Gaston replied with feeling. 'For goodness' sake, listen to yourself, man. Don't you understand marriage is not about *you, you, you*? It is about both of you. It is about making this woman happy, wanting to love her for ever, to give her everything you can. Love, Raoul. I don't think you know the meaning of the word. Frankly, I'm glad she refused you. You don't deserve to tread the ground she steps on.'

With that Gaston got up abruptly and, throwing a few coins on the table, sent his friend a withering glance. 'Wake up, *mon ami*, before it is too late. You've wasted enough time already.'

Without more ado Gaston marched off down the street, leaving Raoul even more bewildered than he'd been when he sat down.

CHAPTER TWENTY-TWO

How could he be so impossibly odious? Natasha wondered, balling her fists and swallowing the tears that she refused to shed. The man didn't deserve even one solitary tear.

Then why did she feel she was dying inside? Why did the mere sight and thought of him still make her want to melt as though she were an ice cream cone left in the sun?

'Damn him,' she muttered, running upstairs to the privacy of her bedroom where, despite her vow not to cry, she fell onto the bed and indulged in a fit of sobbing.

Ten minutes later she pulled herself together and, sniffing into a tissue, sat up. She wouldn't stay here—couldn't stay here. Not while he was about. Not while there was a very strong risk of banging into him.

She'd refused the man she loved for one very good reason: he obviously didn't love her. He wanted her because it pleased him, because he enjoyed her in bed, because—oh, forget all the reasons. They weren't worth going over.

Natasha rose and, pulling a suitcase from her closet, began randomly throwing clothes into it. She didn't care where she went, but get out of here she must.

Half an hour later she was packed and ready, and giving instructions to the staff. This time she would only give her cellphone number so they could reach her. But not her address. Not that she had one to give, she reflected gloomily, revving the car engine. And she was determined that once she did Raoul was not going to get hold of it.

* * *

Of course he should have known that she would run after an incident like this. What a fool he'd been—what an imbecilic fool not to realize what was under his nose the whole time.

He loved her.

Of course he loved her. And he'd thought he'd made that plain to her by asking her to marry him.

But Gaston's words, coupled with his own painful reflections, made him suddenly realize that in truth he had not been very complimentary.

'Quel idiot,' he muttered to himself, recalling Natasha's expression as she refused him. And now he'd spoiled everything. For it was obvious that Henri really didn't know where she'd gone this time around, and neither did Gaston or anyone else.

Raoul knew a sudden rush of panic and despair such as he had never before experienced. What if she'd driven off in a nervous state and had an accident? What if, because of him, at this very moment she was lying by the roadside covered in blood, or at the bottom of a ditch?

As the myriad of horrifying images played out, Raoul realized just how much he loved this woman. But what was worse was the dreadful haunting feeling that it was too late. She'd expected something of him and he hadn't come through. In fact he'd made a complete botch of the whole thing.

For the first time in twenty-five years Raoul dropped his head in his hands and recognized that he wished, more than anything, that he could turn back the clock twenty-four hours.

But that was not possible.

Now only a miracle could save the day.

And, even if ghosts could appear to pass on unspoken messages, a miracle was too much to expect.

* * *

She drove.

For three hours she simply followed country roads with no particular destination in mind, her being in turmoil, her heart in shreds.

But she knew that, despite the pain, her decision was the right one.

Forget marriage on his terms. She was certain that Natasha would have thought the same. The way he envisaged it, things would have been as bad as they were for her ancestor.

Or worse.

For at least Natasha Senior had had the freedom of choice, whereas she, as his wife, would merely find herself subjected to his dominance. And no way, however much she loved him, could she allow that to happen. It was a sure recipe for unhappiness.

But after several hours of wandering Natasha also came to another conclusion as, stopping by the sea, she got out of the car and took a long deep breath: she couldn't run away. She must go back home to the Manoir and face whatever she had to face. It was her home now, her reality. And whether Raoul was close or not was irrelevant. She must stand firm, head high, on her own terrain and confront the situation. Not flee like a scared rabbit.

After several minutes' walking in the bracing sea air Natasha felt better. Gazing out over the grey waters, she let her mind travel back sixty years, to when these very beaches had been bathed in the blood, sweat and tears of those courageous men who'd so bravely fought for the freedom of Europe. Men who had not faltered, she reminded herself, but who had faced the enemy head-on, just as she must.

Without more ado Natasha got back in her vehicle and,

gunning the engine, prepared to drive home, in the knowledge that she too would stand strong.

Whatever the odds.

It was impossible to trace her. No one knew where she'd disappeared to. Should he hire a detective to find her? What if—? Raoul ordered himself to stop imagining the worst and blot out the horrific images that crossed his tormented mind. Perhaps she had merely gone to Paris for the day, or— But then why hadn't she left directions with her staff?

'I don't know where she can be,' he repeated to Gaston for the hundredth time as he paced the Baronial Hall of the Château while his friend sat in one of the high-backed velvet chairs, holding his own counsel. It wouldn't do Raoul any harm to worry about Natasha. He himself wasn't concerned; he was certain that she had gone somewhere to seek some peace and regroup.

'I must find her,' Raoul said at last. 'I can't go on like this, not knowing where she is.'

'But why are you so anxious about a woman for whom you don't have deeper feelings?' Gaston murmured, tongue in cheek.

Raoul stopped in front of him eyes narrowed. 'You know damn well I love her, *mon ami*. It has been hard for me to admit, hard for me to realize, but the truth is I do, and I can't live without her.'

'Then the matter appears quite simple to me.'

'It does?' Raoul's brow flew up and he looked at his friend, bewildered.

'Tell her.' Gaston raised his hands in an expressive gesture. 'Tell her you love her.'

'How can I tell her if I don't know where the heck she is?' he replied, frustrated.

'I have a funny feeling that if you go over to the Manoir

you might find her there. She may have needed a few hours to get her thoughts in line, her ducks in a row. But I don't think Natasha is one to run from adversity.'

'You think she's back?' Raoul's eyes narrowed. 'But what if she doesn't want me even when I tell her that—?' He cut off, stared out of the window, floored by the novelty of the situation. He had always been so sure of himself, in the driving seat, certain of the outcome. Now, suddenly, the tables had turned. And he hadn't a clue what might happen.

'The risk of having your pride trampled is one I'm afraid you'll have to take, *très cher*. Nothing really worthwhile in life is ever conquered easily. And sometimes there is a price to pay for our blindness.'

'Oh, stop all your damn moralizing,' Raoul snapped. 'If you really think she might be back then I should get over there and see that she's all right.'

With that he flung on his shooting jacket and swung out of the castle, determined to find out if his friend was right.

She heard the wheels crunching the gravel, knew instinctively that it was Raoul, and braced herself for a row.

When Henri showed him into the *grand salon*—the formality of which she had so deplored a help now in her moment of need—Natasha straightened her shoulders and prepared to face the music.

'Natasha,' he said, stopping as Henri closed the door discreetly behind him. 'Where have you been?' he demanded.

Natasha took a deep breath, determined to remain calm despite her racing pulse and thumping heart. 'It is not important, Raoul.'

'No,' he said suddenly, looking her over, filling his eyes

with her, too relieved to see her safe. 'It isn't. What matters is that you have returned to me.'

'Raoul, I have not returned to you,' she said quietly, holding on to the small Louis Quinze table to her right for support. 'I came back to my home, that's all.'

He took several quick steps across the room and was standing over her before she could retreat. 'Natasha, I have been a fool and an idiot, and Gaston has spent the better part of the day telling me so.' He gave a quirky smile, very different from any she had seen before. 'Natasha, *mon amour*, I have come to tell you that I am that very fool that Gaston calls me. I am a fool because I saw things through the wrong pair of glasses. I saw them through the lenses of pride and honour and all those things that I have surrounded myself with all my life. I don't know if you will want me any more after the way I have behaved, so idiotically, but before you make any decision I need you to know one thing.' He stopped, gazed down at her, then reached for her left hand and raised it to his lips.

'Wh-what's that?' she whispered hoarsely.

'I love you. *Je t'aime, mon amour*. More than anything or anybody in the world. I never dreamed or thought that I could love like this, that I could feel such intense wonderful feelings for any woman. But you, *ma* Natasha, you have taught me differently. I swear that if you accept to marry me I will be a faithful loving husband to you till the day I die. I want you in every sense—in my arms, in my heart, in my life.'

Natasha felt her fingers tremble in his. She could hardly believe the words tumbling so sincerely from his lips.

'Raoul, I—'

'Tell me you love me too,' he said urgently, pulling her close. 'Tell me that all we have experienced together was as special and wonderful for you as it was for me, that you could never feel the same in the arms of any other man.' His eyes filled with a proprietary gleam.

A small smile escaped her. 'Oh, Raoul, my darling, you'll never change, will you?' she said, a tiny tender smile illuminating her face as her fingers touched his cheek and she read the anxiety and hope in his expression.

'My darling, I have changed. You have changed me. I don't guarantee that I will be—what is it you say in English?—a hen-pecked husband,' he said, his smile tender, 'but I will try and make you happy.'

'God forbid! A hen-pecked husband indeed.' Natasha burst out laughing as he hugged her tight. Then, drawing her against him, Raoul kissed her long and tenderly with a new, deep passion that obliterated any doubt she might still harbour as to his sincerity.

Then, drawing back, Raoul fished something out of his trouser pocket. 'I almost forgot,' he said, opening an ancient velvet pouch.

Natasha looked down, amazed, at the sparkling object lying in his palm, and when he took her left hand in his she swallowed.

'With this ring you become *ma promise*, my promised wife,' he said firmly, his eyes never leaving hers.

'It's beautiful,' she whispered, gazing from him to the ring and back.

'It is the ring Regis had made in Paris before the Revolution, when he planned to marry Natasha. It has been waiting in the vault all this time. Just for you.'

There was nothing left to say, nothing more to do but rest her head lovingly against his shoulder and feel the wondrous strength of his arms around her.

And as she did so a shadow on the terrace caught her eye. 'Look,' she murmured.

Raoul followed her gaze and together they held their

breath. For out there, moving in the distance, were the old-fashioned shadowy figures of a man and a woman, disappearing hand in hand into the autumnal mist.

'We have come full circle,' Raoul whispered, when the moment had passed and all that remained were the leaves on the lawn. 'History has been righted. What a good thing I realized in time,' he muttered, with something of his old self-assurance.

With a shake of her head and a laugh, Natasha looked up at him, her eyes filled with love and mirth. 'Promise me you'll never change, Raoul.'

'But I just told you—' he protested.

'Shush,' she answered, placing her finger over his lips. 'I love you just the way you are.'